"[AN] AFFECTING FIRST ...

Wilentz has accomplished nearly the impossible. . . . She has captured the corrosive moral shortcomings of Israeli and Palestinian leaders and the near helplessness of the people pulled into their wake—yet she renders virtually all of them with a deeply knowing sympathy."

—*The Baltimore Sun*

"With intensity and skill, Amy Wilentz manages to show us the internal life of characters who are usually seen as journalistic subjects, those struggling in the complex and highly charged world of the Palestinians and Israelis. A deeply personal and tragic incident is at the center of this novel. The backdrop is one of political and social conflict, but the subject turns out to be the wider one of being human—of the difficulty of enduring loss and of trying to live by one's beliefs when all the world seems to be against you."

—SUSAN MINOT
Author of *Lust & Other Stories*

"The strength of *Martyrs' Crossing* . . . [is] its authentic and persuasive portraits of people trying to find their way through, and possibly past, the traps of history."

—*Time*

"Amy Wilentz has a deep firsthand understanding of the impossible snarl of politics and daily life in Israel and the West Bank. Even better, she has a subtle and sympathetic understanding of the nuances of the human heart."

—KURT ANDERSON
Author of *Turn of the Century*

"[A] page-turning political thriller."

—*Mother Jones*

Please turn the page for more reviews. . . .

ALSO BY AMY WILENTZ

The Rainy Season: Haiti Since Duvalier

AMY WILENTZ

Martyrs' Crossing

A Novel

Ballantine Books   New York

A Ballantine Book
Published by The Ballantine Publishing Group

Copyright © 2001 by Amy Wilentz

All rights reserved under International and Pan-American
Copyright Conventions. Published in the United States by The
Ballantine Publishing Group, a division of Random House, Inc.,
New York, and simultaneously in Canada by Random House of
Canada Limited, Toronto.

Ballantine is a registered trademark and the Ballantine colophon
is a trademark of Random House, Inc.

www.randomhouse.com/BRC/

Library of Congress Cataloging-in-Publication Data: 2001118933

ISBN 0-345-44983-5

Cover design by Carl Galian
Cover photos : (spot) © Lena Koller/Johner/Photonica;
(background) © Lance Nelson/The Stock Market

This edition published by arrangement with Simon & Schuster, Inc.

Manufactured in the United States of America

First Ballantine Books Edition: January 2002

10   9   8   7   6   5   4   3   2

For Nick
and for Rafe, Gabe, and Noah

Martyrs' Crossing

CHAPTER ONE

S HE WANTED TO BE LIFTED AWAY FROM HERE BY ANGELS, plucked up into the empty sky. Failing angels, she would accept any transportation—no matter how mean, no matter how low. The crowd was squeezing the breath out of her, and Ibrahim's hand kept almost slipping away. Marina picked him up so that she wouldn't lose hold of him. He turned and twisted irritably in her arms. There was too much old sweat here, there were too many bodies close to hers, and the whole thing made her feel like retching, like running. Too many people were breathing down her neck, and whose breath was it? No one who knew her, no one she wanted to know. Strangers, foreigners, was how she thought of them, really, even though they were her own people, standing packed around her. Finally, she was sharing their predicament. She had always thought she wanted to.

They were all treading dust out here on the Ramallah road under the blue winter sky, and Ibrahim was inhaling it, too, like fire. It was scratchy air. He coughed and coughed again, and squirmed in her arms, trying to see what was happening. He was pale and feverish, but there was strength in those little legs. Marina looked down at his flushed cheeks. She looked through the dust up at the sky and saw a string of faded plastic flags fluttering over the road, crisscrossing it. There was a picture of the Chairman on one side of each flag, and on the reverse, a picture of a jowly commando who had been assassinated more than ten years earlier.

She felt an elbow grind into her side. No one liked to be this close to his fellow man—she could say that with certainty. A car alarm yowled. The crowd was approaching the yellow sign: PREPARE YOUR DOCUMENTS FOR INSPECTION. The sky overhead was clear, but there was a threat in the clouds piling up far out to the west over the distant sea. The wind whipped through the cypresses that scrabbled up a hill behind the low stores and houses. Straining toward the rickety watchtower that overlooked Shuhada checkpoint, the faces of the crowd, upturned and expectant, were like faces in religious paintings, the faces of believers waiting for a miracle. Just let me through, Marina thought. A man next to her coughed in Ibrahim's face.

Next time, get him out of there and over to us as fast as you can, Dr. Miller had said. He needs to be on the machines. He needs drips you can't always get at your hospitals. He needs our nebulizers.

She held Ibrahim tightly with one arm, and pushed his hair back from his eyes. He felt hot and he looked frightened, and this was a boy who did not scare easily. Not even when they went to visit Hassan in the prison on the other side. In order to see Daddy, they had to get through the checkpoint, find a taxi, drive into Jerusalem—and then, at the prison, pass through a reinforced steel door while men with big guns watched them and asked questions.

Marina was used to the rituals of crossing over. But today was different. The press of bodies made her feel faint. In the months since Hassan was arrested, she and Ibrahim had become accustomed to lining up. It was more or less civilized. With the right papers you almost always got through—if you had the patience. Sometimes the soldiers didn't check at all; they were naturally unsuspicious and lenient with mothers and children. But if they did run her through the computer, she was ready with her passport and with Ibrahim's medical file from Hadassah Hospital. There would be a few questions about Hassan, because prisoners always turned up on the computer. But then, right through. Marina looked like what she was, a Palestinian, but she was an American citizen, born in Boston, with what had always been a foolproof passport.

But nothing works forever, especially here. Early this morning, there had been two bus bombs in downtown Jerusalem. Bodies had been blown all over a square. These were the first attacks in a long time, and now the checkpoint was like a place she'd never visited before. Marina had never seen a complete closure before, a *towq*, it was called in Arabic. They hadn't done one in years, and she'd never believed they could do it, not really.

Could they? No one knew, not even her doctor in Ramallah. She had run to him this afternoon, when Ibrahim seemed to be getting sicker. The medications he had been expecting for more than a week had been delayed again. Get yourself into Jerusalem, the doctor told her. With your passport, it should be all right.

Turning away from his office door, Marina flagged a cab and headed for the checkpoint. Traffic to the crossing had slowed to a stop a half mile from the Jerusalem line. She got out to finish the trip on foot.

FACING THE CROWD, in the shadow of the watchtower, Lieutenant Ari Doron flicked away his cigarette and tried to decide on a few next steps. In the old days, he might have panicked. But he was a harder man now, he didn't wilt when confronted. That's why his superiors used him for checkpoint duty when the situation got bad. And today it certainly was dangerous. The crowd had grown larger as more and more were refused permission to cross. It was hot out for this time of year, and Doron felt damp beneath his heavy bulletproof vest. He pushed his hair up under his cap and drank some tepid water out of a plastic bottle that was standing on one of the sand-filled, plastic roadblocks the army had set up at the intersection three years ago, as a temporary measure. By now, the checkpoint had become a permanent part of Jerusalem's geography. Since the peace was declared, Doron thought. He tried to brush some of the dust off his shoulders.

Today's disturbance was going down like clockwork, each notch up in the violence coming according to schedule. It was like a drill for the checkpoint soldiers, the angry crowds of rock-throwing young men. Doron was used to it. It started with children, the little boys who slipped through legs and whipped around the crowd and were having the best time, you could see it. It was only a matter of minutes before the young men joined in. They used slingshots, which Doron considered fair practice in the land of David. He wondered whether these were the kind David had used to kill the giant. The contraption looked like a holiday noisemaker, and the Palestinians spun it from the hip so that if you were up close, which you tried not to be, you could hear it whipping the air. The slingshot could send a rock flying at what seemed like the speed of a bullet.

Usually, the soldiers waited until a rock hit its mark, until there were enough men throwing stones, so that they weren't firing into a gaggle of schoolboys. First they shot into the air. Rubber bullets. Then they tried tear gas. When the tear gas didn't work, the soldiers would shoot in the air again, which also never worked, and then they'd begin shooting in earnest, over the heads of the crowd if their aim was good, into the crowd if it wasn't. By then, the men would be angry and nervous and ready to shoot for real, but Doron always tried to avoid this stage. He had never used live ammo at a checkpoint, and could not imagine the situation in which he would give that order. Rubber bullets were bad enough. Or there were sound bombs, a kind of grenade that did not explode but could generally be counted on to send a mob hurtling away. Doron also tended to go extra heavy on the tear gas. He didn't want casualties on his record. Things could escalate quickly into something really bad, something he didn't want to see, didn't want to deal with, didn't want to be responsible for.

Doron had seen the crisis building today as the politicians pulled the closure tighter and tighter. The Palestinians here at the checkpoint were trying to get into Israel for all the usual reasons: work, work, and work. There had been closures before, as punishment for acts of terror, and yet they would still come, desperate to get through, and every day, some of them made it, because usually the closure was not airtight, and there was room for lackadaisical enforcement, there was room for leniency—even sympathy, on occasion.

Like most of the officers in charge of the checkpoints today, Doron had asked headquarters to loosen up—he could feel the place turning into a flashpoint as the pressure built. But Tel Aviv kept tugging on the drawstrings. Responding to terror, the government said, the two bus bombings all over the television, the two suicide boys, dressed up like Israeli soldiers, who packed their kit bags with explosives and got on the buses and blew themselves up. Whose brothers or cousins might explode tomorrow at the mall, the movies, the grocery store. Fifty killed and scores wounded, in two minutes. So. No passage between the West Bank and Israel. No movement among the towns and villages of the West Bank. Even the most urgent cases would be judged harshly today.

The stone throwers were close. Doron called in to headquarters. There was trouble at several of the other crossings. It sounded chaotic over the phone line. He heard other phones ringing and the sound of someone cursing loudly. He hung up and had his men advance a few more meters in front of the watchtower, hoping they would look tough and determined, even though right now he had only seven men on shift, if you didn't count the other two he had diverted to watch the dry, deserted wadi a hundred meters away. Sometimes enterprising Palestinians would walk or drive around the checkpoint through the dry riverbed behind it. The Israelis knew about these violators, but usually ignored them. Today, the wadi was off-limits. Nine men total, a reasonable number. The check-points were not supposed to be war zones.

Zvili came up to him. It amazed him that checkpoint duty always meant working with guys like Zvili.

"They're closing in," Zvili said. He sounded excited.

"They are far away," Doron said.

"We might have to begin firing," Zvili said. He knew that Doron shied away from this.

"I don't think so, not yet." Doron looked at Zvili. The little man had a hard look on his face, like a gargoyle. These little guys shocked Doron with their toughness. They were ready for anything. Unlike Doron.

"Well, what do *you* suggest?" Zvili asked him.

"Nothing," Doron said. "Nothing yet."

"So we're just going to sit here like target practice?" Zvili spat on the ground. He was a gremlin, but he was scared. Doron could see it in his posturing.

"No, we're just going to sit here like grown-ups until we see what's developing," Doron said to him. His tone was condescending, the vocal equivalent of patting Zvili on the head. "For all we know, this is business as usual, but a little more intense. Anyway, they're still too far away to hurt us."

Doron prided himself on his new maturity. He was an old hand, temperate and calm, having found himself—sometime after his twenty-eighth birthday—suddenly quite able to distinguish between a problem and a crisis. Was it a run-of-the-mill melee, or "a situation"? Making that judgment was the essence of Israeli military professionalism. Doron checked the time and calculated how long it would be until nightfall. Even the most violent crowds tended to disperse at sunset. It was a matter of keeping the boys at bay until the earth's rotation came into line with your military strategy. It would be almost an hour, not soon enough. He noticed the dust rising. It made his eyes itch. He sniffed at the air. He listened. A car alarm was going off. From this distance, about a hundred meters, he could only make out beetled brows, and kerchiefs around noses and mouths. It always looked in photographs as if they were seeking anonymity, but in fact it was protection against the gas. The gas slowed them down—it prolonged the time between the hurling of the rock that smashed a soldier's cheek, and the shooting that would repel the stone throwers. That was the only use for the gas, as far as Doron could see. It never really put an end to things.

He nodded to Zvili, and Zvili prepared a tear-gas cartridge. The young men were moving in closer, their pitching arms back. Doron nodded again.

Zvili fired off the cartridge. It soared up into the air and then plummeted down like the tail end of a firework, exploding on descent. The crowd opened up around it. Breaking through the ring of those who were fleeing, a young man with a kerchief around his face ran up to the spewing cartridge, picked it up, and galloped toward the checkpoint like a strange tribal smoke-dancer, stopping finally a few meters from Doron's line of defense to hurl the cartridge back at the Israelis. Doron coughed and bent over, and tears bit at his eyes. He felt for a second as if he were going to black out, the stuff was so fucking strong. Should have shot him, he thought. When Doron stood finally after the cramp in his lungs had abated, he saw the boy scampering back into a rejoicing crowd.

Doron wished these battles did not have to be so intimate. He coughed into the back of his hand. There was something too much like children's games about being at such close quarters with the enemy. It was like hide-and-seek, or a color war. They ran up to you, you chased them back. They conked your guy, you conked theirs. You got to know each other by the end of a day. You could take the measure of certain individuals. He hated seeing their joy at a wounded soldier, and wished he could take the same raw pleasure in their injuries. He wanted to want them dead. But God, he just wished that these people had stayed home today. He wished that they would stay home every day.

"HOLD ON, hold on, hold on here," a voice shouted through the crowd. No one could see who was talking. An old man's walking stick thudded against Marina. People jostled her from both sides, stepped-on toes crunching like pebbles underfoot. The car alarm was still wailing. The crowd lurched forward; someone was pushing from behind. Marina felt one of her shoes come loose, and then it was gone.

The crowd stumbled backward a few paces as the soldiers advanced toward them. Gunfire popped. For a moment, everyone stood still. I have to get out of here, Marina thought. But she couldn't afford to leave. She had to get to the checkpoint, and through it, now. So this was total closure, she thought, an occasion for riot, a mini uprising. And then there were the people, like her, who really needed to get across. Four years in this place, and she still had learned nothing.

A slight breeze blew a cloud of gas over them. Marina put her shirt over Ibrahim's face. He was gasping. Tears were coursing down her own face, too, from the gas. She stood up against the side of a photocopy store, panting. The crowd was running away from the checkpoint, now, but young men still stood around, in corners, behind walls, down alleys, waiting for the next assault.

A man standing next to her offered his handkerchief. He pulled a small plastic bottle of scented toilet water from his bag and poured it over the white square.

"Here," he said.

She took it gratefully and put it over the boy's nose and mouth. The man smiled briefly, and then looked back out at the wildly scattering crowd. He was thin, and his suit was shabby in the local style: a little too long in the cuffs, worn at the elbows, cut too sharply, glossy at the collar, the lapels too broad. A West Bank professional of some kind, Marina guessed. An accountant, or a dentist.

She thanked the man over and over for his kindness.

"It is nothing," he said. "You keep that." He turned away.

Marina closed her eyes. A vision of the Star Market on Mass Ave in Cambridge came abruptly into her head. The piled-up apples. Pyramids of boxes containing macaroni and cheese mix. The wide corridor of frozen foods. The soups with the soups, the dog bones with the dog bones, bags with bags, meat with meat. The spray that rained down on the vegetables every ten minutes like a passing sun shower. The quick click of the cashiers. In every way, life was orderly there.

Marina wanted life to be normal, whatever that was. She wanted to be at home with her baby. She wanted to feel his head and call Dr. Miller's office and have them say, Yes, come in, and then get in a car and drive him over, like a normal person. And have them say, He's fine, don't worry, calm down, everything is going to be fine. Ibrahim had a very bad cold, you'd think it was nothing. But the last time he'd had a cold with a fever, he'd begun to come up short for breath, and then he wasn't breathing right at all, and she ended up rushing him through the checkpoint to Jerusalem, to Hadassah, and Dr. Miller had hurried over to see him. Ibrahim lay in a hospital bed, with his blue eyes looking up over the green plastic nebulizer mask, a drip in his arm, and she had felt like collapsing, but at least Dr. Miller had been there, saying he's going to be fine.

That was last month and all the days before. But now something— many things—had changed. You couldn't even get near the checkpoint because of the demonstrators and the crowd. She thought of her father, who had left Ramallah last week, and the small crowd of admirers who had stood on her doorstep, waving goodbye at his disappearing taxi. He was heading back to America. Marina felt a pang of nostalgia for the Boston winters of her childhood, for snowboots and slush. She imagined her father in snowy Cambridge now, sitting comfortably with his reading glasses down near the tip of his nose or lounging in front of the television watching tennis. *He* would never get caught in a situation like this. During his visits, her father, with all of his ties to the Authority, managed swift and unlimited checkpoint crossings for himself—whenever he wished, which was not very often—each one planned carefully in advance, each strategically fixed: the right car one day, VIP documents the next, a connected driver, whatever it took. But today, Marina had been caught by surprise. No time for arrangements. Ibrahim's breath came in gasps. She watched the crowd rush by. Rabble, that would be the word that would rise to her father's lips, even though he'd never say it.

IT WAS GETTING DARKER. That was help from on high, thought Doron. The clouds might bring darkness earlier than expected. He hoped so, he hoped so. One of Doron's men had been hit. It wasn't serious but blood was flowing down into his eyes, which did not exactly raise morale. Doron looked up at the sky. If only God would send a message down the way he used to, publicly and unmistakably. Instead, rain clouds, gunfire, boys with stones, dust.

Doron watched the kerchiefed boys preparing another onslaught. He knew that what was unhappily called a situation had developed on his watch. Behind the boys, the crowd was moving toward the checkpoint again. Doron thought about percussion grenades, good for stopping animal stampedes—or starting them—and for stopping running crowds in their tracks without causing casualties. Certainly no matter what he ended up doing, it would be found that he had done something wrong, had forgotten to do something, had neglected something that right now, right now, should seem utterly obvious to him as a course of action. He was sure that firing on the crowd at this point would be a mistake. On the other hand, he didn't want to be a sitting duck for some kind of unprecedented attack on the checkpoint.

"Let's launch a sound bomb," Doron said. It was getting too close, they were getting too cocky. It had to end. There was a moment past which you could not let things continue, or the escalation might prove unstoppable. Doron stood out in front of his men while they prepared the percussion weapon. Rocks were coming at him from three sides. It was raining rocks. Doron felt an urgent need to reassert control. He knew he could do it. It was going to happen now. We can always win, he thought. He reminded himself: The one who gains victory in close quarters is the one with superior firepower—and the will to use it. That last bit had always been Doron's problem.

A SHATTERING NOISE shook the ground. They are bombing us, Marina thought. That's impossible. She had never heard of bombs, not at the checkpoints. This one was so loud the shock seemed to continue in waves under her feet like an earthquake. She trembled and thought about natural disasters. She didn't see anyone lying bloody and wounded, the way they would after a bombing. No buildings collapsed.

Another tremor rattled the ground. Maybe they're trying to end it, Marina thought. The windows of the businesses along the street rattled and one or two shattered as another blast shook the street. She closed her eyes tight and prayed that they would get across. She tried to make her way to the checkpoint, but the crowd kept pushing her back.

DORON WATCHED the crowd flee from the waves of the explosion. The blast rippled under his feet and he thought it would toss him into the air. The crowd felt the same thing: it was like an earthquake. He gave a signal to launch another bomb. One or two more, and they'd be so far gone they would never regroup. Doron wished fervently never to see another Palestinian. Dream on, he said to himself, tapping his foot, waiting for the end, his gun at the ready.

In a few minutes, he knew it was over. No shouting, no tramping, no stones. Not a single one.

"Hooray," he heard Zvili say to another man.

Hooray is right, Doron thought. It was over for today. As usual, the sound grenades had worked, combined with a massive dose of tear gas and a few strategic bursts of shots fired into the air. At least there would be an interlude of calm until tomorrow, although it would be an interlude filled with stretchers on the Palestinian side, and exhausted, bleeding soldiers at the checkpoint. His men were gathering around the watchtower.

Now was the time to deal with the aftermath. Normally, the men would all be smoking after such an afternoon, but they were coughing too hard. Dust caked over the bloody face of the man who'd been hit, a private, first time on the checkpoint. He was looking for water and a towel. Doron handed him his water bottle as he passed by. A light injury—but he'd send the man to get stitched up, anyway.

Doron could see several yards of road now, a stretch of beautiful, radiant, black macadam, with no one standing on it. The roadbed. Amazing. He looked at the few yards of blackness as if it were an old buddy returning from war. He wanted to kiss it, slap it on the back, offer it a beer. The road was decorated with dust, dirt, sand, rubble, and stray sandals and shoes lost in the melee.

Not everyone left, of course. There were always a few troublemakers, and some people who, Doron supposed, *were* desperate to get across. But wouldn't. Zvili appeared at his side and handed him a cigarette. Doron took it and looked at Zvili with a pained smile on his face.

"Good work, Lieutenant," Zvili said.

"Thank God it's over," said Doron. They went into the trailer.

It was growing dark fast. Zvili flicked on the fluorescent bulb with an elbow. Two of the men who had been out front had returned to the trailer. One parked himself at the desk near the radio with his feet up, and the other sat backward on a metal folding chair, reading the log sheet. The bleeding soldier stood against the wall in a dark corner, with a bloody piece of someone's old shirt balled in his hand and blood still trickling into his eye and down his face. He shook his head as Doron examined him.

"You've got to have someone see that," Doron said. Doron took the bloody rag and made some swipes at the private's face.

"I'm fine," said the man.

"Don't be brave," said Doron.

Zvili polished his sunglasses on the edges of his flak jacket. He returned them to their case.

"Everything cool?" asked Zvili, looking out. This was code.

"Yes," said Doron. "No one dead, as far as I can tell." They watched as an injured man on a stretcher was carried away in the direction of Ramallah. It was always possible that a couple of Palestinians would turn up dead after the riots finished; people you hadn't noticed go down.

"So what else?" Zvili asked. "What are we going to do with these folks?" He gestured to the stragglers coming up the road. "Look at that guy," he said, pointing at a man in a suit, standing near the bench outside. "Why the fuck does he need to get across, I'd like to know. I mean really."

"Don't worry," said Doron. "He's not going anywhere. One guy came through this morning. Authority. Special plates and a special paper just for today. That's been it. Orders are no exceptions. Headquarters is scared shitless. They don't want anyone sneaking through. They've even closed off the wadi."

"Yeah," said Zvili. "Makes me want to cry."

Sometimes, Doron wished there was something really bad he could do to Zvili, instead of fucking over all these pointless Palestinians. Still, the world would be a better place with no Palestinians in it, he often thought. And Zvili was his comrade, supposedly. He had worked with him before at this checkpoint. He had even had a beer at Zvili's house after a hard day. Once. He tried not to dislike Zvili, but Zvili didn't make it easy. Doron turned to the guardroom.

"Be down in a minute," he said. He walked out and climbed slowly up the metal staircase to the watchtower. He liked to survey things at sundown—this was his personal minaret. The man on watch edged aside, and Doron peered down. Things seemed normal. It looked like every night along this road. It was colder, darker, too, without the headlights from the usual traffic that was deterred tonight. Cypresses rose like the shadows of flames from the crest of the hill running behind the wadi. The rain would start soon.

Down on the road, everyone headed home, shocked by the sound bombs and undone by the growing dark and the storm that was descending. But Marina could not go home. Ibrahim's eyes were closed. He wheezed loudly at the end of each short breath. The crowd was breaking up, each person an individual again, with his own plans for the night. The man stationed up in the watchtower leaned on the window ledge with a bored look on his face, pointing his machine gun down at a straggling line of people who were making their way toward the checkpoint in the near dark.

Marina started to run down the road toward the watchtower, with one shoe gone and Ibrahim panting in her arms. At least now there was space to run. At the guardroom, she would plead her case. Those Israeli soldiers who looked at you as if you weren't the same species. She knew them. Their impassive faces, deathly indifference, like Roman praetorians. She'd have to beg, plead, get down on her knees. She hated having to do it; she liked looking away as she presented her documents, getting through, no arguments, no contact, no humiliation. Nothing personal. She had always sworn that if it came to total closure, she would never beg, never degrade herself that way. She'd happily stay in Ramallah, except for her visits to Hassan. What, after all, did Jerusalem have that Ramallah didn't? But that was before Ibrahim got sick again. She knew the answer to her old question, now: Jerusalem had Hadassah Hospital.

DORON BREATHED IN the wet, fresh air. After a hot dusty day, you almost felt clean, up here in the watchtower. He leaned out the opening and looked down at the stragglers waiting outside the guardroom. The sole bench in front, which seated six or seven, was full. In spite of the rain clouds that were building toward blackness above them, a few small groups huddled in conversation near the bench. And heading down toward the checkpoint trailer across the road, coming at a run, almost, but graceful and dignified, was a slender woman in blue jeans, with long, uncovered hair, a beautiful woman, really, Doron could see, carrying a child. One of her shoes was missing.

CHAPTER TWO

GEORGE WAS TERRIBLY TIRED. THE TRIP BACK TO BOSTON had been long, and he was still edgy with jet lag a week later. He hated traveling: wasted time. And now that he was home, he realized he had been in no condition to deal with the vagaries of his trip. Sitting in the security zone at the airport in Frankfurt for three hours, waiting for a late connection, he had been lonely and bored and irritated. The newspapers bored him, his German was not what it had been, he hadn't brought enough books or magazines he could bear opening, much less reading. It was extremely unpleasant. Just hoisting himself up out of those deep seats to go to the bathroom or to get a cup of coffee, a bad cup of coffee but a necessary cup of coffee, was a physical endeavor more difficult than he could have imagined, after only a four-hour flight from Tel Aviv. He was sick and getting old at the same time, and he was not enjoying it. Before he left Boston on this pointless journey, he had sworn to himself that he was not going to let the terrible fatigue stop him. His credo had always been to do what was necessary, to keep his connection to Palestine alive, to give an important part of his energy to The Cause (he always said those two words in a deep ironic tone, the meaning of which—of course—no other Palestinian, except Sandra, could understand; Palestinians said "the cause" as if it still had real meaning . . .). Do what was necessary for The Cause, no matter the cost, he told himself. But now that he was back, he was wondering.

That movie on the plane out of Tel Aviv! It was the most enjoyable part of this last visit. It was the kind of thing he loved: evil CIA agents, a beautiful blond, a secret installation, a ridiculous gang of swarthy foreigners of uncertain origins. One scene remained fixed in his mind. The towering CIA man gives orders to his shady, third-world ally, and the dark-skinned man bows just slightly from the waist in receiving his commands. That little diffident hint of a bow, both acquiescent and defiant, reminded him of Ahmed. George had seen Ahmed give that little bow only last week, as he dismissed someone he was pretending to respect.

Since his heart attack, it was impossible for George to take the kind of pleasure he used to in the regular events of life. When he went down to New York, to give lectures on Palestine or to attend cardiology conferences, he was tired and at his least sociable, not like in the old days—which weren't so old or so long ago. New York in the old days had been the scene of his glory: parties, congresses, fund-raising banquets, gatherings to whom he spoke about The Cause (without irony, in public), and the fate of his people. But now, with Sandra dead and his heart still unrecovered, he almost always said no. He didn't feel like making the effort. He might have taken his old comfort in the accoutrements of wealth one found at New York parties: the rich upholstery and linens and flatware, the sparkling glasses, the high ceilings, the catered food, the clink and laughter, the talk—it reminded him of evenings in his parents' dining room. But he missed Sandra. And he hated looking down at a full plate and wanting nothing.

At lunchtime on a weekday, his part of Cambridge was silent. Everyone had already gone off to work. George put his cup and saucer down, turned on the television, and leaned back into the easy chair that his father had had carried out of their house in Jerusalem so long ago. The chair that, later, he had taken from Amman to London, and then up to Oxford, that he and Sandra had stuck on a steamer to cross the Atlantic, and then lugged up to Boston in a U-Haul, all of this back when his life was just beginning. George flipped through the channels. Tennis, would it be the Open? Yes, there was Australia in the promotional shots: that odd harbor at Sydney, kangaroos looking perplexed in a parking lot. The defending Czech was playing a Swede.

George hoped the phone would not ring. Some new minuscule section of the so-called peace process was being implemented today—or was it tomorrow? yesterday?—and he was afraid the media deluge might start up again. What was there to say, after all?

Tennis relaxed him. He loved to watch the ball go back and forth. Pock, pock, pock, pock. No sound was more soothing. Now only politics could get him going, bring the blood to his face. He would never have imagined that it was possible, but Palestine was the only thing left that aroused his passion.

Love, forty. Good, the Czech was winning. All those damned get-togethers in Jerusalem. They always invited him very courteously when they had an important cabinet meeting, or if there was a big holiday celebration and they needed a rousing speaker. He was still "advising" Ahmed and the Chairman and the Authority, even though they no longer listened to him, no longer took him seriously. It was the political equivalent of Ahmed's little bow—respect combined with dismissal. You couldn't criticize them and think they would accept you in any way other than formally, nominally. But they needed him, still, they needed him.

Ahmed was his best friend, or used to be—decades and decades ago. They had shared hours and hours at school and in the afternoons, in Jerusalem and later in Amman, over tea or coffee, Ahmed stretched out on the sofa and George lying on the carpet in a corner of Ahmed's father's dark study, talking about politics and girls, daydreaming about returning home. George was still disarmed by Ahmed's brilliant smile, and yet Ahmed was a part of the whole corrupt contraption. He was dispensing jobs to cronies, selling ministries to high bidders, the whole shebang, George thought. He seemed to have lost sight of The Cause. George believed that Ahmed was just getting on with things, business as usual, petty politicking, jabbering with the Chairman as if the two of them were a couple of old hacks. Yet Ahmed was vibrant in some atavistic way. He seemed to store his own heat. On George's last trip, the chill of Palestine's winter had crept into his bones, he'd felt it even in the overheated library in Bethlehem where he'd given a talk. But Ahmed walked in from a cold driving wind blazing like a furnace.

Well, they were all virtually dead now, as Sandra used to say, many of them well past sixty. George always caught himself on the verge of walking out of meetings, leaving Ahmed and the boys behind to natter until the end of time about who should control Abdul's orchard near Dah'riyeh, and who would get those two hectares of scrub brush outside Deir el-Ghuson. The whole rickety edifice made him tap his foot with annoyance. Maybe one day he really would just split and head over to see some big brutal American movie at some big brutal shopping mall on the Israeli side. Wouldn't that shock them? He was running out of patience.

He had accomplished precisely nothing in Palestine this last time, precisely zilch. Marina kept pushing him to leave Ramallah and go for a ride through the other side of Jerusalem, the side where he spent his childhood, the places he had told her so much about when she was small. Just to see, she said, just to see. George couldn't explain to his daughter—who had grown up undisturbed in America—how very much he didn't want to. He still felt—after fifty years—like a child who had been suddenly orphaned; he was still suffering from the shock of the Israeli takeover in that unbelievable spring of 1948. His whole life had been cut off from him when he was only eight years old. When the family fled to Amman, George's world had changed as if he'd been transported to an alien planet. He felt awkward about revisiting a past that had been denied to him for so long, a past that—really—he had never been allowed to experience. Still Marina pushed him—she argued for it with the directness of someone who had only suffered secondhand.

He'd done it, finally, but he hadn't set foot outside the car. Saw a house, and felt for the key his father had given him, that he always took with him on long trips. There it was, in his jacket pocket, long and smooth. It was made of iron and it felt heavy in his hand. The end was wrought into the shape of a fleur-de-lis. He remembered how he had worked to make it one of Marina's favorite objects—*her* talisman, too—when she was little. He had dangled the shining key before her fascinated eyes so many times that she imagined it had magical powers. He held it briefly, and looked up at the house. He saw a path he remembered—it led down to the renters' apartment in the back, and the henhouse and pigeonry that had been tended by his nursemaid. He saw the old arched windows. The towering cypress that hid half the garden. A sign that said LOVERS OF ZION STREET—in Hebrew, *Hovevei Zion*. Well, *that* was new. Funny name for his old street. Saw unfamiliar people, new buildings, paved streets. Blue sky. And then on to another meeting.

All right, I've done it now, he said to Marina.

He would love a sweet, but in Cambridge good Arab sweets were still hard to find. Sweets with coffee, perhaps the only reason left now to visit the West Bank. Pock. Ah, the Czech was clever—a wicked backhand crosscourt, and at net. George sipped at his coffee and remembered the little nests of honey and pistachios from Nazareth that he had eaten while he was visiting Marina and Ibrahim in Ramallah. His daughter seemed happy, he supposed, under the circumstances. She was still missing her mother. She pushed more sweets on him, too much coffee, watching him with judging eyes when she thought he wasn't looking. He hadn't been taken to see the husband, and he assumed that that was no oversight.

Marina looked beautiful, and Ibrahim was very charming, for a baby. The boy smiled often, and spoke both languages, and did not seem at all sick, even though Marina said he was ill. He had had an asthma attack—was it just a month ago?—but he looked fine now to George's medical eye.

George had had asthma as a child. Mothers were always nervous. Ibrahim and George played hide-and-seek—Ibrahim found George wedged in a corner between the armoire and the wall, next to the ironing board. The two of them built traps out of blocks. The color in the baby's cheeks was perhaps a little high, but otherwise he seemed well. Ibrahim was quite dark and blue-eyed, as George's mother had been. It was a lovely and surprising remembrance of her.

My Palestinian grandson, he thought.

George remembered that when Marina sent him the first photographs of her newborn baby, he had been taken by surprise by his own emotion. How could he love someone so much whom he had never even met?

UP IN THE WATCHTOWER parapet, two soldiers leaned against the sides of the opening. They were watching her. Marina's arms were beginning to ache. Ibrahim, almost two and a half years old, was heavy. The watchtower seemed far away as she half walked, half ran toward it, going as fast as she could. The sun had set over the photocopy shop. She imagined again what her father would have to say about her finding herself in this situation. He believed she never planned anything properly. He believed she was still a sloppy teenager living in a room piled high with dirty clothing. He would find the bare foot too degrading in this situation. He would be annoyed to find she had gotten herself into this fix. And he would not be interested in the fact that it was probably inescapable.

Just a few more meters, and she could begin the battle to get the attention of the checkpoint guards. A half dozen or so other people were already sitting on a bench, waiting. The setting sun left a strip of pale pink floating on the horizon behind the checkpoint, and night arrived, abruptly. A lacy drizzle was falling.

In the shadow of the watchtower, Marina sat down on the bench, squeezing between two elderly men in traditional robes. She set her bag down between their walking sticks. She wanted to check Ibrahim before she brought him over to the guardroom, see if she could get him to use the inhaler. Through the rain, the one small bulb in the checkpoint trailer sparkled like a star.

• • •

GEORGE SET DOWN his cup, and experimented with putting his left leg over his right, instead of his right over the left. It relieved the deadening somewhat, he thought. He regained a painful contact with his left foot. He sipped at his coffee, so unlike Marina's. Second set: Czech down two games to love. Hers was really good, boiled over charcoal on the grill, fragrant with cardamom and thick with sugar and the sediment of ground coffee. It was heavy with the taste of home. So Arab. *"Si arabe,"* as Ahmed would say breathily, laughing, imitating an old French flame of his who had been infatuated with the desert peoples. How had Marina become such an authentic Palestinian all of a sudden?

They had never drunk coffee like that while she was growing up in Cambridge. It must have been the husband's influence or the influence of geography. Or her new religion, George thought grimly. The Raads were secular Palestinian Christians; his daughter had made a conversion to Islam. The girl he remembered and the new religion did not seem to go together, but she had done it for love. Perhaps that explained it.

On this last trip to Ramallah, he and Marina had sat out on the roof and drunk her coffee together. She complained too much about the Israelis.

"They are so arrogant at the checkpoint," she said. She poured more coffee. Ibrahim climbed down from her lap. "It's such a frustrating experience, every time."

"It's meant to be. It's meant to teach you a lesson."

George shook his head, remembering the conversation. The Israelis did stupid things, pointless things. What did Marina expect, fellowship, respect? They were a rude and thoughtless people, at best. We are enemies, she knew that. But she'd been worried that with the growing unrest, it might become more difficult to get through for an appointment at the hospital. She already needed medical documents, a doctor's note, et cetera.

George recalled how he'd tuned her out and had begun wondering about the solar panels on the neighbors' roofs. He couldn't listen long to Marina's analysis of The Cause because to him she seemed such a novice. Her observations—he could have made them at the age of eight, as he bounced into Jordan from Palestine, sitting on a suitcase in the backseat of Grandfather's motorcar.

From Marina's roof in Ramallah, he'd noticed an old, rusty bedspring on the Katuls' terrace next door. Katul was such a pleasant fellow, always smiling and whistling and offering to lend George his car. Katul was whistling over in the next yard, as he worked beneath his old Chevy.

What was that song? Katul had something to do with Hamas fund-raising, George had heard. Oh, Hamas. George thought about it every time he heard Katul whistling. A bad and difficult organization, full of cold and rigid men, including his son-in-law. Not Katul, of course.

George remembered feeling that he was being inattentive to Marina, so he'd turned from his study of Katul's terrace, and watched his grandson's face. What an amazing face it was. The boy was bent over a pot full of dirt, digging for worms that were not there, and humming. Now George recognized the song that Katul was whistling as he worked under his car—it was the theme from *The Lion King*. "The cirrrrrrr-cle of life . . ." Ibrahim was humming along with Katul. George and his grandson had watched the movie the other day dubbed into Arabic. *That* was funny. In any case, what was George to do about Marina's problems with the Israelis? She was a big girl, now, and George was not the Israelis. He was not even the fucking Palestinians anymore, particularly. George began humming the *Lion King* song, too, and Ibrahim looked up, smiling. He was picking handfuls of flowers from the flowerpots on the roof. My ticket back, George thought, watching the boy.

The defending champion went down to a sudden and ignominious defeat—and at the hands of a Swede who only liked to hit from the backcourt. Too bad. George switched off the set. What now? It was almost time to go over to the hospital, check out his mail, begin his afternoon procedures. He finished off the cold coffee.

George did not want to think of Marina alone in depressing Ramallah in that apartment with Ibrahim while the father did his hunger strikes and made his protests and conspired with his cellmates and wasted time. She had returned to a place that was not the Palestine George had dreamed of regaining, not the place he'd told her about ever since she could understand. The new Palestine was a place totally unlike that—it was a new world, changed utterly since George and the rest of them had been forced to flee. The Catastrophe, the Palestinians called it, appropriately enough. Forever after, George had felt homeless—unlike most people, when he traveled he did not have a home to go home to. He wasn't a refugee anymore, exactly, but he considered himself one. The worst part was that he never experienced his dislocation more acutely than when he was back in Palestine among the unhappy Palestinians who were surviving the Israeli occupation with a fixed ironic grin or eternal defiance.

He'd made Sandra into his home, and she was gone.

It was a strange life their daughter had chosen, and probably George's fault. It was another reproach, he was sure. Marina had gone "home."

You make Palestine romantic, Sandra had told him. It's not romantic.

In MIDWINTER, Cambridge was covered in snow. The trees that lined Boylston Street looked heavy and tired, wrapped in white, like shrouds. George was beginning to feel his old, hard resentment of America: the cold, unpleasant climate, the long, long winter. Marina liked to ski, he remembered.

"It's almost time, Doctor," Philip said to him from the doorway. Why did Philip always have to sound so young? Six months after Sandra died, it turned out that Philip's lease for his place on Comm Ave had run out and he was looking for a new spot. So George put him up in their basement apartment. Philip was his protégé, a doctoral candidate in the Middle Eastern Studies department at Harvard, and a Palestinian from Beit Jala near Bethlehem. He had always been around, seeking advice or information, having dinner with them or coffee with George. And now George needed companionship to keep him from depression. Now Philip was his assistant. Spirited, faithful, kind. Hardworking, intelligent, learned. Just the sort of thing the doctor ordered, George thought glumly.

"I'm going, I'm going," George said. Wisp of a boy, the phrase kept going through his mind. He pulled himself up and adjusted his robe. Yes, okay, sure, it was just a flannel bathrobe, a dressing gown—as he used to say before he came to America where the names of things were less euphemistic—but somehow the adjustment, the rewrap, the pulling at the sash, made him feel more kingly, more distant.

He started slowly up the stairs. He felt his face. Gray whiskers growing. He stood barefoot on the planks of the dark upstairs landing, feeling around on the wall for the thermostat—ha! there it was. He turned up the heat.

George made his way down the hall, flicking on the lights as he went. He wondered what made him so angry with Ahmed and the Authority. Was it the stupidity of it all, and how this group of thieves thought they represented a "people"? No, it was also the self-congratulatory tone Ahmed always adopted, and the way things were decided these days, how the Chairman—and his sycophants and flunkies—scraped away all the profits and made deals with the Israelis to enjoy the eventual spoils.

Ah, well, and why should the people get anything? They never had and never would. Never missed an opportunity to miss an opportunity. You couldn't put your fate into the Chairman's hands, or Ahmed's hands, and expect to come out of it unscathed. It infuriated him, and yet he could never quite abandon Ahmed, friend of his childhood. *Sadiq at-tufoulah*: it was a classic Arabic formulation. George rinsed the razor and slapped at his face with a cold washcloth. Those connections were impossible to overlook, especially when one had so little else from the past to hold on to. Look how he had clung to his easy chair.

He came downstairs into the front hallway and put on his coat, his fur hat, his scarf, and his gloves. He stepped out onto the stoop. The light this afternoon looked like a winter dawn, gray and dismal. The snow on the ground was not new, and it was caked black along the curbs. He could see the spots where the neighborhood's dogs had been pissing on his tires. His car had not been moved since before the snow.

Ah, he thought, feeling himself hesitate before unlocking the car door. George's wrist would not turn: he was having a terror episode. Calm yourself, he thought, using Grandfather's strict, military voice. George had started having this problem after Najjar got shot in the knees three months earlier, in London. There were rogue elements, Najjar had told him on the phone. Najjar was something like him, a Palestinian writer who objected to the way the peace was being concluded—but Najjar was a poet and had worse enemies, apparently. And an ominous, paranoid turn of mind that had turned out to be prescient. A few days after Najjar was shot, Ahmed had rung George from Jericho to warn him that, as Ahmed had said portentously, "threats were being made."

By whom, George had asked. Against whom?

Don't ask, Ahmed had said. Just be careful.

George didn't believe Ahmed. It didn't make sense. He was pretty sure that you didn't blow up people these days because of what they wrote. Probably, the warnings were just one method the Authority was using now to quiet annoying dissent. But then, look at Najjar. It was bound to make you think.

George tried to control these episodes. Especially since he had had his little coronary problem, he rejected them as redundant worrying. But Najjar's knees and Ahmed's call had forced him to contemplate the renewed volatility of the situation. As a writer who frequently expressed opinions that were at odds with someone or other's—you could count on *that* in Palestine—he was a visible and quite stationary target. And here was his car, bearing his license plate, at his address, in front of his house, which was listed in the Peter Bent's hospital directory, which was public. George stepped back from the car. It seemed untouched. There were no footprints in the snow except his own. And the dogs', of course. He hoped that one could still assume the dogs were innocent.

Well, then. Onward. He bent toward the car and clicked the key in the lock. No explosion. Utter quiet reigned as usual on the quiet boulevards of Cambridge. He straightened and rewound his scarf before lowering himself into the driver's seat. Of course, he had not forgotten that another method was to have the thing detonate upon ignition. He steeled himself. Is it a phobia if it stems from a factual menace? And *was* this menace factual?

"A phobia is irrational," he said out loud.

He had had the opportunity of hearing in some detail how Semtex works, with the explosive's chemistry explained by people who knew. He knew how fast it was, how powerful, how undetectable. Like the pilot knowing how many thousands of bolts, switches, bearings, and meters could fail during takeoff. You just had to forget about it. That was real courage.

"A phobia is irrational," he said again. He heard a noise. A dull thud. He trusted it was not his heart. Someone was rapping on the car's window. It was Philip. George gave him a small wave. Philip gestured at him to lower the window. But he could not do that without turning the key in the ignition. If by some chance, someone had—God, it was ridiculous—planted something, poor faithful Philip would be killed along with Dr. George, the intended victim.

The thought cheered George, somehow. But shit, he was becoming morbid. He turned the key. A little cough, the sound of the motor revving, and otherwise, a resounding silence.

He lowered the passenger window.

"You're still here?" Philip said.

"Apparently," George answered.

"You're going to be late."

"I expect so."

Philip smiled. "Anyway, you started the car, and it didn't explode," he said. "And it actually seems to be running. So you're a lucky man."

Philip was surprisingly not stupid. George watched him clump away in his tremendous galoshes. Only a foreigner would wear those things in America, he thought. Philip was a skinny Palestinian twig, and it looked as if his big rubber boots were holding him to the ground. George watched the boy weave down the street. He put the car into gear and felt the tires spin for a second, spraying snow and slush, before they engaged with the asphalt.

• • •

MARINA WAS SOAKED through. She'd taken a seat on the bench when the storm erupted and some one made space for her. She'd been up and down, now, shouting at the soldiers, begging to get through, and then sitting again, quiet, comforting Ibrahim and trying to get him to take his inhaler. When the rain started in earnest, she pulled him under the jacket that the man in the worn suit had given her, tucked there along with all the medical documents, and sat forlornly under an umbrella—also provided by her protector—while the man went and yelled some more at the Israelis. He was the same man who had given her his handkerchief.

"Why can't you take this woman inside the guardroom?" the man was shouting from the doorway.

Doron looked at the man. He hated this pushy Palestinian, had come to hate him during the past half hour, as he wrestled with headquarters about an older man who said he needed dialysis, always receiving a negative response, and argued with Zvili, and checked the private's bloody eye, and watched the rain begin, with the man's spluttering always going on in the background. Doron was actively considering civilian life. Set up a little business, get married, live in the suburbs.

"No, I've told you. I can't let her in," said Doron to the angry man. "Not yet. Tell her two more minutes, and I'll have permission."

"Lieutenant Doron?" interrupted another young private, who appeared at the door to the trailer, his face dripping with rain. Doron wheeled on him.

"What?"

"We're to send the rest of them home?"

"Yes. Now. Not the woman with the baby."

"Yes, sir."

"Do it now," Doron said. He turned back to the man he hated.

"The baby is sick. He's sick," the man said.

"So you've told me," said Doron. He peered out at the mother and child, sitting on the bench a few yards from the tiny trailer window. "Can't you see I've got a lot to do here? I've already called an ambulance from Hadassah for my man; they can take her too."

"Then let her in. Into the guardroom, I mean. Out of the rain. Do it. You must."

Doron peered out at the drenched woman. It was hard to see detail through the coursing rain, but he saw a woman holding her child inside her coat, trying to put some kind of contraption over his face. It was cold out there. Doron had already put on the blue-jean jacket he kept in the trailer for winter nights. She must be freezing.

The ruling from headquarters was no Palestinians inside the trailers. Doron pushed open the sliding window a crack.

"Come on in, ma'am!" he shouted to her. He saw as she stood and came toward him that she was the woman who had been making her way in their direction at sunset.

She flashed him a resentful look, stood, and started to walk in. Zvili stopped her at the door with his metal detector. He flicked it up one side of her, down the other. In terms of security, his frisk was dangerously superficial: he didn't check the bag or the boy. Really it was just harass-ment, Doron knew. Zvili stepped back from Marina, holding on to his detector, considering what to do next. Doron put his hand on Zvili's arm. Marina was shivering. She stepped inside.

"I would never set foot in here if it were not for my boy," she said in English.

"Thanks for the news bulletin," Doron answered. He noticed her eyes, very deep, very black. "I would never let you in here if it were not for your boy. We agree. Sit down while I deal with headquarters. Fill these out."

The woman was soaked. She seemed to Doron to shake slightly or to vibrate, but maybe that was just the storm plowing and harrowing and exploding around them. She sat down and bent her head over the papers and her child. Doron wished she were not the enemy.

GEORGE ARRIVED at the hospital just in time to scrub up, and the proce-dure went perfectly. The bubble pushed up into the patient's arteries like a worm digging a tunnel. And there it all was on the monitor, George the Worm, unblocking the flow. It was elegant, angioplasty—far better than bloody bypass, which he had observed many times. He liked that shred of distance that angioplasty left him; the illusion, with the monitor and the catheter, that you were not deep inside the bloody workings of another human being. No spurting.

He had one last appointment before he left for the day, with Carol Gerstman's husband. Carol, his patient, was a humorous person, always pleasant even when she was sick, but Joe was a little touchy, and he had the unfortunate American habit of discussing politics as if he were sure you agreed with him. George went into his office and clipped some pictures up on the light walls so Joe could inspect the work George had done for Carol in the cath room last week. He'd update Joe on Carol's progress.

The nurse let Joe in. He looked as if *he* had undergone the procedure, not his wife. He was pale and damp, and smelled of cigarette smoke. He was carrying a newspaper folded under his arm, and he looked at George with a knot of concern between his eyes.

For some of his patients, it was hard to trust a doctor with a foreign name. George knew that. Joe was Jewish, which probably didn't help the situation. Although Joe had always been correct with George, even genial, George continued to have just that little suspicion, and there was something in Joe's face, now, that got George's attention. He hoped what he saw was just the stress of Carol's illness.

"It went perfectly, Joe," George said. "Perfectly. You *know* that. She's fine. You can relax for a good long while now." Joe smiled wanly. Be hearty, man, George thought. Be proud. Be relieved.

"It was a textbook procedure, which is rare. Here's what we did." George beckoned to Joe, who allowed himself to be toured around the X rays, as George explained each one. Joe didn't seem to be focusing, but then again, the explanations were a bit technical.

"Uh-hunh," Joe said, as they finished with each picture.

Then they sat down. George had no family photographs on his desk. His only decorations were a single piece of Palestinian embroidery on the wall and his certificates from Harvard. The other diplomas and certificates he had stuck in a drawer. On the floor, in an unused corner, there was a small Shirvan carpet from his father's lost house in Jerusalem, a real jewel.

Joe picked up his newspaper and looked up from it at George with pale, beseeching eyes. George waited for the unavoidable questions about prognosis. He did not like this part.

"How do you explain *this*?" Joe held up a section of the paper and whacked at one story with the back of his hand.

"What?" George was taken aback.

"Look," Joe said. He threw the paper onto George's desk.

George looked at the upper-right-hand column. Oh, yes, the two Israeli settlers who had been killed in a drive-by shooting.

"Yes," George said.

"A man and his wife. Young people."

Joe's wife was sick, for Chrissakes, and *this* is what he wants to talk about? Well, maybe that was the explanation for the outburst—maybe Joe was trying to take his mind off her condition.

"*I* didn't shoot them, Joe," he said. He tried to make his voice gentle.

"No, but you think it's okay?" Joe looked at him. "How can you go around saving people's lives and then think it's okay to do this?"

The picture was gruesome: a machine-gunned car, blood, an arm dangling out the window.

"I didn't say it's okay. It's complicated," George said. I will be patient and kind, he thought.

"Being dead is not too complicated, is it?"

"People get killed in wars, and not just soldiers." Oh, he'd said that so many times. Everything about The Cause was repetitive. He felt a wave of fatigue. Thank God he didn't have to live in Palestine. He remembered Marina on the roof, bending over the coffee.

"A war?" Joe was plainly outraged. "Killing people driving their car home from the supermarket?"

"To the people who did this, those two were not just driving their car home. They are part of an occupying force. The settler certainly thought he was fighting a war."

"And now they're dead."

"Yes."

George took it back, a little. "I don't mean 'that's okay.' You're right. It's dreadful. But that's what happens. They came to live in a place for political reasons; and they're not wanted there. They bring their children into this place, they put their children in danger by deciding to live in a place where they are not wanted. Where they're seen as the advance troops of the enemy."

"Oh, come on. You guys just hate them because they're Israeli."

"We would hate anyone who took our land away from us. We believe we are at war—that's why we're negotiating a peace. You can't have a war and then get squeamish because people die. The Israelis never said sorry when they blew up the British, and why should they have?"

"You don't even really believe in peace, do you?"

George felt defensive.

"I believe in peace, but this is a loser's peace," George said. "It's corrupt, the people who are doing it are corrupt." Said it so many times; it was his refrain. He picked up his prescription pad and put it down again. "Victory is for winners, peace is for losers. The only reason the Chairman wants this peace is because he's old and tired and desperate."

"Better to just go on shooting innocent people and tossing crippled men off boats, and like that, right?" Joe asked. "Is that your argument?"

"Come on, Joe, you *know* me." George was truly appalled. He knew these feelings lurked out there, but he'd rarely had them addressed to him in person. He preferred being criticized in print, where it was less emotionally immediate, and he could respond logically and calmly. "You know I don't believe in cruelty."

"I don't know anything about you except that you're one of the best cardiologists in the world." Joe was standing now, holding his newspaper as if it were Exhibit A. "I don't want to fight with you. Actually, I thought you'd be as revolted as I am by this attack."

"You did."

"I did. I hoped, anyway. But I won't pursue it, George," Joe said. He looked down at the Shirvan. "You're too important in my life right now for me to feel comfortable saying what I really think. Maybe some other time."

"It's okay. I think you've made your feelings clear," George said. He hoped he didn't sound huffy.

"Sorry if I've upset you," Joe said.

"Not at all, believe me. I'm used to it." George felt Joe was now trying to placate his wife's doctor. That he was nervous. Poor guy.

"I know you're not well, either," Joe said. "I shouldn't have . . ."

"I'm fine." George bristled. He looked up from his desk. "Just fine."

"Well, that's good to hear." Joe picked up his coat. "Carol was worried."

"You tell her not to worry," George said. "I'll tell her not to worry. She has enough to worry about without adding me to the list." The two men shook hands.

"Thanks for everything, George," Joe said. He walked out of the office, his shoulders drooping.

Down in the parking lot, George walked through the slush to his reserved space, but his car wasn't there. He stood for a moment in wonder. Had it been stolen? Impossible. The locks and alarms on it were too good, the parking lot too well protected for a car thief to consider. He was befuddled. He felt lost and stranded. How would he get home? He would have to call a cab. He turned back to the hospital entrance, resigned, when he remembered. Of course. He had parked the car elsewhere. After his panic of the morning, he hadn't wanted it sitting in the space marked DR. GEORGE RAAD. Now, the car was anonymous. But lost. Lost in the Peter Bent's enormous visitors' lot. What an ass he was. George the Worm. The intended victim, indeed. An old ass. Was this how he seemed to Ahmed's boys? Worse, was this how he seemed to Ahmed?

• • •

DORON HELD ON to the phone like a lifeline. The boy didn't look so bad, but he was straining for breath.

"See?" his mother said. "See?" She tugged on Doron's sleeve. "It's getting worse, it's getting worse. I can't wait for your ambulance." She had heard him talking about the ambulance to Zvili, in Hebrew. She understood some words.

Doron knew the issue was even less clear. It wasn't about the ambulance; the ambulance was for his injured man. But what if he couldn't get headquarters to let her in? The computer said she was the wife of Hassan Hajimi, a terrorist who was in jail on the Israeli side. So? If he couldn't get her through, then she and the boy would be stuck, ambulance or no ambulance. He trusted her feelings about the boy's condition. She knew, after all, didn't she? This was a medical crisis, not a terrorist ruse. Even a terrorist's kid can't help being sick.

She was murmuring to the child; Doron couldn't hear the words. She hardly looked up. Headquarters had put Doron on hold again; they had a lot to deal with at all the checkpoints, but still. He kept having to identify himself and explain the urgency of the predicament. How many times did they have to hear it? He was listening to computerized ragtime. She ran her fingers through the boy's hair.

With one ear on the phone, Doron turned to the man who had been her advocate. He was tired of the guy's presence. "You get out, now. You've done your duty. Go home." The man shrugged.

"I'm glad you're in, miss," the man said to the woman, in Arabic.

She said nothing. He shrugged again, and turned and walked away from the trailer door. Doron watched him trudge up the road toward Ramallah.

Doron hung up and called again. On hold again, more mouse music. An operator, another operator. It was too late to get through to the normal numbers. He didn't even know who he was waiting for. He had already ordered the fucking ambulance, he kept pointing out to whoever would listen. All he needed was permission to let the woman and her son cross over. The phone receiver felt like a toy in his hand.

"I'll take a taxi," she said. "Just let me through, and I'll take a taxi from here." There was always a line of taxis waiting on either side of the checkpoint, even during a closure. God, he just wanted to zip her across. She was right, a taxi would be faster. Who knew when the damned ambulance would come? He had told them his man had a light injury. They were probably busy.

Her dark eyes were imploring.

He shook his head and pointed at the phone.

The boy started to gasp. Her eyes widened. Doron wanted to hurl the receiver across the guardroom and watch it shatter, but instead, he sat there, mentally screaming for them to pick the fuck up. Pick it up. Pick it up. Another operator gave him a secure number to call. He scrawled it across the back of an empty cigarette pack before he dialed. It rang and rang, and then, surprise, someone picked up. They asked for the woman's name. Which checkpoint? they asked. Shuhada, Doron said. Then there was more waiting. Finally, they came back on.

They are not permitted to enter Israel, the voice on the other end said.

But her papers seem in order.

Not permitted, Lieutenant.

But she goes back and forth all the time.

Not during closure, the voice said. Not during *this* closure.

But an ambulance is already on its way.

Not permitted.

The ambulance is here. Doron slammed down the phone. Lights were flashing through the slits in the guardroom. He heard a siren wailing. He stuffed the empty cigarette pack into his jacket pocket and stood.

"I am so sorry," he said to the woman. "They just won't permit it. I don't know what to say. Sorry."

She didn't even look at him.

"Where's my injured man?" Doron asked. The men pointed. The private was standing quietly in a different corner. His wound was still bleeding—they'd hit a part of the face that bleeds profusely even when the injury is not serious.

"Your ambulance is here, go on." The private started moving out delicately, as if he thought any motion would increase the bleeding.

Doron heard a low voice.

"And what ambulance are we going to take?" It was the first time she looked directly into his eyes.

He looked back at her. What was he going to do with her?

The child looked up at him from her lap with panicky eyes.

Oh, God.

He watched her fumble with the inhaler again. It never seemed to work.

"Lieutenant," she said.

The child was turning blue.

"Okay. Okay. I'm letting you through," he said to the woman. "Come on, get up." He gathered up her jacket and documents and the inhaler. She picked up the boy, who hung limp in her arms. Doron looked at him and felt the panic gather in his stomach like a hard ball.

Zvili blocked their way.

"Move, Sergeant," Doron said.

"No," said Zvili.

"No?" Doron said. "No?"

"The woman is the wife of a terrorist," Zvili said.

"Move, Zvili," Doron said.

"No," Zvili said, planting his feet at both sides of the doorjamb. "She could be a part of some plan. What do we know? Headquarters said she can't come in; I heard you talking to them. You can't let her in."

"You better get out of his way, Zvil!" another soldier shouted from behind them.

"Have you looked at the boy, Zvili?" Doron asked the question in a very even tone with spaces between the words. Marina stood very close to Doron. He looked down at Ibrahim. Was he breathing at all? Still, behind Doron's ball of panic over the boy, he worried, he worried—was he doing the right thing? Was Zvili right?

"Hurry, hurry," she said.

She turned to Doron.

"Look at my boy," she whispered to him.

He looked again.

"Okay, that's it," Doron said, and Zvili moved aside.

They all rushed through the door together, as the emergency medical crew of the ambulance rushed toward them. The doors to the back of the ambulance had just opened. A man in a white coat ran to the injured private, who was just ahead of Marina and Doron and holding the red rag against his cheek.

"No," shouted Doron at them. "Here, here." He pointed, and the white-coated man saw the boy. Doron saw a look of concern pass over the man's face.

The man felt the boy's pulse and he put his hand above Ibrahim's mouth. He bent down and put his ear against the child's chest.

He stood and started shouting and everything began to jump around Doron and Marina. Now everyone was acknowledging an emergency.

The white-coated man plucked the child out of his mother's arms and rushed him into the back of the ambulance. Marina ran after them and Doron followed her. The bleeding private stood off to the side, watching, dabbing at his eye. Everyone inside the ambulance was shouting, green monitors beeped, a nurse leaned over. The child lay pale against the white stretcher, a mask over his face, a white hospital blanket thrown across him, emblazoned with big black Hebrew letters. Marina kept trying to push through the technicians to get to him. Finally they let her hold his hand.

The siren was still going. Doron stood outside thinking, I am the enemy, I am the enemy. The ambulance's spinning light made the rubble at his feet appear and disappear. The little bits of glass and pebble seemed to dance around him in a circle, flickering. He saw Zvili walking back to the trailer. The private's damaged face flashed in and out of view. In the artificial light, the slender-legged watchtower with its searchlight at the top looked pitifully fragile. It looked as if a child could blow it out like a candle.

The next thing Doron knew, the man in white was walking stoop-shouldered over to the bleeding private. Doron turned and looked toward the ambulance. It was as if everything had come to a halt. A nurse sniffled loudly. There was an odd silence except for the mother sobbing against the side of the ambulance. Everyone was watching her, unmoving. They looked frightened. Doron walked toward her. He hesitated. She was shaking with sobs. He put his hand on her arm. She let it stay there for a moment. She turned and looked at him. He knew right then that he would give anything to forget that look. Then she shook him off with a violent movement of her arm, and climbed into the ambulance to be with her boy.

CHAPTER THREE

*T*HE WINTER WIND BLEW THROUGH THE CYPRESS STANDS AT the edge of the graveyard. The first line of mourners approached the family plot, followed by a small bier borne by two men over the stone-strewn yard. Behind George and Philip, hundreds more filed into the small cemetery. Marina had been left at home with her sisters-in-law. Women did not attend Muslim funerals, Philip had reminded George. The mourners wore sunglasses and shaded their eyes.

"Get out of my way," George heard someone yell. Philip wheeled around to see who was disturbing the quiet. It was the press corps. The television people were up ahead, behind a police fence. The still-rising sun cast long bony shadows over the headstones and mausoleums.

The photographers and cameramen, shoving for position, clambered up the graveyard wall, and tumbled down. Some had hauled themselves and their equipment up into the cedar branches. Others stood on aluminum ladders they had brought along. As the wind shifted, they appeared and disappeared among the branches. Down the hill and blanketing the small street that connected the graveyard to East Jerusalem, George could see the procession coming, hats, scarves, and keffiyehs, and bareheaded young men by the hundreds, and above it all the green banners of Hamas, and then, farther back, the red, white, green, and black of the Palestinian flag. George wondered what all the young men in the crowd would do if they could get their hands on an Israeli soldier—any Israeli soldier—now, right now. Oh, Ibrahim. The cameras were pointed at the mourners like the open mouths of fish.

George was exhausted today beyond imagining. Jet lag in one direction, jet lag back. For no one but Marina would George have roused himself once more in his condition, much less flown halfway round the world and walked for a mile in front of cameras to a place where he would have to stand for at least an hour in a cold, unpitying wind.

The first callers had merely stunned him, and left him cold with incredulity, suspecting some kind of a hoax. But Marina, calling from Ramallah, had convinced him, and sent George into a torrent of action. He knew it was Marina because when he picked up the receiver, no one spoke. He kept saying, "Darling, darling," and on the other end there was nothing but the oceanic emptiness of an international connection.

This *never* happened to him, this inability, this fear of confronting whatever was coming to meet him. What could he say that would help her? Nothing, nothing. It was beyond his control. She was two oceans away, Christ, thousands of miles, a world away, no comfort could reach her. I'm coming, he said to her. Finally, he heard her click off. Blood seemed to drain away from him. He felt himself fading and grabbed onto the edge of his desk for support. He dumped himself into his desk chair.

"Philip," he'd called. His voice sounded faint, even to him. But Philip came in.

He must have been waiting just outside the door, expecting to be summoned. Obviously, he already knew everything. He came too close. George waved him back a little. George saw tears in his eyes.

"No, no, no," George said to him, sinking farther back in his chair and covering his own eyes with his forearm. "Philip. That's too much sympathy. I can't stand it, really."

"I'm sorry, Doctor," Philip said, standing there with his hands oddly clasped together.

"Just don't touch me, if you were thinking of it," George said.

"No," Philip said. "No, I won't."

And now here Philip was, in a graveyard in East Jerusalem, bothering to be furious at some noisy cameraman. Dear boy. What a good idea to bring him. Philip was having all George's emotions for him. Philip was in charge of emotions and political thought: outrage at the Israelis, lucid understanding of the Palestinian politicians who were making hay out of the tragedy, canny but diplomatic. Very useful. George might as well be dead already. As he watched them pray over the small, shrouded body, he wished he were.

Reading *Al-Quds* over the breakfast he could not bring himself to taste that morning, George had felt tears sting his eyes for the first time. That was typical of him, to feel something only when it was in writing, only at that safe, mediated distance, when it was more like art or spectacle than like something that was really happening, and to him. He had emotions the way a pornography enthusiast had sex. There was something about the use of the word *gasp* that did it. The editors of *Al-Quds* wrote that Ibrahim had been detained at the checkpoint because he was Hassan Hajimi's child. Hajimi, they reminded their readers, was a disaffected young follower of the Chairman who had turned to Hamas in the past two years.

They wrote that the boy had been visibly gasping—that word—for two hours while his mother, incidentally the daughter of George Raad, the physician and writer ("incidentally"—George noticed that), waited for the officers at the checkpoint to examine and approve the boy's medical documents. That a new, superstrong U.S.-issued tear gas had been used, for the first time, on the crowd at the checkpoint, and had gravely exacerbated the child's respiratory distress. The editors noted that Ibrahim Hajimi was Hassan Hajimi's only child and George Raad's only grandchild. Hajimi, they went on, had been in and out of Israeli prisons since he was first arrested in a general sweep in Jenin in 1992. They added that Raad had recently been ill. Somehow, they managed to imply that all of this—the desperation of the Palestinian people, the prisons, the lack of offspring in Marina's family, the gasping, George's own condition—was the fault of the officers at the checkpoint. Philip was drinking coffee and reading over George's shoulder. George looked up at him, and Philip shook his head, pointing down to several errors in the Arabic typography, and an incorrect identification of George's great-grandfather, the family patriarch, in an old photograph. Ignoring painful content. Attaboy, Philip—trained at the foot of the master.

He was glad Philip was with him, because it was so hard right now to be with Marina. George could barely bring himself to talk to her or to touch her, she seemed so alien and past helping. Her sorrow was transforming her. She had welcomed him the morning he arrived by walking into his arms and sobbing there for a long minute, as he could recall her having done when she was little. He held her and remembered all the stooping and hugging he'd done then, the enclosing arms and bent head and pathetic useless doglike murmurs that were meant to console his child for the broken dolls and spilled glitter and fights with friends and ruined dresses. He cherished those few moments after he arrived back in Ramallah, moments during which he felt himself give way the smallest bit, felt himself feel something along with her, felt the loss of her little boy who had been so delightful and full of interest and amusement. His grandson. He knew it would catch up with him later, when he wasn't trying, wasn't ready for it.

After that initial outburst, Marina retreated. She seemed distant, even when she was not sitting curled up in a corner with her head buried in her hands and her hands buried in her hair. George busied himself with plans for her trip down to see Hassan at al-Moscobiyyeh, the lockup in downtown Jerusalem, when he realized that she didn't need documents, special plates, VIP papers, or an okay from the Chairman now. She could just take a taxi to the checkpoint, walk across, and take another taxi into town. No one at the checkpoint minded now who her husband was, not after what had happened. The closure was still on, but the Israelis would not stop her again.

IN THE CORNER of the cemetery, a shadow flickered between two of the grand old Arab cenotaphs. Doron was trying to hide himself, here in alien territory. Just a few days ago, he had been a good soldier, in a smart uniform. Today, he was the unnamed baby-killer, dressed in civilian clothes. He huddled in a corner and tightened his blue-jean jacket. This was the kind of place he had never been to, a place where he would never go: in Arab Jerusalem, among the enemy. But Doron couldn't help himself, he had to be there, it was an obligation. He still couldn't believe what had happened; he had never seen a dead child before, not in all his days on the checkpoints, not in Lebanon, even.

Doron did not know what to do with himself. He fidgeted, smoked a cigarette. He hoped he could not be seen over here, kicking at a stone, stepping over sage and sorrel plants, half hidden behind a big gray mausoleum and a dusty, swaying willow. He did not think any Israeli would survive being discovered in this place right now. He could just make out the individual mourners—the boy's grandfather was there, he saw, a dark young man at his side. Doron watched the procession coming down that hill toward him. He remembered the back of the mother's bent head as she sobbed over her boy. Her whole life came to an end right there in front of him, and he could do nothing for her. "Please help me," she'd said toward the very end. He'd had an impulse to console her, to offer kind platitudes, the way he was used to doing with the bereaved. Instead, he had to stand there like a soldier, and take it. When he finally touched her arm, after, she recoiled. He remembered that. Well, she was right.

Tomorrow he was to appear before a military investigator. Headquarters would stand by him, of course. He would tell them about the man he finally reached somewhere, working late in some office in the high tower of the Defense Department in Tel Aviv, who had ordered him not to allow the Hajimi family to cross. Maybe he could even show them the secure number. He might have it somewhere, stuffed into a pocket.

His mother had tried to console him, as if that were possible. He could hear the worry in her voice over the phone.

"Look," she'd said to him. "The army will stand by you if you stand by them. They believe that protecting your name is the same as protecting theirs."

"Yeah."

"You did your best," she said. "Poor little child."

How had the boy ended up dead? Doron didn't understand it. Someone on the phone in a distant city by the sea had told him not to let them in, but he didn't even get the man's name. And in any case, you didn't always have to follow orders. Well, he hadn't really. The ambulance had come, he had contacted headquarters, they had refused her request, he had been about to let them in anyway, over Zvili's indignant protest, and it was fate alone that had brought help there only after the boy was beyond saving. He told himself all this. But he knew he should have let them through the minute they appeared at the trailer door.

He still wasn't hungry. He had barely eaten since he left the checkpoint. When he focused on the graveyard crowd again, he thought he might be hallucinating, there were so many people flowing down to the graveyard, covering the hillside, too many for a funeral by far. Too many. With flags and banners. Flags and banners, so unkind, so festive and inappropriate. But of course, this was not just any funeral. This was his own funeral, Doron kept thinking. Up front, where a white-turbaned sheikh was standing, Doron could see Raad, in black, slender, erect.

The Raad family. An old Palestinian family, he had read. They looked as if they were people just like his own family. But they weren't. They were Palestinians. And now they were going to be victims: a family with a martyr. Their little boy was dead. The banners were waving for Ibrahim. Now Doron knew the child's name. Another banner slowly unfurled at the top of the hill. IN ISRAEL, it read in English, SOLDIERS KILL BABIES. Doron leaned against the willow. He could hear the crowd roaring and chanting. The banners flickered and waved in the wind. They snapped and flickered, and his head hurt. He needed to eat.

He was afraid to see the bier go down. He crushed out his cigarette and wandered up the hill, making sure to keep some distance from the watchful cameramen and the crowd. Not that anyone would recognize him. When he reached the crest, Doron looked down over the heads of the crowd and the backs of the banners to the valley where a little bunch of people was locked in a knot around the burial mound. Doron wished that women were allowed to attend. He remembered the exact tilt of Marina Raad's head as she sat desperately filling out her forms, the exact color of her dark eyes, the exact anger in her penetrating, dismissive regard. Then again, he was grateful that women were forbidden. He didn't think he could bear to see her. And what if she saw him?

GEORGE LISTENED TO the old man talking. Normally, George loved funerals. Who wouldn't? The sheer joy at not being dead, the delight in the presence of dozens of other living beings, the uplifting thought that you get to carry on eating and fucking and breathing and shitting, while some other poor mortal is going down to nothingness. But the funeral of a child was different and the funeral of this child was not something he was prepared for.

He looked at the sheikh. He was nervous about the old man standing there in his turban; he mistrusted anything left to the discretion of clergymen. George dreaded the eulogy, which was not traditional at Muslim funerals, and was bound to be political (what else could you say about a baby's short life?), but Marina had accepted it when it was suggested by friends of Hassan's. The sheikh's white-wrapped fez—a sign that he had made the haj to Mecca—reflected the strong sun. He gave a dry cough of self-importance, and began to speak.

"We are all here today because, again, a Palestinian has died at the hands of the Israelis," he said in a low voice. He paused dramatically.

No, no, no. George wanted to correct him. I beg to differ. That isn't why I came here today, haji. I came because my little boy is dead.

"A Palestinian, a fine baby boy. A boy who flourished in his parents' love, but who was never to learn about his people and his stolen homeland, never to become another brave warrior in the battle for Palestinian liberation." The sheikh shook his head somberly and looked down at his notes. Notes? What could notes for such palpable drivel say? Pal boy innocent . . . /Zionist enemy to blame . . . /Pal people must advance to final goal . . . /Push Zionist enemy into sea . . . /Burn ground beneath feet of Zionist occupation force???

"When we consider this young boy's mother," the sheikh went on, squinting up at the crowd, "we cannot help but feel a burst of pride, pride in her composure, her courage, her stubborn will, her clear desire to continue the battle no matter the cost." George felt Philip tremble next to him. The Palestinian people, thought George. He sensed their impending introduction into the funeral oration. He could always predict the moment when The Palestinian People would enter the speeches of Palestinians. Almost invariably, he was correct. By now it had become a joke between him and Philip.

At the back of the crowd, listening to the doddering ancient prattle away, the young men who were supposed to be today's brave warriors cheered wildly and leaped up and down and made the bright banners they were holding wiggle like eels flashing and glinting in the sun. This is the Palestinian people, George reflected as he heard the cheering get louder, then fade, then start up again. What are they cheering about?

"She is a shining example to the Palestinian people," the sheikh continued. Although vindicated, George found himself overtaken by a wave of helpless anger. He tried to imagine Marina as a kind of heroic female standard-bearer for the future Palestinian liberation, but all he could see was the lonely creature he had left at the door to the kitchen in the house in Ramallah, in her stark veil, surrounded by the silent sisters-in-law. My daughter, who used to wear ribbons in her hair and play Chinese jump rope on an American playground. After all, she had only been trying to get her boy to the doctor. If Ibrahim had made it across alive, Marina would have been just another desperate Palestinian mother accommodating herself to humiliating Israeli demands. It was only her dead child in that awful shroud that gave her this sudden political stature. George wanted to spit the empty words back into the sheikh's face. But the poor stupid old geezbag was only doing his job, and life also was stupid.

George succumbed to a flash of unsummoned memory: Ibrahim leaping off the foldout bed at Marina's, wearing his floppy red slippers and waving a golden plastic sword. Ibrahim with a sword—it played on George's love of Palestinian history; at school in Jerusalem, every boy in his class wanted more than anything to ride in the saber-wielding cavalry of a nineteenth-century Middle Eastern army. And Ibrahim that day was like a cavalryman. He hurled himself into the air with no thought to his own safety and utter trust that he would land on his feet. George remembered. The gold blade flashed.

George wanted to go back in time. What if he'd been there at the checkpoint, been in charge of his family, hadn't left Ramallah to return to comfortable Cambridge? He could have fixed things, saved the boy, stepped in. George wanted a time machine, only for this one thing. Time machine: he hadn't even thought of those two words since his school days. But now he did. Open the door. Fasten the seat belt. Press the button, pull the lever. Zap, and there you were, in the past. Not to right the wrongs done his people nor to rewrite history, nor to do any of the historic deeds he'd planned and failed to accomplish, but just to do that one simple small thing. In memory the boy kept falling and falling through the bright air, sword flashing, down toward the bottom of the world, where his grandfather scooped him up before he hurt himself, and kissed him.

George felt as if he might black out. He wondered if his childhood asthma was returning. Shortness of breath often precedes a heart attack, he well knew. But perhaps it was sympathetic asthma, adult onset. Just behind the sheikh's left shoulder, he saw Ahmed Amr whispering to a flunky who had a cell phone at his other ear. George did not want to fall apart here, in front of everyone.

He looked down into the hole next to the bier. Why did the time after death seem so different from the time before birth? You've already managed not to exist quite nicely during the one, he thought. You'll probably get through the other. You couldn't say that one black period was longer than the other, or qualitatively better or worse. But having been alive, you felt somehow a morbid nostalgia for living when it came to flinging the mind forward into the grave. History—dinosaurs, wars, harvest festivals, trilobites, druids, plagues, diplomacy, droughts, music, and the like, worms, snails, and starfish—came before birth, full of facts and events. Eternity, empty and blank and possibly unpleasant, came after.

As a doctor, George had come to the ugly conclusion that fate existed, biologically, even though he'd rejected the concept long ago as philosophically repugnant. How many hearts had he watched detonate, just as the hearts of the preceding generation had and the generation before that one, so many in one family dying early of a final, dramatic coronary seizure. What was in your genes had been in the genes of your ancestors millennia ago: prehistoric hairy peoples who wandered the steppes or the plains or the jungles, who carried sharp weapons and wore negligible clothing and did not read books. Maybe in George's own asthmatic chromosomes, it was written that his grandson would die of asthma, and given the family's geographic origins, it could be predicted that the boy would die of that asthma in Palestine, and given history, why should it not happen during a closure, at a checkpoint between Israel and the West Bank?

History and genetics were not so far removed from each other, just like geology and biology. The primordial ooze was still pretty much the primordial ooze, pushed and shoved into different packages down through the eons. All life was like a cartoon monster arising from the squelching swamp, feet trailing mud. Why, for example, should human life require zinc or potassium or iron or salt? But it did. The holy texts said we were made of dirt, and on that point at least they were not wrong. Ooze, all of us. He remembered sitting quietly with Ibrahim on his lap while Marina snapped their picture. The boy laughed for each photo, but only after the flash went off and the picture had been taken. And so the smile was lost.

George looked up again and saw Amr's beard behind the sheikh. He looked away, but in that brief glance, he had already seen too much. Most of The Cause's brave warriors were dead, but the ones who remained—could you really be brave, if after the long years of struggle, you were still among the living?—were all standing here in the cemetery, listening to the sheikh's foolishness, all except the Chairman, who couldn't get there. Detained in Gaza, as usual. Across that hole that seemed to reach down forever at George's feet, he'd seen them. Across the hole, suits, ties, moustaches, grave faces. He raised his eyes again. Behind the sheikh, George saw Ahmed, half hidden but vigilant. George nodded his head unconsciously, and shifted his gaze to another man. But Ahmed, who had always been the braver of the two, did not falter. His sharp eyes sought out George's.

George did not want Ahmed's pity. It would be unendurable, after their disagreements, and the endless wondering about Najjar's shooting, about the threat against himself. How much, really, had Ahmed known? Stay away, stay away, George thought. At the same time, he felt a hateful urge to throw himself at Ahmed's feet and beg for his affection.

George looked around at the remnants of the long battle. Salah was here, alongside Ahmed and Bassim and Hayder. Khalil and Hussein and Kamal and Wa'il would have been here, too, if they had survived—there were always ghosts at any Palestinian reunion. The younger men, assistants and aides-de-camp and sycophants and power seekers, stood farther back, each group behind its particular protector. Ahmed had his coterie: all the boys who had been in his youth battalion and were now grown; a selection of valiant counselors who taught rifle assembly and kidnapping at the summer camps he ran, and all the other dazzling militants he had collected since then. These were the ones who thought of George as a man who had turned and run from the fight. So unfair—George Raad, who should have been their great hero, who was more brilliant than all of them put together, who, back when he was a young man, had even fancied himself a future elder, being worshipped and followed and listened to by just such fellows. Because of his great wisdom, of course. Back when he was a young man and in exile with Ahmed in Amman and Beirut. Back when he had participated in his one small raid. Before he left the guerrilla life and went on to America, while the rest of them remained.

And now here he was, feeling like a sack of bones, staring out at these former militants and future functionaries and bureaucrats. At least his son-in-law was not a bureaucrat. George was reminded of Hassan's importance by the presence of all the young men, the lads, the *shabab*, as they were called in Arabic, at the back and sides of the funeral procession. The green Hamas banners with their fancy glittering silver mottoes would be for Hassan, carried by his people, George supposed. There were so many, slapping against the sky. Ahmed's boys waved Palestinian flags. One other banner drooped over the heads of the crowd, all alone, dull and homely. It was written in unsophisticated Arabic script across a strip of white bedsheet, and gave the command: FIND THE SOLDIER.

Must mean the checkpoint commander, George thought. Finding him didn't seem likely. How would you find him? What the Israelis didn't want you to know, they did not exactly give away. And then, what would you do with him if you did find him? George was sure the fellows carrying the banner had several ideas on this score.

Looking up the hill at the huge descending crowd, George lost his balance, and felt his heart flutter. He lurched and began to slip at the edge of the grave. Only the old sheikh, jumping forward with surprising strength and swiftness and grabbing him under the arms, spared him by seconds from the ignominy of falling down into the hole after Ibrahim's bier. Bag of bones, bag of bones, he kept thinking. He heard what he took to be a suppressed snicker from the other side of the chasm. He looked up, but saw nothing, nothing. No evidence. Only young moustachioed faces full of concern. Ahmed, looking curious, tilting his head. Wondering what was wrong. George dusted himself off. He smoothed his hair back, shaking himself, trying to rid himself of that feeling of fragility, of brittleness. Soon enough, he would fall. Soon enough, he would be an old person who had broken his hip. He would have a pelvic fracture. Only a matter of time, he imagined, before he would have to be wheeled melodramatically from one place to another with a blanket over his lap. Perhaps then he would buy a small dog with a good pedigree and a squashed-in face. Have it sit on his lap and snarl. Marina had barely managed to say goodbye as he departed for the funeral, he recalled. That would be his life, then: Philip pushing, and a Pekinese. Christ.

Chapter Four

THIS WAS SURELY THE LONGEST DAY OF HIS LIFE, GEORGE thought as he woke from a short nap and unexpectedly pleasant dreams of a crisp Cambridge day, the Charles River meandering, sailboats. Sandra. Apples? Something sweet. A ringing telephone and what sounded like a party down the hall had awakened him from a sleep made deep by his exhaustion after the funeral. He pulled himself slowly out of bed, sneaked through the hallway to the bathroom to splash some reviving water on his face, straightened his clothes, and walked bravely out into the gathering. I do not want to do this, he thought. Where is the coffee?

George felt heat pouring from the living room as he walked down the hall. It was a formal room—it had been Hassan's mother's house and this central, public room was done in what George thought of as West Bank Gothic, with too many high-backed, uncomfortable chairs and too many sofas; it wasn't a big room and it was crowded even when it was empty. For tonight, someone had pushed all the furniture up against the walls and stretched the two coffee tables, now laden with food, down the middle of the carpet. About forty people were stuffed into the room now, after the funeral. George plunged in and they made way for him. He located Philip in a corner near the telephone.

George walked over. A young cousin had the telephone receiver in one hand, holding it far away from his body. The Chairman was calling with condolences.

Philip shrugged and took the receiver.

He knew just what to make of condolences from the Chairman. George went and sat down near the coffee table, in the back. Books on the table, he noticed, right away. He didn't care what they were about, they were books. He opened one and listened to Philip talking.

Quite the diplomat.

"Kind of you to offer," Philip said. There was a long pause, and Philip listened patiently.

"Oh, no, no," Philip said. "Please. You are too kind. It's unnecessary, quite unnecessary."

Again, that attentive silence.

"He's fine. Fine. A little indisposed after a long day, you can imagine. Of course, I'll tell him you called."

More listening.

"Really, he doesn't want to cause you any inconvenience. You've already honored the family with your notice," Philip said in a formal Arabic George did not realize he had mastered. "Dr. Raad thanks you."

George winced. He looked down at the book of photographs that lay open in his lap. *All That Remains*, it was called. In its pages were many stories of fathers and sons from the past—the Palestinian Past, before Israel—people like George and Philip, and wedding photos of pretty girls like Marina. White dresses, veils framing old-fashioned faces. Correct young husbands in morning suits. A time irretrievably lost. George looked up, searching for his daughter. Nowhere. He supposed she had gone off again, lying on her bed, no doubt, staring at the ceiling, or sobbing in the bathroom, the only room in the house with a lock. He should look for her.

He tried to but each time he set off across the room to the door, someone pounced on him. Neighbors, friends, distant family, acquaintances, political allies and rivals filtered in and out. Finally, he abandoned any idea of finding Marina, and sat back down with his book. People searched him out in his little corner. Every few minutes, George had to stand again and shake someone's hand and quietly exchange traditional expressions of grief.

"Thank you for your kind expressions of sympathy."

"I am honored by your presence here this evening."

"The tragedy is overwhelming, but with God's help we will endure."

George looked at their sad faces with what he hoped was an appropriate display of grief, and said the appropriate words. He would not permit himself to think about what had happened and what was happening. Someone came up and handed him a little cup of coffee. He sat down again under the lamp, and took up his book. It was dark out and each time the door opened to admit another guest, a wind rushed in and he heard cars stalling and honking and crashing down on the Ramallah road.

• • •

YES, SHE HAD WATCHED the funeral on the television this morning, while the sisters and cousins prepared for the evening gathering. She was the one who wrapped the little naked body in the winding sheet, who chose Hassan's prayer rug to cover the bier. Who kissed the cold cheeks she had kissed so often and habitually when they were still warm, and who kissed the dimpled hands inside and out, and smoothed the dark hair, and watched the men take him away forever. The hearse pulled down the street, and she turned away back up the narrow path forever. Later, watching them parade him down to the graveyard, she saw that these big men carrying the bier, and the television cameras, and all the flags and banners, had turned her little boy who loved lollipops into a figure from history. On the television in the bedroom, she watched the green banners wave. She heard the crowd shout and rejoice. She saw an old clip of Hassan walking down a street in Ramallah. She watched her father standing next to the bier, with his eyes closed, and she saw Uncle Ahmed watching him. She heard the sheikh and, from the other side of the bedroom door, the oven door opening and shutting, the gas igniting, soft feminine conversation. Aunts and cousins were heating up *qidreh*—rice and meat—that they had brought with them for the mourners. Water for coffee. The sheikh spoke of brave warriors.

Marina watched as the camera zoomed in on the red-and-green prayer rug waiting there beside a hole in the ground. The legs and the muddy shoes of all those men who were gathered around, watching. She couldn't begin to acknowledge that that ugly unfinished hole was for him. To put a boy underground. The camera panned up. You could see men talking on cell phones, whispering to each other, looking interestedly out at the crowd. They didn't care about the rug and the shroud. They had no idea. Her father had looked so lonely, standing there leaning on Philip. She'd turned off the television. She heard the clanking noise of plates and silverware, and smelled the *qidreh* warming. She was profoundly not hungry. She had gone into her beloved bathroom, and when the female relations had gone, she'd come out again, and lain back down on her bed, waiting for the visits to begin.

THE FRONT DOOR OPENED and George felt a cold breeze. The sisters-in-law, who had gone home during the afternoon, were arriving back at the house, under their veils. Marina emerged briefly from the back hallway to greet them. George harrumphed to himself. Religious people, more religious than their brother had ever been, he recalled Marina saying. As she talked to the sisters-in-law, Marina waved at her father across the room without looking at him, a little wave of a hand that hung at her side. Like a secret message of recognition, that little wave. He treasured it and returned it as soon as she cast her eyes at him. A little friendly twinkle of the fingers that suggested a separate connection between the two of them. We are not among our people here among our people, George thought. Surrounded by the sisters-in-law, Marina disappeared back toward the kitchen.

He still had *All That Remains* on his lap. The book held his attention better than the visitors. There was the old mufti of Jerusalem in the fez of the haji, looking stern and austere and Muslim among the Christian elders of the city—the same noble-looking mufti who later wrote the infamous, abject letter to Hitler, offering to help with the führer's Jewish problem. The mufti: another geezbag. And there was the picture of George's grandfather with his huge moustaches and three-piece suit and medals, and the family—all the turbulent cousins—spread out for a picnic under the arching olive tree in the courtyard at Abu Ghosh, George not yet born. Pictures of burning buses and exploded houses and the smoking remnants of the King David Hotel, blown up by the Jews—photos of the Irgun, the Stern Gang, and Menachem Begin with his wild hair back when he had hair, looking Dostoevskian, dark, furtive, mad.

Another few pages of Palestinian guerrillas on horseback and beautiful girls wearing the coins of dowry, and then he came upon the picture of little Wa'il Zu'aiter, taken in 1935. Wa'il the militant, as a baby. George heard Philip on the phone thanking Salah for his condolences and inviting him to come by.

George looked down at the book again. As a baby, Wa'il Zu'aiter looked like Ibrahim, with fat arms and a thick thatch of black baby hair. There he was, sitting majestically on his father's lap in Nablus, more than ten years before Israel became a state. He was wearing a hooded white christening outfit, the tie of one of his crocheted booties undone and hanging like a tassel between his father's knees. George picked up his coffee again absently, and drank without looking—a mouthful of mud. Dah! he exclaimed mentally, recoiling. It was a syllable he and Ahmed used in the old days to express both mock and real horror.

Dah! That's what happened if you weren't careful, George! He had forgotten the simplest rule of the West Bank. Look before you drink. And before you eat, before you sleep, before everything, look. The lesson of Ahmed's warning call, the lesson of Najjar's shattered knees, and of the whole stupid battle. Mouth of mud. George tried to locate the roving coffee tray, but it seemed to have retired to the kitchen. The sharp bitter taste of the dregs stayed with him. In the picture, Wa'il's big brother Umar stood at his father's side, in velvet shorts, a satin bow tie fastened carefully around his collar, luxurious brown curls framing his sad, romantic face.

A hush had come over the room, and suddenly George noticed that everyone had turned to face the door. When he looked in that direction, George saw the backs of suits and dresses and robes, and—set off by the door frame like an official portrait of a king—Ahmed Amr, facing the gathering. He wore a black suit and a superbly woven black-and-white keffiyeh. The light from the room cut his figure out from the black background of the night. Ahmed said nothing to anyone, as he looked around, searching, George imagined, for one of his boys. The guests turned away from him, one by one, resuming interrupted conversations. Someone came up to Ahmed with a tea tray, but he waved the man away. Philip rushed across the room toward the new guest, and George half stood. No matter how they sparred, George felt it would be ill-bred not to acknowledge him. As George rose, Ahmed spotted him, strode across the room, and grabbed him by the shoulders.

"George," Ahmed said to him, as if the name by itself signified something. Do not be false, Ahmed, George thought. He felt desperate—if Ahmed was insincere under these circumstances, then Palestine was lost to George. Don't do it, George thought.

"Friend of my childhood," George said.

"You are my family," Ahmed said to George, looking him full in the face. Something about the claim seemed brazen to George. Or, worse, staged. Others were watching them, they both knew. "We are brothers."

"We are what we have left, I suppose," George said quietly.

"Your loss is my loss," Ahmed went on. "Oh, George, I am so sorry, so sorry." Tears fogged Ahmed's eyes. George blinked at him. Possibly he cares, George thought. Possibly, on the other hand, he is overwhelmed by his own performance. George put a hand out and touched his friend's forearm, then grasped it and held on. He remembered with precise visual clarity the swing and the sandbox in the park overlooking Bethlehem Road. Ahmed's sand castle; the domes and walls and battlements they both worked hard to create, every Sunday afternoon of their childhood. "I shall be Salah al-Din!" he recalled Ahmed crying out, when they'd staged their wars to conquer or defend the city of sand. That was Amr, always working in the name of the conqueror.

"Look at this," George said to Ahmed. He pulled his friend down on the sofa with him, and picked up the opened book.

In the photograph, Wa'il's father looked proudly down, through dark-rimmed spectacles, at the boy on his lap.

"Do you know who that child is?" George asked Ahmed.

"Not sure, really," Ahmed replied. Curiosity and caution combined in his voice. He shifted uncomfortably.

"It's Wa'il," George said.

"Wa'il Zu'aiter?" asked Ahmed. He fiddled with the tassels of his keffiyeh.

George nodded.

"Amazing," said Ahmed, picking the book up out of George's hands to examine the photograph more closely.

"He died in Rome, I remember," Ahmed said. "That must be his father, the lawyer, wasn't it?"

In the picture, Wa'il's father had a happy but tense expression on his long face, and George imagined that this sitting might well have marked the first time that Baby Wa'il had been placed on the august paternal lap. From that precarious perch, Wa'il squinted into the sun. He already had a very grown-up expression.

"Sad, isn't it," said Ahmed, laying the book down.

"Yes," said George.

"Sandra liked him, I recall."

"She certainly did."

Wa'il had been assassinated by the Israelis in Rome; he must have been thirty-five, or thirty-six. The picture in *The New York Times*, which George remembered vividly, had shown a long, thin body facedown in the street, and a trickle of blood running down to the photo's edge. That was the black-haired baby's destiny. This pretty baby with his untied bootie. Would Ibrahim's fate have been different? Could all this idiocy continue?

"Sad," Ahmed said again. "We grow old, my friend."

"We're *too* old," George said. Sad, sad—that was all Ahmed could think to say.

"He was a real fighter," Ahmed said.

"Yes, he was," George said. Was Ahmed reproaching him?

"It will end, it will end," Ahmed said. "The struggle will end. Soon."

"Do you think?" George asked. "Oh, I doubt it, Ahmed, I highly doubt it."

"We will end it. But we have to get there, George. You know that. I thought you were the one who believed that we were still at war, no? We can't just throw up our hands. The peace talks are the last best way to continue the struggle, that's what you don't see. Every moment has its own strategy. And we have to pull the Israelis by the balls to bring them to peace."

Ahmed looked at George, who was shaking his head.

"You're just a visitor, George," Ahmed said. "Visits don't count, *habibi*. You've been away a long time. You don't understand what's going on here. This is the final conflict."

This?? George wanted to say. But he chose to maintain a friendly tone.

"I've been watching you, though," he said to Ahmed. "I've had my eye on you, Salah al-Din. You all make a lot of declarations. You talk a lot. And talk is fine, I know, I agree. But you don't need to use everything that comes to hand."

Ahmed shook his head.

"We've *always* used whatever tools were available to us, George."

"What does that mean? It sounds sinister." George flipped through the index of the book, looking for his own family name, for Ahmed's, for Wa'il's. But he wasn't concentrating.

"Oh, you know what I mean," Ahmed said. "When we had only knives, we used knives. We got guns, we used them. TNT, then plastics, Semtex. We used raids, actions, operations, hijacking, explosives, and when that stopped working, we used the intifada. Every mistake they made, we exploited for every ounce of usefulness, and we must keep doing that. Until the end, we must keep doing that."

"I think I know what you're trying to say," George said, after a minute. "But you have enough weapons at your disposal. You have enough bargaining chips. You don't need to use my grandson to spur on the masses. He's not a blunt instrument, Ahmed." George looked down. He riffled through the pages of his book.

"We use the tools that are given to us, George."

George raised his eyes.

"Oh, don't look at me like *that*, Raad. Don't be so angry with me. I'm only doing what you would be doing if our roles were reversed." Ahmed fixed him with those bright, penetrating eyes. "I want you to join forces with me.

"Listen," Ahmed said. "I mean it, really listen, George. Right now is unfortunately when the rest of us—and that means me, too, no matter our connection—right now is when the rest of us have to keep pushing. We have to. Hamas bombed those buses to stop the Israelis from negotiating with us. And it worked, too, of course. Hamas is our enemy. Now, the Chairman wants to put a little gentle political pressure on the Israelis to bring them back to the talks."

"Go on," George said. He wanted to hear the whole bloody rationale.

"You know it all already, George." Ahmed shut his eyes for a second. Was he showing exasperation? George wondered. How irritating.

"We need the boys to come out to the checkpoints and stir things up again. As usual, riots at the crossings will be the one thing that convinces the Israelis we mean business. You know how they hate seeing Israeli soldiers shooting Palestinian kids on CNN."

George nodded.

"To get the boys to come out," Ahmed said, "the Chairman needs something to fire their imagination. He has to push with whatever he has—whatever incident—and I think you and I both know just what it is he has right now."

Ahmed looked at George's face. What did he expect to see there?

"Don't hate me, George," he said. "Just listen to me. A violinist who's a soldier can't say as he marches onto the battlefield, 'Well, my bow arm is too valuable, too sensitive—I'll just fight with my left arm.' He'd be cut to bits in a matter of moments. Or he'd lose his left arm: No more music in any case. If you're serious, you have to use what you have, no matter the cost. I'd like to have you on board. It matters to me, and it would help. It would help very much."

George looked back down at the open book that was balanced on his lap.

"I hate it, Ahmed," he said in a low voice. Wa'il looked up at him with large innocent eyes.

"George, what can I do?" Ahmed asked. "I can't promise you anything. The Chairman is not going to see it from your point of view, that much I can say. The Chairman rarely wastes a political opportunity."

The Chairman, George wanted to say. I don't think this is about the Chairman.

• • •

ANOTHER SECOND OF it and Marina thought she would collapse absolutely. Female relatives kept coming into the kitchen and looking at her expectantly, as if *she* were supposed to say something kind and sympathetic to *them*. She pushed her chair away from the table and walked out. They were all looking at her, she knew, and when she was gone they would start to discuss her.

She went into the bathroom. She loved the bathroom, her refuge. The closed seat of the toilet was hard, but at least private. The fluorescent light zipped and hummed and flickered. It was her noisy but undemanding companion. And there was something about tile: smooth, white; it had an appealing blankness. She let her eyes drift over it, and then occupied herself in the study of the arabesque border design, whose repeating pattern could be fiddled with mentally for minutes at a time, to distraction. The pattern had endless possibilities, and no meaning. She locked the door with the key and removed the key from the keyhole.

Everything you could possibly need was here, Marina thought. Water. A small window, through which you could see a single tree. Reams of tissue paper. A place to sit. A place to lie down—the bathtub. Pills and razors.

She was still living only because going on living was what you did. But she had no interest in it. Her heart felt dark and empty. She couldn't suppress the feeling that she was responsible. She was his *mother.* This bathroom was the little prison cell where she came to hide her guilt. She ran a finger around the rim of the sink. She put her feet up on the toilet seat and wrapped her arms around her knees. She leaned her head against the cool white tiles behind the toilet. The evening breeze blew over her. In the mirror, she could see her tree swaying in the light of a streetlamp.

CHAPTER FIVE

YIZHAR'S RUBBER SOLES MADE A SPONGY NOISE AS HE WALKED past the yellowing, grime-stained, malfunctioning Xerox machine toward his office. At this hour, the hallway on the fifth floor of The Building was always nearly empty. That was one reason why Yizhar liked to keep late hours, free himself from the watchful if unobservant eyes of the human beast. You needed privacy for his kind of work. Yizhar's beat was scandals and fuck-ups and security lapses. He had a reputation for *handling* things. The Prime Minister was always praising Yizhar for fixing the things—the very *simple* things—that the Prime Minister had somehow fucked up. Like last year. Last year, Yizhar took Israel's failed assassination of a Hamas official and spun it into an attempt by Israel to *save* the guy from assassination. Not bad, not bad.

When he arrived finally at the wall-to-wall carpet that marked off his office from the hallway, Yizhar smiled at last year's coup. Even the Hamas guy, formerly certain that he understood and could explain every little thing that happened in this chaotic, random, inscrutable universe, was no longer—and Yizhar knew this for a fact—no longer *really* sure whether the Israelis had been his saviors or his assassins. Yizhar imagined the guy fiddling with his beard.

"Packaging problems"—that was how the Prime Minister liked to put it.

So of course, the minute Yizhar heard that the boy at the Shuhada checkpoint had died, he had asked to be put on it. Naturally. Yizhar did not like to push for things that would come to him anyway, simply because of the army's colossal bureaucratic inertia, but for this one, he pushed. He was afraid to miss it. He had to admit to himself that he had his own personal interest in what had happened, but then, as number two in charge of West Bank security, he was also someone to whom they would naturally come. Packaging this "problem" was a perfect job for Yizhar. It was high profile, and delicate. It needed a proper army investigation, and thorough army spin.

If a situation demanded a straightforward treatment, entirely aboveboard, Colonel Daniel Yizhar was happy with that: he could be direct and open. But also, he had no problem with the little distortion, the white lie, the stretching of truth to fit necessity. He could look quite honest and innocent with that kind of situation, too. He had a law degree. He had military standing. He cared about the army, thought it was an institution that was probably worth respecting. He was a lifer, as far as the army was concerned. He had gone to them and asked for this one, and he knew why they had chosen him. He was glad.

The main thing was to get the story out there, Our Way.

Irit brought him the file. Why did she always have to have that piece of white stomach sticking out between her tight little sweater and her tight pants? It was all he saw when he considered her from behind his desk. She must be under the impression that it was appealing in some way. He should send her home soon.

"Look at these," she said. Of course Colonel Daniel Yizhar would have to have a secretary with a stripe of white stomach who felt it was her right as a citizen to look at—and probably memorize, and probably recite for her friends over morning coffee while also making time to discuss her boss's waistline and hairline and extreme lack of social life—who thought it was her right to peruse every little secret scrap of paper that blew across her desk. She had to have seen the stamp that said CONFIDENTIAL on the soldier's file, on the checkpoint file, on Hajimi's file. She had probably stamped them herself, when you came down to it. And there she stood, not going away. Yizhar considered pinching that piece of flesh.

"Coffee, by any chance?" he said. Irit knew he needed the hourly fix.

"Right." Her tone was sullen, but she went. She wanted him to let her go home. That's why he was keeping her here. This was one of the sorry things that constituted his life's daily amusement. He couldn't help it, it did. He enjoyed this petty toying. He suspected she did too, in her negative pouting way.

He opened Lieutenant Doron's file. So the boy was handsome. A handsome, open face. He looked nice. For a fleeting second, Yizhar thought, I wish I had a son like that. But he quickly folded up that thought and put it away. Futile fantasy. Business, business. Yizhar wondered about the boy's character. Doron came from a good Labor family with a father who had been a career officer. The father grew up on a kibbutz, fought in the '67 war, died of his wounds years later. Good man, good fighter, faithful army stock—Yizhar hoped the boy was made of the same mettle. How would a boy like this react to what had happened? With too many feelings, probably. But army loyalty would dominate. He thumbed through the rest of Doron's papers: copy of identification card, a résumé with very little on it other than army, army, army, a Xerox of an old photograph of the father being decorated, medical reports—a boy in the pink of health.

Inside the checkpoint file was yesterday's report from one of Yizhar's Bethlehem men. Someone down there was scribbling on the walls: FIND THE SOLDIER, the scribbling said. A couple of angry guys with a can of spray paint. Another report came from Ramallah: the same graffiti on the walls near the checkpoint. Using stencils. Stencils, hmmm. And stencils in Jenin, also, before today's big demonstration there. The same stencils, he could see from the Polaroids his men had taken. Stencils, hah! That degree of uniformity could mean the long arm of the Authority, trying to milk the dead baby for everything he was worth. Or it could just be some fundamentalist jerks attempting to rile up the rabble.

But Yizhar wasn't worried. He was indifferent to violence. Sure, since the kid's death the *shabab* had seriously upped the slingshot ante—and the Authority's policemen were backing them up with gunfire. But fortunately, those guys didn't have what they call "muzzle discipline" in the army. Which is to say, they couldn't shoot straight, so they didn't inflict much intentional damage. Mostly got their own guys in the back. The violence could escalate many notches before it would crease Yizhar's brow, despite all the complaining and whining of the usual politicians. He knew that the Israelis could keep things reasonably in check. As long as Doron behaved. If the soldier fucked up, then things could spin out of control, although even in that case, it was hard for Yizhar to imagine losing the reins of this thing. And headquarters had already warned Doron not to talk to anyone but Yizhar. That was the first thing they told him: keep a low profile.

IRIT BROUGHT IN his Nescafé, plunking it down on its usual spot with particular vehemence. He watched the milky brew slosh from side to side in the cup. He needed a pick-me-up—he'd been working too hard on itty-bitty cases. The little things bothered him. Like crumbs at the bottom of a box of cereal, they couldn't satisfy a man's appetite. Yizhar was itching for something big. With Israel's usual bad luck, this Hajimi thing could turn into a manhunt for the soldier, a sort of *fatwa*, which was not a tiny thing. Yizhar looked forward to the fray. If the Palestinians decided to make an issue of the child, they'd go looking for Doron—the Authority might join the hunt, along with the child's family, freelance terror artists, other factions, who knew? And the Chairman probably *would* make an issue out of it, since the Palestinians, Yizhar had noticed over the years, had a natural flair—was that the word?—for drama and p.r., if not for negotiating or self-government. Everyone would be trying to find poor Doron, Yizhar's little lamb.

Yizhar let his eyes stray over the pictures on his desk. Like everyone else in the army, he had the famous photo of the three exhausted generals walking side by side the day the war ended, on their way to claim the Old City of Jerusalem. He also had a more recent snapshot of himself bringing in Farouz Gara, an infamous freelance terror artist from the Hebron area. But dearest to his heart was the group photo of his old company. Fresh faces, bright eyes, everything you expected to see in young soldiers. There was Yizhar, second row, third from left, standing, second in command. He had his rifle barrel shouldered. Fourth from left, Shimon Gertler, bright-eyed too, a shock of hair falling over one eye. Yizhar's commander. It was a fierce company, but when Yizhar looked at it, he didn't see a group of men. He just saw Yizhar and Gertler, as if their two faces had been circled with red crayon. A mere memento, people thought, just like the other photographs sitting there on the desk of a middle-aged officer. But Yizhar knew its historical significance. Let others think it was a simple souvenir. He picked it up to scrutinize it more thoroughly. He and Gertler looked like brothers.

Irit worshipped Gertler.

"That's Shimon Gertler, there, next to you, isn't it?" she'd asked him once, when he came upon her examining the picture one evening. She pointed with a purple nail.

"Yes," he said. Didn't she know the story, he wondered.

"He was such a hero," she said.

"He's a naturally brave man," Yizhar said. He looked at Shimon. Shimon was smiling, unlike the rest of the company, who had on their manly, brave faces, himself included. He and Shimon had just come from giving the boys a big pep talk: the country, the challenge, the menace, And We

Shall Prevail. After all, he and Shimon had been in charge. They said what they had to say. The boys went into battle that afternoon, fateful day for all of them.

"Poor fellow," Irit said.

"People don't usually say that about someone who's been prime minister," he said.

"I know," she said, looking at the picture again, tenderly. "But still."

Yizhar recalled that conversation in detail: the tender voice, from beneath the bluish sheen of mascara. Oh, she knew, she understood.

His gaze wandered from the picture he held in his hand to the surface of his old metal desk. The desk depressed him. It was the only desk he had ever heard of that was rusting. The turned metal edges and the rolling parts of the drawers were orange, and flaking, like the fenders of an old car. This was where he was supposed to work, and interview people, and appear to be important. It was something that no working person would ever dream of complaining about. My desk is rusting. Your desk is rusting? What?

He took a sweet sip of coffee and ran a finger over a rusty spot. The dust came off like pollen on his fingertip.

A knock, and Reuven popped his head in.

The sergeant's whole entire large body followed slowly through the half-open door. God, he was a presence. When he stood in front of it, the door was barely visible.

"What," Yizhar said, looking up briefly.

"I'm leaving," Reuven replied. "That okay?"

"Why not?" Yizhar said.

"You okay?"

"Yes, of course."

"The Hajimi thing . . ." Reuven looked at him, his head cocked to one side—like a friendly dog.

"Yes?" Yizhar said. It always took Reuven a long time to get to the point. Yizhar realized he was still holding the company's picture in his hand. Well, he'd just have to go on holding it. To put it down now would surely spark Reuven's slow-burning but inexorable curiosity.

Ah, damage already done. Here he comes. Reuven lumbered toward the desk, and came around behind it. He looked at Yizhar to see if he would be stopped or scolded, then peered over Yizhar's shoulder.

"Oh, yeah," he said. The picture was a familiar one to Reuven, who spent about half of every working day in Yizhar's office. "Gertler."

Yizhar put the picture back down on his desk.

"Irit's got a thing for him," Reuven said.

"Does she?" he asked.

"She's weird."

Reuven was so insightful.

"Lots of women like him," Reuven went on.

"He was always very attractive," Yizhar said. "Especially in uniform."

"Hunh," Reuven replied, picking up the picture. He held it up to his face, almost touching his nose. He turned it this way and that, like a faceted jewel. "You know, it's funny. You can smell a drunk, just by the way he looks. Something about the eyes."

Reuven was not an articulate man, but he had instinct.

"Yes," Yizhar said.

Reuven put the picture down.

"You'll manage Hajimi, too, Colonel," Reuven said.

"Thanks so much, Sergeant," he said. But all irony, in fact, all subtlety, was lost on Reuven. Like everyone in the army, Reuven knew almost every military story there was to know, whatever there was to know of it. There had been rumors about Gertler's case, on the outside, but on the inside everyone had what they thought was a pretty firm grasp of the *facts*. After what had happened to poor Shimon, Yizhar was left with the results: Gertler was a shell of a man, a general who failed at the most important moment in the battle. It had been Yizhar's first experience packaging problems for Israel.

"Well," Reuven said. He looked around the room, then back at Yizhar. "Don't work too late."

"Don't you worry, Sergeant," Yizhar said. *"Hakol b'seder."* Everything's okay.

IRIT CLOMPED OUT at seven-thirty. It was always good to see her go, although tonight, he felt a little wistful about that stripe of white flesh. Maybe he wasn't being generous enough. Something about her little line of nakedness, her one bolt of daring, seemed vulnerable, and maybe not so unappealing. Maybe that little stripe was a highway that led in to her inmost being, and Yizhar was always looking for a way in to anyone's character.

He closed up the files, and put his keys and his electronic identification card into his pocket. Dinner from the Thais down the street, he thought. Outside in the cool evening air, the hush and murmur of nighttime put him out of sorts. He was exhausted and the streets sounded like sleep—the gentle buzz of generators, the hum and sputter of old lightbulbs in flickering signs, the quiet, insistent rumble of police vans patrolling the streets, the sound of tires on newly laid tar—but he was not sleeping. When he walked down King George, he noticed that the big clock at the Hamashbir department store was off by an hour, even though it had been almost five months since the time had moved back. One year, they hadn't bothered to change the clock at all, just waited until the time moved forward again. Oh, Jerusalem, Yizhar thought. What did an hour matter?

In front of the pharmacy on Jaffa, under the impassive gaze of the winged Assyrian lion that was carved into the cornice of the Generali building, a bomb squad wearing extreme protective regalia inspected parked cars. As if flesh could be protected from fire and dynamite by thick plastic shields. Yizhar shook his head. He and the Generali lion were old midnight comrades, two cynical ancient beasts. At night, when the blinds of his office windows were open, the creature looked in on him from a safe distance.

A rush of steam blew out into the street as he entered the Thai shop. Garlic. He breathed it happily. The boys behind the counter were most certainly not Thai. Still, nice feeling in here, he thought, and so good not to be in The Building. He usually ate his depressing meals without ever leaving his desk. Irit fetched yellow cheese sandwiches or tuna from a place up the street. Sad little sandwiches in plastic wrap, with a Diet Coke. Yizhar walked over to the counter. Three woks were burning up on the black stove behind the boys. Steam fogged the open kitchen. The cooks kept throwing new things into the woks, rushing in and out from some secret place in the back. In the corner, a man with a rifle over his shoulder sat on a stool, eating stringy stuff. At least Doron hadn't *shot* the child. Yizhar ordered a noodle dish to go.

Most colleagues would tell Yizhar that this assignment was a solemn one: Doron's future was riding on it. Yizhar's too, possibly. Israel's international reputation. But Yizhar was a fatalist, because he had learned on the job that this was the safest, wisest approach. He knew about destiny: how it came in different guises, and not usually with a drumroll. Sometimes with the honk of a horn just before impact. Sometimes with the whistle of the artillery shell before it hit. Sometimes, just a shout or a phone's insistent ring.

He paid and took the poorly wrapped package from the cashier, who *was* Thai. With the steaming bag in his hand, he walked quickly back up Jaffa. Three soldiers passed him heading in the other direction, down to Zion Square. Yizhar could imagine Doron walking with them, a nice boy, good soldier, whatever that meant. But to Yizhar, he was just a figure in the big game. Whatever happened, it was not Yizhar's personal responsibility. It was fate, and fate would pull the boy out of it or it would let him drown and Yizhar was just an instrument, too. His role was incidental.

The correctness of an action lay in its outcome, a Gertler motto. You could claim that the outcome was the result of your masterly strategy, your brilliant cover-up, your clever ruses, your unpredictable subterfuges, but in fact, it was all preordained, and your little part in it was mapped out beforehand, and really, you had little or nothing to do with the end result no matter how deep you were in it. Destiny was destiny, and no other thing. Character did not play a part in it, Yizhar believed. Good actions were as useless as bad ones. He had known this ever since Gertler's breakdown. The man fell apart in war, fell absolutely apart, and then went on to become prime minister! Fate was fate.

This is what happened to your thinking when you lived in Jerusalem, even if you weren't religious—and Yizhar had never prayed in his life and never would. You became a fatalist, and superstitious. You went along with the master plan. One thing Yizhar did not believe in was going against the tide. He did not see value in vain gestures. That was Daniel Yizhar's religion, so-called, of which you had to have some kind if you were going to survive in this hateful city. If you weren't going to wear black bloomers and homburgs and bathrobes and stockings and sidecurls, or run around screaming about Allah and blowing up buses and yourself, you still had to find some ground to stand on with the Lord, and Yizhar's ground was soft and he could dig a trench in it and let the Lord pass over on his march toward the end of everybody, including this nice young soldier, who probably would normally have been out eating Thai food with his girlfriend in Zion Square if only he hadn't let a baby die in the rain somewhere outside the ancient floodlit walls of this holy place.

There was too much history here for Yizhar to worry too desperately about the outcome of a single moment in the rapid flow. What did an hour matter? He would just do his bit and save himself and let history rush onward. History would rush onward, regardless of him and Doron and the dead boy, he knew. The Zen of working for the Israeli Defense Forces, he thought to himself.

It was too bad for Doron that the baby had turned out to be a virtual Arab dignitary. Yizhar himself had personally never heard of George Raad before, although Hajimi's name was of course familiar to him. Hamas bigwig—great. It was seriously and really too bad the kid had to be Hajimi's son. Son of a political prisoner, Yizhar had read in the *International Herald Tribune*. Right, he thought. Translation from the bullshit: Son of a jailed terrorist. And even more too bad that the child had to be the grandson of some wild-eyed Pal intellectual type. A doctor—why were they always doctors? But this guy was not some local dentist who had organized terror cells or some oddball gynecologist who happened to be the Chairman's closest confidant. The Raad guy was known throughout the world, it seemed, he was highly respectable, apparently, a brilliant writer, and famous as a doctor, too, even if he, Yizhar, who thought of himself as not entirely brainless, had never heard of him and neither had anyone he knew. Israelis never knew shit about Palestinians, Yizhar always said. Anyway, suddenly this Raad was practically a Nobel prize–winner, now that his grandson turned out to be the kid who died. That was fate and the onward rush. A phone ringing in the middle of the night.

So now a little boy who would have just been some Palestinian toddler who had the misfortune to have an asthma attack at the wrong political moment turns out to be an international cause célèbre. Died at Shuhada crossing, where else? *Shuhada* meant "martyr" in Arabic, and Yizhar had noticed over the years that any Palestinian who ever died anywhere was immediately transformed by the Authority or by whoever was speaking for the Palestinians into some kind of glorified god, an Allah-inspired victim of the evil Israelis.

Yizhar imagined a small boy in a head scarf and white robes, with a golden sword strapped to his side, and gold medals hanging from his neck, and gold braid around his waist, like a Palestinian warrior from the days before statehood. A cause célèbre and a major big problem for the Israeli Defense Forces, and Yizhar will have to stay up late for this night and many other nights, to say nothing of having to hear ad nauseam and to the nth degree the pathetic and lame and possibly whining excuses of this Doron fellow and his other nameless buddies at the checkpoint.

Yizhar didn't want to hear it. What was the point? He already knew exactly what had happened. We'd just get it out our way, and then never let the media know who the guys at the checkpoint were, don't give them any idea who was responsible. The mere possibility of being on television could make a man start spouting information, either because he was scared or because he was excited. Yizhar feared the Israeli press, who knew everyone and everything and who were always faxing the international media top secret documents from the army hours before the head of central command had seen them. After the Israelis, he feared the English, who read the Hebrew media—or got someone to translate it for them—and then extrapolated and embroidered till you had a story there in front of you that at least seemed to make sense, even if it was a tissue of vividly constructed lies. And he feared the wide-eyed international human-rights people. The foreign, hunger-striking, nose-sticking, meddling, prattling, babbling, sermonizing, peace-loving, underdoggy folks. Lord, they were a dangerous crew. Sometimes when he listened to them he wondered if they could possibly mean what they were saying. They lived in some other world where things were very very safe and very very certain.

He unlocked the door of The Building with his card and took the elevator up. Inside the steel and plastic box, it smelled of cigarette smoke, and, more subtly, of piss. A couple of late-season mosquitoes zinged around the light, trapped here forever. He would have to call Avram Shell. Shell worked at *Ha'aretz*, and he was smart, even though he was a journalist. The elevator gave an occasional lazy ding as it passed some of the floors. This was a country in need of repairs. Don't forget, Yizhar often told his colleagues, this is the Third World. He stepped out of the elevator to the sound of a vacuum cleaner rumbling around the hallways.

He called Shell. Avram was always busy. Yizhar imagined him in his tiny cubicle with his white shirt, his one nod to respectability, all crumpled and untucked, and actual ink stains on his fingers, as if it weren't already clear enough what his job was from his stoop and his squint and the way he hunched over a phone.

"So what about it?" Shell asked, without responding to Yizhar's hello. "This baby. Give it to me, Danny."

"On deepest background," Yizhar began. He took a forkful of his noodles.

"Please," Shell said. "I know, I know."

"On deepest background, this baby, first of all, was not a baby."

"Baby not a baby," said Shell. "Okay, I got that. Thanks. Bye." He waited for Yizhar to go on.

"He was two and a half years old," said Yizhar, "so let's not go imagining a swaddling babe in his little blue blankie. He was a toddler."

"Right. Point taken. Next?"

"Next: He was not showing visible signs of distress when he arrived at the checkpoint. Period. No distress."

"I heard different."

"Yes, but this you're hearing from *me*. The soldiers at Ramallah had no idea it was an emergency. Between you and me, they thought the mother was hysterical, but don't print that."

"You're concerned for the family's grief, et cetera? Very moving, Daniel," Shell said. There was just a hint of a laugh in his voice. "What are you eating there?"

"Noodles." Yizhar took another bite. The vacuum cleaner was passing before his door. He heard it grow louder, then recede.

"From the Thais?"

"Yeah," Yizhar said. Oh, it was a tight and nasty little world they lived in. They all worked in the same three-block area, all ate at the same places, knew the same people and stories.

"How many guys you talked to?" Shell asked.

"A bunch."

"Commanding officer?"

"Not yet. Soon."

"When?"

"Soon, Avram."

"Okay, okay."

"Look, the boys simply put her through the document check that we're doing under this closure, and yes, it is a rigorous check, much tighter than usual, we acknowledge that. We're proud of that. We think it's necessary, we think . . ."

"Yah, yah, yah, got you, okay."

"No, really, I want to say we think the new security regs are justified by the recent wave of bombings. I mean, has everyone forgotten? In case they've forgotten, you might want to remind them about the bus bombs and also about the major riot these guys had to deal with at that very checkpoint, just preceding the incident."

"There were injuries to the men, right?"

"Of course, as usual. And the men did a damned good job, acquitted themselves in a very responsible way, with no serious injuries among the Palestinians."

Avram was taking it all down.

"So understandably," Yizhar went on, "the soldiers were being extra careful—maybe a little too careful, that can happen. How careful do you need to be with the wife of a jailed Hamas terrorist, by the way?"

"Right. Hajimi. He's Hamas?"

"We both have his file, Avram," said Yizhar.

In any case, Yizhar told Shell, the woman was given clearance after only a fifteen-minute wait, which is not long even in proven cases of medical emergency, and only after she was cleared through did the child begin to show signs of medical distress. An ambulance was already there at the checkpoint when the child went into cardiac arrest. The soldiers had gone by the book, their behavior had been correct in every way, and it's just simply too bad the child died, and everyone feels terrible about it, especially the young men who were on duty that night. Questions?

Avram was taking it, going with it, even if he didn't entirely believe it. That was the beauty of the relationship. Both Yizhar and Shell knew what was important: security. They were patriots; they didn't even have to think about it. Of course, Yizhar had other concerns, but he didn't need to explain all that to Avram. Those concerns didn't change his behavior, or his story. He did not mention the officer at headquarters in Tel Aviv who—Zvili had said when he was questioned—had forbidden Doron to let the woman through. Doron was the source for that bit of Zvili's information, and it was impossible that Doron could identify the man who had been on the other end of the line. To anyone without firsthand knowledge of the call, it would sound like something Doron had invented to protect himself. Yizhar was counting on that, not that anyone would ever even hear about that call. Yizhar also happened to know that after-hours calls to certain safe numbers in Tel Aviv were bounced to a secure number in The Building in Jerusalem after three rings. Only top officers—the officers likely to receive such calls, the diligent ones, who worked late—knew that. No one else, not even Avram Shell. As he listened to the toggle and tap of Avram's keyboard, Yizhar could feel tomorrow's story taking shape. Good. Step one.

Yizhar felt no remorse. His version of the story was not a lie! It was true! For the most part. It was certainly true to the testimony he'd extracted from Zvili. Of course, even an old war-toughened type like himself felt bad about a baby's death, any old goddamned kid. It was sad and too bad. And finished. And now, this. This is how we do things and this is how we get things done and this is how we get through situations. Simple, simple. There was only the question of handling Doron, and what Doron would have to say about things and how he would feel about the story. And a slight, nagging worry about little Zvili—Yizhar had told him to keep quiet. Would he turn out to be a blabbermouth?

Would Doron? Yizhar doubted it, and that was good, because he didn't want Doron to say much, not even to Yizhar. He wanted to feel the boy out, see what his story was overall, and find out how much he knew about the details: who was the baby, his family, had Doron himself ever heard of Hajimi? Did he understand the national implications, and the implications for the army? And how about that supposed phone call and the man who answered it? Otherwise, Yizhar had already heard all he needed. The other checkpoint soldiers whom Yizhar had interviewed were comfortable with the army's version of events, but except for Zvili, they had not been directly involved in the incident with the kid.

Yizhar knew the persuasive powers of Colonel Daniel Yizhar, and he had no doubt that Ari Doron, whatever his background, whatever his psychological profile, whatever his ideas about politics and Palestinians, whatever he remembered from that night, would eventually go along with Yizhar when he was shown what the situation was exactly. When he began to understand who Hajimi was exactly, and Raad. When he began to comprehend the implications and repercussions, because this was about repercussions, not about the incident. You had to identify the people to whom something had happened, and then you had to decide: Who was the victim, really? And who was the perpetrator? What was at stake, and what was the value of the factual narrative of events? Who would profit from it? This was about the truth, not the facts.

CHAPTER SIX

DORON PUSHED BACK HIS CHAIR IN THE READING ROOM, and closed his eyes. He could hear a dusty thud each time the librarian piled another book up on the stack at her station. He tried a relaxation technique one of his girlfriends had taught him: imagine empty spaces, she said. Not easy to do with the geography they grew up in, but Doron made an effort. The Kinneret. He pictured its shores on a Sunday afternoon, no one around: grass, dirt and sand, litter—broken bottles and flattened Styrofoam cups, cigarette stubs; but then the sea, flat, gray, shallow, and on the other side, distant but there, the flowering hills rising up and away. He imagined swimming in it. Stroke after stroke. The breathing. Did it calm him? You weren't supposed to ask yourself that question: it interrupted the concentration, intensified the stress. Did it calm him?

He opened his eyes again: this place was empty, too, and musty. One scholar sat at a far table, bent over a decaying monograph. Doron had never been to the Islamic library before; he hadn't even known that this odd artifact of Muslim culture existed in his part of Jerusalem. The reading room was an upstairs afterthought in a museum that seemed to be dedicated to numbing exhibits of Islamic calligraphy or Arab copperware. Thick, sparkling dust floated in great rays of sunlight that swept down from the high windows. It was cold up here, as if the heat hadn't been turned on all winter. The librarian was watching him—she was a helpful, middle-aged lady, and she wore glasses, just like a good librarian. She let him use the Xerox machine for free, because he was a soldier.

He had read three books by George Raad so far, including *The Perils of Peace*, the famous one that had been translated into Arabic by his daughter. The book was dedicated to her: "For my daughter Marina."

It was an amazing book, to Doron. Maybe wrong, obviously anti-Israeli, possibly crazy, clearly full of bitterness. The guy said he supported peace and then went on to undermine every Palestinian associated with the process—shit, they must be angry at him. Poor Raad. He was a man who never got over losing his family home—a spoiled little rich boy. Still, Raad had a Palestinian point of view and Doron had never read anything by a Palestinian before. He examined the photograph of Raad on the book jacket. He looked patrician and arrogant. He actually looked down his nose, and he had a cast of face that said, I'm clever. There was a strength in his features that was like his daughter's, Doron thought. Not the kind of people you want to cross. Father and daughter had a light of intelligence and temper in their eyes. George Raad was a handsome man, Doron could see that. He felt strongly that Raad was not someone he himself would like, but then, they were enemies.

Doron had an appointment to see Colonel Daniel Yizhar at one o'clock. He didn't want to go. He'd been in The Building only once before, to get his ID card. Official Israeli buildings were depressing, filled with depressing people. He'd rather go to the beach, or even to the Kinneret, he'd rather flee, but that wasn't an option. Doron felt trapped, and he knew the feeling was not going to go away. Shortness of breath was a symptom of panic, he learned that in training. It had come on him while the boy was dying, and he still felt as if his lungs ended at the top of his rib cage.

HE WAS LONGING for the comfort of his mother's terrace. He took a bus from the library up to King George Street, and walked through the dust and mud stirred up by a team of backhoes and bulldozers over to the house. Doron's old neighborhood was filled with children getting out of school. A handful of kids sputtered from the bakery, eating powdery cookies and drinking Diet Cokes. One of Jerusalem's many daily rush hours was building. A group of young soldiers in olive drab walked by, their rifles swinging from their shoulder straps and clicking against one another. The street filled up with cars and red buses. A soldier with a rifle guarded each bus stop, and the bus stops were crowded again, in spite of the bombings. Short lines formed at the kiosks that sold stamps and lotto tickets and blue municipal parking cards. Faded Israeli flags hung across a few high terraces.

As Doron passed the butcher's, a young mother in blue jeans pushed through the doors, lifted a stroller down the stoop, and headed off.

Doron followed her. She was relaxed, walking lightly, easily, comfortably. At the florist's she stopped and Doron stopped a few yards behind her. She leaned over a bucket of red roses and breathed. A bunch of delphiniums brushed her cheek. She pulled a rose from the bucket and waved it in front of the stroller's occupant. Satisfied, she put the rose back. She adjusted the plastic bags that swung and slid along the stroller's handles, shifted her small, neat backpack from one shoulder to the other, and moved on, stopping halfway down the block to kick off the heel of her shoe and remove a pebble. Then she turned down a tree-lined side street near the chocolate shop, and was gone.

Doron had to lean up against the florist's to catch his breath. He stood in front of the flower stall, staring at the selection. He tried to remember the name of every flower before him, the names his mother had taught him so painstakingly over the years. Roses and delphiniums, lilies and geraniums and pansies for potted gardens, and hyssops and cyclamen to grow out of terrace walls. Rockrose, hawthorn, and Spanish broom, onion flowers and crocus and lavender. He would not be sending flowers to Ibrahim's mother. The crocus looked so tender; he remembered the little yellow ones from his own front yard. When he was small, he used to pick them and make soup: water, mud, and crocus petals. He imagined himself with tenderness, a little boy kneeling in the mud.

"You're breathing funny," his mother said when she came to the door. She held on to his arm and inspected him.

"I feel a little light-headed," Doron told her. He was more comfortable outside where the air was light and wafting. Inside, it was dark and heavy. His mother had too many Persian carpets. One after another, the rugs seemed to spin Doron down the hallway as he followed his mother's backlit figure, her hair a halo of red fuzz, to the French doors that opened onto the terrace. He sat down heavily on the old, faded couch, and she lowered herself down next to him. She was getting smaller and wider and stiff with age.

Doron and his mother sat out in the cold on the terrace, eating olives companionably. The salt seemed to conquer his nausea. His mother was wearing sandals and a comforting faded housedress printed with huge leaves and tropical flowers. In the garden on the terrace, it served almost as camouflage. His mother kept stealing little looks at Doron when she felt he might not notice. For a long time, they didn't speak, sitting there side by side, picking olives out of the glass dish and listening to the sound of the olive pits slipping back onto the glass table. A mourning dove cooed in the old olive tree around the corner. "A tree from the time of the Crucifixion!" his mother liked to announce to her guests, gleefully. She believed visitors to Jerusalem thought that everything that was old in the Holy Land dated from the Crucifixion. Just beyond the terrace wall, Doron could see that the lemon trees were full of fruit. A few big yellow globes had dropped onto the terrace floor and rolled under the flowerbeds.

"The bird sounds sad today, doesn't he?" Doron said.

"Please," she said. "The bird sounds the way he always sounds."

"Probably," said Doron. "Good olives, Mother." He took another.

"Red pepper-cured. Listen, what is going on?" she said. She smoothed his cheek with her hand, and he knew she was worried. Normally, she was circumspect about showing her affection.

"You've read the paper?" she asked.

"I can't."

"Why not?" his mother asked. He knew she wouldn't question him about details of the incident—she was not a soldier's widow for nothing.

"I don't know. I tried yesterday but it makes me too nervous. Too upset, I guess. I don't want to know too much about what they're saying. I feel ashamed. Not having them mention your name, it's as if something just too shameful has happened to you. You can read them for me."

"You may not want to know too much, but you have to know what the army is saying, and what the Authority is saying," she said. "You have to protect yourself. Wait." She patted his leg. "I'll read it to you. Will that be okay?"

She left the terrace to get her glasses, came back with the paper, and read some paragraphs to her son. It was the army spin: the Israeli Defense Forces were always on top of a story like this one, Doron knew. *Ha'aretz* said that as far as the top command knew at this point, the men at the checkpoint had gone by the book. The fifteen minutes the boy and his mother had waited were consistent with procedure for medical *laisser-passer*s.

"Fifteen minutes, Mother?" Doron said. "God, it was much longer than that."

"Time can seem to go slowly in a crisis," she replied.

There had been some concern about the woman's husband, an alleged Hamas mastermind, and possibly part of the ring responsible for

the recent bus bombings, according to military sources. "The duty officers' behavior was exemplary," the reporter had written.

The army spokesman described George Raad, the boy's grandfather,
as a former confidant of the Chairman who had criticized the Authority,
and Hajimi as a "jailed terrorist." The army did not give out names of soldiers at checkpoints: it was standard practice to guard the identities of soldiers involved in "incidents." Doron had a bad feeling, though. It did not
relieve him that the boy was the son of a jailed terrorist. Because he
remembered the boy; he knew the boy. The story read to Doron as if the
soldiers at the checkpoint had committed a crime. Hiding made him feel
worse, not better. Hiding behind the wall of the army, hiding from one
Palestinian woman: it was low, it was dishonorable.

Shake it off, he told himself. That's what his father had always said
when Doron hurt himself as a boy, and he had tried to respect his father's
dictum, because his father was a war hero and a good man. Almost lost a
leg. Bullet through the shoulder, too. Shake it off.

"I have an appointment with Daniel Yizhar at one," he told his mother.

"They picked Yizhar, eh?" she said. "A good choice, for them. I know
the family. Did you know his father was a mathematician? And his grandfather or his great-uncle, I can't remember which, lived in a tent and built
the highways. A very clever family."

The two of them each picked out an olive.

"I'm just going to tell him what happened," Doron said, standing,
bending down low to pick up one of the fallen lemons.

"Did anyone tell you not to, darling?" asked his mother. "Aren't the
lemons beautiful this year?"

Doron bit off the top of the lemon's skin and began peeling it. He
threw the peels off the terrace piece by piece, and sectioned the fruit. He
handed his mother half, and sat back down.

"I also read in the paper that the Palestinians are saying the baby had
to wait for more than an hour at the checkpoint," she said. She broke off
a lemon section and put it in her mouth.

"Is that what they're saying?" Doron asked, looking at her squarely.
Her frown was odd, tight and disapproving, he thought, until he realized
it was the lemon juice.

"If you could have seen this boy, Mother," he said. He wanted to say
more, but couldn't.

"It's a beautiful family," she said.

"Yeah." He ate a lemon section. It was gratifyingly sour.

"They look very good in the pictures. The mother walking the child down the street. And that one of the boy on his grandfather's lap, very respectable."

"They are respectable, Mother."

"Yes," she said. "For Palestinians. I notice the picture of the boy's father is just a little not so respectable. I suppose the picture must come from the IDF. It's just you can see that he's in a cell."

"Oh, come on, Mother. To Palestinians, that *makes* him respectable. Every family has someone who's been in an Israeli prison."

"Don't begin to get sentimental, sweetheart. It's dangerous. You're not in a good position to start feeling sentimental about the situation. Things are what they are."

"Thanks for the information, Mother."

"You're welcome, dear," she said, collecting their discarded olive pits in her cupped palm. As she bent toward him, he noticed a new line of worry between her eyebrows.

His mother cleared the table. For a minute, Doron was left to himself. He sat there looking out at the trees. The doves made their morning noise, even though the day was well under way. The smell of lemons hung in the air, a crisp smell like a clean electric desert wind. He and his mother had always eaten them; lemon eating was a shared eccentricity, even when he was a small boy. Like eating the sun, she would say. He remembered her young face puckered up in a funny kiss.

COLONEL YIZHAR and three members of his staff were waiting for Doron just within the massive main door of The Building. As Doron crossed the threshold, the three staffers seemed to jump out at him, and he took a quick step backward, nearly stumbling as he did. Yizhar remained in the background, smiling and sticking out his hand. His team looked indomitable. Doron did not feel as if they were on his side. But they were friendly. Yizhar's assistant, a big man named Reuven, a sergeant, was known as a former bone breaker who used to work over Palestinian prisoners at the Russian Compound. He'd been the terror of al-Moscobiyyeh, as the Palestinians called the compound. Maybe desk work had softened him. Doron doubted it. Reuven was blocking the path to Yizhar and Yizhar's outstretched hand. Reuven had dark hair and the palest skin. He smiled broadly at Doron.

Doron looked down, and his gaze fell on Reuven's hands, which were swinging lightly as if to help the big man retain his balance. They seemed swollen and rubbery, swinging at his sides like surgical gloves inflated with water. Reuven was huge and white, an atavistic snowman. Doron looked at Reuven's glossy knuckles and remembered the things he did not like about the army. It was nice that the knuckles were not meant for Doron's jaw, but still.

Finally Reuven stepped aside, gracefully for a man his size, and Yizhar grabbed Doron's hand and reeled him in.

"How are you, Lieutenant?" Yizhar's handshake was strong, and he did not let go. Doron looked at him patiently. Yizhar's eyes were an odd green; they looked like olives. He peered at Doron. He had the stance of an old boxer, barrel-chested and muscular, and eyes that were hooded now, but looked as if they once might have been bright, before the skin beneath the eyebrows began to sag.

"Do you mind if I call you Ari?" Yizhar asked, in a slightly too loud, slightly too articulated voice, pulling Doron over toward the elevator, keeping hold of him and putting his other arm around Doron's shoulders. It was awkward to walk while still in his grasp.

"Do you have the feeling we've met before?" Yizhar asked.

"No, sir," Doron said. What an odd question. Yizhar was not the kind of person you would forget.

"I've been looking at your record," Yizhar said, then paused, watching Doron as if he were waiting for something that didn't happen. He exhaled. "It's impressive. I know you're scheduled to begin another officers' course this spring, wonderful. Your fellow officers say only the best things about you." Yizhar fell silent. His eyes darted over Doron's face.

Doron supposed some response was necessary.

"I'm glad they like me," he said. He looked down at their linked hands. "Are we going to hold hands all the way to your office, sir?"

"Oh, sorry," Yizhar said, with a half-laugh, almost throwing Doron's hand away. God, was the boy going to be difficult?

The five men negotiated their way into a narrow elevator. As they rode up, the air was close and warm. Doron felt like a prisoner. He wondered what would happen if suddenly he could make Reuven's uniform melt away. Fssst! He used his laser gun on Reuven's shirt. No more sleeves, no more epaulets, no more braid! Hanging, swinging underarms, double-chinned elbows. Wrists rolled with fat. Another pull of the trigger: Fssst! Buttons pop off, shirt disintegrates. Big hairy breasts rise and fall. Fssst! Belt unbuckles. Pants, shorts drop away. Doron stopped himself. The thing was too dreadful to contemplate. He watched as Reuven clenched and un-clenched his hands. He wondered what Reuven was thinking about, if you could use that word in that context. He wondered if Reuven was a good man to have as an assistant, and what he did to assist. When the door opened, the men hustled Doron down the hallway to Yizhar's office.

The hallway was buzzing with the officers who worked on this floor of The Building, popping in and out of offices, smoking, hitching up their pants, zipping their flies as they emerged from the men's room. Except for Yizhar, they seemed to be potbellied, with belts slung beneath their stom-achs, and the buttons of their khaki shirts pulling against their ample pec-torals. They hired secretaries they thought were sexy, but the secretaries were always too dumpy, too middle-aged. Doron looked at Yizhar's secre-tary as they passed through her reception area. She was filing something. Reuven stopped in front of her and put out his hand. The men did not speak with her as she handed three or four files to Reuven. Ah, she was typ-ical, Doron thought. Her hair was a deep red and her midriff regrettably ex-posed—though, left to the imagination, it would improve only slightly. She was the kind of woman you didn't want to imagine naked. She and the rest of them in The Building—all now spending their precious non-coffee-break moments going over his dossier looking for sexual perversion or drug abuse or instances of juvenile delinquency—*they* were the people who killed that boy, Doron told himself. It was their fault, with their long purple nails. Putting Doron on hold, forcing him to call down to fucking Tel Aviv, mak-ing him listen while that computer-generated mouse music played ragtime, and Marina Raad sat there watching him with her iron eyes, her rain-soaked hair hanging down over Ibrahim like a mermaid's. Doron had been afraid to return her regard. He was ineffectual, she could see that, and the situation was desperate, he could see that. He remembered the end-of-the-world sound of each rasping breath the boy could not quite take.

Yizhar sat Doron down on a straight-backed metal chair in front of his desk. He smiled at Doron; he was always smiling but he didn't seem sunny. He looked like a green-eyed owl, beaky, clever, probably ruthless. He was perched on the side of his desk, waiting. Doron waited, too. He had plenty of time; he had been taken off Shuhada checkpoint, and was waiting for a new assignment. It had been four days since what had hap-pened happened. He had nowhere to go, except back to the Islamic Museum's library. Yizhar looked at Doron, sitting there. Doron seemed quite calm and relaxed. Yizhar asked everyone but Reuven to leave the room. Doron looked at Yizhar and tried to imagine what it must be like to be such a stereotype of what you are, such a self-parody. Well, to Yizhar, he himself probably looked like some kind of a parody, too, a dumb young fuck-up soldier sitting there, looking a little too relaxed, given his situation. That's probably how he looked to Yizhar, though it was far from how he felt. Zvili would be relaxed in this situation, because he had no conscience. He wondered if Yizhar intended to interview Zvili. Or if he already had. Zvili, who'd had the nerve to brush his metal detector over the mother's body while her baby was gasping.

"Ari? This is Sergeant Reuven, my assistant," Yizhar said, with a sweep of his hand. Over in the corner with the plants and the file cabinet, Reuven looked up. He nodded slowly at Doron, who saluted from his chair.

Yizhar surveyed the room. Doron thought: He's surveying the room. Yizhar looked at the door. Now he's going to lock the door, Doron thought. Yizhar slid off his desk and went to lock his office door. He leaned out into the reception area first, and said "No calls" to his secretary. Lord help me, thought Doron. Yizhar returned to his perch.

"You could be in deep-shit trouble, kid, do you know that?" Yizhar asked.

"I'm aware there's a problem, yes, sir."

"You know who that child was, the other day?"

"Yes, sir, I am aware of the baby's family, if that's what you mean. I know who they are. When they came into the guardroom, I didn't know."

Yizhar picked up a glass cup filled with coffee. It had been sitting on his desk when they arrived: old milk had settled on the top and was beginning to crust. With both hands, Yizhar held the cup up in front of his face and looked at its contents with a practiced, scientific eye. He shrugged once, and sipped at it. He swallowed. He nodded to himself, and put the cup back down, a little farther away from him than it had been.

"It was because of who he was that the baby was delayed. They knew at headquarters," Doron said.

"What?" Yizhar said.

"They *knew*," Doron said. "Someone told me expressly that I was not to allow the Hajimis to enter."

"Someone? Please. Who?" Yizhar sniffed.

"A guy I talked to on the phone at headquarters," Doron said.

"At that hour it may have been the janitor for all you know. Could have been the Defense Minister's driver. What was this person's name?" Yizhar gingerly fingered a tiny tape machine.

"I didn't ask," said Doron. He felt like a fool. "I wrote down the number somewhere." He fumbled at his pockets—of course he didn't have it now; no jacket. He must have left it at his mother's.

Yizhar ignored the fumbling as if it were just simply too pathetic a ruse. He fiddled with his tape machine.

"Neat little item, isn't it?" Yizhar said to Doron, looking over at him as he set the thing down at the edge of his desk. Doron noticed that the desk on which the impossibly small, impossibly thin, brilliantly black recorder sat was rusting. Rusting. God, the army and its priorities.

"Right, Ari. We'll look into that call, okay? If you find the number, great," he said. "Let us know."

Doron thought he detected a hint of sarcasm in Yizhar's voice.

"Right now," Yizhar went on, "I'd like to sit here and tell you just what happened from the time you first became aware that Marina Hajimi and her son were trying to cross into Israel until the ambulance arrived."

"Excuse me, sir?"

"Yes?" Yizhar said.

"You're going to tell *me?*" said Doron. "I thought this was an investigation."

"Yes, yes," Yizhar said. "Let me explain. For the next few weeks, until this dies down? I am you and you are me. I mean, right now, you are the Israeli army, and obviously so am I, and I'm just going to take over for you here for a while, so you can relax and calm down, and let me do the heavy steering. Got it?"

"But you want to hear what *happened*, don't you?"

"Look, if you tell me what happened, it's only going to be what you *believe* happened, am I right? No one knows everything. You don't. The kid's mother doesn't. The other men don't. I don't want to get turned around here, with too many versions. I've heard a couple of witnesses, and that's enough. They told me what I need to know, and now, I'm just going to put everything together. And that will be it."

"Huh," said Doron. He looked at Yizhar with a new respect, and fear.

"Yes." Yizhar smiled. "It's easy. I've done it before. In the end, it will be our word against theirs, or against hers. It's not like it's going to end up in a court of law. It's p.r., not justice."

"But there were other Palestinians there."

"As I said, our word against theirs. Sheukhi, you must mean."

"Sheukhi? I don't know. Some guy in a tie who was butting in and trying to help her. In his way."

"Yeah. That would be Sheukhi. The lawyer. Lawyer who talks a lot."

"A lawyer?" said Doron. "Oh, no."

Yizhar got up off his desk and went around behind it to his chair. He sat down, and looked fondly at his tape recorder.

"Don't worry," said Yizhar. "Sheukhi may be a lawyer, but he's a Palestinian lawyer. We've checked him out already. Not a great reputation, even among Palestinians. Not worth worrying about, for us. The testimony of an Israeli garbageman would carry more weight."

Doron looked down at the floor.

"So tell me what happened," Doron said softly, addressing the linoleum.

"I was recovering from the earlier unrest at the checkpoint," Yizhar said. "There was a storm. A woman and her child sought entry into the trailer. I could see the child was ill, so I took them in out of the rain. The boy did not look as if he was in need of attention when I first saw them. The woman gave me the boy's medical documents, which I examined and found in order. In normal circumstances, I would have passed them through right away. But given the closure, I decided to run her through the computer. I discovered her husband was in jail, and so I took the name and ran it past a few of my superiors. I called, they checked her out, I explained the child's predicament, and some fifteen minutes after she arrived at the trailer, an ambulance was on its way to pick them up. Unfortunately, it arrived a few moments too late." He looked over at Doron, who was still looking down.

"What do you think?" Yizhar asked with a note of pride, but with some gentleness, too. "Good, no? Not inaccurate."

"I don't know what to say," Doron said. "She was there too, you know. She knows how long it took. She knows that the ambulance was actually ordered for one of my men, she knows what calls got made, what the answers were."

"She is the wife of a jailed terrorist, Lieutenant."

"Yeah."

"So. What do you think of our story?"

"I don't know what to say."

"Say: 'Very good, sir.'"

"But I . . ."

"Say it, Lieutenant. I know you can. You're a smart boy."

"The boy *died*, sir."

"I know that," Yizhar said, suddenly not flippant.

"She lost her baby."

"Yes, she did. And now he's gone," Yizhar said. Am I going to have to spell out everything? he wondered. "And there's nothing we can do about that. Too bad, we would all like to bring him back. But we're dealing with what's possible here. We want to save what we can out of the wreckage. Pull out the survivors. You want to be one of the survivors, don't you? The Israeli army is one of the survivors. We are not all going to go down with that—baby, as you call him. He *was* two and a half, by the way."

"Right," said Doron.

"Not a baby, is all I'm saying."

Doron finally looked up from the floor at Yizhar, who was watching with fascination as Reuven groomed himself. The big man gently inserted the tip of a paper clip beneath a nail, pulled it from one end to the other, then lifted it and flicked its burden across the room in the general direction of a stack of *Jane's Defence Weekly* magazines that was sitting in the corner in the shadows of Yizhar's coatrack.

"It's a crucial distinction." Yizhar put out his arms over the back of his chair. "Babies—babies are innocent. Can't talk. Big-eyed nobodies. Little boys are sweet, too, but they are real people. Identifiably somebody. Have personalities. Will obviously become members of their families, resemble their families already. If you see what I mean. The boy looked just like his grandfather, for example. I don't want to be cynical, but in people's minds, little boys can be future explosives experts, future jailed terrorists, future suicide bombers. Babies, it's harder to imagine. But I'm sure that somewhere out there is a photograph of little Hassan Hajimi, Hamas deputy for political information or whatever the fuck, in short pants, sitting on *his* grandfather's lap or holding *his* mother's hand."

Yizhar sat forward.

"Maybe we should find that picture," he said, turning to Reuven. "It must exist. Get it out to the media. Just to make a psychological point."

Reuven grunted, nodded. Wrote something down in a small notebook that he eased out of his back pocket.

Yizhar took up a pen from his desk and began playing with it, flicking the tip in and out, clicking it, opening it, squeezing its spring, putting it back together, reclosing it. He picked up a notepad and applied the pen to it, then thought better of the impulse, and put the paper back down again. He looked up at Doron and smiled. Doron assumed Yizhar must like that small smile, must think it looked good on him. There was a long silence. No clicking. Reuven stopped picking at his cuticles. Yizhar stopped smiling.

"What do you make of the mother?" he asked.

"What do you mean?" Doron asked.

"I mean, how do you assess her character: Is she strong, determined, intelligent? Or maybe she is meek, defenseless, shy? What do you think she's like?"

"Well, remembering that the time I spent with her was maybe an hour and that her son was dying on her lap, I guess I'd say she is very tough, strong-willed. Angry. Vengeful now, probably."

"All Arabs are vengeful," Yizhar said. He was throwing it out, to see how the boy would react.

"Oh," said Doron.

Yizhar looked at the soldier. "Oh" was not your typical army response to such an observation.

Doron caught the look. "Well, her boy did die at an Israeli checkpoint," he said. "She might think she has a reason to be vengeful."

"The mother has no right to feel vengeful," Yizhar replied, sharply. "Maybe she's to blame, ever think of that? Maybe she should have gotten him to the checkpoint earlier, maybe she should have figured out a way to have her famous daddy find her a good place in Ramallah, a good enough doctor on her side of the line. She had other possibilities."

"I've considered that," Doron said.

"Good."

"I'm sure she has, too," Doron said.

"Possibly. But possibly not. After all, Ari, the Authority has pointed out a very convenient scapegoat for her. . . . And you seem pretty eager for the job. . . ."

Reuven coughed. Yizhar looked over at him. Reuven pointed to his watch. Yizhar looked up at the clock. Maybe that was Reuven's role as an assistant, Doron thought. Telling time.

"Listen, Lieutenant," Yizhar said. "In any situation, any incident, anyone could be to blame; it all depends on your point of view, that's what I say. I just want you to be aware of the story we're giving to the press. I'm sure it's close to yours, with a few minor emendations from the interviews we've had with the other men who were there. What we've said is this: Mrs. Hajimi waited a quarter of an hour. The child was not showing signs of distress before the ambulance was called. Procedure was followed to the letter. The boy's death is unfortunate, but there was nothing more the men at the checkpoint could have done. That's all we've said for now."

Doron looked at him. "And my phone calls? Getting put on hold? The orders I was given?"

"Extraneous. All that comes under following procedure to the letter. We don't need to say more than that."

"And when she and her father and her husband and this lawyer all tell the reporters that your story is not true, that we held them for much longer, what will you do?" Doron looked at Yizhar.

"I'll look the reporters in the eye," said Yizhar, "and tell them that we stand by our men, and by their version of events. Basically, I'll say that it's a case of an Israeli lieutenant's word against the word of a terrorist's wife."

"I wonder who they'll believe."

"That's up to them, Ari. But we will provide transcripts of interviews with the men, a tape of the IDF's call for the ambulance you requested, and a report by the emergency medical team about the boy's condition when they arrived at the scene."

"He was nearly dead."

"That's one thing that their report says, but medical personnel are professionally trained to observe more about a decedent than you can, Lieutenant. How close he was to dead, what he eventually died of. How long it might have taken him to die, to be blunt. If saving him was ever a possibility. That kind of thing."

"Ah," said Doron.

"Ah" was also not a typical soldier's response, but Yizhar ignored it. He had no doubt that the boy was getting the message, but did not want to give in without a battle. It was all about Doron's ideas of truth and morality, and Yizhar was sure he could rein him in by showing him how much he would have to sacrifice to uphold his so-called standards, if he happened to be so inclined.

Yizhar considered Doron again. The lieutenant still looked a little too confident in his metal chair, with his long legs sprawled out and his feet resting on the heels, not with the soles planted on the floor, as they would be in someone showing proper awe.

"And the final and most important thing," Yizhar went on, in a deeper, more gravelly tone, "something that I cannot stress enough, is that you and the other men who were at the checkpoint are absolutely forbidden to speak to any member of the media, foreign or domestic, or to anyone else about any aspect of the incident. Anyone who is found to have spoken with the media or with any third party who ends up talking to the press—and that includes your mother, and your girlfriends, and your second cousin's cousin, Lieutenant—will face a court martial. Mere suspicion of the same will mean immediate suspension. Understood?"

"Yes, sir. I'm not about to start running amok."

Yizhar slammed his fist down on the desk and all his little toys jumped. Doron flinched, the noise was so cracklingly loud. Didn't the man give a thought to his tape recorder?

"I don't really care what the fuck you think you're about to do, Lieutenant. I just want you to do what I say. I hope that's clear. You're one piece of this puzzle, one piece."

It was, to Doron, uncanny how quickly Yizhar got himself back under control, as if—and it was only too possible—hitting the desk had been part of an elaborate act. He's West Bank security, Doron reminded himself. This is an interrogation.

"I just want to be sure you understand," Yizhar said. "Any violation of these proscriptions could lead to something really bad, something worse than what has already happened. I want to be very clear about this. It's not only to uphold Israel's integrity. It's also for your own protection and security, do you realize?"

"Yes, sir. I believe I understand," Doron said.

"You don't want them to know your name, believe me." Yizhar looked him in the eye. "Or your address. Do you think she knows your name, by the way?"

"She could, sir. I've thought about that. She could. So could the lawyer."

He was a smart boy, Yizhar thought. Good mind. Yizhar believed that Doron would not self-destruct. But you could never be a hundred percent sure. Yizhar stood, adjusted his belt and his crotch, and then walked over and unlocked the door.

"Oh, and Lieutenant? There's one thing more I want to be sure you understand," Yizhar said. "No matter how we end up spinning this story, guilt is not a useful emotion. The only mistake you made, really, was going by the book, right? You could have let them through on your own responsibility, but didn't. You're a soldier. You wanted an okay from your higher-ups. Fair enough; that's what we teach the average man, and that's what the average man does. The average man gets put on hold. The average man ends up in a predicament.

"Sometimes, you have to assess the value of disobedience. Disobedience can be useful in the army. All of our heroes have disobeyed at one time or another, sometimes with heroic results. But you say you had to ask headquarters for approval. You had to ask them, didn't you? You waited too long, didn't you? With the boy dying in front of you, you didn't even consider disobeying."

"I did consider it, sir," Doron said. "But, yes, it was too late." He remembered himself saying Sorry, sorry. He remembered Zvili's hopping-mad face, the angry exchange, the ambulance staff rushing up, and turning to look at the boy again, and the child had just, just, collapsed, and lay there limp in his mother's arms. Marina looked up at Doron. Her eyes seemed to beg. For what? Doron remembered his rush of nausea. He felt it again, beneath his heart.

There was a long silence. Yizhar did not look at him. Doron felt fear welling up inside him, a physical thing, at the bottom of his stomach. He hadn't felt so scared since the boy started turning blue. Maybe Yizhar was not on his side at all. Maybe he had a fallback position: blame everything on Doron.

"Will that be all, sir?" Doron asked.

"For now." Yizhar thought he detected a shaking in Doron's voice, maybe. He hoped so. Got to make him quake in his boots, that's the way to keep a man in line. Yizhar came back to his desk and looked down, sorting through some meaningless papers as a sign of dismissal.

Reuven stood up. Yizhar nodded at him.

"Lieutenant Doron can see his own way out, Sergeant," Yizhar said.

REUVEN LEFT FOR the day. Yizhar was alone, which was how he liked it. The boy was a smart boy, and he would come around, because this was his country and he was army. You could rely on that, almost invariably. You could count on all those feelings inculcated through years of schooling and training, you could count on the entire fucking patriotic spirit of the country. It was a comfort finally to know you could fall back on the culture, except in the case of an extreme personality—which did not describe Doron. The culture would bring Doron safe to harbor, and there would be Yizhar, waving and saluting from the dock. He sat back in his chair and put his feet up on his poor old desk. He could see a blue dusk beginning to fall over the powerful shoulders and wings of the Generali lion. Thick gray clouds were piling up down at the end of Jaffa Road. Whenever he turned his attention to it, he could hear the sporadic noise of the traffic stopping and going at the light beneath his window. If he listened hard, he could hear the sound of the pedestrians' shoes falling as they crossed the four-way crosswalk below. Where were they all going, so busily?

This was where he'd ended up. It wasn't what he would have chosen for himself, but it wasn't bad either. He was suited to investigation. He would have preferred defense, but that was not to be. That was not to be—funny phrase, "not to be," a phrase full of destiny and fate, but always used in hindsight. Sometimes he agreed with the Torah-kissing nuts: the ways of the Lord were mysterious to man. If you looked at Doron, or at Gertler, for that matter, you'd have to agree. Of course, when the religious talked about mysteries they were not necessarily interested in an individual man's curriculum vitae, but Yizhar was.

Yizhar remembered the facts of Gertler's case with the kind of painful clarity that only youth and war inspire. Shimon said a man is only worth his courage, and Shimon was blindly brave. The end came during the Six-Day War, a heroic time for Israel, not like now. Gertler—the hero, a man who joked while missiles rained down—panicked. Too many people were dying. His boys, the enemy's boys. Gertler couldn't handle the responsibility. That was his flaw: too much compassion.

Yizhar was sure that that, and drink, had unmanned Gertler. Compassion—or its simulacrum—was a useful thing if you were trying to run the human beast. But, lesson one, Lieutenant Doron: It is not a good thing if you let it take you over. Especially in a war, when you needed to do as much damage as possible. In war, even a little bit of feeling was already too much if it was wasted on the other guy. Understand the other guy, okay, but feel only for yourself, Yizhar thought. Yizhar held to this in peacetime, too. In Israel, peacetime was wartime.

Dusk fell suddenly into night. The spotlight went on across the street, and the lion leaped into relief against the sky. With bombs going off in nearby neighborhoods, Yizhar had watched Gertler, in command, sit with trembling hands in front of a shortwave radio for ten long minutes, incapable of action—when what the nation needed was one final assault, and that, fucking quick and fucking huge. There was Shimon, who was supposed to give such orders, sitting dumbstruck and immobile—a man who normally never stopped moving, never stopped talking. He had been drinking, too. Yizhar picked up the photograph again and studied it. The smiling face. That was before everything happened.

Yizhar drank up the cold dregs of his Nescafé, and remembered the three empty glasses on Shimon's desk that afternoon, glinting in the sun. The man drank whiskey the way sand soaks up water. He absorbed it. The other officers were running around madly, trying to cover over Gertler's failure and keep things moving, but Yizhar felt as if he and Shimon were in a small empty space, alone, at two in the afternoon with the sunlight streaming in and the enemy's automatic fire bouncing off the building. Yizhar saw the empty bottle of Scotch in the garbage can, tossed there and lying at a gay angle as if this were a midnight bachelor's party instead of command central in the middle of the day in the middle of a war. Shimon looked where Yizhar was looking and then smiled ruefully up at him from behind the radio. He shrugged and raised his hands as if to say, Why not? and then he slumped. Shimon had failed the nation, and the army, at a time of crisis.

It was a great national tragedy and Yizhar was sorry for his friend, somewhat sorry. At the time, Yizhar thought that this was certainly the end for Gertler, that this unforgivable binge and breakdown would destroy him. After the war Gertler would be quietly and gently relieved of duties, Yizhar was sure. Yizhar could hope now for a brighter future for himself. He was next in line.

This was when Yizhar's spinning avocation started. The chief of staff begged him to come up with a plausible public explanation for Gertler's collapse. Yizhar didn't want to do it, he wanted to let it lie, let the public remember Gertler's failure and interpret it on their own, but the chief of staff insisted, and so Yizhar complied. Because Gertler *was* Israel.

"Exhaustion" was how he had described Gertler's condition at the end of the short war.

"He's suffering from exhaustion," Yizhar had told the assembled microphones and cameras and tape recorders. The reporters looked at him quizzically. "Exhaustion" was a word for Judy Garland or Elvis Presley. It was the first time Israelis had ever considered the possibility that an Israeli could be tired or worn out—and it saved Gertler's name.

Back then, Yizhar was hopeful. He still didn't understand. He loved Shimon, after a fashion, but Shimon was weak and Shimon . . . well, Yizhar thought Shimon could do other things. Shimon could become head of Hebrew University, Yizhar thought. That was Yizhar's plan for Shimon, a nice, safe, comfortable seat. Leather, tweed, tobacco, and enough respect, while Yizhar would go on to lead the Israeli Defense Forces. But instead, unbelievably, the "exhausted" Gertler was decorated and promoted and history marched on, carrying Gertler on its shoulders to higher and higher rank and position, even though everyone in the army and almost everyone in the government and almost everyone in the country, when you came down to it, knew that the man had fallen apart in the face of battle, if not exactly why.

This gave Yizhar early insight into how history—at least in this country—was written. Certain fates you could not change. Gertler was destined for posterity, no matter how much Scotch he poured into himself.

Another star for you, General Shimon! And Gertler, shuffling and inarticulate, is escorted from the command room once again, in the endless tape of Yizhar's memory, and while others pursue the war to its inevitable triumphant finale, Gertler sits in a chair near a window, his blond hair brushed by wind from the fields, in seclusion with his fiancée, under guard in a breezy farmhouse far from any action. The army could do things with its own back then that it couldn't do today. Today, sequestration was out of the question.

But what if it was for the good of the nation? No, it was impossible. An idle daydream.

Doron's file lay open on the edge of Yizhar's desk. There were other options.

In this job, you had to be creative.

DORON HAD TAKEN the two tabloids from his mother's house. He sat down at Moment Cafe on Aza Street and opened *Yediot* to the photo spread. The open paper covered the whole tiny table.

And there they were. He looked at them, trying to absorb some meaning from their faces. How had they ended up with him? And more to the point, how had he ended up with them? Marina and the boy were holding hands and walking toward the camera on the main street in downtown Ramallah. You could see a stand that sold walking sticks to their left and a jeweler's to their right. The boy was toddling; must have been taken within the year. And by whom? The father, perhaps, in between incarcerations.

A small picture of the father at the bottom; clearly the work of an Israeli Defense Forces photographer, with the cell's sink visible in a corner of the shot. Hajimi looked furtive and downcast, as if he were trying vainly to avert his eyes, hoping to avoid entirely the humiliation of being photographed by some army hack, for the prison record.

Raad with the boy on his lap. Never were there two more serious faces. Doron looked and looked. He had stolen this boy from this man. He looked at the grandfather's hand resting lightly on the boy's leg and thought: They will come after me.

Why shouldn't they?

CHAPTER SEVEN

AHMED AMR WAS DRIVING IN OVER THE DESERT FROM JERIcho. In the passenger seat, Rana slipped off her shoes and tucked her legs under her. The days in Jericho had been slow, filled with legislative business that went nowhere, full of wrangling with the Chairman by telephone in Gaza, where the poor man was stuck as usual—hooray! The meeting in Jerusalem today would be something else entirely. No Chairman, no legislative procedure, no Robert's Rules of fucking Order. Just Ahmed Amr at the helm, in the big chair, and the rest of the cabinet, meeting in semisecret, and, as honored guest, George Raad. Friend of my childhood, Amr thought. That's what George had called him and that's what he was. Uncle Ahmed, to Marina. This time, the invitation was not just pro forma. This time, Ahmed needed George—if the Authority could get him on board, the next stage would really go smoothly. George could work a crowd. But he was so touchy and recalcitrant. Oh, we'll see, we'll see, Ahmed thought.

He loved the ride through the bald hills down into Jerusalem, especially today, with Rana next to him. Sometimes he pictured himself as Bedouin royalty, a camel-riding princeling in heavy, costly robes, surging in over the dry mountains to the holy city, with a vast army accompanying him, and wives, servants, and a whole entire city following behind to support him and supply his every need. The heroic fantasy was left over from youth, but it still struck him now and then, when he was alone in the car and driving a decent distance. Of course today he was not wearing robes—he would only put on his *abayeh* at home when no visitors were expected, or to meet his closest Palestinian friends in private quarters. Today he was wearing a suit and tie, and a keffiyeh. He and the Chairman were the only ones in the cabinet who wore the keffiyeh, but the Chairman wore it for extenuating reasons—to hide his utter, complete, and absolute baldness. Amr wore it for effect. A Frenchwoman in Beirut had once said to him, when he was wearing it: *"Ah, tu fais si arabe."* She thought it was romantic, and his eyes had been opened. Rana, on the other hand, was not impressed. He looked over at her. She had her hand out the window and was letting the wind blow back her hair.

Nowadays, he liked to present Western observers with what they thought was the conundrum of the keffiyeh and the suit and tie. The ensemble confused and intrigued them, and Amr enjoyed that. He liked wearing the keffiyeh and sitting behind a desk in an office with a cell phone and a laptop, and reading about himself afterward in the Western press. How they fell for it! The advanced Arab, the chief negotiator in his head rag, calling Washington via satellite. They never failed to mention the phone, the fax, the keffiyeh. In reality, of course, thousands of keffiyeh-wearing Arabs, including Palestinians, worked at desks or in offices or factories or on cranes and bulldozers or in other areas of the modern, technological world. What else was left for them to do in their ancient headgear? Nothing authentic, to speak of. The keffiyeh was vestigial. The Palestinians' land had been stolen from them, and there was little of it left to work in the old traditional ways, with a keffiyeh to shield you from the sun, a flock of sheep, a long Biblical beard, and a walking stick. Who wanted sheep, anyway?

Amr liked being an Arab in a Mercedes with a beautiful girl by his side. It was part of his grand fuck-you to the world. He was one of very few council members who had bought his own car with his own money and who drove it himself. I alone have integrity, he said to himself. He loved the feel of the car. It wasn't new. It wasn't a limo, it didn't have smoked or bulletproof windows. In fact, it was old. But it was heavy, and powerful, and it handled well. It churned up the desert dust as well as any new car could. The stick itself had a thick, heavy, leather-covered richness in his grasp. The car smelled like leather and saddle soap. Why give a driver or bodyguard these pleasures, when he could have them for himself? Amr was the captain of his car. Besides, he hated the dreadful intimacy of drivers and other personal attendants. Following you around from place to place, waiting outside like a signpost for all the world to read, that you were there. Driving you from spot to spot. A driver always knew where you were, who you were avoiding, where you could be reached. He always knew who you were fucking.

It was still bizarre to be back in Palestine in broad daylight with all the proper documentation. Amr had come back after the beginnings of the peace talks to take his expected place at the Chairman's side, but still, he was always looking over his shoulder, waiting to be handcuffed, beaten, brought in. Watching for a tail. Waiting for hitmen from the Mossad, or maybe here, it would be considered internal—the Shabak. It was impossible to forget the famished months in the Israeli-run camp in Lebanon, the long terrifying, exhilarating years leading raids from Jordan into Israel, the weeks and months in solitary at Moscobiyyeh. Now Amr had a car with special Authority plates, accredited to him by the Israeli government.

He kept the two front windows down as the car thrust higher into the desert's peaks and the tropical dampness of the Jericho plain evaporated. The open windows made an attack easier, but only marginally. The breeze, the sandy smell: it was worth the risk. He checked his mirrors. No tail, no one, nothing. The hills looked like the beaten backs of Bedouin donkeys. A tuft of brush here, a dusty tumbleweed blown up against a rocky outcrop, but otherwise dry dirt, and packed solid. Nothing alive, or growing, or about to grow. Nothing his weary, cosmopolitan eyes could see, anyway.

He switched on Kol Israel, the Israeli news.

"No, put on music," Rana said.

He laughed and shook his head.

Blah, blah, the chief of security, the Defense Minister, blah, blah, security is a priority, cannot negotiate with terrorists, without security there can be no peace, blah, blah. Then the Israeli leftists: Talks must continue, blah, without peace there can be no security, the Prime Minister is corrupt, blah, blah. When they were yowling among themselves, the Israelis were like cats. You could never tell if they were fighting or fucking. Then the Palestinian response: Whine, whine, the closure is unjust. People are without medicine, blah, blah, a baby has died, victim of inhumane Israeli policy, the talks cannot continue, how can we negotiate with these people, whine, whine, and on and on.

"So boring," Rana said. "How can you stand it?"

"I love it," he said.

"I know." She shook her head. "Crazy."

This was a low-rent desert. It was hard to imagine an Arab army descending dramatically down one of these scrubby, dirty mounds, although they had, they had. Everything that remained in the possession of the Palestinians was low-rent, low-budget, and this of course was not even theirs, not anymore, not for the moment.

A flock of sheep was wobbling over a rise. These were tended by a scrawny yipping dog and a young Bedouin wearing a rag tied around his head against the sun and a sweatshirt that had a university escutcheon on it, Amr could not make out which. Of course it was mid-morning, and the boy was not in school, much less at university. What did all his sheep eat? There seemed to be nothing for anyone in this place.

Poor George. The most brilliant man in the world. Our voice in the West—or in America anyway, which counted for something. The most amusing man, to Ahmed—but now, not amusing. George had not looked at all well at the funeral, and he seemed not himself at the Hajimis', afterward. Frail, although still capable of summoning the patriarchal glare. The man was sick. Dah! Amr thought to himself, using George's favorite exclamation. Amr had heard from one of Salah's deputies that Raad was not well, but he had not heard any prognosis. Something with the heart, he said. Amr wondered. He would miss George if George died: it was an old bond they had and one that somehow could not be broken by distance. Whenever something important happened to Ahmed, he always found himself wanting to call George. Lately, he didn't.

Ahmed still remembered that hot, hot day from so long ago that seemed, in memory, the beginning of their long association. They were neighbors and schoolmates. He remembered running down to George's— only a few blocks away—to tell him that the Amrs were packing up their things, what little they could take with them, and eight-year-old George standing there in his short formal pants and jacket, in the violent sunlight after school let out, guarding the front of the Raads' house, his legs planted as though he could never be moved from that one spot, his long fingers nervously pulling on the leaves at the end of a low branch of the mulberry tree, saying: "*I'm* not leaving. I'm supposed to be on the junior tennis team this summer. Aren't you?" The tennis team. Ahmed wondered if George remembered *that*. Or was he too caught up in The Cause? And then of course George turning up at the Amrs' in Amman for supper one evening a few weeks later, looking proud but embarrassed, with the rest of his family. He remembered how George had come to him in the hallway after sweets, and said: "Father says now we are poor."

The threats that had been made against George—after he wrote that ridiculous book—had been troubling Ahmed's usually serene conscience, now that George was around. He kept saying to himself—as he had for months, since the threats had come to nothing (thank God!)—that it wasn't his responsibility. He had warned George, he reminded himself, he had done what was right, and then—even better—nothing had happened. Nothing! But he wondered whether George held him and the Chairman responsible for the threat. Oh well, Ahmed thought, in the end fate had been on George's side, that time, in spite of all the information—and it was good, hard information—that Ahmed had got. After all, George had only written a book—and it wasn't an entirely bad book, Ahmed recalled, although George's criticisms of the Chairman's conduct and the Authority's corruption were a little outlandish. Yes, George had only written a book.

Of course, Najjar had only written books, too, and Ahmed hadn't been able to save Najjar's legs. But then, he hadn't tried as hard for Najjar as he had for George, had he?

Ahmed downshifted. A slight hiccup in the otherwise pleasing purr of the old Mercedes, and up she went, up another rise, and up and up, and the desert spread itself before him like a vast blank terrain waiting to be conquered: it was no Sahara, but for a moment he thought he caught it shimmering. Rana was fiddling with the radio. Ahmed flicked the tail of his keffiyeh behind his shoulder, and looked at himself in the rearview mirror. Handsome, imperial. He wondered for the thousandth time how the Chairman managed to achieve such a disarrayed look in a garment that was so very noble, so very formal.

Wretched, enduring bugger.

He caught Rana watching him look at himself. He turned to her and smiled.

"You are vain," she said. She shook a reprimanding finger at him.

"I'm vain because I must be very, very attractive to have someone like you sitting next to me," he said.

She smiled tolerantly.

"Will you see Dr. Raad today?" she asked. She was fascinated by George, Ahmed had noticed. A man of conscience, she thought. Well, maybe he was. All the young students worshipped him, all the kids who were growing tired of the rest of the old farts—the former commandos who ran the Authority. Familiarity, et cetera. Ahmed himself still had the gloss of the guerrilla about him, but he knew that that was fading.

"Yes, of course, of course," Ahmed answered. "My oldest friend. I will see him every chance I get."

But would he? George had always taken things hard, unlike Ahmed or the Chairman, who rolled with the punches and worked with what life dealt them, which was what Palestinians had to do. You were chased, you fled. You got arrested, you escaped. You were attacked, you fought back. But you stayed what little ground you had as well as you could, unlike George who had done the one unforgivable thing, unforgivable by the fighters like Ahmed and many others in the Authority. George had left and made his life—a real, normal life—in the new world, a life that went on as if, in a certain way, nothing had happened back in 1948 when the State of Israel was created and they all ended up somewhere else.

Ahmed was not particularly impressed by George's career. A lifetime writing about the place, about all their issues, making a name for himself while they fought the battles, and sometimes died. Good for him, and so bloody what. What was so impressive about that? From time to time, George was useful. Otherwise, politically, he was a heart doctor from the U.S., as far as Ahmed was concerned.

Nonetheless, Ahmed had forgiven him years ago for the abandonment. The only problem was, having left them all behind to fight the fight, George had felt—what was it?—guilt or embarrassment, and so he'd become more intransigent than all the rest of them, more radical. George was more Palestinian than the Palestinians.

And now poor George was back again, this time right back in the thick of it. Really, if you looked at it personally, the boy's death put him smack dab in the middle of the action, just where he'd always tried not to be—not writing about it, not pontificating, but in fact a part of it. How odd it must be for him. See? You can't escape, Ahmed wanted to tell him. It's in our blood, old chap. The loss of the grandson meant that George could not just sit back and comment from the depths of his father's beaten-up, overstuffed armchair, about which Ahmed had heard so much from George back in the Amman days.

Damn sentiment! Damn objects carried over oceans! Damn romance! This desert, these cities, these orchards and groves, these plains: this was a real place with a real struggle. Like everyone else at the funeral, Ahmed had seen that moment when George nearly stumbled into the boy's grave. The question for Ahmed was whether George would join forces with the friend of his childhood, or turn away again. He so much wanted George beside him for this one. It would be so useful. The grandfather—and what a famous, eloquent grandfather. A truly perfect spokesman for Ahmed's new campaign. Ahmed felt himself rubbing his hands together, mentally. What should they do with the Raad baby?

The Hajimi baby, even more to the point. Ahmed Amr had never met Hassan Hajimi—old Authority types didn't really mingle with Hamasniks—but Hajimi was a legend to the next generation, much as Amr himself had been a legend to his own. Hajimi was a brilliant speaker and a strategist, and all the propaganda the Israelis disseminated about him, how he was an explosives expert, a terror mastermind, blah, blah, blah, had not hurt his reputation among young Palestinians—it didn't matter what was true or not true. Hajimi had a natural popular touch that top Hamas militants often sadly lacked, thank God, or they would be running the Authority. Some of them were as self-regarding and condescending as a pasha, Ahmed had noticed in his dealings with them.

In spite of what the Israelis now said, Ahmed was sure Hajimi had little if anything to do with the recent bombings—but that didn't mean the young fellow disapproved of terror or the goals of the bombers. Marina may not have married an explosives engineer, but she had hooked up with something volatile. People return to their heritage in bizarre ways. Ahmed had barely talked to the girl since she was a child, after all. Maybe Hajimi was her way back to what her father had left behind. Clearly she wanted something more authentic than what her father had on offer. If you were born in the U.S., you didn't settle in Ramallah for nothing. With Marina, maybe it was just love. Fell in love with Hajimi, and embraced Palestine. You had to love someone or believe in something to live on the West Bank out of choice.

"I am now the voice of reason," Ahmed said to Rana.

She looked at him.

"So you say," she said. "History is a funny thing." She patted his knee and smiled.

Imagine that: Ahmed Amr, the voice of reason, he thought, smiling at the windshield. And just ten years ago, he was organizing hijackings and sneaking over the Jordanian border to do raids. Hmmmm. Everything in this world was upside down. The Israelis now call me a moderate. He checked his mirrors again. What a world. The radicals blew up buses to achieve conservative, fundamentalist goals. The most traditional among his compatriots, the upstanding, the righteous—this was Raad—was on his way toward becoming an extremist, edging close to rejecting their peace because, get this, the Chairman was corrupt and because George found it distasteful to negotiate with the Israelis. Well, who else were you going to negotiate with?

"Collaborators"—himself among them—were now the honorable men. Ahmed Amr was deep into talks with the Israelis! The evil Zionist occupier turned out to be some sweaty, dumpy guy sitting across the Formica negotiating table, eating a dried-out tuna sandwich. This was what fifty years of war had brought them to. And the logical conclusion? Here it is: Bus bombs had been used to abort the embryonic peace. Now let's use a dead baby to revive it. The boy was dead, a martyr. His little lungs exhausted with crying, with just plain breathing. Asthmatic, as his grandfather had been. Each dusty breath came hard here in Desertland. Well, let the martyr serve the cause, as a martyr should. Come on, George! We'll give little Ibrahim to the street. That'll bring the Israelis back to the talks. We'll have demonstrations, unrest, an uprising!

Poor little chap.

Ahmed shifted and took Rana's hand. The Mercedes plowed onward.

CHAPTER EIGHT

THE WASHING MACHINE WOULDN'T WORK. IT WAS DOING it on purpose. Slothful, temperamental, lazy machine. Marina was developing a sour relationship with it, just the way ladies did in the old days with their servants. She sat down on the floor in front of it and closed her eyes. It was made in Eastern Europe. Usually, you just had to kick it gently, slightly to the left of the door latch, and it would cough into action, those mesmerizing two-hour cycles of heating water to a boil and then laboriously spinning a hundred and eighty degrees clockwise—spinning was the American word; you couldn't really call what a washing machine did here by the same name—hiccuping for a few seconds, and then, exhausted, rotating painfully in the other direction until it had achieved what village girls used to achieve with an eighth of the energy, the time, the pain, and the cost only a few short years ago, before everyone had one of these unfriendly things perched on their roof in a jury-rigged shelter alongside the solar panels and the boiler, and the discarded furniture that, who knew?, might come in handy one day.

She was washing Ibrahim's clothes. She wanted to put them away somewhere. Maybe back in his dresser. It was a normal laundry day, and she was doing the baby's clothes. His two blue jumpers, his blue jeans, the black sweatshirt with a Ninja Turtle on it that the wife of one of Hassan's friends had bought for the baby in Ramallah, the thin Palestinian socks his aunts had given him that wouldn't last two more washes. His bibs she had set aside because she couldn't bear to wash them just yet, his bibs, and the foot pajamas that still gave off the sweet smell of the sleeping child.

Her father came out onto the roof in his bathrobe. She looked up at him from the floor.

"You don't look very comfortable down there," he said.

"I'm contemplating technology," Marina answered, gesturing toward the washing machine. She bit her lip.

"Ah," George said. "But contemplation does not seem to be leading to action in your case." He got down on his knees slowly, and stared into the dark interior of the machine. "Not working?"

"I kicked it, but it won't start."

"Well, it's not a donkey, sweetheart."

"No, really. That's how you start it. You kick it here," she said, and pointed to a spot where, upon closer inspection, George could see a faint indentation. He stood.

"Did you hear me creak?" he asked her.

"Please, Dad."

"No, I actually creak, like some old chair or door."

"Maybe you can only hear it inside of you," she suggested.

He cast an adversarial look at the machine and kicked it. Nothing happened.

"See?" Marina said.

He tried again.

"I'm beginning to feel slightly ridiculous," he said, looking down at her. She was surrounded by his shirts and Philip's jeans and the general household buildup of towels and sheets. "You look like part of the laundry down there."

He leaned down and opened the washing machine door. He noticed Ibrahim's things.

"Hello," he called into the small, dark cavity.

He closed the door to the machine again, and kicked it softly.

"Not quite hard enough," she said.

He kicked it harder. He checked the plug. It was connected.

He looked at the machine thoughtfully, tugging on an imaginary beard.

She laughed briefly. Her own laughter sounded harsh to her.

"Aha," he said, and leaned forward abruptly to push a button. A red light turned on. He kicked the machine again, and they both felt a grateful shudder as it rose to the morning's task. He looked at her again.

"You have to turn it on, dear," he said.

She looked up at him. Circles of fatigue made her dark eyes look sunken.

"I'm tired, Dad," she said. Behind the concave window of the washing machine, she could see Ibrahim's blue jeans and his sweatshirt flopping from the top of the rotation down into the suds below, over and over, as if they were caught in a storm at sea. *Clean* was the word that repeated itself to her. She gazed down at the topography of laundry that surrounded her.

"Come on, then," George said, using Grandfather's bluff military tone. "Let's fix coffee."

He extended his hand to help her up, as if he could give any help.

SHE SAT AT THE kitchen table while he boiled water, spooned out coffee, complained about the state of her mugs. "Chipped," he kept saying. "In the land of low-cost ceramics." He felt the way he did sometimes—rarely, he liked to think—when he gave a lecture and the audience wasn't really following, as if there were a vast emptiness out there, an echoing amphitheater filled with no one, a void that he was trying to impress and amuse, as if a mere human could impress the void. She was looking at the backs of her hands.

"I'm getting old," she said, interrupting his flow.

"Everything's relative," he said, putting her coffee down in front of her, and looking at her hands also. "They're beautiful. A bit like your mother's, strong and square, but with my long fingers."

"Vanity, vanity," she said. She looked up at him, and he thought he detected a brief passing of amusement in her gaze. He hoped.

"I can reach much more than an octave, dear." He smiled at her above the steam from his mug, and sat down across from her. "So you're going to see Hassan's lawyer today?" he asked her.

"Yes," she said. "Is Philip still asleep?"

"Yes."

"After his great exertions," she said.

"He did acquit himself admirably, didn't he?" George said, nodding. Philip was born to be a funeral director, George remembered thinking. Or a politician.

"He said something about coming with me to Orient House, after," George said. "There's another meeting."

There was a silence.

"Hassan says those meetings are like publicity stunts," Marina said.

"He does, does he?" said George. It was rare that he was offered even the smallest glimpse of the man. "He's not far wrong, I must say. Except that publicity stunts have to be amusing or at least interesting."

There was another pause in the conversation. They both felt it. This was the moment when they would naturally have turned to Ibrahim and let his presence undo the silence between them. But now they were both busy not talking about Ibrahim. Marina stood and turned off the kitchen light. She went to the window, and pushed out the metal shutters that she used for blocking the early morning sun, which got in her eyes in winter in that kitchen no matter where she sat. She looked at her father.

It was odd to have him here. She had finally admitted to herself that he was the reason she had decided to study at Bir Zeit, decided to get to know the Homeland. George sipped his coffee and looked at the headlines in *Al-Quds*, which was lying on the breakfast table. Her mother had been resigned and stubbornly unromantic about Palestine, but her father was quite the opposite. Marina had ended up in Ramallah, she thought, because of all her father had taught her. Her father would call her into his study in the evening, when she imagined he was reading medical treatises, and show her the key, the old key to the Raad family house in Jerusalem, the house he was now so reluctant to visit, and tell her stories from her great-grandfather's day, about men on horseback with swords held aloft, and about the wounds of the fabled fighter Ibrahim Abu Dayyeh, who fled in his pajamas from the hospital in order to continue his defense of the neighborhoods of Jerusalem in 1948 up until the last minute.

"What do you say, shall we flee tomorrow?" That was what George told her were her grandfather's sarcastic words every evening before the family went to bed.

It was a way of thinking about the world: in her father's heart, the Raads were refugees, exiles, and outsiders, no matter how American Marina might have felt growing up, with her mood rings and her prowess at Monopoly and her comfortable way of life. At the house in Cambridge, news items from the Middle East were like letters from family in the old country, discussed and dissected at the breakfast table and then at the dinner table—every day, all day. The Chairman and Uncle Ahmed had been her adolescent heroes, and she'd made The Cause, as her father would say, her whole life, in a way. She studied Palestinian history at Harvard; she had her master's degree in Middle Eastern political science when she arrived at Bir Zeit. (Of course, her father never took her master's seriously; *he* was the one who had *lived* through the Catastrophe. He was the one who was *born* in Palestine, and of course he was also the world's acknowledged authority on the subject.) Marrying Hassan was a way of gaining authenticity, she realized a long time after she fell in love with him—and having Ibrahim, too, who was a Palestinian born in Palestine.

"The editors of *Al-Quds* seem to think they'll find this soldier," George said. He folded the paper and looked over at her.

"And they are all-knowing," she said. Each time she thought about the soldier, she saw his scared face, heard the panic in his voice as things got worse.

"Will you need to see a doctor while you're here?" Marina asked George.

He noticed that she had changed the subject.

"It depends how long I stay," he said.

"You mean you want to know how long you are invited for?" she asked, managing to smile. She didn't want him to leave, she realized. The house was already too empty.

"I can really only stay a week, I think," he said. He straightened his back, and tightened his robe. "I'm not feeling entirely well. It would be nice to get home." Home, he heard himself say. He'd always taught her that this was home.

Marina looked out the window. Of course he wouldn't allow her to extend an invitation. He had to be in charge. It was good to know that she could so easily summon the energy to be annoyed at him; it was a sign that some part of her was still intact.

He was glad to see it, too, that impatient turning away. Maybe disgust would help pull her out of her torpor and depression—if he simply continued to behave like an insensitive father. And it came so naturally to him. But possibly, he thought, it was time to take matters in hand. Possibly, he thought, now was the moment for him to do something for Marina, protect his only child from the situation, The Cause—too late, he knew, but there was still a defense to be mounted. He had taught her to love Palestine; in some way, he had inflicted this terrible trial on her, and it was his obligation to help her now. He didn't want her caught up in some futile and dangerous retribution against this soldier, whoever he was. But what could George do? What could he do? Without Ibrahim, she was even more alone. It would be like Marina, with her sense of loyalty, to stay in Ramallah just to be near the husband's prison. And was Hassan interested in personal revenge? George wondered.

He heard an electronic beep coming from somewhere just outside the house—the roof, was it?

"What's that?" he asked Marina.

"Oh," she said. "The washing machine. It's changing cycles, or so it claims."

MARINA WENT TO find the ironing board, which she hadn't seen in months. She found it folded up behind the armoire in the hallway. A few pushes and shoves dislodged it, and she carried it to the laundry room and set it up. This was how she was going to spend the rest of her life: washing, sorting, ironing, and folding. Philip's collar wouldn't stay down. She sprayed it. She sprayed blue jeans and tee shirts and underwear. Her iron made everything flat. She did Ibrahim's little shirts and even his socks. Flat, and flatter. It was a relief to watch the wrinkles disappear beneath the iron. Heat was passing over everything. The heavy iron sank into the folds of her father's blue shirt like an ocean liner, flattening the waves as it moved. It was a beautiful, magic eradication. She looked forward to ironing an infinity of cotton sheets.

LATER, ON HIS WAY from the kitchen to find Philip, George passed Marina in the hallway. She was holding Ibrahim's neatly folded clothes ahead of her on her flat palms like some Oriental offering. George stopped her by putting a hand on her shoulder. He kissed her cheek and then looked at her closely. The hallway was dark. Half open on either side of them were closets overflowing with stacked linens wafting a fresh smell into the air. At the far end of the hall, a door to a bathroom where the shower had just been turned off was open, and a fog of steam swept down toward them. The carpeting was soft underfoot. George felt inappropriately uplifted, as if he were walking beneath a bower with a young girl on a spring night near the sea. Marina shook herself free as he inspected her face, and fled down the stairs to the baby's room.

CHAPTER NINE

To venture into enemy territory, that was how Doron thought of it at first. He located the Hajimi house through police records at the Russian Compound, where Hassan Hajimi was imprisoned. It was like a research project: First, Raad's books at the library. Then some treatises on Islam, and books of Muhammad's sayings. Now this. As he flipped through the long document—which listed former as well as current prisoners—Doron began to wonder who all these political prisoners were. The sergeant on duty watched him with folded arms. Doron was in civilian clothes: black jeans, a white tee shirt.

"Here it is," Doron said to the sergeant, because the man seemed to require communication. Doron jotted the address down on a matchbook. He nodded at the sergeant, whose eyes flickered over Doron's face. He raised two skeptical eyebrows and quickly came over and took the heavy notebook from Doron.

Doron walked down through Musrara and across King David to the Old City. Enemy territory, he thought. Man with a mission. He was looking for a new wardrobe. He wound his way to Jaffa Gate and the souk, and began descending the main thoroughfare. He tried not to look out of place, but he felt huge and awkward and surrounded. He zigzagged through the crowds down to the bottom of the tourist market, past stalls selling tee shirts, chess sets, ceramics, candles and candelabras, round leather ottomans, silver jewelry, and gilt-sheathed daggers, and then turned left and headed toward Damascus Gate and the real market, where they sold things people needed. The place was crowded; Doron was certain he was the only Israeli here—if you were Israeli, you stayed well within the Jewish Quarter in the Old City unless you were looking for a fight.

He passed through the food market. Imploring wide-socketed skulls of butchered animals hung at waist height. Goats and cattle, possibly sheep, Doron couldn't tell. Behind the exotic aromas of cumin and coriander from the spice market, you could smell death. The broad stones of the alley were slick and black with water and bloody runoff from the butcher stalls. Women with shopping baskets and bags engaged in a cacophony of negotiation with the stall keepers. Bright oranges and lemons lit up the dark alleyways.

He turned down a narrow roofed alleyway and emerged from a world of skinned chickens into aisles piled with pants, stacked with scarves, festooned with hanging dresses, leggings, and children's clothes. Eager faces looked out at him from the stalls. It was less crowded here.

If he spoke Hebrew—no, he didn't even want to think about that. But if he spoke Arabic, his accent would give him away, he was sure. So, English—maybe they would not be able to detect his accent in a foreign language.

"Pants," he said to a smiling man.

"Pants?" the man asked.

Doron pointed at the stack.

"Ah, trousers," the man said.

"Yes, for me," Doron said, pointing to his legs. The man showed him a pair of black polyester pants with a sharp crease down the front.

"You like?" he asked.

"Yes," Doron said. He was assembling his disguise. He felt the excitement of adventure. Dress-up.

The man started wrapping the folded pants, and looked sideways up at Doron. Doron caught the look, and understood: Why was this foreigner buying these things? It didn't make sense.

Should he get a keffiyeh? They were hanging from a rack a few stalls down. Too obvious, he thought. And not everyone wears them. And could he ever figure out how to wrap one? Never. He settled on a scarf, a long woolen one. Palestinian men tied them around their necks with the two ends hanging down in front. Guaranteed to look authentic, Doron thought, as he put the scarf in his little black plastic bag along with the pants. Now a close-fitting knitted hat and a sweater-vest, and I'm ready.

He took everything back to his mother's empty house, and changed quickly, shoving his real clothes into the back of a closet. He didn't want to think too much about what he was doing. This would be normal, he thought, if I were doing it for the army, for some undercover unit, for some good reason. The greatest generals always had some story of dressing up like women and assassinating terrorists in distant Arab cities. But for him, there was no good reason. He was doing this simply because he felt compelled. He needed to know more; so far, he could explain nothing to himself. Not the boy's death, not the mother's strange allure, not his own involvement. If he got closer, maybe he'd see things more clearly.

And maybe not. But he had to try. He wanted more than anything to see Marina Raad again. He wondered: Was this normal? In any way? He turned her over in his mind. The black hair, the way it curled in the rain, and her frightened face, which she tried so hard to keep distant and haughty.

When he looked in the mirror, he thought he'd done a pretty good job. He wondered if Palestinians had a different way of walking; he thought so. Israelis moved aggressively; the Palestinians were more cautious. He would try a cautious walk, then, and keep himself as invisible as possible. He pulled his hat down low over his forehead, put one hand in his pocket, and fitted the other with a cigarette. He looked at himself again, and a Palestinian looked back.

FROM THE STREET, you could barely see the house. It was perched on a hill overlooking the Ramallah road, and only its roof was visible from the street that was listed as its mailing address. Fig trees grew in the garden. Their dark green tops rattled up against the roof in the sandy winter wind. There was a rusting red tricycle sitting in a corner of the rooftop. Some old, dusty, machine-made prayer rugs had been scattered here and there. In front of one section that had been covered with makeshift tin, a clothesline ran. Flowered sheets whipped along it. The flapping sheets waved him away, warned him off. The day was dark and the sky was an ochre color that signaled that the *hamsin* was coming again.

Doron hated the desert wind: it coated cars with a film of yellow sand, it got up your nose, it made you cough, and worst of all, it reminded you that Jerusalem, with its McDonald's and Burger Kings and nice red buses and nice red post offices and its green gardens and flowering terraces and public buildings flanked by fountains, was actually right on the edge of an ancient desert where camels and cactuses and Bedouins were the only successful species.

He saw that there was no door from the house onto this street. He left his unhappy taxi driver waiting and went around the corner. He hoped no one would see him; they would probably be able to spot him as an impostor right away. Down the hill was the Ramallah road, always busy, its intersections and lanes filled with potential and actual car crashes. Across from the house was a big empty lot. Bits of paper trash skittered along its broken ground, and piles of construction materials—tiles, cement blocks, bags of sand—stood in heaps waiting for the day, long distant, no doubt, when someone would manage to scrape up the money to build something here and also get around to doing it. Facing the Hajimis' driveway was a big green overflowing garbage dumpster. Doron decided he would stand just a little behind it and wait for Marina to come out.

He pulled his wool hat down a bit further around his head. He put the collar of his shirt up against the wind, pulled his sweater-vest tighter, and double-wrapped his long wool scarf, letting its tails hang down at the sides of his neck. He lit a cigarette. Now he looked like someone he would normally avoid. He move farther behind the dumpster, so that he could just see around it. Certainly she would come out. A Muslim mother was not allowed a long mourning period, especially if her son had died a martyr. Not that Doron imagined that Marina Raad was a particularly devout Muslim.

Doron hadn't learned much about Islam in his few short days in the library, but he had dipped into a few handbooks in Hebrew and English. First of all, Muhammad ("Peace Be Upon Him," as they said in the books) was always on horseback, which seemed oddly heroic to Doron, who imagined his own prophets as outcasts with mud-caked hair, ranting on street corners, or elderly men with long beards and shepherds' crooks—their transportation at its best an old jackass. The Prophet of Allah (Peace Be Upon Him) rode horses and pitched tents and dug trenches for battle, working with shovels and pickaxes. He was like an Israeli pioneer. He made miracles in which rocks turned to sand and a girl's apronful of dates was made to feed hundreds of trench diggers. He caused lightning to flash from beneath the blow of his pickax. He claimed Abraham, Isaac, Jacob, and Jesus as early prophets of Islam. Like so many of these fellows who purveyed the word of God, Muhammad (PBUH—they abbreviated it in the books) seemed to have had a quirky mind, with opinions on everything. "Do not wear silk," he is supposed to have told Muslim men. The sexual proscriptions and advice were particularly interesting: according to another book, the Prophet said, "A man is not allowed to have a woman and her paternal aunt as two wives simultaneously, nor a woman and her maternal aunt." Probably the translations were not great, Doron thought.

In any case, you could certainly find equally silly precepts in Judaism. Do not wear blends of linen and wool. Why? And the other day, Doron had heard that an important rabbi in Jerusalem—some jerk with an Old Testament name who wore a high hat and a rich cape encrusted with gold and jewels—had advised religious men not to walk between two women, just as it is written that a man should not walk between two donkeys or two camels, for fear of becoming like them. And that same rabbi declared—no doubt after giving it a lot of thought—that it *was* permissible for an Orthodox man to pick his nose on the Sabbath, but Alka-Seltzer was off-limits because it fizzed. Doron could never take religion seriously.

Doron stood there and inhaled the dust and fumes from the Ramallah road, along with his own cigarette smoke. There were things no Israeli did. No Israeli went to Ramallah: it was enemy territory, a place where they wanted to kill you, like certain places in the Old City. The Authority was in charge in Ramallah. If an Israeli walked down the street in Ramallah, these days, he'd get knifed, people said. But there was no avoiding it for Doron—this little wasteland in Ramallah, his post at the dumpster. He was afraid that Marina might see him—that if she did, she would recognize him, and after that, who knew what might happen. And there was some little, contrary, dangerous feeling in him, too: he hoped maybe she would see him.

Two men were walking down the hill, talking. Doron tried to look relaxed as they approached. They squinted at him, and he thought, What if they speak to me? He drew on his cigarette in what he hoped was a Palestinian way, and kicked at the dirt, looking down, waiting for them to go on. They stopped. He didn't look up. He heard the sound of a lighter being flicked, an exchange of words. He kept his eyes on the ground. The men stood for a moment more, then continued on. Doron lifted his eyes after they passed, and watched them recede down the hill. He tossed his cigarette and tucked himself behind the dumpster.

The whole neighborhood used the dumpster, and a bad smell spilled out of it—old canned fish, dirty diapers. He closed his eyes, and the scene at the checkpoint came back to him. He saw himself at the communications controls. He remembered Zvili's angry face and the boy's scared blue eyes. At the bottom of the hill, a car screeched, glass shattered, and there was distant heated shouting. Closer to Doron, a man's voice said goodbye. In English. A door opened.

Doron peered around the dumpster. Marina was coming out of the garden gate, walking toward the street with the young man Doron had seen at the funeral with her father. Her face was half hidden by a silk scarf and sunglasses. The two of them stood there, silent, staring across the street at the dumpster and the empty lot, and for a moment, Doron thought they had seen him. He pulled his head back a few centimeters. The young man looked at his watch, and then checked the street. He shook his head. Marina stood stiffly apart. She leaned lightly against the wall of the garden. An askadinia tree brushed its thick pointed leaves against her shoulder.

They waited. Doron waited with them. He was beginning to feel imprisoned by the vigil when finally their taxi arrived and they set off. Doron hurried up the hill and around the corner to his waiting cab and jumped in. He watched Marina's taxi as it plunged and bucked through the traffic on the Ramallah road.

At the side of the street, small children walked with their mothers to the market. At every intersection, young men were waiting to be picked up by jitneys and driven across the checkpoint to the Israeli side of Jerusalem for day work. Today they would wait in vain—the closure was still in force—but they were eternally desperate and eternally hopeful. Through the small crack in his cab's curtains, Doron saw a fresh graffito on the walls that were bouncing past. Then he saw it again. He tried to sound it out in his iffy Arabic each time he passed it, translating as he went along. He saw it again. Ah, an "s" sound. He heard himself hissing, "Ssssss, sssssssss." And then he realized what it said. FIND THE SOLDIER. Find the soldier. Soldier, he recognized the whole word, now. It was a word he had learned in training, a long time ago. The CD disk that his driver had hung with a red ribbon from the rearview mirror jumped up and down to the rhythm of the traffic like some kind of measuring device, a meter of impending disaster. Specks of light flicked off it. Doron had always assumed that the disks must be symbolic in some way for Muslims, like the rounded-off crescents that topped so many mosques and minarets. Endless frittering useless thoughts crackled across his brain. He sat back. His stomach bounced. He let himself relax into the car's worn vinyl upholstery. His taxi followed the same rocking trajectory as Marina's. Find the soldier. Like a child's game.

CHAPTER TEN

GEORGE COULD FEEL EVERYONE LOOKING AT HIM WHEN HE entered the meeting room at Orient House. He used to enjoy being the center of attention when he came to these gatherings, but not anymore and not under these circumstances. Were they looking at him in a new light because of Ibrahim? Philip stayed close, but offered no real protection against the onslaught. He had come to Jerusalem this morning with Marina to see Hassan's lawyer and met George just outside Orient House. Ahmed boomed up to George with his big, healthy body. You hardly noticed the dozen or so other men, Ahmed was so imposing.

"George," he said, embracing him and kissing him on both cheeks and then taking his hand—actually grabbing it as it hung at George's side, lifting it up and taking it. George looked down at his hand. He looked up at Ahmed.

"Come," Ahmed said, dropping George's hand. How like Ahmed not to mention Ibrahim, here, to understand instinctively what was called for and, more to the point, what was not. George was uncharacteristically eager to belong, not to feel the wrenching alienation he'd been overwhelmed by since his last visit. Look at Ahmed: Here was the man who had stood by him in spite of their differences. George tried to convince himself that here, he was protected.

"Thank you," George whispered to him as they made their way across the room to the conference table. He held Ahmed's strong, sinewy arm. It had been decades since they leaned against each other in this familiar way, not considering politics and the oceans that divided them. Possibly, George thought, this is the meaning of home. There was something about the warmth of Ahmed's greeting that made George believe he had come around to George's way of thinking—that Ibrahim was no longer to be used as part of the Authority's negotiating arsenal.

"Sit," said Ahmed, pulling out a high-backed chair at the table for George. He laid a proprietary hand on George's shoulder after he was seated. He looked at the others, who were talking, smoking, and nodding in small groups around the room.

"Let's begin," Ahmed said. He sat down at the head of the table, his knee touching George's. George looked around the table.

Philip leaned over to George and whispered, "I don't like it."

Philip must be feeling something I'm not, George thought. Something I should get that I'm not getting. Am I being used, trapped?

"They're up to something," Philip said. "Don't you feel it?"

Up to no good, Grandfather would say.

Again, Philip leaned and spoke into George's ear. "'Find the soldier,'" he said. They had commented on the recurring graffiti as they rode in from Ramallah.

"Yah?" whispered George.

"That's what this is about," said Philip. "Watch."

Ahmed began to speak. He riffled through a large loose-leaf notebook as he talked, but it was plain that he was not reading from its contents. It was a prop. A relief map of Palestine hung on the wall behind him.

"Many things have happened in the past few weeks," Ahmed said. "I am sure you are all aware." He looked around the table, letting his eyes meet each man's, before going on. Ahmed motioned to a slender man standing behind him, who approached the table.

"More coffee," Ahmed said quietly, dismissing him to his task with a small backward wave of the hand. A platter of symmetrically arranged sweets sat in the middle of the conference table. Ahmed plucked one out and took a small bite of it. He wiped his lips neatly with a napkin.

"We have seen the closing of the checkpoints." He turned a page in his notebook, as if marking off that example.

"We have seen the arrest of scores of our young men." He turned another page. George speculated on the actual contents of the notebook: Maps of borders described in the peace agreements? Details of the February operating costs for Orient House? Old printouts of foreign-aid disbursements?

"The Israelis have demanded that we arrest certain Hamas figures, and we have done so—some of them are still in our custody. Yet since the bombings the other day, the Israelis have abandoned the talks as if they thought the *Authority* were responsible," he said. Another page.

"And finally, there has been the recent murder of a Palestinian baby," said Ahmed, gazing mildly down the center of the table, avoiding all eyes. George stared at the notebook as Ahmed slowly turned another page. Philip kicked him under the table.

"The Israelis are not serious about peace, as we know. We've tried to work with them, to negotiate. We have given them everything we can give them, in order to advance the process. We have waited for them to recover from violence before. But that moment has passed." He gave them the all-encompassing look again. The others seated around the table wagged their heads. Ahmed pulled at the ends of his keffiyeh, an addition to his wardrobe that George found irritating. Here come The Palestinian People, he thought.

"The Palestinian people will no longer tolerate inaction in the face of Israeli intransigence," Ahmed said. George looked at him over the steeple of his long surgeon's fingers. Ahmed was looking at him. Coffee arrived and Ahmed poured it into their tiny cups. Big men with tiny cups. Ahmed was dangerous, with his glinting eyes and his keffiyeh and his tiny sweet cup of coffee. That's what Philip would say. George considered the concept.

"And that is why, beginning today, we are going to start—quietly and with dignity—to encourage the people to continue coming out to the checkpoints to protest the inhumane treatment of Palestinians at the hands of Israelis." Ahmed looked around at the nodding table.

"We are encouraging the natural anger of the Palestinian people over the murder of this little boy." Nods. "And the people are demanding that the Israelis produce the soldier who murdered Ibrahim Raad." Ahmed closed up his notebook.

"Hajimi," George corrected, without looking up from the table.

"Hajimi," said Ahmed. Ahmed surveyed the table. All his councillors nodded.

They are *all* in it together, George thought. All except me.

"My friends, I see this is a day of rare unanimity," Ahmed said. "Sweets?" He picked up the tray. "George?" he said, offering the platter.

George closed his eyes. He thinks he has me. He actually thinks I will go along with this, even after what I said to him the other night at Marina's. He thinks that he can trip me up, seduce me, as usual. He's always done it in the past. He thinks I will approve. Can he believe that?

George opened his eyes and stared at Ahmed, trying to see beyond the dancing eyes. Ahmed was serving sweets to his councillors, amusing himself by playing the obedient servant. Ah, Ahmed was having fun. He made his way around the table with the tray of sweets, serving each man. He bowed low before Salah, and the two men laughed. George tried to perceive his old friend. He stared and stared, but he had lost whole degrees of observation, his distance from Palestine had made the place inscrutable to him and now he couldn't even read the expression on the face of his, his, his . . . George no longer knew how to categorize Ahmed: his old school chum?

Ahmed sat back down in his throne at the head of the table. George looked up and saw that he was watching him. Ahmed raised his eyebrows at George. He's wondering, George thought. He too is off his game, not quite sure of me. George felt his hands, his own hands, trembling on his lap. He longed for a sense of mastery. He felt set up. Ahmed always won at all their games.

But. This time, Ahmed loses. This is a different time, different circumstances—a new historical moment. Or at any rate, thought George, I have a personal involvement that I cannot deny. Oh yes, he repeated to himself, oh yes, I know the old routines, the norm; I know the drill. You find something, something good, something that really sparks the people because it comes from deep down, and you pump it. Something like the torture of a prisoner, the assassination of a poet—the murder of a child. He remembered Ahmed's lecture on manipulating the fortuitous in history: History can change a man's standing overnight. A speech, a coup, an unforeseen incident. Pump it till it's dry.

But Ahmed misjudged him. George was sick of letting people die for nothing, as Ibrahim had. Time was short. Ahmed was just a wrongheaded Bedouin astride a fiery stallion, recklessly leading boys to their deaths in the name of something he imagined was called victory. Come what may, George was going to make his stand against that charge. Here was his chance to defend his daughter. Probably Ahmed would trample him like dust beneath the hooves of the cavalry, but still, if he was to be mowed down in any case, why not go out with a flourish, with a bit of the old Arab glory?

Ahmed pushed his throne back and stood. George, too, pushed back his chair. Ahmed smiled at him across the table. As he rose, George caught a glimpse of the title written on the spine of Ahmed's notebook: "Expenses for the Deputy Irrigation Coordinator, Palestinian Authority, May 1994." Christ. He held on to the corner of the table, testing his hands along the table's edge. He tilted his head to one side, looked at

Ahmed again, carefully, took in the black-and-white keffiyeh and the level regard of the handsome eyes. Everyone was watching them. Salah had crumbs and honey on his open lips. They were all still. George held on to the table, and he remembered holding on to that bottom branch of the mulberry tree outside his house, holding on to it for dear life, while Ahmed stood before him in tennis whites, fresh from a game across the street, and told him that the Jews were winning the war and that George's mummy and dad would have to leave, and that the Raads were going to have to lock up the house, the farm in Nazareth, his grandfather's estate at Abu Ghosh. They would all be gone for weeks, months maybe, Ahmed had told him in a childish hectoring voice that George could still recall. They would lose their chance to play on the junior tennis team. They would have to start this school term over again when they returned, he said. Funny now how innocent they all had been about history, even the adults. Nothing happens in weeks or months.

George looked right into those same eyes that still had him fixed, as if neither of them had ever moved from that spot beneath the mulberry tree. And then shaking his gaze free, George let go of the table, tapped Philip on the shoulder, and with Philip in his wake walked out of the room and down the hallway under the dull, ugly glare of the circular fluorescent hall lights, past the young receptionist typing away beneath the smiling photograph of the Chairman, and past the two old Italianate wall fountains that had long ago run dry, over the cool checkerboard marble floors, and out the heavy iron doors into the midday sun. The others, gathered in the office at the corner of the table, watched as George's back receded down the hallway toward the exit.

Outside, it was hot and the sky was filled with orange light. Salah's bodyguard stood chatting with the gardener. Mercedes limousines crowded the parking lot. A young man George knew approached him, holding a small basket, and from it offered him chocolates wrapped in red and gold foil to celebrate the birth of his second child. George took two and said congratulations. The birth of a second child. He stood there with his chocolates, trying to concentrate. Was it a joke of some kind? Philip was trying to bustle George out of the parking lot.

A dry wind swept through the parking lot. I am making tired gestures, George thought. Defending the honor of dead babies. He stood in the glare, unwrapping a chocolate. Yet I must do it: it is my obligation. He crumpled the golden foil in his hand. I will block their way. I will give them bloody hell. I will rescue my little boy from their old claws.

Please, Philip said. Ahmed was out on the terrace like a prince watching his guests depart. George did not see him. He put the chocolate in his mouth and let the thick, sweet taste of childhood transport him. Old school chum, farewell. He pushed his hair back from his eyes. Now, he said. We can go. They passed through the black gates.

CHAPTER ELEVEN

IN THE CENTRAL SQUARE OF RAMALLAH, THE CHRISTMAS TREE had finally come down. Mahmoud Sheukhi was walking back from evening prayers at the mosque two blocks away. He rarely went to the mosque but he was searching now for a bit of guidance. Sometimes after prayers he felt uplifted, but tonight, unfortunately, he hardly noticed that he had prayed. He passed the hairdressing salon and the candy store, and walked behind the stall out front where the old man sold nuts and sponges and hairbrushes and grilled corn and bread coated in salty *za'tar.* He dodged between cars parked up on the sidewalk, fished in his pocket, and turned the key in the outside lock of his office building. The walls of the entrance hall three floors below the office of Sheukhi & Sheukhi were covered with a film of greasy black exhaust from the wrecks that stalled and puffed all day outside on the road, waiting to get around the square. Sheukhi entered the building, carefully avoiding coming into contact with any surface.

His poor brother Adnan was dealing with that glass factory-case. So tedious. It was coming to trial in a week, and Adnan was working double time. Probably he'd be upstairs now, with his son Jibril in front of the television and Adnan trying to concentrate at his desk. The glassmakers hired Sheukhi & Sheukhi because they were a respectable local firm that was not expensive. They hired Adnan in particular because his younger brother Mahmoud was considered a smart man but something of a dreamer, and not too diligent. Mahmoud enjoyed his checkered reputation.

He vaulted up the stairs in the dusk toward the office. The hallway light was still out. He knew it irritated Adnan that his little brother had been privileged to see a crucial moment in history, whereas, of course,

Adnan had not. It was Mahmoud's topic of the week—he always had a topic. This week he'd been tormenting his older brother with the violent storm, the arrogant Israeli commander, the beautiful tragic mother, and with, of course, Mahmoud, her defender, and his jacket, his handkerchief, his umbrella, and his vitriol. Oh, it had been bothering Adnan.

Of course Adnan hadn't been there. He was never anywhere at night except in bed or in this cursed office, working either on the glassmakers' case or one in a series of dull battles over village land titles. That was always the way it had been between the brothers. "My Adnan, pillar of the family," their father used to say when they were little, and Adnan would step forward solemnly to kiss a visitor. And then: "And this, this is Mahmoud. Listen to him recite poetry. Ah, Mahmoud." Mahmoud recalled his chubby self, clambering awkwardly onto a chair, standing up proudly, his hands behind his back, and beginning his passionate recitation.

Mahmoud passed the thick little rosemary bush that sat in a clay pot on the third-floor landing, waiting for tomorrow's sun to strike it through the skylight three stories above. The Sheukhis were village people, and every time he came to the office—usually in the evenings to watch the news—the sight of this poor solitary plant twisted some string of nostalgia in his gut. It made him think of the land behind his father's house, the terraced olive groves, the almond trees, the rock-strewn hillside, the stone walls that wandered here and there with rosemary sprouting in great arcs from them, and the small vineyard that belonged to his neighbors, who were also his cousins. Thank God he didn't live there anymore.

On the next floor was the office. He walked in. Adnan was behind the desk, Jibril in a metal folding chair in front of the set, his long legs sticking out halfway across the room, and another chair empty beside him waiting for Uncle Mahmoud.

"What brings you here?" Adnan asked from among his papers. It was his habitual salutation to his wayward brother. Mahmoud didn't answer with more than an acknowledging grunt. He sat down and offered Jibril a cigarette. Jibril said yes and looked at his uncle appreciatively. Uncle and nephew began to smoke in front of the battered old black-and-white television, waiting for the news to come on. They looked alike, long legs, broad moustaches, slender, each with a dimple in his right cheek. Mahmoud was frowning, a frown of concentration that Adnan had always mistaken, since childhood, for a frown of disapproval. Jibril had made coffee and he and his uncle drank it out of thin plastic cups.

"They're running another bunch of Bedouins off their land," Mahmoud said, pointing at the screen with his cigarette. His frown grew deeper. Adnan came around to face the set. The scene was so predictable that Mahmoud felt it must be file footage.

"Have you noticed?" Mahmoud asked. "When they cover the Bedouins, the Israeli cameramen always focus on the sheep to make people think the Bedouins are a bunch of backward nomads, *ya'ni*—they want you to think that this guy has no right to live in any particular place. Humble sheepherder." Mahmoud elbowed Jibril. "Look at those fucking sheep; stupid just like their masters: that's what you're supposed to think."

He listened to the Bedouin's complaint for a moment.

"Of course the guy *is* as stupid as his sheep, but still," he went on. "No reason he should have to move from the Jerusalem suburbs down to, *ya'ni*, the fucking Negev." Jibril laughed. Mahmoud stubbed out his cigarette and pulled a set of jade prayer beads from his jacket pocket. He sat there with his elbows on his thighs, the green beads hanging from one hand, his cup of coffee balanced precariously on the other knee. He thumbed his beads inattentively.

Footage of an old building in East Jerusalem came on. Orient House, the unacknowledged Jerusalem headquarters of the Authority. There had been a high-level meeting there today. Mahmoud watched George Raad leaving Orient House. The man looked old. Every life has a sad ending, Mahmoud thought. He felt a romantic sympathy for tragic old radicals.

A picture of Ibrahim Hajimi came on, big-eyed and unsmiling.

"Cute," said Adnan.

"Yes, such a tragedy," Mahmoud said.

Footage of the checkpoint came on, from this afternoon. It looked just like the riot before the boy died, Mahmoud thought: smoke, a lot of people running, boys throwing stones, soldiers crouching at the ready. The sight of the watchtower made Mahmoud wince.

The Israeli prime minister came on.

"Ah, His Excellency the Prime Minister," said Mahmoud. He pointed at the television with his chin. A press conference in Tel Aviv. Meanwhile, Mahmoud fiddled over the name of that soldier. Had he heard it? Had he? He thought maybe he had, when the fellow was making his calls. Right before he kicked Mahmoud out. He thought he knew the first name. Definitely.

Prime Minister walked to the podium purposefully.

"This guy," Jibril said.

"Let's listen," Mahmoud said. It was always an option when an Israeli official came on, to quit listening, shut off the volume.

Bulbs flashed and the crowd of microphones attached to the podium made the Prime Minister look as if he were sprouting from behind a stand of fuzzy gray bulrushes. The television camera panned across the gathered reporters; there weren't enough seats for them, and some were standing with their arms forced to their sides, lining the walls. The Prime Minister took it all in with his heavy-lidded, vigilant eyes.

"Yes, Yoni," the Prime Minister said, opening the press conference with customary informality.

"How is Israel going to deal with this new Palestinian campaign?" the *Ha'aretz* reporter asked.

"Campaign?" asked the Prime Minister. "I'm not aware of any campaign."

"They want Israel to hand over the officer who was in charge on the night the Hajimi baby died. 'Find the soldier.' That's what the crowds are shouting at the checkpoints today."

"Please," said the Prime Minister, coughing in a special way that signified he wanted silence, attention. The press corps grew less raucous.

"Israel spends its time rescuing members of its armed forces, not handing them over," the Prime Minister said. "We don't hand over soldiers to anyone, ever. Period."

"But it's not the enemy who's asking for this," said a *Ma'ariv* reporter. "It's our partner at the negotiating table, Mr. Prime Minister."

A thin whinny of appreciative laughter issued from the press corps.

The Prime Minister did not smile.

Mahmoud did not smile.

"Why won't you allow us to interview him?" asked a loud voice in English. "What are you hiding?"

"We are not hiding anything," the Prime Minister responded, in his almost unaccented English. Then back to Hebrew, with the Arabic voice-over translation: "The account being given by the IDF is taken from testimony provided by the commanding officer and his men. It is strictly their account that you are getting. We see no need to violate their security and their privacy by providing their names to you." He looked down at the crowd of journalists.

"Is anything being done to protect those men from revenge, from an attack?" a voice shouted from the back of the room.

"Any one of them who is threatened is receiving protection," the Prime Minister responded.

"That would be the commanding officer, I assume," another reporter asked.

"Yes," said the Prime Minister.

"Can you believe this shit?" asked Jibril after a few minutes. He looked over at his uncle. Mahmoud did not respond.

Adnan sat down at his desk and began going through recent letters and documents about the glass factory. It was difficult to concentrate over the sound of the Prime Minister's nasal voice.

"Find the soldier? Find the soldier?" said Mahmoud. "Great. But will anyone have the guts to really go after him? Oh, I doubt it." Adnan looked up. The Prime Minister was shaking his head, looking fierce, his spectacles nearly tumbling from his nose. The announcer was talking about a rally in Ramallah that was to be held in two days to protest the fate of the Hajimi boy and other baby martyrs.

"You can help them find the soldier, Mahmoud," Adnan said after listening for a moment. "You've met the fellow, after all." He gave a brief laugh, and returned to his work.

"Meeting is not finding," Mahmoud said. "Wish I knew the guy's name."

"Moshe, Schlomo, Yitzhak," said Jibril.

"Avram, Chaim, Pinhas," suggested Adnan.

Mahmoud did not laugh with them. "I think it's Ari," he said.

They both looked at him with wide-open eyes.

"That's something," said Adnan. "I mean it's half of the puzzle. It's a beginning."

"I've tried to remember," Mahmoud said. "Did I ever hear his name? It was not a very calm situation, *ya'ni*. . . . But I think I did hear it. She must have heard it, too. Really, it's hard to remember anything except her face, and a lot of phone calls and radioing, people running around. Amazing." He twiddled his beads. "There was so much movement and still, nothing getting done. I should have just taken them across. What worse could have happened?"

"They would have shot you, brother," said Adnan.

"Then I would have died honorably," said Mahmoud.

He lit another cigarette and considered the Prime Minister, who was wiping his glasses.

"Instead of living dishonorably," Adnan said, smiling into his papers.

"Don't tease me, *habibi*, I am not in the mood," Mahmoud said. "What are you working on there, anyway?" He looked over at his brother's desk.

"The glass factory."

"The glass factory," said Mahmoud. His eyes clouded. A merest hint of apology passed over his face. It had been a long while since he'd pored over a brief or shown his face in court. He tried again to recall the soldier's name, but only the name of the factory owner would come to him. He turned his eyes to the press conference. The Prime Minister was on his way out. The man was wearing a very loud necktie.

"Glassblowers. A dull case," Mahmoud said, turning to Jibril, who smiled at his uncle from his slouch on the folding chair.

Mahmoud was remembering that the last time he'd been over to the courthouse, filing some paper in this very long glassblowing case, he had run into Ruby Horowitz, again. She liked him, he could tell. She was a hip-swinger who wore a waist-length bum-freezer leather jacket. She wore tight skirts and moved her hips in a twitchy way that made him jump inside. Her boyfriend was a soldier who had been assigned as security to the courthouse, so she was often around when the boyfriend was busy elsewhere in the compound. She'd come over after work; she was a low-level secretary for some low-level bureaucrat in Defense. She said it was an okay job. Mahmoud thought about it. He would bet that she had unimagined access to information.

He wondered about Jewish women. When they were at all friendly, they seemed so forward, so ready for it. Ruby spoke some Arabic. That was a kick: her parents were from Morocco. She told Mahmoud that she used her Arabic on the job, and then she sat back, looking proud. He laid a heavy hand on Ruby's knee and said things to her in Arabic the gist of which he was sure she could understand. The question crossed his mind, as it was bound to cross a mind like his: was she a Pal-symp, or did she just like Arab men? Fine line between the two, Mahmoud, fine line. She was enjoying the idea that he was taboo. Oh, Ruby.

"Well, I'm off," Mahmoud said. "Anything you need me for, Adnan? Any papers you need me to take to the courthouse?"

Adnan looked around the office, shuffled some papers around his desk. Ritual.

"No, I don't think so. Nothing immediate, anyway," Adnan said.

He would go to that rally for the baby martyrs, Mahmoud thought. He wanted to see Marina Hajimi again and take a look at her father. He figured they would probably be there.

Mahmoud tossed his coffee cup across the room into the trash can, pocketed his beads, shrugged on his coat, and folded up the chair he'd been sitting on. He rested it against the wall beside the closet. Adnan and Jibril followed him through the outer office to the door.

"Don't stay out late," Adnan said, as he shut the door behind Mahmoud. It was his little joke. Mahmoud always stayed out late. Adnan heard a low laugh as his brother descended the stairs.

It must have rained during the news. The street was wet and shining like a mirror under the dim buzzing streetlamps. Mahmoud slipped behind the old man's stall, which had been covered in burlap and was pulled up close to the building for the night. Zabaneh's grocery store was shut tight. He walked past the neighborhood mosque and the entrance to the tea shop, a famous old place. Through the foggy window, he saw old men's heads bent over their tea, and a table full of young fathers sitting on reed stools, playing cards. The sweet smell of tobacco burning in a nargileh tempted him for a moment. But he was neither old nor a father, and had other business on his mind. He went on in the cold wind.

Heavy gold for weddings sparkled out from the windows of a jewelry shop. It was a long way home, down through the center of town first, and then up a long steep hill and over its crest to the family's concrete house, in a refugee camp that had after fifty years become a permanent part of what could be called greater Ramallah. Mahmoud ran down a flight of stairs between two buildings and came out at the big intersection where a toy store and a pizza parlor faced a sweet shop and a dusty old hardware store. Outside the crowded pizza parlor stood a group of foreigners, waiting to get in, shivering. He trudged past them with his head down against the wind. They were speaking Dutch? Finnish? Norwegian? The toy shop was brightly lit. All the gay pink little bicycles had been strung up from the ceiling until morning, when the shop owner would stack them against each other again, out on the sidewalk. Faded plastic shrink-wrapped Uzis and realistic pistols were laid out in the window. A tower of yellow Legos had been built by some ingenious employee and little plastic soldiers stood at the ready in its windows and on its ramparts. Three blond dolls with vacant blue eyes sat next to a pair of neon-colored walkie-talkies. *Lieutenant Doron, here.* Circles of caps for boys' guns spread themselves in a geometric pattern at the dolls' feet. Inflated swimming rings were piled in a corner one upon the other like a totem pole. Mahmoud caught a glimpse of Mickey Mouse. Inane face. *Ari Doron.*

That was the name, Mahmoud didn't doubt it for a second once it came hurtling back into his mind. He looked down at the ground as he walked, and the black street shone up at him. It was a common Israeli name, and it was the soldier's name.

Doron, Doron. What to do with him. Where to go. How did you

take a name like that and find the soldier? There were places to go with information like this. Yes. Definitely. He could think of a few. Hajimi's cell at al-Moscobiyyeh, if only you could get in. The Chairman's office. Or simply to Raad. Raad. He'd think about it. Tonight, he would not stay out late. Tonight, he would fix himself some tea, and lie down on his bed, and decide.

CHAPTER TWELVE

THE RAIN CAME PELTING DOWN LIKE AN ASSAULT. IT WOULD stop for ten minutes, then start again with renewed vehemence. Tonight, it seemed almost personal to Doron. The wind whipped around the stone houses on Kakal Street and made the tops of the pine trees dance. Doron shivered; his shirt was soaked with rain. He'd looked for his blue-jean jacket but he couldn't find it, so now he was cold, and the empty cigarette pack with the military phone number he'd called in Tel Aviv was missing. He was sure the pack was in the jacket pocket. He opened the door to his mother's old jalopy, an ancient boat that had once been a taxi, and climbed in. His mother never used it, but she loved to brag about how inexpensive it had been. They both had a set of keys. Doron thought he could find the way up to Zvili's, even though he'd been there only once before. He needed to know what Zvili had told Yizhar.

Find the soldier. Now that they were out looking for him, he knew he would never feel the same blankness. They had selected him. It was as if they were acknowledging his role. The writing on the walls was about him—a night in his life, an incident, witnesses. He felt an eerie solidarity with whoever had scrawled those words.

It was an amazing sensation, like being hit dead-on in the chest with a mallet. He was a target. He felt the concentric circles narrowing; he was looking down into them, he was being sucked down into a grim nowhere. It brought him starkly back to himself, Ari Doron, a man who was born in Jerusalem, who was an Israeli, who had picked strawberries, camped by the Kinneret, shined his father's shoes, who had been in charge that night. The soldier.

The windshield wipers were on, making their own odd rhythm, and there was static on the obsolete radio, punctuated by blaring bits of incomprehensible voice and music. Something was always wrong with the car, it suffered from negligence, and tonight of course it would be the windshield wipers. They were on, but not working properly. The streetlights made a smear across the windshield. Doron could barely see. He hunched forward, peering out through the small double crescents that the wipers managed to clear. His world was filled with blackness. No one would think of going out in Jerusalem on a night like this. Only the monumental, immovable beggar woman who never left her corner on King George. He caught a glimpse of her, crouching with all her blankets under the pale light of a bus shelter at the Ben Yehuda intersection, looking like a shadowy hillock. The only good thing about the rain was that it kept the Palestinians at home. Today for the first time since Find the Soldier began, there had been no protests at the checkpoints. But that just meant that the rioting would be worse the day after tomorrow, when they were planning to hold a rally in Ramallah to mark the death of what they called the baby martyr.

Doron was feeling guilty. Here came his military side: he didn't like feeling guilty. Shake it off! Guilt was like a side of meat hanging around your shoulders, some repulsive thing about you that everyone could see. It was not permitted. Not here in his hometown. This was the place of no regrets, no apologies. No one does wrong here. You do what you have to do for your country—that was Doron's ethic, what he'd been raised on, in school, in the army. His father, a stalwart old soldier, preached this credo. His mother was different, but she too believed.

Do what you have to do. Doron thought about it. It was so seductive. And with all his penance, with all his guilt, he did recognize in himself an unmistakable panting desire for self-preservation, not learned but organic. Live with it. Shake it off. Like Yizhar, Doron was a simple soldier. Find the soldier; he thought: That's me! Ready or not.

He wondered what would happen. Maybe by now, while Doron sat shivering behind the wheel of the jalopy, maybe by now Marina had already given his name to Hajimi. Maybe by now, the whole terrorist network was gathering its forces to find him, get him, deal with him. He doubted it: it was hard to imagine himself as that important. For a simple soldier, it was not easy to be frightened of something until it was actually holding a gun to your head. Doron believed—no, he knew, now—that Ibrahim's death had been an accident, an inevitability that Ibrahim and Doron and everyone else involved had somehow stumbled into. It was difficult for him to imagine that anyone could see it—seriously—any other way. That was the line he was feeding himself today.

But what if he were the boy's father, cut off, in prison, his wife alone and undefended on the outside, the Israelis his eternal enemy and the boy his only child?

And then there was always the Palestinians' paranoia to take into consideration. For them, no accident was accidental.

As Doron drove up HaNevi'im Street, the skies cleared momentarily, and in patches of moonlight and cloud, the low houses of Musrara with their red roofs appeared and then disappeared. He turned left onto Highway 1. The Dome of the Rock was on his right, its shining cap bursting out of the Old City into the sporadic moonlight. Doron drove up toward Ramallah. Before the Jericho turnoff, the rains began again. He turned right onto the Jericho road, and then left again, off Jericho, toward Pisgat Ze'ev, the Jerusalem suburb where Zvili lived. Zvili had invited him many times and finally he'd had to say yes. Doron remembered that afternoon barbecue. He'd tripped over his own feet in the little backyard, and spilled his beer on the new Mrs. Zvili. Pink dress. She was a good sport.

The road curved up and around a precipice, and Doron passed the darkened fronts of the dry cleaners, the Co-op supermarket, the pizza shop, the SuperPharm, the hardware store, the health insurance office, all along the main drag, until he looped off into the residential area, where the houses were built like little castles, with crenellated turrets and bits of balustrade made of concrete and stucco and brick, and terra-cotta tiles. From the edge of the short cliffs on which the suburb had been erected, you could see down into the West Bank, into the winking Arab villages, with their minarets and domes and flat roofs that shone tonight like patches of a silver quilt whenever the rain let up. During the day, if it was clear, you could see the Dead Sea's salty oblong through Zvili's picture window, evaporating along the Jordanian border.

Zvili and his wife lived in one of Pisgat Ze'ev's tight little castles. Next to his place, a new house was going up, and Zvili complained a lot about the Palestinian workers who were building it. Most of the lights were out in Zvili's neighborhood now. It was almost ten, but Doron was in no mood to be polite. He honked his horn. He honked again, and some lights went on, but not at Zvili's. Finally, Zvili came to the door. He turned on an outside light—the short brick path up to the house sprang out of the dark. He stood in the lit doorway, a small wizardly figure in white underwear and a streaming white bathrobe.

"Who is it?" Zvili yelled through the storm, shading his eyes from the rain as if he were looking at the sun.

"Me," shouted Doron. It was hard to hear above the hammering of the rain.

"Ah, you," Zvili shouted. "Come in. What's wrong?"

"No, you get in the car," Doron yelled.

"Into that car?" Zvili shouted back. "With a madman at the wheel? No way." He lifted the shoulders of his bathrobe up over his head and ran over to Doron's car. "What's up, Ar?" he asked, peering into the window.

"Just get in," said Doron. "We have to talk."

"Actually, we do," said Zvili. He ran back to the house and shouted some words into the doorway, picked something up, and dashed back to Doron's car, letting himself in to the passenger seat after a brief tussle with the car's door handle. He was wet.

"You should kiss me," Zvili said, as he sat down.

"What?" said Doron, looking at Zvili as if perhaps he hadn't heard right. "That's not what I had in mind, really." He started up the car again. It coughed before turning over.

"Kiss me. I'm gonna be a father," Zvili said, turning to Doron with a wide, lecherous grin. He lit a cigarette, and shifted his gun around on the elastic holster belt he had snapped around his waist.

"Alana's pregnant?"

"You think it would be someone else? Yeah, she's pregnant. We found out today." Zvili let his bathrobe fall open wide, and he played with the hair on his thighs.

Doron drove.

"Aren't you going to say congratulations?" Zvili asked. There was a note of hurt in his voice.

"Oh, congratulations, of course." Doron turned to him briefly and smiled. "That's great." These days, everyone wanted him to give the appropriate answer.

"You planning to have kids?" Zvili asked.

"Yeah. I guess. Maybe someday." More appropriate answers. Doron hunched over the steering wheel.

"Where are we going?" Zvili asked.

"Nowhere," said Doron.

"Nice night to go nowhere."

"You want to go somewhere? Where?"

"Actually, home to my wife," said Zvili. "We were just, you know, getting into it, if you must know, when you started blowing that fucking horn. Shit, man, what's wrong with you? Arriving unannounced at ten at night. What's up?"

"I'm a little stressed out."

"So who isn't in Jerusalem?"

Doron gave a short laugh.

"You're freaked about the Hajimi kid." Zvili tapped a cigarette on the dashboard.

"Right."

"You see they're going to have a rally for him? Those people are crazy. It's going to be wild."

"Yeah. Sounds like fun."

"Hey, Ari, lighten up. Yizhar has it all worked out."

"Oh?"

"Yeah," Zvili said. "When's the last time you talked to him?"

"Yesterday."

"He's got it covered."

"Oh, good," said Doron.

"Come on. Yizhar's our savior, Ari. Remember that."

"He's not telling the truth."

"Big deal."

"It's going to blow up in our faces."

"Not in my face, buddy. And not in yours, I hope. He won't let it."

"Don't kid yourself," said Doron. "If people find out the story is not true, we're the ones who'll catch the flak for it, not Yizhar. The only one he'll stand by is whoever it was who told us not to let them through."

"You mean, whoever told *you*," Zvili corrected him.

"Right."

"Was there *really* someone who did that?"

"Come on, man," said Doron, looking at Zvili out of the side of his eye. A truck came out from behind them and passed them going fast. Its tires sucked up rain from the road and swept Doron's windshield with water.

"Yizhar doesn't mention it, if you know what I mean," Zvili said.

"No, I don't know what you mean."

"I mean it's not in the story."

"Yeah, I noticed," Doron said. "He also doesn't mention you jumping up and down like a madman and trying to stop me from letting them through. Or that I called the ambulance for a guy with a scratch on his face, not for the kid." Doron slowed the car down for the light at Hebron Road. The walls of the Old City were shining through the rain. They drove past the Ariel Hotel near the corner, with its imposing facade—a huge concrete reproduction of the stone tablets of the Ten Commandments. In the distance, the lights of the Talpiot commercial zone twinkled. "Yizhar did the story for me. Boom. Boom. Boom. He's got it down cold. Did he give you a chance to tell him what happened?"

"Yes."

"Not me. Did you tell him about the guy on the phone?"

"Of course," said Zvili. "He didn't seem interested. He said: 'That's what Lieutenant Doron says.'"

"I'm fucked." Doron shook his head. "I assume you didn't tell him about your, um, behavior."

"Of course not. Did you tell him?"

"No," said Doron. "Of course not." He could hear Zvili's relief.

"You know what I've got somewhere?" Doron said. "I've got that number somewhere, the one I called that night? I wrote it down on a matchbook or a cigarette pack, and now I can't find it. But I will."

"And what good will that do?"

"I'll give it to Yizhar, to prove I called someone. Not that it will mean much, I guess. I'm still fucked."

"You are not fucked in any way, Ari," Zvili said, holding on to Doron's shoulder and shaking him. "Buck up, man. Yizhar's on your side."

"You don't even know which side I'm on."

"Oh, yes, I do, Ari. I know better than you do," Zvili said. He shook his head in annoyance as if Doron just didn't get it. "You're on my side. We're on the same side, *habibi*, even if you don't like it. I swear, Ari. You're an army boy, and that's it."

Doron listened. He felt that Zvili's words could comfort him, he just had to let them seep in. Fall back on what you know. Relax into the shelter of the army. It sounded good.

"I feel really bad about the kid, too, Ari," Zvili said. "I'm not a heartless creep, no matter what you think. After all, I'm about to have a kid of my own. But what can we do? He's gone. So now you're going to tell the world that some IDF bigwig ordered you to keep him out? What would happen if you did that? Which you would never do, I know. First, no one in Israel would believe you—Yizhar will deny it, you can be sure. You'd sound like a coward to most people, blaming everything on a nameless somebody. Second, there would be, like, a *major* international uproar, because even if the Israelis wouldn't believe you, everyone else in the world would.

"Let's just keep a lid on the thing, for God's sake. Let's get all our stories straight and then over time the thing will die down. The less information out there, the better. Because if the Authority *finds* the soldier, then they damn well have to do something with your ass."

Doron drove for a while in silence. He hated it when Zvili acted like his superior. It had been the same at the checkpoint. Zvili always thought he had everything under control, and the worst part was, he did. Unlike Doron, who did not have things under control. Not now. He hated little Zvili, who was always more sensible than he was. Who was always more practical and *realistic*. Zvili *was* his superior. Who wants to be realistic, Doron's mother had always asked, when he complained that she wasn't. The answer was: Doron. Doron wanted to be. He never wanted to dither around in a sentimental dream world, like his mother and her sister, with their fantasies of peace. He wanted to be hard and firm and masculine and see the big picture, get what was really happening. Was that realistic? He remembered Marina standing under the askadinia, distant and glamorous in her sunglasses and scarf.

"I know you're right," Doron said to Zvili, and he meant it. "You make a lot of sense." He made a U-turn on Bethlehem Road and steered the car back across the old railroad tracks toward town. He wondered if Zvili would repeat this conversation verbatim to Yizhar.

"I feel like shit," Doron said. "I want to do something to make me feel better. I don't like lying to a mother whose baby is dead."

"You're not lying to her. But telling the truth isn't always useful, either." Zvili pushed his foot down on an imaginary brake, and Doron sped up just a little more in response. "Like, you don't want to tell the truth just because it's, I don't know, *the truth*. So fucking what? That's not going to make you *feel* better. You tell what you have to tell. You do the right thing. That's what I'm going to do. Don't look to me to support you if you do something crazy, Ari. Or even something that's just not what Yizhar wants us to do. I won't help you out. Only if you're on board. Go talk to Yizhar. He has some ideas."

Talk to Yizhar. The streets were still wet but the moon was out in a cold and brilliant sky. Talk to Yizhar. Driving down from Zvili's house, Doron let those words play inside his brain. They had a peaceful ring to them, maybe it would be like seeing a therapist. He'd piss out all his bad thoughts to Yizhar, and then Yizhar would tell him what to do. Not to worry. Everything will be all right. Doron shook his head at the thought. He smiled to himself. The idea that Yizhar would somehow comfort him—it was ridiculous. A mouse doesn't go to a hawk and nestle under its wing. Yizhar was not on his side. He was not on anyone's side.

CHAPTER THIRTEEN

After the prison door shut behind them, Marina and Philip and Hassan's lawyer walked through the dark receiving vestibule and then out into the blazing courtyard. The prisoners who were taking the air stood and parted to make way for her, to show their respect. Marina kept her eyes down on the sandy ground, ignoring the lanky Israeli guard who walked to one side and focusing all her attention on getting to the little door that led to the hallway that led to the cell where Hassan would be waiting. Aloni, the Israeli lawyer, was walking next to Philip. He was the one who would be helping to get Hassan, and two others, out of this place, soon. He was very correct, very businesslike—he was their escort. You couldn't get in to see political prisoners without the prisoner's attorney. Philip and Marina had arranged everything with him yesterday morning.

Marina blinked as the door to Hassan's cell opened and they went again from dark to light. Hassan was sitting as usual on a straight-backed metal chair near the high window, and the light fell across his face like a stroke of white paint. His face looked so thin this morning. The room was empty without Ibrahim. The guard shifted from foot to foot.

"Well, we'll leave you," the lawyer said gruffly, taking Philip by the elbow. The guard went out with them, leaving the door slightly ajar. The guard always stood right there.

Marina walked toward Hassan, and Hassan stood up slowly, his clothes hanging down from his shoulders and his hips like sheets. His face was so thin it made his round eyes look even more surprised. He had a habitual look of pleased surprise, and as he stood, she felt that look fall on her and her heart lifted as it always did. He was a small man, sinewy, with elegant long muscles in his arms. His eyes were a blazing blue, like

Ibrahim's, and the skin around them was delicate and wrinkled as if he were much older than he was. The lines that came out from the corners of his eyes like sun's rays were more visible now that he was growing thinner and his face was burned from too much time in the bright courtyard. His sleeves were rolled up in big bunches at the elbows.

Hassan stood there, looking at her. He seemed frightened, as if he didn't know what to do. Marina went to him and put her arms around him. They stayed like that.

After a minute, she said, "My life is over."

"Don't say it, don't say it," he said. He kissed her veil and her hair.

Her legs felt so tired, as if she'd been standing forever. She leaned against him, but pulled back quickly. It seemed as if he might collapse from her weight.

"Are you getting enough to eat?" she asked him. It was better not to talk about Ibrahim. Hassan's wrists were bony. She could see the form of the bone protruding.

"What a question," he said. "Yes, I get enough food. It's just that right now, I am not eating."

"But you have to eat, Hassan, you're getting too thin. You look ill. I . . ."

He put a silencing finger against her lips, and she kissed it. He kept it there.

"Kiss again," he said. She did. She heard him take a quick breath of air, like a swimmer. He let it out. He looked at the door, where one of the guard's legs was visible.

"I've been on a diet," Hassan said. He looked down at the floor.

She took his whole hand and kissed the palm. It was dry and sweet.

He took his hand away from her and laid it on her shoulder. He looked into her eyes.

"Don't let this destroy us," he said.

She looked back. He leaned over and kissed her softly. She held on to him. Then they moved apart. She looked at the wall.

"How is your father?" Hassan asked.

"Oh, you know," she said. Again she felt more comfortable. Anything was better than talking about it. "The same. Sadder. Sicker. More spoiled."

"I'm glad he's there with you, though, still."

"Yes, I suppose," she said. She didn't want to talk about her father. She didn't want to talk about anything. She just wanted to be in this little cell with Hassan, and to look at the wall.

He shook his head. "You're feeling hopeless. Me too."

"I think I'll feel that way forever, now," she said. "I miss him so much." Her voice broke. "There's no one left."

"There is always hope in this world, Marina," Hassan said. "They say."

"I don't see it," she said.

"I'm still here," he said. "I know it's not much to offer, but I am."

"I know," she said. She could hear that her own voice was flat. "That's the problem. You're here. In this place." She looked at the heavy steel door, with the little peephole slat the jailers could open. The door seemed brutal, like a door to a place where you were keeping money or precious metals, not men. Not men with long muscles and hard ribs and blue eyes.

"You're so beautiful, Marina," Hassan said.

"Tired." She looked away. Her eyes kept coming back to that blank wall under the window.

He looked around at the tiny visiting cell. "When I get out, we should move to Boston."

"Boston," she said. She looked at him. "Boston would be okay," she said.

She stood there for a few seconds.

"You can become a stockbroker," she said.

"Yes," he said in his accented English. "I will be trading on your American Stock Exchange. I will cook on the barbecue and be mowing the lawn."

"You'd make a perfect Red Sox fan," she said.

He smiled back. "I love the baseball," he said, again in English. He looked down at her hands and then up again into her eyes. The smile went out of his face.

"I miss you so much," he said.

"I miss you," she said. She thought that she would like to go back to Boston. Then she thought: That's treachery. And leave him here, alone?

"It's hard being in here," said Hassan. "Knowing you're out there and I can't comfort you. At night I lie down with men breathing and snoring all around me, you know, male, very male, and I try to remember every part of you. The arch of your foot." He sat down again, as if in exhaustion. "I was remembering that last night."

Marina closed her eyes. The cell was hot and close. She opened her eyes again. He was still examining her. He looked so hungry. She held his hands and pulled him up out of his chair. He was light as air.

"The small of your back. I think about that, too," Hassan said. He held her hands tighter. "Lips." He touched her lips. He gave a short laugh and shook his head. "It's like a shopping list."

She smiled at him, but her lips trembled. She put her arms around him and hid her face in his shoulder, so he wouldn't see. His body felt fragile beneath the shirt, like a folded-up umbrella.

"I think of everything, imagine everything." He squinted through the sunlight that came in through the window. "Remembering. What we do. Did. I'm thinking of those things now, right now."

"Me too," she said into his shirt.

"I want to make another baby with you now."

"Another time," she said. She kept her arms around him.

"In Boston," he said.

"Yes, back home," she said to him. She looked up at him, and moved back slightly. She knew he would never go to Boston. Not even after all this. Especially not after all this. He had spent four years in Chicago, studying, and that was enough, he'd said.

He put her hand on his chest where his shirt was open. She felt the warm skin there, and the bones too. His rib cage, like a cage really holding something in. His heart was beating strongly. He looked straight at her, and they stood there like that for a minute.

"Justice will be done, Marina," Hassan said. "My mother would say, 'Things like this happen. It is God's will.' But I can't be so accepting. Crimes like this must not go unpunished."

She looked at him. Her hand was still over his heart. She remembered the face of the Israeli soldier at the checkpoint. She had not forgotten him.

"Well, I won't be here forever," Hassan said quietly.

"What are you talking about?" she asked. She let her hand fall.

"Nothing," he said. "I just think the release will be coming soon. And soon we will talk about that night, whenever you are ready to talk to me." He kicked at the angle where the wall met the floor.

Something about the way he said it sounded threatening. He wasn't trying to comfort her now. It was a new sensation for her, to feel even the tiniest chill of fear about him.

"Do you remember anything, Marina?"

"Some things." She pulled her scarf more tightly around her head.

"I've had a message today from Ahmed Amr, you know," Hassan said. "Wise old Uncle Ahmed." He laughed. "He was pretty optimistic. So if Allah is willing, we will prevail."

"If Allah is willing, you will be careful, not do anything crazy, and come home to me soon," Marina said. *Inshallah.* If Allah is willing. She remembered what Uncle Ahmed was famous for saying: History can change a man's standing overnight. Her father used to quote it to her. She imagined Hassan free: all she could think of was the beach, and his bare feet along the water's edge, and Ibrahim running ahead of them in the froth of the waves. She felt weak, sunstruck, foreign. She could picture Hassan—more easily, more vividly—lying in the dust in his prison pajamas, in a corner of the courtyard, shot down off a wall.

For now, her hunger striker was just standing over there, kicking at the wall. She inhaled sharply. What was he doing in here? He had nothing to do with suicide bombs, with killing women and children. On the other hand, she knew the people Hassan knew. She knew what those men did, she knew the operations they ran. She knew very well what they believed in—what *he* believed in. She wanted to tell Hassan the name of the checkpoint soldier, because Hassan was her husband and because she always told him everything and because there was no secret worth having that wasn't shared with him, but she said nothing. What good would it do anyone? If anything happened to the soldier, they'd keep Hassan in prison forever. They would believe he'd ordered it. They would say he had, anyway, even if they didn't believe it.

"We should ask Aloni back in, now. It's been too long," Hassan said.

"Just a few more minutes here," Marina said. She put her hand on his arm. She could see the guard's boot outside the door, and his olive trouser leg tucked in at the ankle.

"No, we can't," Hassan said. He moved back, away from her, but she did not let go of him. She had the terrible feeling that she might never see him again, that somehow, if she stepped outside the door right now, now, she would lose him, too. It was a magic door, and as long as she stayed inside it, he existed, but if she were to leave now, he would disappear forever. When she walked out the door, she'd leave him in the enemy's hands, and the image of Ibrahim's bier waiting at the edge of that hole came into her head.

"Marina, Marina, stop, stop," Hassan said. He was shocked by her sobs. He held on to her, kissing her over and over. "Stop now, you must, you must." He moved back, away from her, and she looked up and tried to smile.

"Oh, Marina." The wrinkles at the corners of his eyes squeezed tight and the corners of his mouth went down. He looked old to her for the first time, and he wasn't old. His neck when he inclined toward her seemed bent under some painful burden. "Really, you have to go now."

He kissed her, and she pulled him up against her. She felt his familiar pressure.

"We've been alone too long," he said. He kissed her again. She didn't want him to stop. He pulled away and looked at her, pushing her scarf back from her hair. He breathed out and shook his head for a second as if he were trying to clear his mind.

"Go now. Go. You never know when they're going to get tough," he said. "I don't want to give them any excuse to stop you from visiting next time, or to delay the release."

"I'll go," she said. He took her hand and led her to the door, then let go of her and called out to Aloni.

Just outside the door, Hassan could see Philip sitting on a low wall, surrounded by men, talking intently. Aloni had been standing by himself near a pillar. He came up now to Hassan, who shook hands with Aloni and Philip. Hassan watched the two of them start off with his wife.

Marina's shoulders were hunched.

To save Ibrahim, Hassan thought, I would renounce a whole lifetime of allegiance and commitment. But he had not been given that choice. Now, his boy was dead, and he could blame the Israelis. He did blame them, but he blamed himself more—he couldn't help it. He saw too clearly the line that connected Hassan Hajimi to Ibrahim's fatal delay at the checkpoint. He hoped Marina would not see it. He watched her go.

Marina, Marina. She was wearing the veil and a long shapeless robe today, but Hassan remembered her at home, with her long black hair brushed out, and he remembered her sitting on a low wall on the Bir Zeit campus the first time he saw her, in her jeans and white blouse, with her hair tied back loosely in a braid, and stray wisps of it framing her face.

The men grew quiet again as she emerged from the cell. A few came up and offered her quiet congratulations on the ascent of her martyr. She looked at them, and they looked away. She imagined them remembering: The woman is not a Muslim by birth. She will never understand. They were right. She did not want congratulations. There were Muslim mothers who lost sons, and they were proud, she knew. She thought they must believe in their children as martyrs for Islam or they could not manage the rituals men had invented for them. Who could eat sweets and dance to celebrate the death of a toddler?

At least Hassan hadn't asked her to rejoice. He hadn't mentioned congratulations.

If Allah is willing. The saying was a sort of joke between them: If

Allah is willing, this toaster will not burn the bread, she would say, and Hassan would permit the implicit heresy. The old lamb will soften, if the Lord is willing. You did use the phrase that way in common parlance among Muslims. But when Marina said it, Hassan knew what she meant.

Inshallah. Did God have a will? She had always doubted it. Now more than ever. She pulled her head scarf forward. After all, Ibrahim was dead. Her baby was gone. What was she doing here, among these men? She swallowed hard and took a few steps into the hot courtyard. Then she turned for one last look back at the door of the visitors' cell. He was still standing there in the doorway, watching them go, and she shielded her eyes from the sun and looked as deep as she could into her husband's unfathomable blue eyes. He stepped back. The guard shut the door.

Chapter Fourteen

PHILIP PARKED THEIR LITTLE RENTED CAR AND POPPED OUT, rushing to open the door for George on the passenger side. Good manners, thought George. But he knew it was more than manners. Philip was always trying to curb George's physical activities. He extended an arm and gave George a modest, almost unnoticeable lift out of his seat. George was more grateful for the subtlety than for the help. They walked together across the hotel's driveway and into the lobby.

It was crowded before lunch. This was East Jerusalem, the Arab side of town, where people took their time about eating—there was the walk-up to lunch, there was lunch, and then, there was after-lunch. Development workers, foreign-aid donors, members of multinational forces, Canadians, Finns, Swedes, Frenchmen, and Italians, Palestinian businessmen, a handful of tourists, and foreign correspondents: that was the mix. More neckties concentrated in this lobby than anywhere else in the Holy Land, a scattering of military epaulets and berets, scores of drooping moustaches. Coffee and whiskey, cigarettes. Brass coffee tables—big shining circular trays held up on delicate wrought-iron legs. Next to the concierge's desk, a tile arrangement depicting the tree of life.

Over near the door, a man with his legs stretched out straight was holding a cell phone between his ear and shoulder, a copy of *Al-Ayyam* open on his knees, lighting a pipe, talking intently between sucks, nodding. Philip hid his hand and pointed to the headline in the man's lap: The Chairman Says: Find the Soldier. George shook his head. He was feeling weak, although for the first time since he'd come back for Ibrahim's funeral, he had had a full night's sleep. Last night's rain had lulled him, the sound of rain hitting the roof, the grill, the old rusted bedsprings, the hot water tank—and the broad askadinia leaves rattling in the wet breeze.

Across the lobby in a corner George saw one of the nodders from yesterday's meeting. He looked away quickly.

"They're everywhere," Philip said.

A man George did not recognize came up to them and began talking quietly to Philip.

"Get us a table, will you?" George said to Philip, interrupting. The man looked at him. George turned and walked away into the courtyard.

It was still too cold for eating outdoors. Too bad—this courtyard made him happy, always had. It had real Arab grace—it was the atrium of another old family palace. A room off the courtyard, that would be ideal. Quite a step up from his room off the bathroom in Ramallah. He looked down at the small fishpond beneath the courtyard fountain. He had read somewhere, probably in the science section of the *Times*, that goldfish were so overbred that some swam upside down in order to eat. Something about dappled goldfish and their swim bladders. Those science reporters, they take the mystery out of everything.

Ah, yes. There. There was one black-and-orange fellow, happily dashing around upside down through the green water, chasing a flaky lunch above an old rusting bucket that lay at the bottom of the pond. It was true, then! Fact! Evidence, George loved evidence. He peered downward. The water below him swirled with fish.

Genetics is a curious thing. Fish swimming upside down. Look how a useless thing like asthma could run in families, George thought. It hopped from the DNA strand of one generation to the next, possibly over thousands of years, as pointless as blue eyes or upside-down eating. The spotted fish finally managed to snatch his food. Beneath him and his comrades, a few vain coins glittered dimly from the pool's depths. George smelled garlic, and strong coffee brewing. He wanted his lunch. Faint stirrings rippled through his belly. It had been a long time since he'd experienced anything like the desire to eat. He wasn't sure he recognized it.

"Dr. Raad," said the maitre d'. "Welcome."

George nodded in acknowledgment. He scanned the room. Ah, there was Philip, in the corner near the window, but sitting with an unfamiliar man. How annoying! It would ruin lunch. What could Philip be thinking? He knew George hated surprises. Philip saw him and jumped up from the table, came across the room and took his arm.

"Who is that man?" George asked.

"He's a lawyer from Ramallah," Philip said. They passed several tables full of men speaking in undertones.

"Please, Philip, I do not want to have lunches with Ramallah lawyers." A man at one table looked over at George and spoke quietly to his companion.

"Well, *this* Ramallah lawyer was at the checkpoint the other night," Philip said.

"Oh." George felt a disturbing tightening in his heart. He looked at the man from a decent distance. Not too close. Fear. "Can't we sit somewhere else?"

"I don't think so. He has something he wants to tell you."

"Mmm."

"He says he knows the soldier's name."

They arrived at the table.

"Hello," George said.

The man returned his greeting. Then he said: "Mahmoud Sheukhi."

At first George thought, That can't be. The soldier's name. What does he mean? Then the man put out his hand and George understood.

"Ahhh. George Raad," said George, taking the proffered hand briefly.

"Yes, I know," Sheukhi said. He looked intently at George. George knew the look: Sheukhi was measuring the man in front of him against his reputation.

"I honor the memory of your martyr," Sheukhi said.

"What?" said George. "Oh. Yes. Thanks." He put his napkin on his lap. Why did he feel there was something rude about this intrusion? The man was handsome but his face was flushed, overexcited. George shifted his gaze away from the thick black hairs of Sheukhi's moustache—they looked like hairs under a microscope. He stared down at his own lap, examined his hands resting on the blank napkin. I need to get away from this place, he thought. He picked at the napkin's edge, pushed back his hair, and looked up. He saw his own reflection in the dull back of a soup-spoon. Face it, he thought. Face whatever it is.

"I have many things to tell you that you will want to hear," Mahmoud said.

"No doubt, no doubt," said George. So formal. Too bad I can't tell him I don't want to hear any of it. Because although I dislike this man so intensely, I do want to hear. I need to know certain things.

"You know your daughter waited there in the rain under my umbrella for at least a half an hour," Sheukhi said.

"Something like that, I had heard, yes," George said.

"That was before they agreed to see her," Sheukhi said. "They knew the boy was in trouble. It was an outrage."

"Outrages are what the Israelis commit by nature," George said. He felt it sounded reflexive, like a maxim. Well, it was. He did not want to think about the incident. Did not want to pour himself into a conversation about it. Did not want to be having this conversation with this sudden stranger—or with anyone. Hadn't had it yet with Marina, for example, though that was as much her doing as his. He only wanted one piece of information, but you couldn't just ask a man like this bluntly for what you wanted to know. You had to sit there patiently and take it. Which was not George's style.

He didn't want to think about the tragedy and he especially didn't want to think about Ibrahim's last minutes. There are details in life that one can live without. My poor little boy, in the rain. With this man. The picture George had struggled not to see was becoming more specific. It was like Ibrahim's pad of magic pictures. He had shown it to George: you drew the flat of your pencil over the pages lightly in no particular pattern, and with no warning Mickey Mouse appeared as the Sorcerer's Apprentice, in that funny hat, surrounded by his cohort and his appurtenances, bucket, broom, fountain, flood. He remembered Ibrahim looking up from the page with a serious look of accomplishment.

"How did they know he was in trouble?" Philip asked.

"I told them," Sheukhi said, with a measure of self-satisfaction. His moustache bristled as he dipped a piece of pita into the plate of humus in the middle of the table. "The boy could barely breathe. I mean, I'm no doctor, *ya'ni*, but you don't have to have a degree in internal medicine to notice a kid turning blue." He looked up from the pita at George, saw the pallor. "Oh, God, I'm so sorry. Excuse me." He popped another piece of pita into his mouth. "Thoughtless."

George leaned back in his chair and breathed deeply. "It's all right," he managed to say. "I'm just not used to the idea, yet. Having a little trouble."

"He was a good-looking little boy, Doctor," Mahmoud said, trying to recoup.

George stared at him. The Sorcerer's Apprentice. This terrible man was making the bad story come true. It hadn't been real before. Now it was real.

"So," said Philip, resting a hand on George's knee lightly, fleetingly. "You told them the child was ill. And then?"

"Oh, they were all exhausted from the day's work, you know," said Sheukhi. "There was a riot at their checkpoint and they were sort of unfocused, like soldiers after a battle, you know? The *shabab* threw their tear gas back at them, and it exploded, did you hear?" He smiled. "So anyway, I was trying to concentrate their minds on this pathetic picture outside, but of course, *ya'ni*, they hate someone like me so much that they can barely see you, much less listen to what you're saying. You could be telling them that the sky is about to fall on their heads, they wouldn't hear it."

"That *is* in effect what you were telling them, as it turned out," George said.

"Hmm?" said Sheukhi. "Oh, yes, I see what you mean. Well, they didn't realize that then, did they?"

"Apparently not," said Philip.

"So I'm standing in the door of their trailer, yelling at them, because of course they can't let a Palestinian into the fucking miserable little office, and this other little dick there wants to put handcuffs on me, actually threatens me, *ya'ni* . . . while your girl is sitting in the storm."

George kept staring at him. Why had fate selected this particular man to be his daughter's protector? It was cruel, a cruel joke played on George, who would have had them wrapped up in a mackintosh and on their way to the hospital in no time. Instead, fate had seen fit to choose a weak man, a well-meaning man but a man of no authority, of no weight, a man who could not command the attention of a dog, with his *ya'ni*, *ya'ni* and his bristling moustache with humus adhering to it like foam. A Ramallah lawyer. George closed his eyes tight shut for a second, then opened them, but the man did not go away.

"What kind of law is it that you practice?" George asked suddenly.

Sheukhi looked uncomprehending.

George kept his eyebrows up, his head bent in curiosity, not relenting, offering a tiny unfriendly smile.

"Oh, you know," answered Sheukhi, bravely facing the look. "The usual local mix. Questions of property, title, family stuff, small claims. Like that. My brother and I."

"Ah," George said.

Philip shook his head at George. One unnoticeable disapproving shake.

Oh, I'll behave, George thought. Don't worry. I won't let loose.

"Just wondered," George said. He gave the little smile again.

"So half an hour after the rain began, I finally got the commanding officer to let her in. Some little jerk frisked her first with a metal detector."

George flinched.

"They can't resist a chance to humiliate us, you know? She's lost a shoe, she's soaking wet, she's got this child on her hands, and they frisk her like she's some security threat. I couldn't believe it."

"May I say something here?" George said.

"Yes, sure," said Sheukhi.

"We don't require every detail."

"No?" asked Sheukhi.

"Just a few facts. A very few facts."

Sheukhi wiped his moustache with a napkin. "Are you sure?" he asked.

"Yes. I'm sure."

"Because I imagine that every detail is important. Or will be."

"What you imagine does not concern me. Will be when? When the Israelis bring their men to trial for the death of a Palestinian child?" George looked at Sheukhi. "When was the last time that happened? Tell me. Or when the Palestinians take the fellow into custody and try him in a court of law? Is that when the details will be pertinent? What was the man's name, for God's sake?" George asked.

Sheukhi looked at Raad.

"He's upset," Philip said to Sheukhi. "Please. Don't be offended."

George gave Philip a murderous look.

"His name was Ari Doron, Lieutenant Ari Doron," Sheukhi said. Raad was not someone he was going to understand, much less like.

"Ari Doron," said George. That's like Muhammad Abdallah, he thought. Lieutenant John Doe. It has no specificity, a meaningless identifier. It tells me nothing. It was as if Sheukhi had said the Israeli soldier's name was Israeli Soldier. Lieutenant Israeli Soldier.

"I suppose that's something," George said. "Philip, is that something?"

"Oh, yes, certainly it is," said Philip.

"Not sure what, though," said George, exclusively to Philip.

Sheukhi watched. These two were politicians, he could see. The younger man, too, with his delicate face. They seemed to be deciding what the information was worth.

"What will you do with it?" he asked them, interrupting their quiet discussion.

"Do with it?" George said, looking at Philip. "I don't know."

"You must do something, you know. The Palestinian people are demanding justice," Sheukhi said. "Something must be done."

"You are so right," George said in an unexpectedly loud voice, his hearty military voice. "And something will be, something will be. By the way, did you like the humus? This place has some of the best. Unfortunately, I lost my appetite. Would you like something else? You've been really very helpful, hasn't he, Philip?" Here, George clapped Philip on the shoulder.

Philip nodded, rising.

"Very helpful, indeed," said George, nodding at Sheukhi.

Philip was helping Sheukhi up from the table.

"So farewell," George said. "And thanks, *habibi*."

Sheukhi was halfway across the dining room, escorted by Philip, when he suddenly turned on his heel and headed back toward the table.

"You know," he said to George, leaning down so close that George could smell the chickpea and garlic on his breath, "you know your daughter heard the name, too. I'm certain of it. Several times she heard it. Why hasn't she said anything? Why hasn't she come forward? She must come forward. I'm sure she will. Don't you think? She knows better than any of us what he represents, this Ari Doron. Don't you agree? That poor little boy."

Of course she knew. It had not occurred to George even to think about it, but now that Sheukhi had made his point, George realized the man must be right. So Marina knew, and wasn't saying. Wasn't telling George, at least. He hoped she hadn't told Hassan. Because if something happened to the soldier, to this Doron, they could all be in big trouble, especially Hassan. George didn't doubt that his son-in-law was capable of stirring up something fatal, even from inside an Israeli prison, but even if Hassan did nothing, he would be blamed.

He pushed back his chair and stood up to face the man.

"Listen to me, *habibi*," George said. "Don't you go around peddling this piece of information as if it were a bushel of figs."

Sheukhi looked at him.

"One moment of irresponsible behavior," George said, "and I will march over and give your name to the Israelis as a possible threat. I have no compunction where protecting my family is concerned. Do not dream of going to my son-in-law with this. I will not have my daughter or my son-in-law taking responsibility for the fate of this soldier. Do you hear me?"

Sheukhi began to laugh.

"You know what, Raad?" he said, sticking his face right up into George's. "You don't scare me. You've just confirmed something for me; before I wasn't sure if you were a coward, even though you abandoned the struggle. But now, I know. Goodbye, Doctor."

George wanted to hit the man, but instead, he turned away, and Sheukhi sauntered out.

CHAPTER FIFTEEN

MARINA PUSHED THE CART THROUGH THE NARROW aisles. First you had to navigate around the island of nuts and chocolates and pink and blue marshmallows near the entrance. It was odd buying for men only: meat and coffee, pita, the occasional cake. Her father loved lamb, she bought lamb. Meat for men. Not like before: chocolate treats and breakfast cereals, macaroni and cheese, hot dogs, sliced white bread, diapers. Or before that, when she shopped for herself and Hassan: chicken and rice, onions, Diet Coke, and Turkish delight, a repulsive sweet he loved. There wasn't much in the cart today, but she was finished. It seemed sad and empty, diminished. She stopped at the counter where Ibrahim liked to pick out a lollipop. If she made a hundred men happy, it would never satisfy her as much as one single smile of Ibrahim's—looking up at her with a lollipop stuck in his mouth, his cheeks hollow with sucking, the lips curled up at the sides with a grin like the drunken one that had come when he finally noticed for the first time who was nursing him, only two years earlier. The edges of the mouth smiling while the rest was occupied with something else. It was a devastating look he used to have, and she tried to face it squarely now, as she pictured him sitting in the pull-back section of the carriage, kicking his legs through the holes, sucking on his red lolly.

Adel was behind the counter. Marina put her stuff next to the register for him to tally. He gave her a rueful smile. She gave one back.

"How is your husband?" he asked.

"He is fine, thank God," she said. You always had to mention God.

"The Lord be praised," Adel answered. He turned over her package of meat. "This lamb is not so fresh."

"Oh," said Marina. "That's okay. I can cook it forever. It will soften, the Lord willing."

"Let me see if we have something newer in the back," said Adel, and he was gone.

On the radio that morning, they'd been talking about unrest at the crossings. People kept flooding to the roadblocks to demand that the Israelis hand over the soldier. Marina never wanted to go near a checkpoint again, and she wouldn't, except to cross over to visit Hassan. The night before, during the Prime Minister's press conference, they had shown boys throwing stones and Israeli soldiers shooting, as usual. And she saw it. The small white trailer at the Ramallah checkpoint. It looked just the same as ever, as if nothing of note had ever happened there. The soldiers outside it could have been her soldiers. That's how she thought of them now: hers.

Adel came back with a better piece of meat, and she paid him and carried her father's lamb out of the store in a plastic bag. Next to the popsicle freezer beyond the doors, four or five folded strollers were piled up against the wall.

As Marina walked up the hill to her house, she read the graffiti scrawled along the wall. FIND THE SOLDIER. It was scribbled again in poorly executed script on the green dumpster in the dusty lot across from her house. She wondered where her soldier was now, right now. What he was thinking.

A car festooned with rippling white ribbons and pink balloons was coming down the hill. As it passed by, its hot exhaust brushed her and she caught a glimpse of a bride's rouged downcast face. It was her wedding day, the day of photographs, the groom on horseback on a hill in the park, and the bride primly standing in front of an arch with her hands at the sides of her big white dress. Marina had seen it all a hundred times, she knew it all by now. The customs of her homeland. Hassan looking like a prince in his white wedding suit. She remembered Hassan from the photos more than from the event itself, Hassan squinting into the sun, the lines webbing out around his eyes, a small smile playing like sunlight over his beautiful face.

She felt like a liar. She had kept something from him: and it was not some frivolous girlish thing. It was the name of the enemy. Not just the enemy of her family, but the enemy now of the entire Palestinian people. That's how Hassan would think of it, she was sure. At first, she had forgotten the lieutenant and her West Bank protector and everything that happened before, during, and after—and remembered only Ibrahim's face amid a hubbub of useless whirring activity. But now she could picture the soldier. Little by little, he was coming back to her. It had been a week now. She remembered his eyes were scared. He was useless, but he tried. He crouched over that radio as if it could save him, as if it were something you could rub and a miracle would happen. But it was just communications equipment, and on the other end were Israelis, doing what Israelis do.

And why was she there, anyway? Dr. Miller and her doctor in Ramallah had told her that when it was bad, Ibrahim's case could be critical, and he might need extreme measures that they could not provide on the Palestinian side. Still, they had to have had something better than the pointless inhaler that she had tried to use so many times and then finally left behind. She hated the Israelis, hated the soldiers, hated her own sad soldier. His face afterward, the shock trickling out of the corners of his eyes—it wasn't *his* loss.

The Palestinian people were calling for his blood, and she still hadn't told anyone his name.

Was she protecting Ari Doron? She didn't think so.

She was protecting Hassan, protecting him from what she imagined might be his natural reaction. If a man wants revenge and you give him the information he needs to get it, he'll use it. If something happened to Doron, Hassan was the likely suspect, in Israeli eyes. But maybe Hassan was above revenge; and maybe he would have understood if she'd told him everything about the soldier—the small good things, the big bad things.

WHEN SHE ARRIVED home with the groceries, her father was sitting in front of the television, watching tennis. His feet were up on a hassock, his left sock had a hole in it. His shirt was undone at the collar. His hair was rumpled, as if he'd been running his hand through it.

"If all those people who think you're God could see you now, they would be utterly shocked," she said. She looked at him over the tops of her grocery bags.

He put up a finger, didn't take his eyes off the screen.

"Ah, good, good," he said, watching the end of a point. "Sorry," he said, looking over at her. "Even God is allowed to put his feet up once in a while. What did you get?" His eyes brightened.

"Lamb."

"Lamb," he said. "You're wonderful."

"Have you had lunch?" she asked.

"Yes," he said. He gave her a penetrating look for a second, then went back to the tennis. She raised her eyebrows and went to unload her bags.

When she came out of the kitchen, he was still spread-eagle in front of his match, but he had fallen asleep.

He seemed so relaxed, so unlike himself. One arm was flung over the side of the chair, and his trouser legs had both crept up so she could see that sad, vulnerable spot between the end of pants and the beginning of socks. The twin patches of calf were pale white, and the hair on them was sparse. Her legendary father was an old man now, with bald legs. He was snoring gently. He did not look elegant. His glasses had fallen down so that the spectacles were under his chin. He looked like an old Irish character actor on Broadway; all he needed to complete the picture was a tweed cap gone askew. His mouth was slack. Until Hassan, Marina thought, the man I loved best in the world. He would die, too, and then she would be completely alone: Ibrahim dead, Hassan in prison, Daddy dead.

Two women in whites took their places on opposing sides of the court, and applause came from the television like static, the sound of thousands of tiny hands clapping halfway across the world.

She sat down and watched, her sewing box on her lap, her father sleeping next to her, a shirt of his—missing a button—in her hands, two women on the screen, batting the ball between them. Not telling Hassan—it was a gross betrayal of their marriage. But things were different now between them from the way they had been at the beginning. Hassan was isolated and frozen, and Marina was on the outside. With Ibrahim, their greatest connection had disappeared. Hassan had been in prison on and off for Ibrahim's entire lifetime. He'd been at Moscobiyyeh so long that he had grown fuzzy in Marina's imagination, like a dead person. Sometimes between visits she almost forgot the timbre of her husband's voice. That voice was one of his chief attractions, a lithe baritone that could turn sharp and stinging.

She remembered Hassan in a white shirt standing in the corner of the library at Bir Zeit, where everything was supposed to be hushed and reverential, the two windows behind him facing the desert, and the hot wind streaming in. He was holding some novel between two fingers of one disgusted hand and pointing at its pages as the wind riffled through them, his blues eyes alternately blazing and twinkling, his voice rough, and then sweet, laughing as he deconstructed the bad prose, the bad ideas, making unkind but entirely reasonable jokes at the author's expense while a crowd of rapt students listened from their library pods to the eloquent storm of his words, denouncing the winner of a Nobel prize.

She had that mental picture of him, and many others, but each time her private remembrance of him was brought up to date with an actual visit, he seemed to have turned into someone else, a flat empty thing with only one characteristic: one month an angry man, the next, a thin man; one month, a lonely man, the next, hopeless—and not the vivid, complete, compact, brilliant, magnetic person he was when they married. He had slipped out of the stream of humanity. Prison was turning him into a "Palestinian"—after all, he was a political prisoner, and he was in prison not because he was charming and handsome or sad and lonely, but because he was Palestinian. Over time, he was conforming to his jailers' preconceptions, becoming a distillation of stereotypes of his own refugee race: thin, sun-blasted, angry, hopeless, voluble yet unreachable.

One of the women came to the net and hit a hard crosscourt backhand that left her opponent looking disheartened and woebegone. Marina heard her father's breath go in and out, a slow, reassuring sound. Hassan's hands and his voice and his belief—the man he was—had been her visa back into Palestine, a Palestine other than the dead romantic one her father had envisioned for her, that fairyland of cypress and palm and stone. Hassan had taken her and led her into another place, where there were no wealthy landholding grandfathers, no grass tennis courts, no country tours on velocipede, but instead the yearning call to prayer, and refugee camps and villages on windblown hillsides.

Teaching her about her homeland had been a passion: You call yourself a Palestinian? Hassan would ask, when she would say something particularly naive. And then he would instruct her. He had pulled her out of her father's Jerusalem of a half century earlier, and into Ramallah now. She remembered him holding Ibrahim in the visitors' cell. At least my son is free, he would say at the end of every visit, forgetting he had said it the time before. She was afraid for Hassan now that Ibrahim was dead, and afraid of him at the same time. Even his tenderness was aggressive.

They had been trying to get Marina and her father to go to that rally tomorrow. The head of the student league at Bir Zeit had called, ostensibly to offer his condolences but really to invite them. He said the students wanted her to speak, as well as George. She might just go to the rally—she would never speak, but she might accompany her father if he decided to go. Family solidarity. She could hide behind him.

George stirred as the commercials came on: commercials were always louder than the regular programming. Marina coughed to wake him. She wanted company. She coughed again, louder. She'd sewn his button on, admittedly slightly off-center, but nonetheless undeniably attached.

Marina looked over at her father: he was waking up, reassembling his features, putting the mask back on.

She tossed the shirt to him and it landed in his lap.

He picked it up.

"Oh, right," he said, adjusting his glasses. "Thanks."

He looked at the television.

"Who's winning?" he asked.

She shrugged.

"Doesn't matter," he said.

Philip came in, coughing a little as he usually did to announce his presence.

"Whatever is cooking smells wonderful," he said. He smiled at Marina with those generous, compassionate brown eyes. She felt tears come into her own. God, was she so vulnerable that a compliment on her cooking could make her cry?

Philip handed a newspaper to George.

"They are disgraceful," Philip said. Marina could see a large spread of photographs, and headlines in Hebrew.

George looked at the paper, and made a small noise of disgust. He shook his head.

"Oh my, Philip," he said.

Philip nodded.

"I am *so* sorry, Marina," Philip said. He shook his head at her and left the room.

"What is it?" she asked her father.

"This," he said, and handed her newspaper. It was *Ha'aretz*, she saw.

She only looked at it for half a second, and then she stood and walked quickly from the room with the paper rolled in her hand.

"Marina!" her father shouted after her.

She locked the bathroom door, sat down, and stared at the thing. She couldn't read the Hebrew, but she knew what they were saying. There was her husband as a boy, holding the hand of his older sister Fatima. Next to that old picture was one that had been used once already, on the day after the incident, a picture of Marina walking Ibrahim down a street in Ramallah. The pictures were so similar, it could have been the same street. And Hassan and Ibrahim looked so much alike—she had never noticed it before. But the Israelis certainly had. Daddy terrorist, baby terrorist. That was the implication; she knew without being able to read. All she could see was Ibrahim. On her lap. She covered the pictures with her hands.

After a while, she put the paper aside, folded, and stood up to wash her face. She looked at herself: bedraggled, woebegone. Her black hair hung straight down around her face. Under her eyes were circles.

She walked into the living room where her father was standing, waiting for her return. He shook his head at her. She put the folded newspaper into his outstretched hands, not looking at him. She wanted to remain in control. Pushing aside her sewing kit, she sat down.

A bus's horn blared out from down on the road.

Let's cause her more pain, George said to himself. The conversation could not wait, he had decided when she ran out of the room. She knew the same secret he knew. Here I go, Lord help me.

"I had a most peculiar lunch today," George said.

"What happened?" Marina asked dully. She clicked off the set and pulled her chair around to face his.

"It was the company that was strange, actually." She was so sweet-looking with her hair down, like a dark Rapunzel, gazing at him without her habitual hostility, for some reason. Well, that was about to end.

"Wasn't Philip with you?"

"He brought someone, a lawyer from Ramallah. Actually the lawyer said he was there at the checkpoint the other night."

"Oh," Marina said.

"Yup," said George. He pulled up his socks, and looked around for his shoes. Even in front of his daughter, he did not like to be unkempt.

"So how was Moscobiyyeh today, by the way?" he asked her as he bent over his shoelaces.

"Fine."

"And what does he think?"

"Say his name, Daddy." It was hard for her father to bend all the way over his shoes, she noticed. He was breathing hard.

"What?"

"Say his name."

He looked up at her. He could hear his heart beating. He did not want to pick his head up too fast.

"Hassan," he said. "What does Hassan think?"

"What does he think? About what?"

"What does he want to do with the name, Marina?"

"I don't think he knows the soldier's name," she said. "Is that what we're talking about?"

"Yes," said George. "Yes, that's exactly what we're talking about." He summoned a flinty glare for Marina, a look she hadn't seen in a long time, but not one she had forgotten.

"Do you know the name, Marina?" George asked. The flinty glare was gone. "Because I do."

"The lawyer from Ramallah," she said after a pause. "He told you?"

"Yup," George said. "He told me. Seemed to feel it was his duty. He says he forced the soldier to let you into the trailer."

"That's when everything started to get really bad," Marina said. She remembered the heat of Ibrahim's flushed skin against her hands as she sat on that flimsy metal chair. She had put her hands under his sweatshirt to see how bad his retractions were. She remembered the feel of him heating up in her arms.

She stood up, turning away from her father. She picked her sewing kit up from the small rattan table next to her chair, and zipped it shut.

"It was a very bad night, sweetheart," George said to her.

Her back shook slightly. He wanted to go over to her, but he wasn't sure. Could she stand it? Could he?

"I can't, I still can't talk about it," she said.

"We don't have to," George said.

"Maybe we do have to," Marina said, her face still averted. "But I can't."

"Do you want me to go to Ahmed with the name?"

"Uncle Ahmed?" Marina asked. "No. No. Why should we tell Uncle Ahmed? I haven't even told Hassan."

Good, George thought.

"And Hassan deserves to know," she said. "Ahmed doesn't. This is what I think: The soldier was there. That makes him a useful symbol: that's why my *uncle* is so interested in him. But there's more to it. There's more."

"Like?"

"He was trying to get an okay for us to go across. But there was a problem."

"A problem."

"On the phone. He ran into a problem; it was all set, and then there was a problem."

"What was the problem?"

"*Who* was the problem. There was someone he was talking to, he got bumped up from person to person, and at the end there was a problem with who we were, or something, he kept saying 'Hajimi, Hajimi,' and things like 'I don't care who the father is the boy is sick, sick, sick— *mamash, mamash choleh*'—I couldn't understand everything, it was in Hebrew, but I understood that."

"So?"

"So then, well, at first I could see he was just going to do what they said, obey orders. He kept saying sorry to me, as if that would make it all right. But then a little while later, he looked at us again and he could see it was so bad, so bad, and he said, basically, he was going to let us in. I could hear the ambulance coming, but . . ."

George looked at her back. Tears surprised him, overflowing his eyes. He wiped them away quickly.

"It seemed so quick, all of a sudden," she said.

"Oh, Marina," he said.

There was a long silence. Her shoulders trembled, but there were no sobs. The afternoon light filtered in through the shutters. The neighbors' television droned on and on.

"So," she said finally. "So, I just feel something about him."

"You mean, the Israeli."

"Yes, him. The commanding officer."

"And what's the something you feel, sweetheart?"

"That we went through it together. That he was trying to be on my side." There. She had said it. It wasn't something she wanted to admit. She was furious with the soldier. She couldn't bear the thought of him. But there was no denying one thing. He had been trying to be on their side. She could never admit it to Hassan, because Hassan could never allow it to be true. His whole world was built on another point of view. Drunken dogs, killers, usurpers, evil, the devil. She knew the litany, had never argued with it. She agreed more or less. Her father was pretty much in accord, too.

But her father would be able to understand her confusion. Confusion was repugnant to Hassan. Whereas George's element was ambiguity, ambivalence.

"That's what I think, anyway," she said. "And that I don't want my husband to get involved with this. Finding the soldier is beside the point to me. Not to Uncle Ahmed, but to me. One stupid soldier is not to blame."

"Maybe." George looked at the blank television screen.

"You would say: 'It's not the individual, it is the state. The state is criminal, the individual is merely acting in accordance with an inhuman and unacceptable system.'"

"Is that what I'd say?"

"It's what you *have* said, actually." She sat back down on the chair that faced his.

"And yet, there are Israelis and there are Israelis."

"Not according to my husband."

"Say his name, Marina."

"Hassan says, and I know he's dogmatic, that you cannot—you *must not*—distinguish among Israelis: each one is a criminal, because the state is criminal. He starts from your proposition, but reaches the opposite conclusion."

That's why she loves him, thought George.

"Ahhhh," he said. "A hard man. No exemption for the innocent."

She sat quietly for a minute. "He's not a hard man, Daddy."

"Yes he is, rabbit. He's hard. Just not to you. I hope."

"He's not hard at all. He's broken, now." She began to cry, but without drama. Just tears coming down.

"Life is wretched," George said. He watched her, but even under his scrutiny, she did not stop crying. Slowly, he cranked himself up from his chair and went over to her. She just sat there, staring blankly at his now-empty chair, with tears running down her cheeks and falling onto her sewing kit. There he was, next to her. He put a hand on her shoulder and she put one of hers up to cover his, as if in thanks. Thanks for what, he asked himself. Thanks for nothing.

Marina looked like a refugee, still wearing the long dark robe she often wore for shopping. He wanted to whisk her away from all this. She should be living in a split-ranch with a station wagon in the driveway, poor darling—or in a bohemian Parisian penthouse. Not in these drab Ramallah quarters. And her husband. He should be an orthodontist in Chicago—or an artist or a professor, not a bitter, deprived man, incarcerated in some sandy dungeon, gloomily plotting the destruction of his enemies. Her baby should not be moldering in the grave. Her father should not be leaving her this terrible legacy. George was growing impatient. He wanted to do something, not just go pat, pat, pat, there, there.

Marina wiped her eyes and moved away from her father's comforting hand.

"I'm going to go fix dinner," she said. She folded his mended shirt and put it on the coffee table.

"Can I help?" George asked.

She looked at him and shook her head. He watched her leave.

PHILIP CAME BACK into the room, as if he'd been waiting just outside for the correct moment to return.

George looked at Philip, shrugged, and lifted his open hands in a gesture of befuddlement.

"So?" asked Philip.

George sat down heavily in front of the television.

"Well, as far as I'm concerned, Philip, absolutely nothing has changed."

"Meaning?"

"I intend to sit here with this fellow's name in my lap and do nothing about it."

"I assumed," said Philip. He looked at George and then down at the Israeli newspaper, which was half hidden by the shirt Marina had sewn. "What about the rally tomorrow? Are you going?"

"Oh, I don't know. I certainly don't want to." George sat there. "I'm tired." He folded his hands in his lap. He supposed he should go to the damned rally. The students had asked him. Not Ahmed. Maybe that was the place to make a stand.

"Just because Ahmed will be there doesn't mean you can't say what you think, you know," Philip said. "Just because he's from a Ramallah family doesn't mean he's in charge."

"You're right. I do have some sort of cultural reluctance to disagree with him live and in public," George said. "That's partly why I don't want to go. Don't want to be rude. Spoil his fun."

"Uh-hunh." Philip picked up the paper and looked at the pictures of Ibrahim and Hassan. "I'm a novice at all this, Doctor, but maybe you could try to . . . redirect the debate tomorrow. It can be *your* forum. You know how to do it; I've seen you do it a hundred times. Remember? You always say: 'I hijacked it.' So, hijack Ahmed's program. I know you want to. Take control; run away with it."

"Yah," said George. "Maybe." He lapsed into silence. He was listening to his heart tumbling in his chest, rumbling and tumbling like a deep-sea acrobat. He didn't tell Philip. If you told Philip, you ended up in the emergency room. George figured he himself knew enough to decide when it was a crisis and when it was just fatigue and the normal tumbling of a human heart.

There was definitely some satisfaction in knowing the name and not sharing it. Sheukhi had wanted George to rush off to Hassan or the Chairman with the Israeli lieutenant's name. But George was not in any hurry about this business. He didn't know what Hassan was capable of, but he didn't want his son-in-law reunited with Marina only to be re-arrested by the Israelis when the soldier disappeared. And he simply refused to give the information to Ahmed, to offer Ahmed another weapon in the political campaign he was waging in Ibrahim's name.

George felt like a small boy hoarding his new marbles. Marina was miserable because she hadn't told Hassan what she knew, but George did not feel even a twinge of remorse about keeping a secret from Ahmed. No, he was delighted. He only wished there was some way to inform Ahmed that he knew the soldier's name and was withholding it. It was a victory of inaction, because surely the Authority would get the soldier's name if they really wanted it, which he doubted.

Still it was a triumph—a small and passing triumph. He knew that what he was doing—or not doing—was right and there was satisfaction in that, as well. Talking to Marina today had only confirmed what he already believed: that the commanding officer was not the guilty party. Life is more complicated. The problem of Palestine was that everyone wanted things simple: everyone was an extremist because everyone wanted things simple. It was the problem of humanity. Good and evil, as if there were only those two.

The interesting thing was to seek truth and then face it, even if the truth was that the commanding officer was not a cruel, birdbrained, Palestinian-hating, Zionist murderer. Even if the truth turned out to be that Marina loved a man who believed in terror and in death, even if the truth was that Ahmed was probably not such a bad man after all. Even if the truth was that George was nearly finished with the thing.

And yet there was one more item on the agenda. Philip raised the question: Should he speak at this rally? Philip said: Take your opportunity. Use it for your own purposes. It doesn't matter who provides the occasion, the platform. Remember? Hijack it. Hijack it. George thought: I just might.

Chapter Sixteen

THE MONTH OF RAMADAN WAS COMING UP. HE NOTICED the clear plastic bags of seasonal tamarind juice hanging from the stalls outside Damascus Gate as he drove a circuitous route back down toward The Building from the police station up on King David. Yizhar was sure it would make the problems at the checkpoints even worse. It was like the fucking Intifada out there, these days.

He lowered the windshield visor to protect his eyes from the late afternoon sun. Yizhar hated Ramadan, and so did the entire Israeli security apparatus. Purification of the soul was arguably something desirable—perhaps not Yizhar's cup of tea, but still conceivably worthwhile—but Ramadan put the Palestinians in a worse mood than usual, if that was possible. Their eternal unhappy mix of depression and resentment turned into something even less palatable during the monthlong fast. They were ravenous from sunup to sundown, and then stuffed themselves all night and got hardly any sleep. In the morning, they were so exhausted from eating all night that they could barely get out of bed, much less go to work, and so the whole rickety Palestinian economy virtually collapsed. Then, too, they went to the mosque more than usual, which meant they had nothing to do but listen to a bunch of foul sheikhs spew anti-Israel Islamist propaganda. It was a time for conspiracies and festering plots to come to fruition. At the end of the month, they were low on calories but full of ideas, which was always a volatile combination. So what do they do? They get together by the tens of thousands for a final starvation-driven prayer at the Dome of the Rock. Who knew what mischief they'd get into afterward? Their holy men used to shoot off a 78-millimeter cannon to signal the end of fasting, but a few years earlier, the Israelis had put an end to that. We didn't want them handling any kind of heavy artillery in the middle of Jerusalem. No way. Even though the gun was made in 1918, and rusting, and perched at the edge of a cemetery.

Yizhar looked down briefly at the passenger seat next to him. The beautiful front page lay open beneath his new cell phone. He felt almost gleeful. His trophy was a photograph of a big-eyed little boy, about four years old, in formal pants, solid-looking shoes, a white shirt, and a little jacket, holding on to a big girl's hand, one of his older sisters, as it turned out. Veiled, of course. Yizhar wished it were the boy's mother, not his sister, but you couldn't have everything in this world and this picture was a little gift from God. A fucking bauble, a treasure. That sweet little boy looking up at his sister with big trusting eyes was Hassan Hajimi, the infamous Hamasnik. The picture hadn't been easy to get: Yizhar had had to use one of their best men on the West Bank, and it was a risk to put such a good man in danger on such a theoretical propaganda exercise, but Yizhar thought the public-opinion payback would be worth it, and he persuaded his boss to get the go-ahead from intelligence. Everything went according to Yizhar's plan, for once, and he'd seen the picture on every newsstand in every superette this morning, next to the picture everyone had already seen, of big-eyed little Ibrahim holding his mother's hand. No Israeli would fail to get the point: cute little Palestinians grow up to be big Palestinians.

Pieces were falling into place. Yizhar was more or less pleased with the Hajimi case, it was going well. Damage control was fun, although there was a lot of damage to control on this one. The Find the Soldier thing was really very irritating: as if anyone who had any power to find him would want to. What would the Authority do with an Israeli soldier? It wasn't as if the Chairman were still in charge of a terrorist organization, even though he probably still thought of himself as a rifle-toting commando—he wasn't about to take an Israeli soldier and summarily execute him, which is what the population would probably want. No, today the Chairman was just an old bald man with a quivering lower lip and shaking hands. And yet the thing kept on going. Only yesterday, two Palestinians had been killed and twenty wounded in riots at the checkpoints. The Authority was calling out the troops, using the *shabab* again. They thought that the Israelis might succumb to the pressures of violence and make a concession or two in the negotiations.

Of course the concept of the Israelis succumbing to anything was ill-founded. No one forced the Israelis to do anything. The country was a law unto itself, and Yizhar liked it that way: a rogue nation riding roughshod over others, trampling norms and shoving aside accepted wisdom. Small but scrappy. We were the new cowboys—yeah, it was outmoded to think this way, but then again, Yizhar was an old-fashioned guy.

Doron was the only meaningful variable. If he went along, then everything worked. If he didn't, chaos. There wasn't much difference between Doron's story and Yizhar's story, but still, the discrepancy was enough to make a controversy, if you felt like making a controversy, which everyone did, the Palestinians, the media, the "international community"—whoever the fuck that was; basically, it was the rest of the world, which always supported the Palestinians. The minute the boy started talking about phone calls and superiors and orders from above, the whole thing could get seriously out of hand.

It was too risky. There might actually be records of actual calls that actually had been made. Real facts could come out. Yizhar hated real facts because their revelation could create uncontrollable situations. Doron must toe the line, keep to the story. Even a whisper of a hint about that alleged call meant trouble, if the information came from an Israeli. *Alleged*, Yizhar liked that word. The call, the orders, a high-ranking officer at work at night. Yizhar had told Doron and Zvili that no one on earth could possibly believe such a story but in fact, the opposite was true. Everyone would believe Doron: the boy was unassailably honest. Anyone capable of doing a quick read of character would know immediately that it would not occur to such a soldier to lie to save his own ass. Yizhar would keep Doron quiet. He knew how to manipulate the human beast—his life's work, really. The soldier's little piece of information was too dangerous. Of all things, Yizhar did not want the man who gave Doron the orders to be found, to even be imagined.

Yizhar had been thinking about the human beast recently. Precious, useful creature. Zvili was a good example. Zvili wanted to do well in life. Zvili was just a little afraid of his wife, and very afraid of Yizhar. And Zvili was worried, also. He knew he had not acquitted himself well at the time of the incident, that he had let reflexive anger get the better of him, when a cooler head should have prevailed. Zvili knew Doron should not be shouldering all the guilt for the child's death. But Zvili was human, and when he saw Doron feeling guilty, his own guilt—what little he felt—dissipated. Doron felt guilty? Why then, he probably *was* guilty. That was how Zvili rationalized. It was the usual self-protective, self-serving, survivor's instinct that Yizhar had come to expect from the beast. It made Zvili into a good ally.

God, what an assignment, Yizhar thought, shaking his head. He was becoming a smarter person for it, and smart, he reminded himself, did not mean evil. Smart was smart. Smart survived. Dumb died. One of Yizhar's rules of war. His cell phone beeped. He pressed the special button on the dashboard.

"Yizhar, here," he said.

"Sir, it's Zvili."

He *knew* the boy would come through.

"Yes, Sergeant," said Yizhar.

"Sorry to bother you, sir," Zvili said.

"Not at all," said Yizhar. "What's up, Sergeant?"

"I saw our man," Zvili said.

"Yeah?"

"He's upset. He says he wants to do something to make everything all right."

"Like what?" asked Yizhar. Talk like this made him nervous. Make everything all right? That was impossible. "What do you think he meant?"

"I don't know, talking to the media, maybe. Telling his side." Zvili paused. "He seemed upset that you had, uh, taken control of the story. He seemed to feel you weren't interested in certain things he told you."

"Yes, well, he's right." Maybe he had been too aggressive with Doron, too arrogant. Not caring and sensitive enough—but really. What did the boy expect? Therapy? A rap session?

"I told him you were on his side. That you were trying to help him. He said that I didn't know which side he was on."

Damn, damn.

"I should call him," Yizhar said.

"If he doesn't call you. I gave him this number, hope that wasn't wrong."

"No, no, best thing you could do. Thanks."

"You're welcome, sir."

"Anything else?"

"No, sir." Zvili hesitated slightly. "Oh, yes. He told me he's got the number he dialed that night somewhere, and he's looking for it."

Yizhar closed his eyes.

"There was no such number," he heard himself say.

"That's basically what I told him, sir," Zvili said.

"Anything else?" Yizhar asked. But what else could there be, really?

He heard a sudden shyness overcome his blunt sergeant.

"Oh, actually, yes, sir," Zvili said. He hesitated, then plunged. "My wife is pregnant."

"Well, congratulations, Sergeant. *Mazel tov.*" What? Why should Yizhar give a shit? "Best thing in the world."

"Thank you, sir."

"Well, stay on the case, Sergeant. It'll take your mind off the impending event."

"Yes, sir."

"You're a good man. Don't worry about your buddy. He'll be fine. You're right, I'm on his side. And *I* know what side he's on, even if he doesn't."

"Yes, sir."

"Okay, thanks. See you later, *habibi.*" Some soldiers just loved it when you called them *habibi.* It made them feel comfortable, as if you considered them your equal. He'd never call Doron *habibi,* because Doron was proud, and an officer, and would feel and resent the condescension. But Zvili was easy. Kick, kick, touch of the whip applied to this flank, a pull on the reins, a subtle shifting of weight to the right, and there you were: exactly where you wanted to be.

ALL NIGHT, Yizhar sat at his desk, his new desk, looking at his cell phone, waiting. He filed a few papers, examined his sad philodendron, didn't water it. He rearranged the supplies with which he had stocked the desk drawers. He listened to the late-night radio news, leafed through a few recent issues of *Jane's Defence*—submarines were his passion—and used the office phone to call Avram Shell at *Ha'aretz* to thank him for the nice placement of the Hajimi photographs. He noticed a spot on the left edge of his desk as they talked. Already decaying like the old one. Shell was planning a series on checkpoints, and Yizhar gave him some information about closure policy, which he'd been studying during the past few days. He told Shell there might be the possibility of an interview in the next few days with the checkpoint soldier, and Shell leaped on it of course; he did a lunchtime interview every day on Army Radio.

As he talked to Shell, Yizhar leaned over to peer at the spot on his new desk. Where the hell had it come from? It was black and ugly.

Shell understood the army and its requirements. He would do a good interview. He knew the right questions to ask—and the right answers.

And of course, Yizhar would do a little pre-interview with the command-ing officer just to let him know what the conversation was to be about. So the soldier wouldn't waste Shell's tape, because of course the interview would be taped—to avoid any embarrassing mistakes.

During their conversation, Yizhar did not put his feet up on his new desk. No feet on the desk: that was his new policy. He didn't want scuff marks.

After he finished with Shell, he wetted a paper towel in the men's-room sink and then kneeled by the side of his new desk to rub off the spot. While he was down there scrubbing, he noticed a new scratch across the desk's left corner. Damn. His desk was made of good bourgeois deco-rator wood this time, not hideous bureaucratic socialist metal, but he expected it to start rusting, too, anyway. Story of his life. Every time you get things fixed up, a new glitch appears. The cell phone refused to ring.

The Russian cleaning woman was vacuuming offices and polishing the linoleum in the hallway outside his door. He was used to her silent reproach—conveyed through sullen glares and a stubborn refusal to move her noisy equipment elsewhere when he was on the telephone—which meant: What can you be doing here getting in my way at this hour of the night? Don't you have a family to go home to? To which he could have responded: If you never go home to your family, you end up having no family to go home to. It was a simple equation in which zero equaled zero and he was sure that the cleaning woman would understand—since, if she was like the rest of Israel's Russian cleaning women and cashiers and garbagemen and orderlies and bank tellers, she probably had a Ph.D. in applied mathematics from Leningrad University or used to be a tenured physics professor at Moscow U.

Yizhar tried to figure out what would go wrong next. He doubted that Doron would go running to the media—anyway, Doron would certainly hint at it if he were about to, because such a big step would scare him. It *was* possible that Hajimi would discover Doron's name and his where-abouts, and this was more worrisome. Inside prison or out, Hajimi was a tough bird, with connections. From the files Yizhar had read on him, Hajimi emerged as a hard man, narrow, directed, vigilant, adamant, immovable. Not susceptible to pressure. And soon to be released, along with a bunch of other prisoners—Yizhar himself was urging Hajimi's release to cool the flames at the checkpoints. After all, Hajimi was just a Hamas detainee; there was no evidence against him, nothing the Israelis could come up with that showed him to have been involved in any specific incident, probably because he hadn't been, not closely, at any rate. With his son dead, why not release Hajimi now, along with the rest? Offer his release to the Palestinians as a blanket to throw over their street fires. It made sense.

They'd gotten what they could out of the man already. Hajimi had been through it all, Yizhar knew, during his different incarcerations. It was all there in the files. Subjected to *tiltul*, which was shaking: you shook the man so much that it would almost break his neck. His brains would rattle in his skull. It was very frightening and disorienting for the victim, and left no outward marks. Hajimi did not flinch. You put him in the little chair, tied him up for hours and hours on end. Hajimi never broke. Solitary for weeks. Nothing. He gave away nothing. No names, no events, no plans. Imagining such a man on the outside and on Doron's trail—it gave Yizhar a cramp.

On the other hand, if Doron was getting ready to do something stupid, it might not be such a bad idea to have Hajimi out there, after him.

Yizhar knew what he was going to tell Doron to do. It was just a matter of getting in touch with him. The boy was bound to call sooner or later. The problem was it had to be sooner, or who knew what Doron might get up to in the interim, and Yizhar would end up along with all the rest of them, trying to find the soldier. Where *was* the man? What had he been doing between the time he had left Zvili and now? Yizhar jiggled his leg nervously.

He wanted Doron to call him, and not the other way around—it was psychologically preferable—but if Yizhar began to get too worried, Yizhar would be the one doing the calling. He had no doubt that if Hajimi did not yet know the soldier's name, if the Authority did not yet, they all would, and soon. No one on the Palestinian side had mentioned the soldier's phone call, his conversation with his superiors. But they would, they would—if it hadn't actually happened, they would have had to invent it.

Yizhar had narrowed down the possibilities himself. There *were* witnesses. The Hajimi woman, first of all. The lawyer from Ramallah, Mr. Bigmouth. Some of the others who had been waiting. Someone must have heard the name. Zvili, too, was a talker, and you never knew how fast talk could hop from one side of the situation to the other. Yizhar was not looking forward to watching the Chairman on television, asking for the extradition of Lieutenant Ari Doron. Because even if the Authority didn't really want him and wouldn't have the least idea what to do with him, the

Israelis would still never hand him over. The Chairman would count on that, and push as hard as he could, in public.

DORON SAT IN front of his mother's house. He didn't want to go up. She might be awake—she kept odd hours. Down the street, he could hear the roosters beginning to squawk in the courtyard of the International Christian Embassy. Could there be roosters there? It seemed to him that roosters always crowed long before dawn broke, in spite of their reputation. It was just a few minutes to four in the morning. He could hear the call to prayer wafting on the end of a night breeze; the distance made it sound off-key. He wondered where it was coming from. Silwan, the Palestinian village that sat on a hillside across from the Old City walls? Or from the Old City itself, from the Muslim quarter? Might be both. Sometimes you thought you were just hearing one call to prayer when actually it was the call going out from loudspeakers installed on dozens of minarets. The muezzin—or the recordings of the muezzin—were like the roosters: all starting at the same time, singing the same song. Back behind his house, where there was a small, one-room synagogue run by an old Moroccan rabbi, the Jews began to sing their morning prayer, too. Without thinking, Doron followed the words: "Listen, Israel . . ."

His poor little country. Beautiful Arab prayers wafting over it from all corners, and it couldn't absorb them, because if you let those prayers filter in, twenty minutes later the whole damned horde would be riding down from the desert to take back everything that had been won so hard. Doron knew how hard, he knew. It wasn't for nothing that he had fought in Lebanon, or watched his father's slow death from the wounds in his leg and shoulder. But was protecting it worth the pain of that poor little boy and his mother? Was it? Was a country worth that loss? Probably it was, *this* country was, anyway. "Civilians die when wars are fought," his father used to say. "A war is not just about soldiers." But now, after Ibrahim's death, Doron wasn't sure. He wasn't sure of anything. He wanted to strike out savagely at Yizhar, and he wanted to tell the Palestinians to shut up with their fucking prayers and daily pilgrimage to the checkpoints, shut up and stay away. Don't risk it, he wanted to say.

His cell phone was sitting in the open glove compartment of his mother's car, which was parked in the sheltered space beneath the house. Next to the phone was his *Yediot* with Yizhar's direct number scrawled in a corner by Zvili. Doron knew Yizhar would be trying to get in touch; he was not the kind of man to tolerate uncertainty for long. Tomorrow was the rally to honor Ibrahim Hajimi and other child martyrs of the Israeli Occupation. It was a relief to know that *his* dead baby was not the only one. That news had really brightened Doron's day. Ten thousand people were supposed to show up for the demonstration, and Doron was going to be among them. The phone rang. He did not pick it up. He wasn't ready yet. He had to pull his nerves together. You couldn't face Yizhar in an emotional mess. You couldn't walk into his office seething and boiling. Doron tried to picture himself wearing his Palestinian costume and sitting in the chair facing Yizhar's desk. A slight smile twisted his lips. But what else would he wear? He never wanted to put his army uniform on again. Never. And he felt uncomfortable in his own clothes. In his own fucking skin.

CHAPTER SEVENTEEN

THE GLASSBLOWERS WERE IN TROUBLE, WHICH MEANT Mahmoud's brother was in trouble. The day before, in spite of Adnan's brilliant arguments and unquestionable documentation, a judge had handed down a ruling awarding the land the glass factory was on to a family that hadn't lived there since the Prophet defeated the infidel at Badr, if ever. Adnan never understood. He thought that justice was supposed to triumph in this business, but the law was so profoundly corrupt that justice was shunted to the side when it was not completely ignored. Adnan would never believe it, no matter how many times he saw it. Mahmoud had laughed when he heard about the decision, and shook a gently mocking finger in Adnan's face.

A blue glass vase from the factory in question sat in Sheukhi & Sheukhi's fourth-floor window. As schools of clouds moved across the sky, sunlight shot through the vase in bursts, splashing royal blue light over the single metal bookcase, the single file cabinet, and the old television in the corner. Mahmoud stood next to the file cabinet, looking over the judge's decision. Laughable. It smelled of money passing from hand to hand. That was life under the Authority. The blue light flashed over his face. Through the closed window, he heard a siren in the square below. He threw the document onto the desk, went over to the window, and looked down.

A very large crowd for so early, Mahmoud thought. Good. It was only ten in the morning. A group of students with keffiyehs wrapped around their necks stood under snapping green and silver Hamas pennants. Green was the color of Muslim celebration. Snapping and fluttering in unison, the flags looked medieval, like banners waving over a cavalry descending to attack. TO DIE FOR ALLAH IS OUR HIGHEST GOAL, Mahmoud read. LITTLE IBRAHIM DIED FOR ALLAH. HONOR TO HIM. Mahmoud remained unconvinced. He died for the Palestinian people, Mahmoud corrected. He wondered if his nephew Jibril was down there. Soon he himself would join the crowd. He wanted to see Marina Hajimi again, and hear Raad speak. The legendary Raad no longer seemed so legendary to Mahmoud. What would the man say? What *could* he say? Would he announce the name of the soldier? From Raad's attitude yesterday, Mahmoud doubted it.

But it didn't matter, because Mahmoud had Ruby. Kind, goodhearted Ruby Horowitz, Mahmoud's agent within the Israeli government! He laughed to himself. What an agent, in her little leather jacket. For nothing, she had done his work for him. All he needed was an address for this guy, he told her. It was for a legal matter. She said it was easy, no problem.

"I'll do it on the computer," she said. "I mean, after all, it's not like it's classified information." Big smile.

And she got it, too: 21 Keren Kayemit Leumi Street. The Israelis called it by its nickname: KKL, or Kakal. "No problem!" Ruby said, as she handed him the printout. *"Ain baya!"* He took it from his pocket now, and tossed it into Adnan's garbage. He wouldn't forget that information.

A flatbed truck full of people was making slow progress through the crowd below, swathed in bunting the colors of the Palestinian flag, green, black, red, and white. That would be the Authority. Already, three hundred or four hundred people had gathered, and more were streaming in from the streets that ran into the square. Normal people not under any banner seemed to be arriving, too, as well as those who were openly affiliated. He saw them gathering in their sensible workaday clothes, the ironed trousers and knitted vests, the matrons' unsexy skirts, the puffy, quilted jackets, the tight high black pants of nonreligious girls. It was cold and all the men were smoking and drinking coffee or tea.

Four black limousines came speeding by, sirens wailing, with an escort of eight police officers on motorcycle. The Chairman, maybe, or Ahmed Amr and his retinue. Mahmoud had once seen the Chairman land in Ramallah in his helicopter, with green and red smoke bombs going off all around it, on an inconceivably small landing pad ringed by security vehicles. He couldn't tell whether the bombs were celebratory or designed to ward off attacks on the Chairman's helicopter. It was said that the Chairman never traveled without a decoy vehicle, and that he often used a personal double, though it was hard to imagine mistaking anyone else for the short little Chairman, invariably damp and unshaven, with his decoratively tied keffiyeh and his way of always looking as if gravity had some kind of moral sway over him, as if it were pulling him down more than others. You wouldn't want to be known as his double, let's put it that way, Mahmoud thought. But today, the highest official was likely to be Amr, because the Israelis did not usually allow the Chairman to come to Ramallah from his Gaza headquarters. He had to ask their permission. Intolerable. Little Palestinian flags waved from the limousines' antennae. The windows were smoked black.

THE MOTORCADE CAME to a dramatic halt in front of The Sheikh's, sirens blaring and then all of a sudden extinguished. One of the Chairman's Ramallah bodyguards leaped out of the front limousine and opened Ahmed's door. He reached out a hand to assist Ahmed, but Ahmed declined it, springing out like a film star at an awards ceremony. Ahmed was sorry to have left the Mercedes behind, but he felt it would not look impressive at the head of a limousine motorcade. He half expected a red carpet beneath his feet, his greeting in Ramallah had been so warm—they hated the Chairman in Ramallah, and adored Ahmed. The Sheikh's was Ahmed's favorite teahouse on the West Bank. They knew him here: as if they didn't know him everywhere. Here he was favored, though, because his father's family was from Ramallah.

As Ahmed entered The Sheikh's with his cohort, three whole tables' worth of the teahouse population was displaced to accommodate the Authority and its guests. Ahmed nodded at a distant cousin, embraced "the Sheikh"—actually the last son of a Nablus shoe-factory owner—held the hands and looked deeply into the eyes of a Ramallah neighbor whose daughter had been injured in a car accident a few days earlier, and then took his place in the center of the three tables, ready to preside. He was always presiding. The world was divided into hosts and guests, Ahmed had long ago decided, and he was a natural-born host, even when he was an honored guest at someone else's table.

He sat down on one of The Sheikh's low wooden chairs, and felt it tremble beneath his weight. The crowd was buzzing around him. In the corner near the bathroom, the Chairman's bodyguard was trying to talk on his cell phone. He had one hand over his ear, but he couldn't shout for fear of being overheard. Reporting to Gaza. The Chairman would be stewing in a jealous, impotent rage. Ahmed smiled and ordered a strong pot of tea. He loved to steal the Chairman's thunder, and the Israelis—not allowing the Chairman here today, for example—made it so outrageously easy. They knew about the rivalry. They enjoyed it. They used it.

Ahmed was doing something here at The Sheikh's that would torment the Chairman further. He was arranging the details of Hajimi's release, and when it happened, all of the praise would go to Ahmed. It was going to be beautiful, with street celebrations, rounds of congratulations, interviews with the international media. It would happen soon, maybe even today. Ramadan began in two days. It was his least favorite time of year. He hated its disruption of life's regular cycle of pleasures, and his was not a particularly spiritual nature. It would be good to go into the fast month on the crest of Hajimi's release. Give him something to savor during the long dull days. Not that anyone wanted the man out of prison. If everyone even faintly allied to Hamas could be stuck into an Israeli jail and shut up tight, the world would not be a worse place, Ahmed thought.

He happened to know that he looked particularly good this morning. He'd had a good sleep, and only last week, he had shaved off his now white beard and moustache, and with it a decade of aging. His eyes, often bloodshot from fatigue, were clear, and their hazel color was set off by golden flecks in an otherwise somber, conservative, world-leader-style necktie. Ahmed looked forward to the moment when the crowd's eyes would be upon him. Even sitting down, he towered over other men.

Ahmed smiled broadly at a tall foreigner who was already ensconced at the table. Ted, the American consular officer, had agreed to meet Ahmed here to discuss the final details of Hajimi's release in The Sheikh's back room. Hajimi released in time for Ramadan. What a coup.

"Would you order a nargileh for me, please?" Ted said, leaning over the table to pick a sweet off a silverized plastic tray.

Ted was ready to finish up their talks: what day, what time, where. He smoked a nargileh like an Arab—as if it were a normal thing to do, without too much bullshit, although you could always trust Arab custom to attach some bullshit to every ritual. Ted treated the nargileh as if it were a half a pack of Marlboros. Ahmed could do business efficiently with Ted: if only the two of them could run Palestine together and alone. You couldn't smoke during the days of Ramadan, Ahmed reminded himself with a wince.

"Oh, Ted," said Ahmed. "I nearly forgot to mention it. I was talking to the Chairman yesterday, and he told me what a wonderful job he thinks you've been doing."

Ted nodded. Even the toughest man secretly enjoys flattery, Ahmed knew, and will believe any compliment to some degree or another. Tell a fat man he looks slim—even if at that very moment he is looking in the mirror—and he will think that possibly he's lost a few ounces, or that, possibly, to you, he does seem slim, for some reason. The praise will gladden him even if he knows at some not very deep level that it's untrue. And that you don't mean it. As you watch him take pleasure in your insincerity you feel a small surge of power. Ahmed also knew that a compliment is more likely to be believed if it's secondhand, and that the good feeling generated by secondhand flattery extends even more to the bearer of the praise than to the flatterer himself. At first, Ahmed had been merely an assiduous relater of secondhand compliments, but soon, running low on material, he began fabricating the compliments themselves. It was highly unlikely that he would ever be found out. Would Ted dare go to the Chairman and ask: "Oh, by the way, Mr. Chairman, did you tell Ahmed Amr the other day that I've been doing a wonderful job?" Never.

It was no Versailles, but as far as Ahmed was concerned, The Sheikh's back room—with its red wallpaper and hard-backed, beat-up, vinyl-covered chairs—was almost as good for treaty-making as the reception room at Orient House, or the checkpoint at Erez. Maybe better. This was the kind of place where Ahmed liked to do business: not a boardroom or an office or a dais or the antechamber of a conference room or that ugly little fluorescent-lit, soundproofed, debugged hole in the back of the Chairman's Gaza apartment that was used for supposedly important meetings. For Ahmed, the place where a deal was done always remained a part of the deal, a part of history. The Sheikh's had a stale, authentic West Bank atmosphere.

Things were looking up. Now if only George could remain calm during the rally. And not go spluttering off and ruin all Ahmed's fun. The students who helped organize the thing had wanted the old writer, and so George would be there, and speaking. Dah! George hated Find the Soldier—that was what had made him walk out of Orient House in a fit of babyish pique. Still, Ahmed was hoping that in public, George would stick with them. He straightened his tie. Let's expect the best . . . after all, George was a gentleman.

AND THERE HE WAS, a little late but gorgeous as ever. It was a wonder how a sick man could look so glamorous. Ahmed stared at his old friend through the bobbing heads of the crowd. George looked like no one else there, Ahmed thought. He seemed not larger than life but more intense: slightly taller, somewhat darker, his eyes brighter, his hair thicker, his clothes in some indescribable way better, his whole being poised on the brink of something ineffable, like flight. He is more like me than I am, Ahmed thought.

With his chin tilted up and his whole leonine face raised toward the sky, George seemed to be judging the direction of the wind in preparation for something grandiose and remarkable. The unconquerable arrogance of his character was readable in his every movement and gesture. He looked like a man who feared nothing. As if something had caught his eye and displeased him, George turned his head brusquely away from the clouds, downward, and next to him Ahmed saw a covered woman standing as quiet and unmoving as if she had been alone in a big room. Ahmed's little niece Marina, gazing with deep empty eyes over toward the square where an enormous digital clock sat perched on a pedestal. Around the magnificent, absurd timepiece, the Authority's limousines were parked near a temporary stage where today's speakers were to gather. George said something to his daughter and they began to move toward the clock.

SHE WAS EVEN more impressive in traditional clothes. The white *hijab* covered the thick hair that distracted you from her eyes, and so you saw those eyes in a new way: they were profound and empty and they sucked up light. She rarely blinked, Doron noticed. She stood a good distance from her father, but seemed attached to him, moved when he moved, went where he went, without looking at him, without seeming to think. She held her left wrist with her right hand in what looked like a symbolic gesture from a medieval Christian painting. Her stillness chilled Doron, and excited him. He had moved down to the front of the crowd and he could see every detail, even to the single lashes. She wore so much clothing, like a proper Palestinian lady. No jeans today. He remembered her bare foot, and the rain rattling down. The night so black outside, the closeness of the trailer so hot and damp and bright, and all his men breathing their hot nervous breath down his back. Her wild hair. And here now, distant, correct. It was too much. It unleashed in him an unbridled pack of emotions that he chose not to examine. At least, she would never know what he was feeling. And her father would never know. And her husband.

• • •

UNCLE AHMED was going to introduce them. This was an unbelievable scene in a life that had become unbelievable. The bereft mother stands before the crowd. What was she doing here? She felt a terrible physical feeling of heartache, as if there were pressure against her heart, remembering the photographs in the newspaper. The crowd was solemn and still as Ahmed approached the microphone. Marina looked out at the people, and saw the tops of their heads, their dark hair, their white, beige, blue collars. Their shoulders were hunched against the wind. The glinting rims of sunglasses. White and dark *hijabs* dotted the scene. She saw television cameras. She closed her eyes, listening to Ahmed's low voice, letting it rumble in the back of her consciousness without paying attention to the words.

She heard the name of her son, her husband, her father. She looked down at the plain plywood planks of the stage. Humble, she thought, composed, grief-stricken. They were all looking at her. She felt her father move closer, protectively. It was as protective as he got. He must feel the same shame I do, she thought, standing here, being talked about in front of people. But at least he has a mission. I just want to go home and be alone in Ibrahim's room. He wants to speak to the people. Teach them something. Clear things up, as he said. Okay, let's get it over with.

She looked at her father. He drew his eyebrows down into a violent V, and pulled his scarf tighter around his neck. She could see he was preparing to speak, and that when he did, Uncle Ahmed would not be happy. Never underestimate Dad, she thought. She looked out over the heads of the crowd at the reflection of the moving sky in the windows of a dirty building across the street.

The crowd was full of people she didn't know. Why are they here, she kept thinking. Why aren't my father and I at home, going through picture albums? Why aren't all of these people at home? She looked at the front rows, trying to pierce through to each individual's motivation, his need. It was important for her right now to understand why events happened, if you ever could understand. That old lady, for example, she should be home in her rocker, Marina thought to herself. Those two young men with their neat attachés? Back to the office, on the double. Get out of here. And you, how can you hear on your cell phone in this crowd, stupid man? Miss, your skirt's too short. And this one is bizarre. She felt the tiniest twinge of amusement. Handsome, but doesn't know how to wear a scarf, even, she thought. Then she saw who it was. Her heart turned over. She stared in disbelief. Fear tightened her chest, fear that he would see her looking. Fear of contact. She averted her gaze.

DORON LOOKED at Marina. She had turned her eyes brusquely away from his side of the crowd. She was quiet, unsmiling. He stared at her, trying to judge her feelings. Again he was stirred by her silent, unmoving beauty. The woman he had robbed and destroyed. Doron stared, trying to understand. He looked at her averted eyes, fixing her face in his mind. She was staring out, and her face was blank.

Doron looked at the people closest to him. Was it possible that his getup had actually worked? He couldn't believe that they all did not immediately recognize him as an impostor. But then, it would never occur to them that someone would bother pretending to be them. To his eye, in fact, some of them looked as much like pretend Palestinians as he himself did. Off to his left, for instance, he saw a ridiculous moustachioed man in a suit that was just a little too old and too tight. He seemed stuffed with self-importance, like a B actor in an old comedy. He was trying to get Marina Raad to notice him. Funny, Doron thought. Then he recognized the man. It was the Ramallah lawyer—her knight in shining armor—standing, gnawing on one corner of his moustache and watching her. Doron ducked and turned away. Raad took the microphone.

"I'M SORRY TO BE here today," George said, squinting out at the crowd. They grew silent as they took in those first words, so impolite, the wrong thing to say, yet the truth. It brought the audience up short.

"I have no thanks to offer to my host." George turned to Ahmed and shook his head briefly.

"I am sorry, but I have no thanks to offer, Ahmed—friend of my childhood." Ahmed Amr lowered his eyes. It was rude and very intimate to address someone by his first name only, in front of an audience. Rude to say you had no thanks to give.

George shaded his eyes with his hand for a moment, and swayed slightly. He put his other arm out to Marina, and she walked over to him. He put his arm around her.

"This is my daughter," he said.

"My beloved daughter." He looked at her. Something was wrong, he thought. She seemed to have no expression. But then, everything was wrong.

"My daughter came to Palestine four years ago on her own, after completing her degree in America. I was worried about her, but was glad she felt for Palestine some of what I had always felt. She wanted to begin to know her homeland. She met a man she loved here, at Bir Zeit, where she was studying her country's history, a man who shared her passion for Palestine." George had to stop for a moment as the crowd stomped and applauded Hajimi. He tapped his foot, waiting.

"They married and had a child.

"That child was my grandson, Ibrahim."

George let the crowd savor the story, which they already knew. He heard them sigh. An old woman started to cough. He waited until she had finished.

"My grandson, Ibrahim. Let me tell you about him, if I can." George gripped the sides of the podium to steady himself, letting Marina go. Wind whipped through the square. "Ibrahim was a small boy with blue eyes, calm, clever. He knew how to get his grandfather to give him sweets and tell him stories. He was a lovely child." George turned back toward Marina and put his arm around her again.

"Now, Ibrahim had asthma," George resumed. "Sometimes his asthma was bad, other times, not so bad. The other night, he had a bad asthma attack—he should be in a Jerusalem hospital bed now, on a nebulizer." The wind ruffled George's hair, and he pushed it back. A cloud passed behind the clock tower.

"But he's not.

"And I can tell you why. He's not in a bed in a hospital in Jerusalem because the other night, he ran into trouble at a checkpoint. He ran into trouble because he was sick.

"And because we are at war.

"He did *not* run into trouble because his mother is a courageous Palestinian heroine. She's not. My daughter is his mother. Our little Ibrahim was *not* a brave Palestinian freedom fighter. This was my Palestinian grandson, my boy who was going to have the life in Palestine that history did not permit me to have. The life that history stole from me, and stole from you, Ahmed—stole from us all. Ibrahim was just an innocent little boy—you all have them in your families, innocent little boys—and his memory should be served by respect for the dead, not by political manipulations of his fate."

George took a deep breath, as deep as he could muster. He had stunned the crowd into silence. Marina felt him tremble.

"And let me tell you one other thing, Ahmed, *sadiq at-tufoulah,*" George continued, "if you want to find someone to blame for my grandson's death, look further than the soldier who was at the checkpoint that night. If you want to place blame for my grandson's death, look in the mirror, as well. Look at yourself and the Authority, who've negotiated away our birthright and abandoned Palestinians like my grandson to the whim of the enemy. Who are selling every job in their so-called government, and who have corrupted every official.

"If you want to find the soldier, go hunt yourself down. Arrest yourself, Ahmed."

A section of the audience was applauding loudly—that would be the students—but others were confused.

"I forbid you to use my daughter's child to play politics, Ahmed," George went on, looking right at him across the dais.

"There are other ways, we all know there are other ways. . . ."

It started at the back of the crowd. People began to yell, clapping, screaming. It was an extreme speech, George knew it, yet he was immediately certain that this uproar and tumult were not for him. He could see thousands of triumphant hands raised in the air, applauding. Ahmed stood with his arms folded, looking remarkably unsurprised by the uproar. George heard the name Hajimi from the crowd, and then heard the chant: "Hajimi, Hajimi, Hajimi."

Salah came over and whispered in George's ear. The story was spreading. The rumors were true. Hassan Hajimi was to be released today or tomorrow. George turned to Marina with the news. The people in the crowd were looking to her expectantly. She wondered what emotion they could read on her face. She wondered what they wanted to see there.

This is not happening, Marina thought. She didn't know how to react, but to react in public, that was asking too much. She kept her face perfectly still, and watched Ahmed to see if there had been some mistake, but his face—like hers—was about as full of meaning as the platform's plywood planks. He was watching the crowd's reaction with those lizard eyes of his. Her father was holding on to her wrist now. She looked back at the spot where she thought she had seen the soldier, but he had disappeared.

George stood still for a moment, surveying the scene, then stepped carefully down from the podium; these days, he couldn't trust his balance going down even a single pair of steps—going up was always better, though not good. He looked sideways over at Amr, who was talking to some ferocious-faced man in a suit and nodding. Well, *that* friendship was probably over. George felt overcome by the loss. So few intimates remaining—and he had pushed this one away. But what could he do? It was a family obligation, a loyalty to his blood, after all. Ahmed should know that that was what pushed him to it, pushed him to this extreme. Of all people, Ahmed should understand this repudiation.

George turned to check on Marina. Her face was calm, but he thought he detected something like shock. Her eyes were so still. He leaned on his daughter and she had just begun walking him away from the podium when there was a sudden commotion at the foot of the platform. Marina saw men in dark caps rushing at them and in a few seconds, she and her father were surrounded by big men in dark clothes carrying guns.

"What's going on?" she asked them.

"It's the Palestinian security apparatus in the flesh," her father said. The men jostled them and pushed them down the stairs from the platform. George tripped and he felt himself begin to tumble, but he fell into the back of the man in front of him, and his body righted like a child's tipping toy. He was afraid that he looked drunk.

"My father is ill," Marina said to one of the men, as he continued pushing George down the steps in front of him, using the butt of his gun as a prod.

"We'll take care of him," the man said.

The men shoved Marina into the open door of a waiting car, and then hurried around to the other side with George and stuffed him in. The car drove away.

DORON'S STOMACH was playing games with him. He had to concentrate hard to understand the Arabic around him, but some things were unmistakable. Hassan Hajimi was to be released. He envisioned the guy walking up King George Street, with a keffiyeh wrapped disdainfully around his neck like some pilot from the thirties, and explosives sewn into the lining of his leather jacket, turning down Kakal, and watching Doron's mother's house, checking out the situation. Hajimi was very tough, from what Doron had read about him. Of course, he was the kind of man prison walls would not stop. He had people on the outside who worshipped him, who would do anything he asked. Was Marina ecstatic at the thought of her husband's imminent release? Her face was closed, and who was he to try to measure the extent of her emotions?

Doron tried to push through the crowd and get away, but everything was in turmoil. There had been rousing applause at Raad's final exhortation, only some of which Doron could understand, but that enthusiasm was lost in the news of the Hajimi release, and when people saw Raad and his daughter hustled out like that, the mood had turned more careful. Doron saw Ahmed Amr assessing the situation and deciding whether or not to try addressing the people after Raad's speech.

Doron let himself be pushed and shoved along. Had Marina seen him? She had given no sign, but he was almost sure she had. When Doron had noticed Sheukhi there, he had buried himself deeper in the crowd, and so there had been no chance for him to make some definitive eye contact with her. Well, that was probably for the best, Doron thought. Definitely. All she had to do was point a finger, and he would have been deader than dead. He felt light-headed. He wondered where she was being taken.

"LET'S BE CALM, let's be calm," Ahmed said to the crowd. He couldn't leave the last word to George.

"Instead of recrimination, let's remember our happiness: our brother Hassan Hajimi is to be released." Ahmed twisted a tail of his keffiyeh. The crowd roared with approval. Fools, Ahmed thought. Who wants the man out?

"That is a palpable gain achieved by the Palestinian people, and no one can deny it.

"Not everyone knows how to be grateful for a gift, however. Let's not be enraged by ungrateful behavior." Ahmed thought mildly about what he would like to do to George right now, and dismissed it.

"And let's hope that next time we gather, we will have more good news—and less ingratitude. Thank you all for coming out to show your support."

He left the platform and walked through the crowd surrounded by the Chairman's bodyguards. The people near him were chanting "Hajimi, Hajimi, Hajimi." Ahmed felt a rush of warmth as the door to his limousine opened.

• • •

"THIS IS a little scary," Marina said to her father.

"We're having a Middle Eastern adventure, darling," George said.

"Great," said Marina. "I'm sick of the Middle East."

"Me too," said George.

They sped along. There were four men squeezed into the car with them, not including the driver. Each was carrying a large automatic weapon. It was hot in the car with all these big men. The windows were curtained, so it was hard to make out their direction.

"Where are you taking us?" George asked the driver.

The driver said nothing.

"Hmmmm," said George. "Not very talkative."

They were stopped at a light.

"That was quite a speech you gave," Marina said.

"Apparently," George said. "What did you think of it?"

"I don't know. It seemed true, but very rude."

"How unlike me," George said.

Had the soldier really been there? She did not trust her eyes or her memory. It seemed too unlikely. So dangerous for him.

But she knew it had been him.

"Well, it's over, at least," George said.

"This man is touching my leg with his leg," Marina said, loudly.

"Not allowed," said George to the man, gesturing toward the point of contact and then wagging a finger. "Married lady, you know."

The man moved as far away as he could, which wasn't far.

"See, sweetheart? They still respect tradition. Even in the middle of a kidnapping."

"This is not a kidnapping," the driver said, annoyed. "It's a service. An escort. That's what Mr. Amr said. An escort."

"Where are you escorting us to, may I ask?"

"Home."

"Home?"

"Yes, home. Your daughter's house. Mr. Hajimi's house? In Ramallah? That's where."

"So please," said the man sitting next to Marina. "Don't worry."

"All of a sudden, I'm not feeling entirely well," said George, looking out a sliver of visible window at the passing houses and stores. His head ached and his heart was doing odd tricks it wasn't supposed to do, leaping and thrumming and sending Morse code. It was from the effort of standing there on the podium in the wind. He leaned his head against the cold metal window frame. The shards of light coming in from outside were too bright; he felt a pain at the back of his eyes. The scenery seemed to be whirling past their car, slipping down into a dark, slithering vortex. He felt a cold sweat envelop him.

Then he blacked out.

DORON HAD TO get himself back across the checkpoint now. It had been so easy this morning coming out for the rally in his Palestinian gear: all that the checkpoint soldiers wanted was to get rid of another Palestinian, send him home, out of Israel, onto the West Bank. Whooosh, and you're through—in *that* direction. They didn't even look at him. He hadn't given much thought this morning about how to get back this afternoon. After all, he was Israeli, and a soldier.

But what was this, now? There was so much that did not occur to an Israeli soldier, he thought, as he got out of his taxi, which had been forced to stop when the driver encountered roads completely blocked by crowds. Fuck, there was no mistaking it. People milling all over and the sound of nearby gunfire. And now he was on the wrong side, unarmed, with this stupid scarf around his stupid neck but no slingshot in *his* back pocket. They were all running toward the checkpoint, and he ran too. No choice, really, once you were in it. You were just swept up by the crowd. The sheer stupidity of himself and this situation—oh, it was so easy to fuck up and get killed, especially if you had no plan and did things impulsively. They were near the checkpoint, now, and bullets were whizzing past him right and left. He felt an odd kind of surprise about these bullets, a mirrory feeling that he was firing and being fired on. A man dropped to the ground next to him and Doron tried to help him, but the crowd pushed Doron on. He heard the helicopters before anyone else, and looked up behind the watchtower. Three specks were approaching in a white sky.

I'll go through the wadi, he decided. He thought he would hide himself in the dry riverbed in the shadow of the abandoned buses and trucks, and under the scattered willows. The helicopters have more important business than one poor lone Palestinian.

He pushed slowly and with great difficulty toward the edge of the crowd. As the helicopters neared, people began shifting direction. Doron felt he was trying to part a sea. Finally, he reached a side alley. Everyone was ducking and running and stumbling as the sound bombs exploded, but not Doron, who knew exactly what was happening. It was funny, he thought, how even people who come out every day, day after day, as these guys probably have for at least several days now, are still put off by those bombs. Because they never knew. He supposed they mistrusted the Israelis so much that what had been sound bombs the day before might well be real bombs today. And they were right, because just then, the helicopters began firing down on the crowd.

Doron was crouching behind a row of low commercial buildings, as block by block he took himself farther and farther away from the main road, which meant he had less cover, but was also farther from the action. He felt less threatened now, except that to Palestinians, he would cut an odd figure, a young man ready for action who was distinctly avoiding it. Possibly he wouldn't run into anyone, since everyone from around here was either hiding inside or participating. He sniffed a trace of tear gas in the air but it was far enough away. He ran and ran, keeping low and tight and almost touching the buildings and garden walls.

It was a real fight over by the checkpoint, a firefight. He could hear rounds of machine-gun spray. Thank God he'd pulled away from there. The wadi lay rutted and windswept before him. He was right, by now, the scene at the checkpoint was too intense for the Israelis to spare manpower for the wadi—he saw no one on watch. In any case, getting across to Jerusalem was no longer what these protests were really about. He gritted his teeth and leaned up against a dumpster, trying to decide which was the fastest and safest way down through and across. Trucks and buses had been abandoned down in the wadi, some of them long ago, but many many others only recently, when the Israelis had stopped them and repeatedly refused them entry. The Palestinian truckers left the vehicles there for better political times, took their produce off by hand and found other ways to transport the stuff to other markets. The bus passengers were also forced to make other plans. Thank God, because as Doron scampered down the shallow bald hill, he knew he was going to feel almost safe when he reached the shadows of the long, empty, looming buses. The afternoon light gave him long patches of darkness to hide in, and he flitted from one shadow to the next, always looking up, watching for the choppers that were plying the sky now like swarms of intrusive insects. He tried to catch his breath.

Ping. What was that? Another ping and the sound of a crackle. He saw two black rips in the side of the bus, just a few feet from where he was standing. Someone was shooting at him. He looked up toward where the shots had come from and saw—quite far away at the edge of the wadi—a figure in khakis, looking lonely against the white sky, aiming. Another ping. Doron's heart started to race; he just couldn't believe it. He hesitated for a second between fleeing or calling to the fellow in Hebrew. What would he shout? *"Ani Israeli"*? He would never be believed.

Another shot exploded next to his ankle, and Doron fell to his knees and pulled himself under the bus as a hail of bullets ripped the air where he had been standing, chopping up the dirt beneath the bus's tires. He rolled to the other side of the bus and out from beneath it. He looked up at the slope of the wadi. Damn, he was almost across, really. Would the guy follow him? Doron doubted it. It depended how nutty and paranoid and *dedicated* the guy was. Would he be convinced that this poor Palestinian fuck trying to cross over was a mad terrorist intent on bombing the Knesset, or would he more likely think, Oh, fuck it—one more Palestinian visiting his ailing auntie in East Jerusalem, who gives a flying fuck? That would be the reaction of most of the men Doron had worked with, but then, there was always the possibility of the odd superpatriot taking up the scent. Then you were fucked.

He edged around the truck that was hiding him and looked up toward the spot where the soldier had stood, but the man was gone. Oh, he hoped and hoped again that the guy was not going to give chase on foot. He did not want to be hunted down by one of his own men. What if it were someone who would recognize him? It was unlikely, but they did sometimes put the same guy on duty over and over during these times. What if it was Zvili, for God's sake? But he knew it wasn't: Zvili never watched the wadi. I'm just going to make a run for it now, Doron thought. Not much more than a hundred meters, a good sprint. He was off, the ends of his scarf trailing behind him. The shots followed him up the side of the wadi like a furious animal. Fast, fast. He stumbled and clawed at the ground, and strained his way up the slope, racing against his heartbeat. He didn't look back until he reached the wadi's edge. The boy was standing there on the other side, his gun hanging down, watching Doron go.

And then he was across.

This Dr. George Raad was a very sick man, sick in the head, according to Mahmoud Sheukhi, who had been standing well back in the crowd, watching the proceedings. Mahmoud had one rule: No matter how shitty and stupid a fellow Palestinian was, you *never* criticized him in public where the Zionists might pick it up and use it against your people. Mahmoud despised the Authority, despised Ahmed Amr, too, now, but he would never say it out loud in a place where there were obviously television cameras.

And besides, Dr. Raad knew the damned name of the damned Israeli soldier who was responsible for the boy's death. He *knew*. She knew, too, Mahmoud was sure. So what was going on? Raad was attacking Palestinians, and at the same time protecting an Israeli soldier? It was unheard of, unprecedented, a terrible act of treason. Maybe tragedy had driven the two of them insane—it was the only explanation Mahmoud could think of.

It left Mahmoud in an awkward position. It seemed to him that he was definitely the only other Palestinian who knew Lieutenant Doron's name. The Raads weren't doing anything with this precious information. They were sitting on it as if they had the right to decide what was moral and immoral, as if only they had the right to judge. Just because it was their baby who died.

Raad took him for a fool, but Mahmoud Sheukhi was nobody's fool. Dr. George Raad with his American and British degrees and his long string of publications and all his endless pronouncements on the Palestinian question? Fuck him. He had forgotten what was right and what was wrong. What was acceptable and what was forbidden.

So it was up to Sheukhi. Sheukhi would see to it that the right thing got done.

Chapter Eighteen

"HE WAS AT THAT DEMONSTRATION," REUVEN SAID SLOWLY. "In Ramallah. Baby martyrs . . ." Reuven knew this would irk Yizhar. Reuven was pleased to know something his boss didn't. He looked up for the reaction.

"What? What? You mean yesterday?" Yizhar was nonplussed. His day had hardly begun, and already, this? He was leaning with one hand on his desk. He straightened abruptly, and looked at Reuven.

"How do you know?"

"I saw it on TV," Reuven said.

"I watched it, I watched it," said Yizhar. "I didn't see anything."

"Well, he was there. Right down in front. I saw him. He was wearing some kind of outfit. But it was him, all right."

"At the rally." Yizhar dropped himself onto his chair and shook his head. He exhaled. "He's out of his fucking mind." He shut his eyes. The boy could get himself seriously killed, and it would be—as far as the army was concerned—Yizhar's fault. Irit came in with the newspapers, and dropped them down on his desk. They landed with a clap. Yizhar opened his eyes, said "Coffee" to her back, picked up the papers, selected *Yediot*, and held it almost to his nose for examination. He was hiding, too. He didn't want Reuven to witness the depth of his dismay.

"Palestinians," he said, reading through the report on the rally. "Leave them alone, they'll tear each other to shreds. Look at this," he said, holding up the paper so he could shove a finger at one story and rattle the sheets. "They practically kidnapped the old man. Idiots. They almost managed to kill a man who's already half dead and a fucking symbol of their cause."

Reuven shrugged.

Yediot had more. All the Authority had to do, it seemed, was whisper the words *find the soldier,* and the melodrama would erupt all over again. Two hours after the rally ended, and in spite of the rumors of Hajimi's imminent release, two Israeli soldiers had been wounded, and four Palestinians had been killed and hundreds injured in a huge demonstration at the Ramallah checkpoint. An old woman who lived nearby died of a heart attack, which the Authority was also blaming on the Israelis, of course. If a Palestinian died anywhere in the world, somehow it was Israel's fault. In Ashkelon, Intelligence was still going over the pieces of metal they had collected from a bombing in Tel Aviv three days earlier. *Yediot* had a picture of the scraps sitting in a warehouse somewhere—Yizhar supposed it was Ashdod, but those kinds of facts were never released. The scraps looked like lost pieces of a huge old puzzle. Once, they fit in somewhere, the wall of a SuperPharm, a Super-Sol produce counter, a Bank Leumi teller's booth, Discount Bank, Best Buy. Now, they were a jumble of nothing. Yes, of course—Yizhar ran his finger down the column until he found the name—as usual, they were saying the bomber was a young man from Tzurif, from the Tzurif village Hamas cell. As far as Yizhar could tell, all suicide bombers came from the Tzurif village Hamas cell. We should just go in and raze the place, he thought. Trundle in with the bulldozers, and presto!, no more Tzurif, no more bombers. Simple. It's how we did it in 1948. "We will maintain the remaining property and return it to the owners when the time comes."

Classic. " . . . When the time comes." That's what the army told the Arabs back in 1948, and that's what Yizhar would like to tell the families of Tzurif. (Of course, there was hardly any property remaining back then, and the Arabs also never got it back. The time was not coming.) Yizhar should be in charge, he thought to himself. He understood 1948. He knew it by heart from his grandfather who had been a road builder before the establishment of the state. In 1948, his grandfather had told him, a brave outnumbered fighting force was defending a valiant Jewish population from utter destruction by the vast arrayed armies of Arabia. They were defending the people of Israel—my people, Yizhar thought—who had come from everywhere in the world but especially from Europe, where every nation was bent on their destruction. His grandfather had fled pogroms in the Ukraine, he knew. We were an upright nation back in '48, Yizhar thought. Those were the days of real heroes, and the few Palestinians who were here in the land of David—and who were really Lebanese and Syrian and Jordanian—had to make way for the desperate Jews, it was an imperative of history. We used to call *ourselves* Palestinians,

Yizhar remembered, because we lived in Palestine. In 1948, the Jewish triumph was complete, and it was morally sound.

But nowadays, the Israelis were weak and dispirited. They were modern. Put the village under closure, was all they could come up with. There were too many problems in this world. Without looking up, Yizhar reached out for his coffee mug, which had been placed in its usual spot. He took a long swallow. Sweet, the way he liked it.

At lunchtime, he went over to Chezy. It was a dive, a linoleum and Formica room on the ground floor on Jaffa Road with a plate-glass window that looked out onto an intersection where one of the really spectacular bus bombings had gone off. When the door opened, tobacco smoke poured out. Chezy was the lunch haunt of Likud lifers from City Hall. They looked bad, these middle-aged functionaries. Yizhar sucked in his stomach when he went in to ensure that he wasn't confused with the regulars. They were to the man sickly, spotty, hairy, greasy, fat and stooped, pale and damp. An unhealthy crew who only took the cigarette out long enough to put in the food. They tucked their belts under their stomachs, where belts and buckles disappeared. The only hint that the belts existed was that the pants stayed up despite the pull of a certain principle of physics. They ate well. Plates of falafel and humus and pita, pickles and olives, hot sauce, rice and beans, and the inexplicably popular fried chicken schnitzel. To drink: Coke and Diet Coke, the Israeli national beverages.

Yizhar kept to himself. He sat behind his *Yediot* at a small table under the spiral staircase that led to an upstairs bathroom the size of a single stall. When the toilet flushed, everyone in the restaurant could hear. The skinny man with the collection of warts on his chin was serving today. He brought Yizhar a pile of pita bread and a bowl of vegetable soup with a big yellow potato sitting in the middle like an island. The functionaries' tables buzzed with gossip, and cries issued forth every few minutes for more pita, Coke, pickles. They talk only about each other, Yizhar thought. He could hear Aryeh going on about Zvi, who tried to fuck him over last year, the prick, and now, Aryeh was going to get even, oh yes he was, and with Nitzan too, and Yoel, oh yes. Yizhar returned to *Yediot*. These were the people running Jerusalem, Lord save us, thought Yizhar.

"Nitzan says someone told the soldier to stop the baby and his mother."

Yizhar's ears perked up behind his paper.

"What?"

"The dead Arab baby. The fucking soldier supposedly says someone at Defense told him not to let them in. Can you believe it?"

"How do you know? Nitzan's a committed liar."

"Yes, but everyone says the same thing. Story came out of The Building."

Yizhar peered out from behind *Yediot*. It was a table of four regulars. They were hunched over their Nescafés. As they talked, little silver waves of cigarette smoke curled up from the center of the table and flashed like a school of sardines ascending in the sunlight. Yizhar couldn't see who was saying what.

"I say it's Palestinian disinformation."

"Nah, nah, someone in Defense says the soldier himself says it."

"Hah . . . he tell you himself?"

"The guy's just trying to shift the blame."

"Nope. Straight shooter, they say."

"He could get The Building in big trouble."

"No. It'll never come out. Still, the question is, why is Nitzan spreading the story? He's such a schmuck. He's probably trying to fuck someone—the question is who. What do you think? Is it possible? What he says?"

The half of the yellow potato left in Yizhar's bowl took on a sickening tinge. He put down his spoon and waited for the table of gossips to leave. Who knew who might recognize him? The minute they were out, he stood. He had to get back to The Building, make a plan. The story was spinning away from him. Zvili and his big mouth? Or one of the other soldiers? Or just guys at The Building who hoped it was true, who wanted to get someone in trouble, stir things up, and move people around, free up some jobs. . . . He paid, said goodbye to the man with warts, and made his way to the door, pushing through a group that was about to be seated. He walked quickly past the travel agency and the bookstore whose windows had been blown out by the bus bomb. NEW AND USED, said the bookstore's sign. It was all clean and put back together now, but he remembered the blood on the jagged shards of glass. Little flaps of flesh had hung down from the sign. He needed Doron, now. Yizhar felt his stomach churn and cramp. He was sweating: himself the human beast. The cold afternoon breeze swept over Jaffa Road and pricked the wet skin of his neck.

YIZHAR FAST-FORWARDED the tape of the news through what must have been long, painful minutes of dull political back-patting speeches by boring Arabs. In a corner of the crowd, he caught something wrong or awkward, something artificial. There he is. It's his scarf that looks wrong, and those ill-advised pants with a sharp shiny crease and no cuffs. He's moving at the front of the crowd. And the woman. This is the problem, Yizhar thought, studying Marina Raad. This is the whole damn problem. The beauty of very few women showed beneath the severe contours of the *hijab*. Hers did. She had a kind of radiance, and good bones. Until now, Yizhar had only seen still photos of the bereaved mother, but this person was someone utterly else. Her stare was commanding and she held herself with what must have been innate authority, since this was not a situation she was in charge of. Standing there just apart from her father, she looked like the future prime minister of a third-world country, the one who would inevitably inherit the mantle. Yizhar clicked the remote.

Not permitted, he kept thinking. You are not permitted to go near these people. And Doron looked pathetic in his Palestinian getup. My God. Imagine stooping low enough to put on those *schmattes*. No self-respecting Israeli would ever think of it. Answer: Doron was no longer self-respecting. Couldn't all those people in the crowd detect the impostor in their midst? But they weren't interested. They wanted to see the tragic Raad family, they wanted to see the wife of Hassan Hajimi, and most of all, they wanted to watch the legendary Ahmed Amr, favorite son of Ramallah, Amr's father's ancestral home. Marina Raad was the only one who happened to be paying attention. Yizhar was angry at Doron for being there, but he was fascinated. In all his years upholding, enforcing, and controlling, Yizhar had never seen quite the likes of this one. The new generation has lost its mind, was one of his conclusions. He turns away from me, thought Yizhar, and walks among Them.

Raad was speaking now. Yizhar listened without concentrating hard enough to understand. Content did not matter. Yizhar's Arabic was decent, but Channel Two had voiced over a Hebrew analysis, so that it was almost impossible to hear Raad's voice. Whatever the man was saying was not complimentary to Amr and the Authority. Good, thought Yizhar, create a schism, widen the breach, get 'em fighting. Nothing better than a dogfight. But Yizhar's mind was only half on the tape now that Doron was no longer on camera. The boy must be reined in, Yizhar was thinking. Sequestration, like Gertler? It was his favorite daydream. Idle fantasy. But still, maybe you can spin him again. Take him for one more turn around the room. Then dump him, if you have to. Let them finish him off. Yizhar was glad he had helped with the Hajimi release.

The message light on Yizhar's telephone was blinking red. He pressed in his code and listened. Oh, how rumors travel inside an army—it was almost as if the senior staff were bivouacked along a ridge somewhere, playing a game, repeating things down the line. There were just a few messages, only from men who knew about the secure Jerusalem line. Almost every message asked the same question: Was the story true?

It was getting late; without looking at his watch, he could tell the approximate time because from far down his hall, he could hear the ominous approach of the Russian woman with her vacuum cleaner. Her shift began at ten. The sucking roar—he closed his eyes, put his head back over the edge of his chair, and breathed, and thought about Gertler: failed general, happy if brief prime minister, advising now at Defense. Fate was something Yizhar enjoyed mulling over, but his mind was fuzzy. Historical detail wouldn't come. Yizhar felt as if his tired brain were clogged with dust and lint that the Russian's vacuum could suck up into a disposable dust-filled bag. He did not like to hear gossip about himself, his work. What he did was supposed to be leakproof, yet there were men at Chezy sitting there like stuffed derma and talking about the details of his case. Fabled Israeli intelligence: full of double agents, incompetents, frauds, and blabbermouths. It must be Zvili who was talking; Doron would never talk—not idly, anyway. The vacuum was coming closer, homing in on its target: him.

Yizhar had wanted Gertler's life, but Gertler got it. Gertler got it in spite of himself. After the breakdown, Gertler's brilliance dissipated and his energy vanished, but it never seemed to matter. Instead of falling into a pit of oblivion, he went on to become chief of staff, head of the Labor party, prime minister for a few months, now back to running Labor from behind the scenes, dispensing useless, unheeded pointers to the Defense Minister. He seemed to have led an enviable life, and if Yizhar could have, he would have simply jumped inside the man's skin and assumed his identity.

But instead, Yizhar was left to pace the West Bank, hunting for prey among the sad tin and cinder-block houses, stuck till the light turned blue in the refugee camps, wasting his time on layabout terrorists and two-bit fanatics, reduced further, now, he felt, to a slightly sordid attempt to quash truth and save the country's not unspotted honor, when he should have been running the country. At least the West Bank had been action, but what action was this, now? Second in charge of security during the "peace" turned out to mean public relations, chatting up Avram Shell, controlling the incidents.

· · ·

YIZHAR WAS TRAPPED, hiding up here in his black den with the lights off, listening to the sucking roar of the vacuum cleaner down the hall. He did his best thinking in the dark—the darker the better in this mood. It freed his mind from extraneous details like the latest scratch on the new desk, the dying philodendron. He could examine the most obscure things—for example, he acknowledged to himself, his own emotions, his own intentions—more clearly in this gloom. He leaned back in his chair and put his hands over his open eyes to conjure an even greater dark. On the screen made by his palms, he saw Doron's face. His cupped hands magnified the sound of his own breathing.

If he looked at the situation closely, too closely, it turned out that he was afraid. He was afraid Doron would fly away, out of his hands. Losing control was something Yizhar did not do gracefully, and he would go to great lengths to ensure that he did it very rarely. He stood to open his window. He wanted to let something in—the night air, the dark sky, something besides himself. He clutched at the narrow sill. The rain that had started up after lunch had ended, the clouds had parted, and the moon hung above the winged lion on top of the Generali building. Below, life was a party. The traffic was stopped and honking. Then the light across from his window changed and people crossed the street in a rush. He heard laughter. An angry voice rose up, what was it saying? But Yizhar couldn't make it out: angry gibberish moving away down Jaffa. People were walking up the street and down, off to have a drink, a dance.

Yizhar's cell phone rang. He turned from the window and his heart raced like a lover's. Let it be him. But quickly he convinced himself: It will be Zvili, or Reuven. It will be the dentist canceling an appointment. He opened the phone and put it gingerly to his ear.

"Yes?" he said.

First there was silence. A breath, a sigh. Hesitation and doubt, Yizhar thought.

"Yes?" he said again.

"I've been thinking about you," came the voice.

Yizhar exhaled. It was his man. Doron's voice was low, tense. Yizhar heard cars and pedestrian traffic like an echo in the background. The noises sounded peculiarly familiar.

"Where are you?" asked Yizhar. A mistake—never ask what you want to know.

"Here and there," said Doron.

"Don't be stupid," Yizhar answered. "You are in big trouble."

"Oh?" said Doron.

"Yes," answered Yizhar. "You've been out touring the countryside. Not good."

"Maybe," said Doron, but there was a nuance of superiority in his voice. "Are you at your office?"

"Yes, I'm here," Yizhar said.

"I thought you would be," said Doron. "So am I. Come let me in."

Too IMPATIENT TO WAIT for the elevator, Yizhar took the narrow dark stairway down to open the door for Doron.

Through a grille on the front entryway, he pointed Doron to the side entrance, a low steel door with multiple locks and a computer code that would only open after a personal identification number from a Building staffer was entered. A grown man had to duck his head to come in The Building's side door. As he entered, Doron ducked, and it looked like a gesture of submission and subordination, almost like an unacknowledged salute. But Yizhar was not fooled by appearances. He did not put out his hand for a handshake. The two men looked at each other.

"Come up," Yizhar said, turning his back. He felt just a small nip of fear as he turned away—who knew: the boy might be unhinged—but he turned away.

Doron followed him. They went up flight after flight—Doron lost count trying to keep pace with Yizhar. When they got to Yizhar's floor, Doron heard the roar of something behind them, down the hallway. The linoleum tapped beneath his shoes. This floor of The Building was empty at night. It felt like a cave to Doron, dark, empty, echoing.

Yizhar didn't bother to flick on the lights in his office.

"Come in," he said.

Doron looked around the unlit room.

"Do you always work in the dark?" he asked.

"I think better in the dark," Yizhar said. "It helps when I'm working on something important. And difficult."

"I hope my case is not so difficult."

"I don't understand you, Lieutenant, truly I don't. Sit down. Why are you here?"

"Zvili said you wanted to see me."

"I've seen enough of you already today. On a tape from Channel Two. At that rally in Ramallah."

Doron looked down at the floor.

"So?" he said.

"So? You were there." Yizhar looked at Doron. In the half-light, he caught the knobby outline of the scarf that was wrapped loosely around the soldier's neck. Did he wear this outfit all the time, now? The rope to hang yourself—the phrase passed fleetingly through Yizhar's mind.

"It's a violation of our agreement," Yizhar said. "You're ready to go there again, aren't you? You look foolish."

Doron looked away from the wall he'd been staring at and focused on Yizhar's silhouette against the patch of moonlit sky in the window. Backlit, the brush of the officer's hair stood out from his head like the blade of a hatchet.

Doron was exhausted. He'd spent almost all the previous night wandering around the Old City, disoriented and jangling from his scramble through the wadi. Near dawn, he'd taken a bus over to his mother's and slept for a few hours. The house had been empty. His mother was down in the Negev overnight, teaching at the university. When Doron awoke, he had rummaged through his closet until he found his blue-jean jacket, removed the empty cigarette pack and stuck it in his pants pocket. If he could only get access to a military phone and call the secure number he'd copied down that night, he thought he had a good chance of finding the man who had given him his orders. For what it was worth.

Yizhar walked around the office, moving things in the dark, straightening them, putting papers into piles, kicking the side of the *Jane's Defence* stack.

"Marina Raad is quite pretty, by the way," Yizhar said, looking up at Doron. Even in the shadows, he could see the soldier react. A slight step back, tension in the shoulders, as if he were getting ready to take a blow.

"You think?" asked Doron after a second.

The soldier's shadowy features were unreadable.

"So, are we enemies now?" Doron asked.

"I sincerely hope not," said Yizhar. "That would be very bad for you."

"What do you want?"

"To talk to you, and have you listen."

"Yeah?"

"Yes. And then, to have you do as I say."

Doron sat on a hard chair in front of Yizhar's desk. "It sounds as if your plan hasn't changed much since we last spoke," he said. The moon shone down in patches, touching his shoulders and his hair and brow and the angles of his face with white light. What Yizhar could see of him looked like an ancient stone head of a boy, floating in midair. His eyes were huge and dark. Who was this boy, this man, now? What was he capable of? The roar down the hall was growing louder.

"Why should the plan change?" Yizhar asked.

Doron just looked at him.

"This is my thinking," Yizhar said to him. Doron gazed out the window at the winged lion. "Are you listening to me?"

"Yes, sir." Doron nodded his head curtly.

"We have a problem. The first problem is this: They want you. The second problem is this: You don't know what you want. Except you want to be a hero. Fine."

"I don't want to be a hero."

"Good."

Yizhar sat down at the edge of his desk. He fiddled in the dark with his tape recorder.

"Do you want me to be a hero?" Doron asked.

Yizhar looked up from his fiddling. "I despise heroes."

"Ah. He despises heroes."

"Heroes act, and other people suffer. I hate that."

"You have a very dark view of things," Doron said.

"Everything I am, I became in the army. I'm just an army boy," Yizhar said. "That's what you were supposed to be, too. Before you became a Palestinian."

Doron began to rise from his chair.

Yizhar stood quickly, and came forward and pushed him back down, a light push, gentle, on his breastbone. Doron sat down. Yizhar could hear the man's breath. It was quick and shallow.

"I'm through talking to you," Doron said in a fierce whisper.

"Oh, no. Wrong. We have lots to talk about, *habibi*," Yizhar said. Now he would use that word with Doron. Its familiarity would humiliate the boy, or at least, he would understand that there was an implied condescension.

Yizhar shut the door on the faint light of the hallway, and the room turned a deep blue. Doron could hear Yizhar's voice but could only see his outline as he paced. "Listen: I don't like the bullshit, okay? You talk to those people, you're court-martialed, do you understand? Court-martialed in a secret proceeding. You're finished. Second: Hajimi is going to be released, and very soon. I worked hard for this release, but trust me, you don't want to be standing around Ramallah like some fool in costume when he comes out.

"Satisfy my curiosity, okay?" Yizhar said. "This is what I'm curious about—and let's put it starkly: Are you a patriot or are you a traitor? Let's find out, okay?"

"What's the test, Colonel?"

"This is the test: Tomorrow afternoon, at one o'clock, I've set up a session for you at Army Radio and you are going to go over there and you are going to have a little give-and-take with my friend Avram Shell. A chat, we call it. Sort of impromptu."

Yizhar leaned over his desk and picked up a few pieces of paper from beneath a paperweight that had a blue Star of David embedded in it. He waved the paper at Doron. The white sheets flapped in the moonlight like the wings of an exhausted bird.

Over the architecture of the objects on the desk, Doron looked at the strange dark figure opposite him. Yizhar's face hovered there, and he stuck out his hand with the few sheets of paper in it, and the paper seemed to float above the blue star, above the shadows of two telephones, and above the open cell phone that was lying there open on its back, like a dog waiting to have its stomach scratched.

Doron took the paper.

"I've been working on it all day," Yizhar said. "It's very simple, short. It's perfect. It's true. Avram will ask his questions, and you will give answers that are a lot like the ones you see there. It will spare the country terrible stress and embarrassment. It will save your skin and your career."

"Sounds like a miracle," Doron said. "Let me look."

"Remember, we need this," Yizhar said. "I need to hear it. The Israeli people need to hear it. Most of all, the Palestinians at the checkpoints need to hear it. If you weren't the one who was the commanding officer that night, and if you weren't acting the way you've been acting, I might not ask you to put on this performance. But as things stand now, I've lost my confidence. We need to hear your voice."

Doron held the interview in his hand.

"Do you mind turning on the lights?" he asked.

Yizhar stood and turned on his desk light. The vacuum cleaner was fading away down the corridor. Doron read. Then he went back to the beginning, and read again.

Finally, he looked up at Yizhar. Lit from below, Yizhar's face had taken on an otherworldly pallor. His nostrils glowed, his earlobes shone, the slight dimple in his chin turned shadowy and mysterious. Above it all, his eyes kept watch. Doron shook his head almost imperceptibly, to himself. Yizhar picked up on it immediately.

"You can't say no," Yizhar said. "Don't even try."

"I can," said Doron. "I do. I won't lie. I will not say it was a ten-minute wait. I will not say the boy was not in trouble. I will not say I went by the book, and I won't lie about that phone call."

"It's not a lie. *You* are not remembering correctly. *You* were exhausted, as it says there. *You* did the best you could. Poor boy. Now, the enemies of Israel are trying to use you to injure Israel and her army. But *you* will *not* be a party to their manipulations. You know that the responsibility for the checkpoint that night was entirely yours. Am I right, by the way? Entirely yours, and thus any blame is also entirely yours. Correct?"

Doron said nothing. He folded the sheets of paper carefully. He put the thing in the pocket of his sweater vest.

Yizhar turned off the desk lamp, and seemed to disappear. His voice went on, out of thin air. It was piercing into Doron's brain. Doron felt his fatigue kick in. As Doron's eyes again became accustomed to the gloom, Yizhar's shadow slowly gathered itself before him once more.

"You can't go on taking their side against us, Ari. In your mind, okay, maybe, but on the ground, impossible. We need to establish our *facts*—that's what you do in a case like this. Just because their kid died doesn't make them good or honest. They're not good. They're not honest. The Raads and Hajimis are terrorists and propagandists. They are the lowest of the Arabs, vile Jew-haters. I'm not protecting anyone but you, and I'm protecting you from *them*. Nothing will happen to the boy's family because you and Avram have this little chat. They'll go on being what they are. But *you* will have spared your country an ordeal. I appeal to your patriotism, truly." Yizhar realized as he spoke that he more or less meant what he was saying. *That* felt good—strange, but good. "If you involve the army in some kind of scandal over this relatively minor incident, you will be playing into the hands of the enemies of the Jewish people."

"I am not going to involve the army in any scandal. The army has nothing to do with it," said Doron. "By now."

"Nothing to do with it? You *are* crazy. Anything you do now reflects on the army. You're the target, the bad guy, the guilty party. God, if the Authority finds you in Ramallah, if Hajimi finds you on his turf, hanging out, I don't know what will happen. You see? You involve us, but you don't consult us. How can we protect you and ourselves?" Yizhar looked at Doron as if he were a specimen from a primitive culture.

"I will not go on the radio and tell lies," Doron said.

"We need you to get out there and say this, or something like it. We need *you* to tell Israelis that we did the right thing. And we want the Palestinians to hear it, too. To hear from us that there wasn't an hour wait for this boy, as their people are claiming, to hear that you take full responsibility for your actions that night."

"I won't do it."

Yizhar stood there, tapping a foot, thinking about court-martials. He wondered what he would have to say to get the chiefs of staff to go along. Ah, it would be nice to have Ari Doron under lock and key for a few weeks or months. Yizhar could tell his colleagues that the man was deranged, and, as evidence, show the tape of Doron in Ramallah. The outfit itself was enough to get an Israeli institutionalized.

"Well?" Doron was waiting.

"I'm not sure I see an alternative."

"How about this game plan, Colonel? I don't say anything, you don't say anything, and we let the whole thing die down."

"Yeah." Yizhar sat down again. "Yeah. That would be good." He was silent for a minute. The shuffling shouting sound of the nighttime crowd below poured in through the window. "In fact, that would be the normal thing, the thing I myself would advise. I would advise it, that is, if I hadn't just seen you parading around at a rally organized—I mean, really, targeted—against *you*. If I didn't think that, in some way, you were a dangerous lunatic and a very very loose fucking cannon. You are playing into their hands, no question. The Authority is not going to let this thing 'die down' if they can figure out a way to keep it alive. You're helping them, and if you help them, you will lose our backing. And then, you will be utterly at their mercy."

"What does that mean?"

"It means what it means. We will withdraw our protection from you."

"Protection?"

"Our physical protection. You may not have noticed, but we've been following you with a small security detail." Maybe *that* would put the fear of God into the soldier.

"Right," Doron said. He felt in his pocket for the pack with the number on it. It was his insurance against Yizhar. Doron had devised his own little test for the colonel, and he didn't want to give it away.

Doron seemed bigger to Yizhar in some way since their last meeting, taller, more powerful. Maybe it was the darkness. Yizhar remained quiet. He wondered if he should be just the smallest bit nervous. And yet, he was an old hand. Did Doron think Yizhar didn't know how to do this? West Bank security: it meant interrogation first of all. Yizhar had been a master not just of the physical techniques—the humiliation of the little chair, the electric "stimuli," the shaking methods, deprivations of every kind; all legal, by the way—but especially of the psychological aspects. And the miracle was, it worked with everyone! Hamas, Islamic Jihad, Fatah, the PFLP, the Intifada kids, petty street criminals. All human beasts. They all crumbled and talked and obeyed and collaborated, with the rare exceptional case, like Hajimi. And then they were okay after it. Yizhar didn't have to feel bad. He was a *nice* interrogator. He was gentle, not like some of the other guys. There were no lasting bumps, no visible bruises. No maiming. He would never do anything like that, not even to a terrorist. No. Just a little lesson.

He was a stylish interrogator, and his methods would work on Israelis, too, he imagined. Let's see.

"You're my favorite soldier, Ari." Yizhar let the statement sit there.

Doron said nothing.

"You know why? Know why I like you so much? Because you're different. Because you *care*."

"Fuck you."

"No, I mean it."

"So do I."

"Just listen," Yizhar said. "I care, too. The thing is, right now, we think we care about different things. You care about the family of this boy who died, and I care about Israel. Right?" The boy was bound to assert his patriotism.

"I care about the country, too," Doron said.

"Oh. Well, that's good," said Yizhar. "I thought maybe you didn't feel that anymore."

"I care, but maybe I care in a different way."

"You want it to be a *good* country, right?"

"Don't try to make me sound naive."

"I don't need to," Yizhar said.

"I shouldn't have come here tonight," Doron said.

"You came because you know instinctively that I will help you," Yizhar said. "Why don't you believe me?"

"Because we have a fundamental disagreement."

"Can you tell me what it is?" Yizhar asked.

"You believe nothing bad happened; I believe we killed a baby."

Yizhar stopped on that. He leaned over and shoved his face close up to Doron's.

"We?" he whispered. "We?"

Doron pulled his head back. He looked at Yizhar, the blade of hair, the sharp brow that hid those eyes lying in wait. He was like some great bird of prey, crouching over Doron.

"We, the State of Israel," Doron said.

"Oh," said Yizhar. "We killed a baby."

He said it without emotion, as if he were weighing the statement. "No. No, I don't think so, Ari. We've been over this. A child is dead, is how I would say it."

"I'm tired of this," Doron said. "You can't do this kind of thing and not take responsibility." He stood, and Yizhar noticed how the soldier towered over him. A head taller, at least, my God! But Yizhar never lost his nerve. A man's courage is everything, Gertler had said.

"Where do you think you're going, Lieutenant?" Yizhar asked. "Ramallah?"

"I'll go where I want to," Doron said.

"You'll go to Shell," Yizhar said. "You'll go to the studio tomorrow at one. I don't like to be so crude, but it's an order, Lieutenant."

Doron walked over to Yizhar and stuck his head down so the he was looking right into Yizhar's eyes. It was too dark to see much of anything so close up.

"Your orders don't mean much to me at this point," Doron said. "Not compared to what I think I have to do."

The two men were standing so close together they could have been dancing.

Yizhar stood there, thinking: What next. He thought he heard a noise, then, a noise that was not his panting, not the soldier's breathing, not his own heart.

His office door flew open.

No, Yizhar thought. What? What? He could feel Doron reacting to the sound, his interest failing, attention diverted.

A roar blasted into the room. Blazingly, the lights went on.

Doron wheeled around. In the doorway stood a squarish woman with a babushka tied around her head and the neck of a vacuum cleaner in her hand. Yizhar felt relief flood through him, followed by a wave of hilarity. In her other hand she carried a black garbage bag.

"Oh, God, to excuse me, please, gentlemen. I did not know that anyone was here." Her face was flushed. She put the garbage bag down. "Lights were not on, you see. I am not paying attention." What must she think, Yizhar wondered. A homosexual assignation? They had been standing so close to each other, in the dark, and now both looked so taken aback.

"That's all right," Yizhar said. Finally I know why this hideous creature whom I have always loathed and avoided was put on God's earth, he thought. Fate gathered its strength, the East spewed forth its refugees, and then, suddenly, here she was, Mother Russia, at the door in Jerusalem, with a garbage bag, rescuing me from who knew what fate. Thank you, Lord. Thank you, Kremlin. "We were just finishing up." God is good.

"So I am to be cleaning, Mister? Or what?"

"You go right ahead," said Yizhar.

DORON PUSHED PAST the Russian lady and out the door. He barreled toward the stairway, with Yizhar at his heels. One flight, another, Yizhar always pursuing, until Doron arrived at the side door, a few floors ahead of Yizhar. He could hear the other man's footsteps coming down the stairway above. Doron breathed deeply. He twisted the door handle. It did not move in his hand. Next to it, a red light blinked. He blinked back at it, realizing what it meant. He breathed slowly again, trying to collect himself. The look on the cleaning woman's face. Unexpectedly, he wanted to laugh, but in a second, Yizhar would be there with him. Footsteps clacked down the stairway, some distance above. Doron put his head down and balled his fists into his vest pockets. He felt something there, and pulled out a piece of paper.

Right, the interview Yizhar had scripted for him, the smooth paper folded neatly. He replaced it. He scuffed at the floor. He was waiting for Yizhar, even though the guy had just threatened to court-martial him. It occurred to Doron that this was how he was spending most of his time these days. Waiting for Yizhar to decide, dispense, mete out his fate. That was over. Doron was waiting for Yizhar for the last time, waiting for him to open the door and let Doron out into the world to do whatever he was going to do. The footsteps came to a dead halt behind him. Doron turned and faced his pursuer. Humiliating to try a jailbreak only to end up back in the hands of the warden.

Yizhar looked at him and gave him one of those small smiles, like the one that Doron had seen frozen on his face the first time they met.

"Let me open it for you," Yizhar said, with hyperpoliteness, almost as if he had swept his arm out before him and said, "After you."

Doron waited for him to open the door.

"I'll be listening tomorrow," Yizhar said as he turned one key, then another, in the door.

"You can listen," said Doron.

"Be there." Yizhar's index fingered hovered in the air in front of the computer pad. He looked at Doron. "By the way, we think they know who you are. We think Hajimi knows."

Doron gave him a small smile of his own. But the news jolted him. Should he believe it? His legs weakened for a few seconds as he went out the door.

The dark city opened up before Doron as he moved into the night from the clammy confines of The Building. The enormous black sky. He closed his eyes and thought of the cleaning lady: someday he would go back into The Building and take her in his arms and kiss her right on the lips, adorable thing. The sweet chunk of moon hung like a piece of candy in the heavens. Something was cooking over charcoal—a piece of juicy meat being prepared somewhere for a late-night snack, with a smell that made his stomach cramp with hunger. Across the street, parking meters stood in rows, and the traffic light changed and changed back and changed again in a comforting automatic succession of stops and goes. Rooftops and antennae, domes, steeples, and lit-up signs, alleys that ran off in twisting blocks into darkness, cats crouching with stiff tails—all of this was here, outside, waiting for him.

He heard the door clank satisfyingly shut behind him, with a metallic, prisonlike slam. Turning, Doron surveyed The Building's exterior to make sure Yizhar had not followed him out. He couldn't have withstood any more talk with the night creature. Out here, it felt like freedom, although he knew that that was illusory. For the moment, shadows hid him. He noticed a car double-parked down the block, its engine idling. Was this his security detail? If there was one, which Doron doubted. It was probably just Yizhar's wife, waiting for him to come down. If Yizhar had one, which Doron doubted.

Yizhar only came out after sunset, Doron was beginning to think. Yizhar could see in the dark! He remembered that Yizhar had been linked to Gertler's wartime disgrace in some unknown way, and it didn't surprise him. The man was capable of any stinking trick. Doron leaned against a parking meter near his car. He was exhausted. He'd come near to strangling the man, and put himself at great risk, he was certain of it. Yizhar was always armed. He was not a military man for nothing.

He knew that before it was all over, he would regret not having ripped the creature's head off. Kill it before it kills you. He was beginning to wonder whether, beneath his khaki uniform, Yizhar concealed a pair of shiny black wings like a crow's. After Doron broke his scrawny neck, the wings would spread out across the pavement, broken, with blood and bone, and pink and gray sinew, and feathers splashed everywhere.

CHAPTER NINETEEN

ARINA TRIED TO REMEMBER BACK TO THE DAYS WHEN she was an intelligent person who could think logically. It seemed a long, long time ago. When Uncle Ahmed's men had started driving them away from the rally in Ramallah, she thought, dramatically, that she and her father were finished. They had gotten in the way of the Authority, and Uncle Ahmed, when riled, was ten times more hotheaded and dangerous than the Chairman, whose greatest virtue—and greatest flaw—was his wariness, and his caution. When her father had fainted, sitting in the big black car between those sweaty men in suits, Marina was certain he was going to die, and right there, and she would be all alone with those frightening serious men in the dark car, speeding somewhere up into the empty unlit hills. Her heart raced and pounded as she tried to revive her father while remaining proud and aloof, not an easy assignment. The panic felt familiar. The grotesque bodyguards would dump her father by the roadside and take her away where no one could find her.

Instead, the escort service sped Marina and George over to the Friends Clinic in Ramallah. Uncle Ahmed didn't want dead Dr. Raad on his hands, thanks, no matter how badly George had behaved. Ahmed would have had his thugs punished if they had let her father die, Marina realized later. Ahmed could be vengeful, she had heard, but he was not stupid. At the clinic, she sat in the bright waiting room with other women. A group of old men in drooping gray robes smoked cigarettes in a corner. Sick babies sat politely on their mothers' laps, waiting to be seen. She wondered what would have happened if she'd come here the other night. Probably they too would have sent her to Hadassah.

Right now, her father was in the living room, resting on the couch, with

Philip watching over him. He had recovered quite nicely. In a matter of minutes after coming to himself at the clinic, he began berating nurses, correcting doctors, complaining to her, asking for Philip, and demanding to be taken home. Hospitals make you sicker, he pointed out to the doctors. The doctors told Marina and Philip that a combination of exhaustion and palpitations exacerbated by chronic coronary weakness had caused Dr. Raad to black out. They told them that he needed to be examined soon by a specialist, to see how the heart was functioning, as they put it. It had been a month since his last electrocardiogram. He should go to Hadassah, they implied. George knew it all already, of course. After their consultation, Philip and Marina went into George's room, where, propped up against his white pillowcases, with a copy of *Al-Quds* open across the knobs and bumps of his covered legs, and his glasses pulled way down to the bottom of his nose, he told them exactly what the doctors had just told them, and then said, "Now, get me out of here." When they heard his petition, his doctors nodded and smiled and released Dr. Raad because he asked to be released, and because he was George Raad, eminent cardiologist and political commentator. He was weak, they warned Marina.

The episode scared her, and pushed the rally and Ari Doron straight out of her thoughts. Until now. She whisked lemon juice, garlic, hot pepper, and spices together. She was preparing the *iftar* meal—during Ramadan, the evening meal that breaks the long day's fast. She never thought about cooking, even during Ramadan, when meals took on a painful importance. Cooking was just something she did automatically. Like her mother. She chopped up a couple of chickens and threw them into the bowl with everything else. She turned on the oven, which was not so easy: you had to fiddle with so many knobs. For some reason, the timer always had to be on or the gas would not ignite. Cooking was the only thing in the Middle East that had to be timed. Her father said it was because food was the only thing Arabs profoundly cared about. But Marina pointed out that although the timer had to be on for the oven to light, you could set it for 20 minutes if you liked, and then cook for half a day, and the dial would just sit there at 20 and never move. The alarm would never go off.

"Well, that about sums things up, don't you think?" her father said.

It was a gross violation of everything decent for that soldier to appear at the rally, Marina was thinking. To stick his nose up there, in the front of the crowd. Attending a rally for his own victim: it was too insolent. Parading like that, to make sure she'd see him. A person who would do such a thing, you couldn't know what was going on in his mind. Did he think she forgave him? She hoped not, because she didn't. She couldn't. She was not about to forgive anyone involved, not herself and especially not him. When I forgive myself, then I'll begin to start thinking about forgiving you, Lieutenant. And I will never forgive myself. So don't come near me again. Don't do it. I don't grant absolution. I don't spare evildoers. I was about to tell Uncle Ahmed you were there. Yes, I was. That would have changed the mood of the crowd, wouldn't it? I just didn't have a chance, didn't have time. What saved you wasn't my kindness or my forgiveness. Don't imagine it. What saved you was my father's desperate rush to get his hands on the microphone, and the uproar after.

Leave me alone.

Soon none of this would matter, because Hassan would be home. Her father had been wrong. He thought that Hassan would reject freedom because it had been granted by the enemy. It almost made her want to laugh, how wrong George had been. Her father thought that all a man's actions should be based on lofty principles. It must be nice, Marina thought, to sit in your house in Cambridge, Massachusetts, on a chair that was the only remnant of your life in Palestine—a chair that was a virtual archaeological find—and decide what behavior was appropriate for people ten thousand miles away. George thought it was shameful for Hassan to accept what the Israelis offered, to provide the enemy with even a moment to appear humane—when they were the ones who had let Ibrahim die. He didn't say that to Marina, but she got the gist. Didn't George understand? Hassan was not a hero, he was a man, and he wanted to be with Marina. He was proud to be humiliated. He was doing the correct thing, the honorable thing. He was showing respect for his family. He wanted new babies. At nine tonight, he would be home.

Only a few hours after the announcement of Hassan's release, George told Marina that he and Philip would be moving out of the house in Ramallah.

"I don't think I can handle all the bustle after Hassan's release," he said. "In my weakened condition. Anyway, we'll be just down the road at the American Colony." Marina smiled. She knew what would happen at the hotel. He would install himself, and reign from there. He would create his own bustle, instead of enduring Hassan's. There, it had not escaped her, he would also not be subject to Ramadan's restrictions.

"Marina!" her father called from the living room.

She went in to him, wiping her hands on a dish towel. I am an Arab housewife, she thought.

"One more thing, sweetheart." He jacked himself up a little higher in his chair. "God, that chicken smells delicious."

"Yes? What is it?" She knew he was about to interfere in her affairs. He couldn't resist.

"I think it would be better if Philip answered the doorbell tonight, you know," he said.

"What?" She looked at him as if he were joking. George, the stage manager, she was thinking. Philip was reading a book.

"That way, if there *are* cameras, they won't see us all gathered around in the doorway, pathetically, like some refugee-camp family gratefully accepting their recently released stone thrower."

"I want to be there waiting for him."

"Absolutely not. Waiting there is as bad as putting up decorations or fixing festive sweets."

"This is my house."

"Marina. Think about what I'm saying." George coughed. "You know I'm right." Then he coughed again. Philip looked up from where he had been studiously attempting to keep out of things, a ripple of concern on his face. George kept coughing. His shoulders began to shake and the cough sounded like choking by now. His face was turning white, bluish white. Marina looked at him, watched him. His color was Ibrahim's color, as if a harsh blue light had suddenly been focused on him. When he didn't stop coughing, she began moving toward him, her panic rising slowly. Philip stood up. Marina was at George's side now.

"Dad. Dad?"

George put his hand up toward her and turned his head away. Philip held his shoulder. George coughed and choked and made a retching, spitting noise. His back heaved as if he were sobbing. Then there was silence. A half minute passed. They could see him breathing heavily, but his face was turned away.

"Philip, could you possibly get me a tissue?" He said it sharply, as if he had already asked and been ignored.

Philip swiftly left the room and returned. George wiped the tissue across his mouth, folded it. He turned and looked up at Marina, who was standing next to his chair.

"In any case, it's not your house, it's Hassan's, and this is what he would want."

"Are you all right?" Marina asked, thinking: *You're* speaking for Hassan, now?

"I'm fine. Listen, he doesn't want a greeting committee at the door," George said, "and he doesn't want to be folded into his grieving wife's arms on international television." George patted at his mouth again. "You decide, Marina. But think of your husband's position. Think of the symbolism."

When will you be moving out? she thought.

THE ARMORED VEHICLE came for him after dark. He had finished his evening meal, water and more water and one piece of pita bread—not much of an *iftar*, but fine as a part of his continuing protest. Hassan was no longer hungry—just empty. Protest against what? He no longer knew—protest against his own release? But he couldn't stop not eating. He couldn't help it. He had gotten into the habit, and now he habitually didn't eat. He felt weak. His eyesight was not strong and especially in the dark, he felt half blind. The armored vehicle's huge headlights seemed to hit him at the back of his eyes. They lit the courtyard and cast long shadows of the big soldiers who jumped out to receive him into their custody. Five soldiers, armed with everything, combat ready, riot ready, wearing—strapped onto their belts— gear whose use even he was unsure of. Miniature stun guns? Communications equipment? Incapacitating chemical sprays of some kind he'd never seen before? He couldn't tell, couldn't even see well enough, with those high beams burning into his eyes. Everything seemed artificial in that light. The whole reason for the nighttime release was to ensure secrecy, but under those lights, he felt as if he were being filmed.

The warden had given him back the things he had had on him when he was arrested. They were delivered to his cell in a used plastic bag from a toy store in downtown Jerusalem. Some functionary had scribbled HAJIMI in bold squares of Hebrew over the toy store's logo. There was his wallet, as well as his belt, his shoelaces. Thank God for the belt. Until now, he had nothing to hold up his pants properly. He was so thin he had to roll his trousers at the waist to keep them from falling down around his ankles. Now he had his belt and even his wallet, with his frayed identity card—issued by the Israelis, of course. Among the big Israeli soldiers with their bulky gear, he felt old and breakable. They could snap his body in half right here, now, and no one would be the wiser. What protected him from them? But he was resigned, he would submit to whatever they inflicted. He deserved his punishment, not for their reasons, but for his own. He would come out, he would suffer, and endure.

He had told the Israelis that he was renouncing violence. Now, what could that mean? The big Israeli soldiers hustled him along. He felt their big hands on him. Hassan never had thought of himself as a violent man, but he did believe it was right to repay with violence any violence that was directed against his people. Acts that had to be answered with violence were: forced exile; occupation of territory; torture; illegal imprisonment; assassination; and the killing of innocent demonstrators, innocent worshippers, the killing of mothers and children. That was Hassan's litany, which, he felt, nicely summed up the relationship of the Israelis to the Palestinians. He himself had never placed bombs or detonated them nor had he ordered bombs detonated, but he knew how to build one, and he had never rebuked the bombers, not even when a particular incident revolted him with its cruelty. It was an item of faith for him never to reprimand them unless their activities interfered with long-term strategy—if it was possible to imagine a group like this with a long-term strategy. Hassan often doubted it.

His wallet felt heavy in his pocket as he moved toward the headlights of the dark armored vehicle that stood before the barrier. He hoped it would not drag his pants down in spite of his belt. Of course, there was nothing in the wallet but his ID card. No money. No photographs. He was tired and his stomach felt empty. He wanted to let the strong soldiers carry him, but he summoned up his pride and made his legs move forward. The light was painful, still. They had turned on a searchlight in one of the towers. He felt like an actor.

During their times together, Marina had softened him slightly. She made her own small points, her little, humane inroads. She understood the big battle, but from time to time she raised what Hassan thought of as feminine objections. It moved him when she looked at him with American horror in her eyes, talking about the kind of attack in which nice, working Israelis who had no idea they were a part of a terror machine ended up dead through no fault of their own, exploded on the drive to work or while having a cup of coffee or window-shopping with their kids. She didn't like Israelis much. She found them imperialist and aggressive and arrogant on a personal level, almost without exception (and what Palestinian wouldn't? he wondered. Look at these soldiers here). But she'd still felt compelled to make these incidental victims of the struggle real to him. He'd watched Israelis reacting to bombings on television with new interest, then, and felt a mixture of shame and sadness when one day it dawned on him that he was capable of sympathy for them. He believed that it might just be philosophically admissible that among these victims were innocents.

He tripped over his pant leg and tried to stop for a moment to tug it up from beneath his sole, but the soldiers pulled him onward. The innocent enemy was a new concept to him. He did not tell Marina that her sentiments had begun to bend his habitual rigidity. "Feeling," they called this way of thinking in English. "Feeling" was a way of communicating through emotion that was alien to Hassan, but Marina was teaching him. His thoughts on the innocence of the enemy were still inchoate, and he certainly did not think that such feelings could evolve into policy. The feelings would never be acceptable to others, and they weren't consistent in him, either. The soldier, for example, the commanding officer? No matter how Hassan reasoned, he came to the same conclusion. The soldier was not an innocent—not in any way.

A few meters before Hassan and his handlers got to the armored vehicle, the warden loomed up out of the dark into the spotlight that had been following them.

"Mr. Hajimi," said the warden. It was the first time the warden had used "Mr."

Hassan looked at him.

"Mr. Hajimi, the American consul here just wants to say one last word to you."

The tall man cleared his throat.

"Congratulations," he said, putting out his hand to Hassan.

Hassan did not take it. He looked at it and waited.

"Well, all right," said the consul, with a wry smile. He put his hand down. "Uh, I just want to make sure that one important thing is understood."

"Yes?"

"And that is, that before leaving Ramallah—if you intend to leave Ramallah—you check in with Israeli security." The consul smiled broadly now. "Just to let them know where you're going, you know. It's an arrangement we've worked out with Mr. Amr. For your protection."

"Oh, of course, of course," said Hassan. Ahmed Amr, the old whore, he thought, not for the first time. My savior.

"We wouldn't want anything to happen to you, if you were to be traveling without alerting security. You understand."

"Oh, yes, of course." Hassan looked at him, and smiled back. Marina said that a smile like his could win anyone's trust. He watched the consul's suspicion soften. "I am glad to be leaving this place."

"Well," the warden interrupted brusquely, with what Hassan imagined the man thought was sly humor, "we are glad to be getting rid of you."

"I'm sure." Hassan laughed. "Ramallah will look like paradise to me."

"That in itself is a sorry statement about this place here," said the consul, looking around at the courtyard. He caught himself. "Although Ramallah has its charms."

"Yes," said Hassan. He waited a moment. "What is left of my family is there. For me, that is a charm." He hoped there would not be a big welcoming committee waiting for him. Marina, his sisters, their husbands, the nieces and nephews, his cousins from Jerusalem, George and George's sidekick—what was his name again?—and Katul, the neighbor, and *his* family. . . . The list was endless. But no, it would not turn out that way. Hassan trusted his father-in-law to see to that. There were some things, a few things, that George Raad was good for, and propriety was one. He was unfailingly correct, except when he chose not to be. Hassan wondered if Raad had played a part in his release. Somehow, he doubted it. His father-in-law was above such low maneuvering, such hand-dirtying. And a son-in-law in prison was just fine with George, Hassan imagined. Something to boast about and an irritant avoided, at the same time. Dr. Raad was probably enjoying having his daughter to himself.

Hassan climbed awkwardly into the back of the armored vehicle, the soldiers grabbing at his arms from above and pushing him from behind to help him up. It was more exercise than he had had in the last few months of walking around the courtyard, and it taxed his shoulders, his calves. His weakness shocked him. He did not want to present himself to Marina as a patient, after all this time. One more man to be taken care of. His escort lowered him onto a narrow bench, then sat themselves down heavily on either side of him, and across from him as well, surrounding him. As if he posed a threat. At the checkpoint, they would switch him into the custody of the Authority.

The vehicle pulled out of the courtyard, and Hassan felt his heart lighten. Goodbye to the men, he thought. He loved the pull of that powerful motor. The traction of the treads, pulling him out of wretchedness, toward Marina. Take me away, Israeli military vehicle, take me away. Goodbye, men, goodbye. Goodbye to all their suffering and stories, endless repetitive stories that he had to hear patiently, like some kind of a sheikh or wise man, as if he were wise. He was not wise. He was bored. Goodbye and good riddance. He didn't want to look at one more man. He didn't want to hear one more man's snoring. He never wanted to go to prison again, not like some of the boys he knew, who preferred prison to a woman. He'd been in too long, too many times. Marina, Marina. As they made their way through Jerusalem up toward Ramallah, he watched out the window through the protective iron latticework. Beautiful dark mysterious stone city, he thought. He wanted to kiss every wall, he didn't care which Zionist had built the wall or whose Zionist politician's face was plastered across it, or which damned Palestinian had once lived behind it. He was sick of the words and the stories. He would kiss them all, every wall, every column, every damned balcony and every squat square house and every Zionist oppressor's wall, thank God for freedom. Marina. He didn't dare picture her too clearly. Across from the Old City, the Virgin on the roof of Notre Dame appeared. She was gilded and lit, and holding her boy up to face Jerusalem's walls. Then he remembered Ibrahim not being there, and he hated himself.

IT WAS WORKING splendidly, and everything redounded to his own credit. Ahmed Amr was splendidly pleased with himself. The Mercedes was parked a few blocks from the Hajimi house, and he sat next to his car on a plank bench in front of a corner soda shack and taxi stand, waiting like a contented hen on her eggs for Hajimi's return. Ahmed had had his *iftar*, but he was still hungry and had bought a bag of chips and a Coke from the soda man. And here he was like a mindless teenager, munching and drinking. A television satellite van stood one block closer to the house, its presence there arranged by him. Let George complain now—which he would, no doubt. I have managed the release of Hassan Hajimi, the legendary militant. Who will stand up now and argue that the Authority is not committed to the freedom of all Palestinians? No one. Who will argue that the Authority cannot achieve its goals? No one.

I can tell myself I've done the right thing, Ahmed thought, and then of course, there was Hajimi's poor young wife to think of. It was a humanitarian decision. Find the Soldier? Who needed the soldier now? He was of no use. To reassert its control, the Authority had wielded the little lieutenant and the dead child like a flashing blade. Very efficient tool, and the Israelis had caved and now here was Hajimi on his way home. Now it was over. Ahmed and the Chairman were back in control again.

CHAPTER TWENTY

DORON'S EYES WERE CLOSED. HE FIGURED IT OUT, JUST sitting here behind the wheel in park, letting his mind wander. There was something nipping at the edge. Something in Yizhar's office that had caught his attention. The two phones. Next to the paperweight, two phones on Yizhar's desk. Two, not counting the cell phone.

He started up the car. Poor old car. He was going to pay a little visit to the checkpoint in Ramallah, where he had sworn he would never go again after crossing the wadi two days ago. He would make sure. He was going to visit the checkpoint; avoid Zvili as much as possible while imposing on their so-called friendship. Make a phone call. It was the only military phone he could get access to.

It was quiet out here on the way to the West Bank. Everyone was at home for Ramadan, eating as much possible before the sun rose again. Doron drove past Petra Car Rentals—with their fat little Fiat Unos lined up outside like a cartoon battalion—and past Joulani's Furniture and past the big yellow Paz gas station and Jaffar's Supermarket and past all the tiny Christian missions with their handwritten signs. Each one hoping to save the Palestinian people.

He approached the watchtower, lit up white against the night sky like a symbol waiting to be sewn on a flag.

He pulled his car over to the side. Two soldiers looked at it curiously. It was a wreck.

When Doron walked up to the guardhouse door, Zvili stared at him without embarrassment, but of course Zvili was never embarrassed.

"Hey, man," Zvili said. His squinted and tilted his head to the side. His bunched-up gremlin's body tensed, like a fighter's.

"How are things, Zvil?" Doron offered him a cigarette, the soldier's universal token of friendship. He held out a fresh pack to Zvili. Soldiers are like convicts, Doron thought, always offering each other cigarettes. Doron felt for the crumpled cigarette pack in his other pocket.

"Things are better," Zvili said. "Things were better today." He took a step backward as if to remove himself from Doron's reach. "It just all of a sudden calmed down. Snap, like that," and he snapped his fingers.

"Yeah?" said Doron. "Aren't you lucky?"

"No kidding, man. It has been hot, hot, hot," Zvili said. "Worse than your last day."

Doron looked at him, and Zvili looked right back.

"I doubt it," Doron said.

Zvili took a long, self-conscious puff on his cigarette. "Worse. By far."

"You've had casualties?"

"So many wounded, you can't count them," Zvili said, looking away. "And five dead, so far. That was mostly one day, though. It's the Find the Soldier thing." Zvili looked at him meaningfully. Doron smiled back, gave him a wide, innocent smile. "But I think it's over, now," Zvili said.

"Why is it over?"

"Because of Hajimi's release."

"What?" Doron felt his chest tighten.

"They're releasing Hajimi tonight," Zvili said.

Doron knew that Hajimi's release had been proposed, but he never thought the man would accept it. They never did. But this one did. Doron felt his heart move inside him in some new, surprising way.

"Didn't you know?" Zvili looked at Doron as if he were an alien. "Watch TV, asshole. Listen to the fucking radio." He kicked at the ground. "Yeah, they're sending him home to the bereaved mother. He'll be coming through here." Zvili smirked and sneaked a glance at Doron's face to see if there was a reaction, but Doron kept his face empty.

"Can I borrow the phone?" Doron asked. He looked up the Ramallah road, remembering fate walking toward him.

"What?" asked Zvili.

"Can I use your phone?"

"It's an army line, Ari."

"I know." Doron looked at him. "I'm army."

"Yeah, sure, I guess," said Zvili, moving slightly away to open Doron's path to the guardhouse.

Doron sat down at the communications controls, his stomach swirling. He was a pilot returning to the helm of a crashing plane. Hajimi was coming home and he would reclaim Marina. Doron was in a tight death spiral, plummeting down toward the bare desert hills at more than five hundred miles per hour. Pull up, pull up. Doron stared blankly at the controls; the red blinking lights, the buttons that opened new lines, the switch that lengthened the antennae, the green light that lit when communications were established, the touch-tone pad. I've been here before. He stared at the controls. He was zoning out, disoriented.

Now if Hajimi were in the cockpit, surely all could be saved. Doron has seen pictures of Hajimi; he looked like a Royal Air Force pilot, gritty and heroic, with only the keffiyeh wrapped like a scarf around his neck to give him away as what everyone knows he really is: a black-haired, dark-skinned, moustachioed, rag-wearing Middle Eastern bomb artist. Hajimi knows his vehicles, that's the official wisdom. A crashing plane would not be beyond his ability to control. He knows about switches, they say. Timers. Fuses.

This is the scene of the crime, Doron kept thinking as he looked at the controls, his hands hanging useless at his sides. We're crashing. Shit. *Shit*—the word that was always the last word you heard on the black box after the sappers picked it up from the debris-strewn desert and brought it back to headquarters. The word when all hope is lost.

Doron took the old crushed cigarette pack from his jacket pocket. He squinted at the scribble of numbers. The handwriting was tremulous and spindly, almost not recognizable as his own. He picked up the receiver and pressed the numbers into the pad.

It rang at headquarters down in Tel Aviv. Two rings, three. Then a tiny pause, a jump in the dark silence between rings, unnoticeable if you weren't paying attention, and then a fourth ring, a fifth. A pickup.

"Yes?" said the voice at the other end. It was a man's voice—kind, resonant, and caring.

Doron said nothing. The world was spinning.

"What is it?" said the voice.

"Is there a problem?" the voice asked.

Doron breathed.

"Who's there?" Now suspicion crept in. Doron listened. He was breathing, and so was the man on the other end.

I knew it, Doron thought. I knew it.

There was the click of the hang-up.

Unmistakably, the voice at the other end of the phone was Yizhar's.

• • •

DORON DROVE FURIOUSLY down King David Street. The city was empty at that late hour. Clouds passed over the moon, darkening hills where cypress trees bowed toward him in the wind, and then the clouds moved on, opening up the skies and flooding the valleys with blue light. He drove through light and dark single-mindedly, not looking at the scenery, not imagining a destination. Black birds swooped down over the tombs of the lesser prophets that were carved out of pure rock in the valley between the Old City walls and the village of Silwan. The poor car sputtered under Doron's angry hand. He was in an unallowable rage and he needed to go fast. He tried to sweep Yizhar's betrayal to the side of his concerns.

Instead, his thoughts wound in tighter and tighter circles around another subject. I was the one at the checkpoint, he kept thinking. I was with her. I am the one who knows what happened. I am the one who cares.

They will show Hajimi's release on the news, he thought. Where can I watch that? He remembered the window at Best Buy at the Talpiot circle. He'd go there. The lights of the diamond factory on the road to Bethlehem twinkled against the shifting skies. To his left loomed an old cement watchtower from the war for independence. It was built solidly, like the turret of a castle, with narrow loopholes at the top to shoot down from. He came to Talpiot's commercial district, and drove around the circle over and over, seeing how fast he could make the jalopy go in such a tight curve. Plastic picnic tables were chained to posts outside the entrance to the housewares store.

Three-quarters around the circle at Best Buy, two rows of television sets broadcast to an empty street. They made a bright stroke of light in his peripheral vision as he jockeyed past. Doron circled and circled—no one would disturb him; the police were asleep at this hour. Maybe he would crash the car through Best Buy's window. Smash through the plate glass and upend the televisions, ride up and over the washing machines, and then come to rest, bloody and shattered, in the cool of refrigerator row. Freon. He wanted to breathe it, freeze his insides.

He sped around the circle, where next? What next? Up onto the sidewalk he drove, and right up to the Best Buy window. He got out and stood next to the car, looking in. The televisions aired the news in silence. He could see his own reflection in the dark glass between two sets. He was panting—he hadn't noticed until he saw himself doing it. He shut his mouth and pushed his hair out of his eyes; he was becoming disheveled.

His chin was rough with stubble. His eyes were hooded; they looked like Yizhar's eyes. He looked the way Palestinians expected a checkpoint officer to look: like a bad guy. He looked the way Israelis think a suicide bomber looks in the seconds before he pulls the pin. Bad guy.

A Palestinian police car flanked by motorcycles was pulling up to a sharp stop in front of a house somewhere on the West Bank. The house in Ramallah. Doron recognized it, but the camera angle was new. What seemed like dozens of policemen jumped out from the squad car whose flashing lights lit the scene. One policemen leapt over to curbside from the street, opened the back door of the car, and pulled something out. And then out from among the massed policemen in their dark uniforms stepped a small man in light clothing. It reminded Doron of magic shows he had seen in the Jerusalem theater courtyard as a child. Hajimi, Houdini. Hajimi squinted under the light. The camera focused on him, that handsome, boyish face, and as he noticed the camera's presence, Hajimi looked away. Toward the house. The door was opening.

A thin young man emerged. Thank God it's not her. The young man put out a hand to Hajimi, and as he pulled Hajimi in, Doron saw—just for a second, just behind the young man's shoulder—a woman's covered head. Hajimi moved in her direction and the door shut behind him.

Doron stepped back from the window. He closed his eyes and leaned against his mother's jalopy. He felt the odd tickle behind his eyes that signaled the onset of tears that he would never allow to emerge. The idea that she and Hajimi would just sit and mourn their baby, and receive visitors—Doron tried to comfort himself with this plausible version of the night's unwinding, but he doubted it, he doubted it. He hadn't seen Raad there at the door: maybe she had gotten rid of her chaperone. She and Hajimi could do what they wanted. No one would hear. He let himself feel all of his impermissible feelings. Why not?

Doron had been betrayed. Well, screw Yizhar, then. He knew how to get back at his tormentor. Doron was going to go to Marina. That's what he wanted, he realized now. He'd been wanting to for so long. No contact with the family. We'll see about that, night creature. Doron climbed into his mother's jalopy. No more of Yizhar and his crude scheming. No going cravenly to Shell to tell Yizhar's story. He would do the honorable thing. Put himself at Marina's mercy, and beg for her forgiveness. Offer himself up. For judgment. Let Marina decide.

CHAPTER TWENTY-ONE

*I*T HAD BEEN SO LONG SINCE GEORGE HAD ACTUALLY SET EYES on Hassan Hajimi that he had forgotten the effect his son-in-law's presence had on people. Hassan was so dazzlingly handsome—George had forgotten. The fellow walked in the door and the guests who had assembled there and were chatting drew their breath audibly. Was it because Hassan had done the unbelievable, and had managed to win release? Was it because he was a legend? Was it because of those eyes? Was it because he was good, or because he was evil? Hassan walked through the door and went directly to Marina and touched her shoulder softly, then reached down for her hand. He stood next to her, looking around the room.

George knew that another man in Hassan's position and from his background would probably have greeted his friends and supporters before he would have gone to his wife, but Hassan was different. For others, this would have been a political meeting to reconnect with backers and adherents. George wondered if Hassan had planned a political strategy for dealing with this occasion. He wondered what Hassan was feeling about Ibrahim; George felt connected in a new way to Hassan because of their shared loss. Looking at him, George could see traces of the child's face in the father's smile, in his high cheekbones, his serious eyes. (The thought came to George painfully: Perhaps Ibrahim's blue eyes came from Hassan and *not* from George's mother. . . .)

What a sad homecoming this must be for Hassan. George doubted he was thinking of anything but his family. It seemed unlikely, from his behavior. Standing there, holding tightly on to Marina, Hassan smiled at a few friends, and then saw his father-in-law across the room. He whispered something to his wife and came toward George.

Wish I could disappear, George thought. Wish I could sink beneath the floor. He felt overpoweringly that he had nothing to say that would be right. He felt he had nothing to say at all.

"Hassan," he said.

Hassan embraced him.

"Hassan, congratulations," George began.

Hassan smiled sadly. "Thanks. I'm not feeling much joy."

"I know," said George. George touched his arm gingerly. "The worst thing."

"Coming back to this house," Hassan said. "It's too hard. It's not how I ever thought it would be. When I permitted myself to imagine."

George looked at him. "Life seldom gives us what we imagine it will."

Oh, really, George? Oh, my, how profound. George's discomfort prompted him to issue declarations, but that was no excuse. How like a father-in-law he was, he thought. How despicable. Pompous blowhard—why did he say such a stupid thing? He was wary of Hassan, mistrusted him, but still, they shared so much now. How he must irritate Hassan, who was so immediate and so seemingly intimate. But Hassan's face betrayed no annoyance. His blue eyes looked on his father-in-law with undeserved equanimity and friendliness. Life seldom gives us what we imagine it will.

"That is very true, Doctor," a deep voice said from behind him. He turned. It was Ahmed. Out of the corner of his eye, George saw the big Palestinian photography book he'd been reading the other day. It was still sitting on the coffee table. Although he had read almost every word of it already, he wanted more than anything to pick it up now and rush off into a corner with it, alone.

"'Life seldom gives us what we expect,'" Ahmed intoned. He had a tight smile pasted on an otherwise forbidding expression. He and George had not spoken since the Ramallah rally two days earlier. "Such a profound observation. As we have all come to expect from you, Doctor. Very true. I remember you saying that you yourself did not expect that your son-in-law would accept the terms of his release, for example."

George glared at Ahmed. He recalled how certain he had been that Hassan would not accept a brokered freedom. Then he recalled the car ride after the rally, the thick, stupid-looking back of the driver's neck.

"How are you, George?" Ahmed asked.

"As well as can be expected," George said. George stood next to Hassan, as if there were solidarity between them. Hassan was watching George and Ahmed closely, with that little smile he had that looked so amused and yet was barely even a smile. George could feel the intensity of his son-in-law's observation. "Who invited the television cameras to my house?" George asked.

"*Your* house?" Ahmed smiled. "Your house is in America, George."

"*This* is his house, Uncle," Hassan said.

Ahmed shook his head at the two of them in feigned wonderment. He held a single decorative piece of pink pickled holiday cauliflower between his fingers, and now he waved it over the two of them like a censer.

"George Raad and Hassan Hajimi. Who would have supposed? We are so glad to have you back among us, Abu Ibrahim," Ahmed said to Hassan. Hassan flinched. It was a sign of respect to call a man by the name of his first son. Still, George was shocked. His eyes widened. No one had said Ibrahim's name aloud in George's presence since his return to Jerusalem. Ahmed popped the pickle into his mouth. He swallowed hurriedly, raising his eyebrows at George.

"Dah!" Ahmed said, smiling broadly. "George, I almost forgot to tell you. I saw the Chairman yesterday. He told me that he thinks you've behaved impeccably throughout this ordeal."

An outrageous lie! The only question in George's mind was whether the lie came from the Chairman or from Ahmed. George knew from a dozen sources that the Chairman was furious with him for repudiating the Authority and rejecting its campaign to find the soldier. Yet perhaps the Chairman wanted some kind of entente with George. It was possible.

"And how do *you* think I've behaved?" George asked.

"It has been a very hard time," Ahmed said.

"Thank you for working for my release, Uncle," Hassan said. Ahmed leaned forward and embraced Hassan, and over Hassan's shoulder, he smiled at George. George wanted to punch him. It was bad enough that he had used Ibrahim's death for his own political profit. But now! Whom did he think he was kissing when he kissed Hassan Hajimi? Was he kissing his own rosy political future? Was he embracing Hamas? George noticed that all the hugging and kissing was done away from the eyes of the international and Israeli television cameras, but in front of the very local eyes of all the assembled backers and funders and supporters and checkpoint *shabab* and long-time adherents and militants and anyone else who would find it to Amr's credit that he had negotiated Hassan's release.

George had forgotten his son-in-law's charm, but now it was brought back to him powerfully, as Hassan, released finally from Ahmed's embrace, looked over at his father-in-law and smiled wryly. When you were near him, it was impossible to believe that this gentle, open man could really be some kind of monster, as the Israelis liked to portray him. But if you turned away from that smile and listened to the youthful purveyors of Hassan's legend, to his supporters, everything became clear. Of course—at the very least—he supported the bombings.

Look who his friends were, after all! George surveyed the room: Silent men standing in corners. Excited boys trying to get near the hero. Certain mayors and local pols. That idiot lawyer from Ramallah—what was his name? Businessmen whose businesses had died years ago but who were still wielding power for social and cultural reasons beyond George's exile understanding. George watched as Hassan and the lawyer talked. They put their heads together like two bad boys up to no good. George did not find it inconceivable that one or the other would eventually put a knife to the soldier's throat.

Blow up buses! Burn the land out from under the feet of the Zionist oppressor! Terror is the legitimate war of a people without a state, without an army! Slit the throats of the drunken infidel dogs! Yeah! Go for it! Christ, thought George, looking at Hassan's expectant welcoming face as he turned away from the lawyer and began the long job of receiving each of the guests. He must believe all the propaganda; he probably dreams about The Palestinian People. The passion and commitment of the young. Watch it burn and explode.

George's Jerusalem of olive groves and goat herds and za'tar salesmen and eggplant sandwiches and boys in school uniform playing tennis was now a Boys' World of fire and weaponry and destruction. From the other side of the room, the lawyer was watching George, now, trying to catch his eye. The lawyer had come here to hustle his little secret, no doubt. Lieutenant Ari Doron. Ready, aim, fire! Muskets, cudgels, cutlasses, catapults, battering rams!

George had forgotten the boyish delight of destruction. Now, he simply longed for one final unswerving belief. He felt his joints weakening as Sheukhi approached. Swaying slightly, George watched as the lawyer sauntered across the room—and in the end made his wandering way not to George, but to the table of sweets and pickles. George leaned back against the wall to steady himself, and closed his eyes. He could feel his bones failing, his heart leaping and thrumming like a drummer playing out of time.

A CONSTANT MURMUR came from the living room. Marina sat with the sisters around the kitchen table, listening to their talk. They were eating sweets. The children were piled in the bedroom, watching television and drinking cherry syrup. Marina looked down at her hands, her sad old hands. Soon, Hassan would stop loving her, she thought. She would be sad and old, a virtual spinster, childless, who sat with her sisters-in-law in a kitchen in Ramallah while her dashing husband fought for the freedom of his people. She shook her head. What stereotypes people agree to live by, she thought.

And yet it could happen. The kitchen table, forever. The chipped cups. Ibrahim's bright drawing on the refrigerator door. She would leave it there, forever. She looked at the sisters again. This world, this fluorescent light, the rubble on the rooftop. Nihaya was chewing a nut. Fatima had the baby on her lap. These could be my companions for life, and the nieces, and the nephews. I will be a victim of politics. I already am.

Seeing Hassan out of prison was heartbreaking. He seemed like a refugee, out of place in his own home. She felt the tension in him. He was ready to be doing things, taking up where he left off. And where was that? She did not think that she could remain in Ramallah much longer. Dashing husband. She was afraid that she could no longer go along with the uses to which he put his courage and sangfroid.

Nihaya giggled at some joke of Tamira's, and Marina tried to listen. She had once been curious about the inner lives of these people whom she had known now for more than three years. They gave off few clues. Once, Fatima had smiled at a child on the street. Once, Marina had caught Tamira watching *The Brady Bunch*, by herself. That was about it. Now, Fatima was in on the joke with the others, and the sisters were almost touching heads, as if they were in a rugby scrum. They were laughing. Marina wondered what the joke could possibly be. The sisters were not usually funny. They made a practice of not laughing at Marina's attempts to lighten conversation, and nothing serious could be mocked. Nihaya had told Marina once that she did not like comedy—Marina wondered what that could mean. Not like comedy? Hassan's sister? Yet here Nihaya was, laughing, bent over with laughter; they were eating their sweets and nuts and almost cackling. And then suddenly they went silent and their backs straightened. Marina looked up to see what had caught their attention. Hassan was standing in the kitchen doorway.

Marina stood and went over to him. She put her arm around his waist and he kissed her lightly on the forehead. The sisters giggled, as if they had never seen such a thing. Maybe they hadn't, Marina thought. They stood, too, and awkwardly began clearing the table and putting on water for tea.

"Stop, stop," Hassan said, beginning to laugh. "What are you doing?"

"Making you some tea," Fatima said. She stood there, holding the kettle in midair.

"Tea is not what I want, sisters," he said, smiling at them.

"What do you want, then, Hassan?" Tamira asked.

He still had his arm around Marina. He looked at Tamira and bent his head slightly, raised his eyebrows, and smiled.

"We'll leave you, then," said Fatima, putting down the kettle with a thud.

She gathered the other sisters and the nuts and went into the bedroom with the children. Hassan sat down with Marina at the table.

"I feel I never leave this table," Marina said. He was holding both of her old, sad hands.

"I love this table," Hassan said. "I am so happy to be here with you. So happy. You can't believe it. I love this table so much." He leaned over and kissed the table. He looked up and smiled at her. "What seems unbearable and boring to you is like a fabulous dream to me."

"You are like a fabulous dream to me," she said. She realized she had almost forgotten how much she loved him. "Kiss the table again."

He kissed it with comic fervor. He raised his head after and looked at her. Her face seemed so calm, the Virgin of Notre Dame. He breathed slowly. He reached toward her and unpinned her head scarf. It sank down to her shoulders. Her hair fell around her face. She smiled and then pointed her chin at the table, and he turned away from her and kissed the table again. Doing as he was told. His shoulder blades were sharp under his white shirt. She could see his breath coming and going. His hair fell forward and she reached over to touch his bent head. She wanted to cry but she refused. He turned his face to her, resting his profile on the table's cool tin top. She wished the sisters and the children would go, would leave the bedroom empty, at least. She leaned down to him. As she bent her head to kiss him, she saw Ibrahim's old drawing rising over his shoulder: blue scribble that was sky, yellow stain for a sun, a few green lines of tree. This place will never be the same, was her last thought, and then she kissed the father of her child.

He kissed her back, and stood up slowly, and said, "I'm kicking them out of our room."

"Okay," she said.

"I'll tell them I need to take a nap." He smiled. "I'm tired—from prison, you know. Exhausted." He yawned dramatically.

"Ah," Marina said.

He went through the door, and she heard laughter and complaining and then the silence of the television set. In a few minutes he returned.

"I have kicked them out of our room." He was smiling.

She stood up and walked over to him and they went into their bedroom like a bride and groom. He held her tightly around the waist as if he might fall if she weren't there, and she leaned against him.

"AHMED AMR."

Ahmed whirled around at the sound of his own urgently whispered name, his keffiyeh making a trail of light behind him under the streetlamps outside Hajimi's house. The voice was low and desperate.

And there was its owner, that moustachioed, old-fashioned-looking West Banker, standing next to the green dumpster. He looked familiar, like someone you've seen before but only in a photograph. He had a bit of a hangdog look to him. Who was he, again? Ahmed hoped the fellow was not about to assassinate him. A shame, at a moment of triumph like this one. Maybe I should hire a bodyguard after all, Ahmed thought. Of course, that *would* be my dying thought. That thought, and the taste of those wonderful pink pickles.

He looked at the man.

"Yes," Ahmed said.

"You are Ahmed Amr."

"Yes," Ahmed said again, wondering, Should I admit to being myself?

"I know the name of the soldier."

"What soldier?" Amr asked.

"What soldier? *What* soldier?" Sheukhi looked at Amr, and then began to laugh through his nose.

When he caught his breath, Ahmed was still watching him.

"Okay," Ahmed said. "You've had your fun." Ahmed remembered now who this odd man was.

"My God," said Sheukhi, "your arrogance astounds me. Your cynicism is breathtaking. Your indifference is *royal.* You don't even care. The soldier isn't even remotely on your mind. Forgotten, eh?"

"You don't understand. There is no soldier anymore. What soldier? It's over, my good man," Ahmed said. Perhaps he was being a little grand, but he could afford it. It seemed clear that he was not about to be killed. And it *was* over, as far as Ahmed was concerned. Hajimi was released. Ahmed had had his political victory out of Find the Soldier. He was on to other, bigger things now. Making a new stand on a disputed hill outside Jerusalem. This afternoon, he had pitched a tent near its summit. Bit like the old days.

"'It's over, my good man,'" repeated Sheukhi, in a mocking tone. "Who the fuck do you think you are, effendi?"

"Listen, Sheukhi, I know who *you* are," Ahmed said, tightening his keffiyeh and pulling himself up to his full height. "I know where you live, I know who your family is, I know your practice, I know your upstanding brother, and you had better watch your attitude toward me, sir." Ahmed had never before delivered a speech like this, and it thrilled him, although he would have regarded his behavior as distasteful and embarrassing and even politically incorrect in someone else. We are so forgiving toward ourselves, he thought. He was particularly proud that he had remembered the man's family name.

"Are you threatening me, Excellency?" Sheukhi glared at him, and Ahmed thought, This man is brave. He is capable of action. Who knows what he could do? The glare reminded him of George back in Hajimi's living room. Poor me, Ahmed thought, no one likes me tonight.

"The Authority will take care of the Authority's business," Ahmed said. "*Habibi*, I am not threatening you. I am simply advising you to leave things to us. If we think the matter requires further attention, we will certainly see to it."

"But I know the name." Sheukhi pointed a finger at Ahmed's chest and thrust it forward with each syllable. "I . . . know . . . the . . . name. . . ."

"Well then, out with it, patriot," Ahmed said.

Sheukhi told him.

Ahmed's face registered nothing.

"Not only do I know it," Sheukhi went on. "Raad knows it, his daughter knows it, and her husband, too, now."

A flush began to color Ahmed's face. He was shocked, and even hurt, that George knew the soldier's name and hadn't told him. And now this man knew that George hadn't told him. Embarrassing.

"How long has Raad had this information?" Ahmed asked the man.

"Oh, days, days . . ." Sheukhi said. He sensed a vulnerability and pressed on. "I suppose he didn't want to tell you. Possibly, he was worried that you wouldn't do the right thing or that you might—"

"Thanks for your information, brother." Ahmed interrupted him, turning to go, only remotely expecting to hear the crack of a gunshot.

"What will you do with this information, *habibi?*" Sheukhi asked, putting an extra accent on the "brother," in imitation of Amr.

"Whatever we deem necessary," Ahmed said without turning. Then he remembered—the compliment. He turned.

"Listen, Sheukhi," he said. "I appreciate your coming to me with this. Really. Anything I can do for you, I will do. I think you are a very brave man. I will tell the Chairman what you have done for us. Surely it will not go without notice. Here is my card. You are a real patriot."

Sheukhi took the card but did not look at it. He watched Ahmed depart but did not say thank you—or even goodbye.

I better hire that bodyguard, Ahmed thought.

My FRIEND, COMRADE, thank you for this important piece of the puzzle, Hajimi had said. You have helped me to see things more clearly. I am your servant.

His empty blue eyes were like portholes into the sea. Mahmoud had never seen eyes that were so removed.

And what will you do with what I've told you?

For the moment, nothing. Nothing at all.

Nothing at all?

No, nothing. There is the mourning period to be observed. And it is Ramadan.

Hajimi seemed not even to focus on the soldier's name, maybe he wouldn't even remember it come tomorrow morning. His face had turned blank when Sheukhi started explaining who he was. He shook his head unhappily as it became clear that if Sheukhi knew, then his sweet, lovely wife must know, also. Sheukhi tried to make *that* clear. But the fellow didn't want to hear about it, really. Invoking his religious excuses like a damned imam. Well, Hajimi maybe had other things on his mind for tonight. Marina Raad had color in her cheeks again. She would be a lot of fun, so Sheukhi thought. High-strung girls always were.

So Hajimi was another one who was not interested in finding this soldier. So many Palestinians not interested in doing their duty.

They were all a bunch of snobs, George Raad, Ahmed Amr—Hajimi, too, who had been, until this evening, Mahmoud Sheukhi's hero. Hajimi didn't care, even though it was his very own son who had been murdered. Snob. Sheukhi could read it right away in their faces, their immediate, instinctive cool disregard for him. And why? He came from a good family, a family with a name, a major clan, he had a college education, was a professional. And he could imagine and do what they were incapable of imagining and doing.

The problem was, he was too Palestinian for them, not enough of a citizen of the world. Fuck them. Oh, fuck them extremely and in every way. He spit on Ahmed Amr. He would show them all, even Hassan Hajimi, who had too much on his mind to avenge the blood of his only son.

It would be Mahmoud and Jibril, then, working together, uncle and nephew. Jibril respected him. You are the only adult who still understands the people's struggle, Jibril had said the other night, while Mahmoud was commenting on the news for his nephew in Adnan's office.

Right.

Adnan had snorted, but fuck Adnan, too, and his petty concerns. Mahmoud was sick of them by now. Glassblowers, all. Sitting by the fire and only puffing, blowing air into sand, making bubbles and globes and long, thin breakable necks. No more of that, no more of that prissy, hot, sedentary leisure. He was going to show them what you do with a fiery furnace. He was going to shatter their pretty transparent world. They were too good for the struggle, too pure, too removed. Not he. He was in it. He knew all about it. He would teach them. He was made to be a teacher. Learn your lessons, boys. Don't forget, now.

"WE'RE GOING TO leave you tomorrow," George said, turning to Hassan. The reception had ended, and even the sisters had gone home. It was very late for all of them.

"What? Where are you going to go?" Hassan asked. He twirled a lock of Marina's hair around his finger, and untwirled it, then twirled it again. The automatic way he did it reminded George of the prayer beads of old tea-drinkers. Marina looked happy—happier, anyway. George wondered how long it would last, how long before she realized that her husband's identity and the choices he had made in life were inextricably tied to Ibrahim's fate. Philip had come up from the little guest bedroom, and was standing next to George. He held George's antique leather suitcase (one of his relics, Marina's mother had called it), the one with travelers' stamps on it. Marina recognized it immediately. It was like a prop from an old movie, but real; it was his grandfather's, of course, with stamps on it from Cairo and Alexandria in the 1930s, and from Suez and even the former Transjordan, for Christ's sake.

Philip put the bag next to the front door. He looked up at everyone.

"We're packing," he said brightly, and disappeared again down the hallway.

"We'll go to the hotel," George said to Hassan. "I think there will be enough happening here without me and Philip to increase your caseload."

"We wish you would stay," Hassan said, but George detected relief in his son-in-law's tone. And in his daughter's expression. Finally he was doing the right thing, and what was it? Leaving, naturally. Leaving was what he did best. It made sense that he should have this gift. He had started at a young age.

Hassan sighed. "I wish the celebrations would end," he said.

"You can end them, Hassan," George said. "One simple word from you, and they are finished."

"Yes, yes," Hassan said. "I know. But people feel the need, and then, there is so little to celebrate these days."

"True enough," George said, "true enough." He felt a shocking swell of tears come into his eyes. My God, what's happening to me? Everyone's crying around here, but for God's sake, not me! Christ, was he becoming sentimental? After a lifetime spent in skepticism and hard brutal facts. Are my tears for Ibrahim? For myself, and my imminent departure? For Palestine, of all things? But he realized that it was something about Hassan, his voice. Hassan had the uncanny actor's knack of conveying powerful but inarticulate—and possibly nonexistent—emotion. And just then, he had again looked at George with something very like affection or at least sympathy. There was some new emotional connection between the two of them, George felt. This hard man and I: maybe we are more alike than I had suspected. They both had come to understand, and only recently, the futility of everything they had spent a lifetime doing. Or so George thought. Both were hanging on to a few last shreds of dignity.

George began counting the luggage Philip had been piling up. One, two, three, his typewriter (an antique, like me, he thought), Philip's knapsack, Grandfather's old valise . . . and then he saw that Marina hadn't moved. She might as well have been framed by an arched niche in the wall, her position was so still. He noticed, not for the first time, how beautiful his daughter was. She was standing there near the open door, looking out into the moonlit garden. Like some ancient form of jeweled adornment, tears sparkled down her cheeks.

• • •

She loved Hassan and she knew she had to leave him.

She was lying in bed earlier, looking up out the window at the moon. Hassan's hand was on her knee. Blue shadows moved over them.

"Beautiful sky, isn't it?" he said.

She nodded.

"Sheets are so soft," he said. He moved closer to her.

She turned her head toward him.

"That was nice, wasn't it?" he said, smiling. "We're still good at it."

"Yes," she said, letting him kiss her.

He rested his hand lightly on her hip.

"Tell me about the soldier, Marina," he said.

She was silent.

"You know his name?"

She put two fingers on Hassan's lips, then took them off. He kissed her again.

"I heard it, I'm sure," she said. "But I don't remember it."

"Ah," Hassan said. "Effect of stress, maybe."

She moved closer so that they were facing each other on their sides.

"Post-traumatic stress disorder," he said, stroking her hair.

"Do you think you'd recognize the name if you heard it?" he asked.

"I don't know," she said, turning her head again to look out at the sky. Her heartbeat quickened.

"It's Ari Doron. Does that sound familiar?"

"Yes," she said. "Yes, it does. That could be it."

"Good." He pulled her around to face him. "Again?" he asked, smiling.

"He tried to help us, Hassan," she said. She felt she had to tell him that.

"Uh-hunh. Good," he said. "Good for him." He played with the ends of her hair, and smiled at her. She pushed his hand away gently.

"It wasn't completely his fault," she said.

"Of course not, Marina." He kissed her. "Of course not."

She could feel him thinking, weighing, deciding.

"Of course not," he said. "Still . . ."

He pulled her toward him and they began again.

Leaving Ramallah the next morning was a pleasure, a preview of how liberating it was going to be to leave Palestine entirely, if George could ever, ever, ever get away. Watching the low walls fly by, he thought he understood a little of what it must feel like to be Hassan. Escaping from unrelenting dreariness and hopelessness—George felt that way, *leaving* Ra-mallah, and Hassan must have felt it, too, going in the opposite direction, away from Jerusalem and prison, and home to Ramallah and his wife. George and Philip got through the checkpoint without much trouble, us-ing the VIP pass the Authority had issued to George before his break with Ahmed. Ahmed had not canceled George's card after George walked out of the meeting at Orient House, nor even after the speech at the rally, even though that would be typical Authority protocol, always tit-for-tatting you, George thought. The valid card was a mark of the Chairman's respect, re-spect for George's reputation for making a stink out of anything he chose. Or perhaps it was just a mark of his respect for anyone who was under Ahmed Amr's protection, which George ostensibly still was.

The Israeli soldiers were respectful, deferential even, and it was too early for protests to have begun, if they were going to begin at all, now that Hassan was released. A few trucks had been moved to the shoulder for in-spection, and did not impede their progress. The soldiers practically bowed to George, they were so careful nowadays of anyone named Raad or Ha-jimi. George enjoyed the show, the quick return of his card, no questions asked, the welcoming, after-you-sir wave the weasely little officer gave the car as he let them pass through. You bet you better bow down before me, George thought. He wondered if any of them had been there that night.

Philip was at the wheel of the tinny little Uno. He drove well. He did everything well. George was glad to be getting out of Ramallah and out of Hassan's house and out of the little guest bedroom next to the only bath-room, on the way to the laundry shed. He felt engulfed by the crisis and the situation in a way he hadn't been since the beginning of his political involvement. He didn't want to be involved anymore. He was over-whelmed by the rest of life already, without becoming a part of Ahmed's and Hassan's political games, games that would soon end, possibly wreck-ing everything that remained of what was valuable: his family, his beliefs, his dream of home.

The worst of it was that the man who was destroying the fabric of George's past was a part of that past himself. George couldn't reconcile himself to the paradox. He had never before imagined he was capable of hating someone he loved, but he was beginning to feel he might hate Ahmed now. You loved someone, and then discovered your love was not equally returned, or—in the case of Ahmed—possibly not returned at all. The realization was shaming, and—since shame and embarrassment were the human emotions George experienced most powerfully, more than love and hate, or so he believed—the humiliation began to sour the old affection, began to erode it. George felt it slipping away. How long could we go on squabbling while the rest of the Palestinian people sacrificed endlessly for our mistakes? And Ibrahim was dead.

"WHAT DID YOU THINK of the celebration?" George asked Philip, as they drove down to the great hulking white statue that the Israelis had erected to commemorate the '67 war—George thought it looked like three simultaneously unfurling toilet-paper rolls. They made a left, went past the Hyatt and the monolithic Israeli police complex, down through the former villages of Sheikh Jarrah and Wadi Joz—now part of greater East Jerusalem—to the Street of the Wreckage, as Philip had named it. The Street of the Wreckage was a Palestinian version of an industrial zone— really just a place to pick up a used air-conditioner part or a length of fencing, or get a burst tire mended. The journey recapped the entire Palestinian experience, from lost war and destroyed heritage to the blackened junk pile, ending at the American Colony Hotel, which was George's personal oasis in Jerusalem.

"What did you think, Philip? Come on. Quite a party, eh?"

"Interesting," Philip said. "Good pickles."

"Part of Marina's Palestinian solidarity," George said. "Sisters probably did 'em."

"Hassan was happy to be reunited with his wife," Philip added.

"I'll say," George said. He enjoyed the occasional Americanism.

"She too," Philip said.

"Yup."

"Amr was pleased with himself. As if he had somehow obtained the release all by himself."

"Self-satisfied as ever," said George. "I don't believe he has changed since babyhood. He was probably proud of the way he suckled, knowing Ahmed." George looked out the front window. On the Israeli side of town just across the street from the wall that protected the hotel's pool, a handful of Israeli hotels were being erected.

"He's accomplished an interesting thing, though," Philip said.

"Stop saying 'interesting,' Philip. 'Interesting' is just a refusal to say whatever it is you really think. Say what you think."

"All right. He pushed Find the Soldier."

"That's nothing. Unless you're counting the dead at the checkpoints."

"Oh, not really nothing. As far as he's concerned. It's gotten the Israelis back involved, which is what he intended. They're back at the bargaining table. And Hassan is out of prison. As Amr always says: 'Judge actions only by results.'"

"Despicable motto."

"Tried and true, though," Philip said.

"Besides, the only thing the Israelis are bargaining about is how much of our land they should keep."

"Ahmed would say that it's a miracle they're giving back any at all."

"Please, Philip. You're undercutting my carefully nurtured respect for you. What other 'interesting' things has he accomplished, according to you?"

Philip switched on his blinker while they waited at the light. "His proudest achievement: he has neutralized his greatest enemy."

"What?" George said. "Who?"

Philip hesitated as he turned past the gas station toward the hotel's entrance.

"Who?" George asked again. "Hassan?"

"What?" said Philip, as if he had forgotten what they were talking about.

"His greatest enemy is: The Chairman? The Prime Minister?"

"No," said Philip, shaking his head and almost laughing. "No. You are, of course, Doctor." They turned into the hotel's driveway.

George was stunned. Was it true? No, he wanted to cry, no. Ahmed is my best friend. He is the only one who remembers everything, who knows every detail, understands every nuance.

"Don't say that," he said to Philip.

"Okay, I won't."

"Why am I his worst enemy? Tell me that," George said, folding his arms over his chest as if he had just demanded the impossible.

"Because you believe in something, and he doesn't," Philip said. He stopped the car to wait while a woman piled three children into a minivan and tried to negotiate her way out of the hotel's small parking lot.

"He and I believe in the same thing." George tapped his foot impatiently. He felt uncomfortable in this conversation. Philip was approaching truth: Oh, George hated that.

"What is that? Palestinian statehood, you mean? A 'homeland'?"

Philip put a sarcastic spin on the word. "That's easy, the easy stuff.

I'm talking about the biggest things, Doctor. Imperishable things." George watched the minivan's red brake lights flicker on and off.

"Like?" George asked.

"I'm not answering that question," Philip said. "You know what they are, you're just trying to trap me into sounding stupid by enumerating them. But it can all be distilled into one word." Philip leaned back into his seat, shaking his head as he watched the woman try to get out of her space.

"And that word is?" George asked.

"That word is . . . Ibrahim. I know no one says his name, but he is the key. That's what Ahmed doesn't get. Decency and honor. There, I've mentioned the imperishable things. You happy?"

George was silent. What Philip said was undeniable. Ahmed with his hooded eyes just couldn't give a fuck about that baby's fate. Things and people existed only to serve Ahmed's political aims. But was that wrong? In the long run, was it wrong?

"*What* is she *doing?*" Philip put his hands into the air. The minivan was backing up, then moving forward, failing to emerge from its tight space.

"She's trying to get a good angle, poor thing," George said. "Listen to you, Philip who is from Beit Jala near Bethlehem. 'Decency, honor.' Where did a Palestinian like you pick up this Victorian lingo? You're beginning to sound like a British officer, Philip. People who uphold those ideals are just silly, useless, and pointless. They're suckers."

"Now you're just parroting what Amr would say."

"No. First of all he'd never say it, he'd just think it. And anyway, I'm just saying what I believe is true. If you stand for those old useless things, you're a dead man, like me. And I *am* a dead man, and I can't even manage to stand for those things. I stand for my family, only my family, now, after this business with Ibrahim. Imagine my being reduced to that. A Raad man. If I were more like my grandfather, I'd have a blunderbuss and a saber, instead of a heart condition."

"Still, it's better than being Ahmed," Philip said.

"Ah, there you go, young lady," George said, as the van finally chugged up the hill. "I'm not sure it's better, Philip."

"Ahmed's purely political," Philip said. "And he's a preemptor, a first-striker. He doesn't wait for human feeling to enter in: look how fast he moved into Find the Soldier."

"That came from the street." George looked at Philip hopefully. Ahmed always liked to say: I do not lead the people. The people lead *me*.

"Not entirely, as we know from the meeting at Orient House." Philip parked the car down near the pool, and they sat there. "Do you trust him, really, Doctor?"

"No," George said. "And on the other hand, yes. Yes, implicitly."

"There was a guy there last night." Philip looked over at George.

"Well?" George looked out at the pool's entrance. The gate was closed. "There were lots of guys, Philip. Hassan trades in 'guys.'"

"This guy, this one friend of Hassan's, told me a story."

"Go on, Philip. I know you can't hold back." George wondered what the story could be. He leaned back. By now, I should be able to take what life deals me.

"You won't like it."

"I seldom like anything I hear, especially about Ahmed."

"So?"

"Go on." He closed his eyes.

"This guy, he told me that the threats against you, after *Perils of Peace* was published in Arabic? He said that when Ahmed Amr called you up in Cambridge, he already knew exactly who was threatening you, and that there were two reasons nothing was done to put an end to the threats."

"Uh-hunh. What were the reasons?" George was still sitting back with his eyes closed, but his entire body stiffened.

"One: The people who were threatening you, Amr needed. At the time. These were the guys based in Damascus. And two: No one here cared what might happen to you, except for Amr. He cared, but not too much."

"Mmmm."

"What?" said Philip.

"Oh well." George felt his throat constrict.

"And the attack, the guy said, was to be by letter bomb, and the reason it didn't come off was the usual: incompetence, disorganization. Thank God for idiocy!" Philip sighed. "Anyway, so he said. Could all be lies."

"Probably lies, Philip," George said quietly. "I'm sure."

Philip's shoulders rose like a cat's.

"You just can't bring yourself to condemn him, can you?" Philip asked. "Sentiment, Doctor. You are confused because of your old affection for Ahmed." Philip looked across the front seat at George. "But I don't believe you can let that cloud your judgment."

"Aren't *you* tough as nails," George said. Two waiters in white emerged from the pool gate. They wiped their hands across their aprons.

"Ahmed is." Philip looked at him again.

"I feel much less affection for him than you imagine," George said, using his brisk voice, his professorial clipped inflection. "In fact, right now, I don't think I can bear the sight of him again. So don't feel so sorry for my wasted fondness."

George looked away, and Philip got out.

George clicked down on what appeared to be the Uno's door handle, but the door wouldn't budge. He pushed it down again. Nothing.

What a fool I've been, George thought. He grasped another chrome handle that he thought might open the door, but still, nothing happened.

Philip had come around to the passenger side by now, and was watching.

To imagine that Ahmed was malevolent; it was too much for George. He thought of Ahmed's strong grasp, the way he welcomed George each time as if he were standing at the family hearth, the warmth of his every gesture like a winter's fire, and the light of his eyes under the fold of his keffiyeh . . . and then just the memory of that irritating keffiyeh and all it pretended to stand for but did not stand for, all it suggested but did not *mean*, all the distance it represented that Ahmed had traveled away from their shared childhood, and all the unfair, unfounded reproaches it offered to someone like George, made an acid rise in George's throat. George did not want to think that distrust of Ahmed Amr would become his one final unswerving belief.

Fiddling with all the hooks and handles on the car door, George finally snapped a little clasp that exposed a red bar of color. Yes, he thought grimly. It helps to unlock it. Philip came forward and pulled the door open. George looked up at him. Philip extended a hand.

"I'm fine," George said, refusing the hand and lifting himself out of the car in what seemed like slow motion.

"THANK YOU, thanks, *shukran*," George said, pushing some money into the hand of the bellboy who let them into their suite. The bellboy flipped on the lights, turned on the air-conditioning, motioned to the welcome basket of fruit.

"Have a good day," he said, bowing backward out the door.

George was exhausted. He sat down heavily on his bed.

"I'm going to order some breakfast," Philip said. "Do you want something?"

"I'm not hungry," George said.

Philip looked at him.

"I'll order you some eggs," Philip said.

"You do what you like, Philip."

George fell back on the bed. The high, blank white ceiling comforted him. Today or tomorrow, or soon, anyhow, he would go out into Jerusalem, finally, go to the old house, and to the hospital. The doctors at the Friends Clinic had told George what he knew was correct. If he didn't go in and have his tests in the next day or two and certainly this week, he was taking a serious risk. It was the equivalent, they said, of just resigning yourself. And why not? he thought. But he would go in, and hear the bad news. He could take it.

George wanted to go home. He had been meaning to do it before, and now, he felt he needed to. He would tell Philip: Get the car, I want to go home. He was ready, now, to knock on the door of Grandfather's house and go in. This was what it was all about, wasn't it, in the end? History was history, and not as reversible as we might wish, it turned out. It was to be confronted, not denied. Israelis were living in his house, and were likely to go on living there until the house crumbled, which it might never do given its solid construction, which had already withstood two earthquakes and countless wars and skirmishes. Would Israelis be sitting around *his* dining room table? Would they be looking through the same colored glass in the back window? Perhaps they had had it removed. It was so typically *Arab*. Would they walk over the same enormous pink stones in the courtyard? Would it feel like home? To them? To him?

A waiter came to the door with breakfast. George heard the clanking of the rollable, foldout table in the other room, the stir of silverware. Philip was murmuring directions and thanks. George remained motionless on his bed. He did not want eggs. His body felt empty now; that was good. He felt light, unburdened physically. Now if only his mind would go blank.

He clenched and unclenched his fists. He had read that this was good for releasing tension, in some sidebar in a cardiology self-help guide, next to a chart about situations that provoke anxiety and stress. Laymen were obsessed with stress. Divorce was always number one. Death of a loved one, number two. Moving or changing domiciles, number three. He wondered where threatened assassination ranked. Clench, unclench. Betrayal of friendship?

Loss of homeland? Came under "changing domiciles," probably.

He tried deep breathing, but only felt a terrible, shattering loss of self as he waited to take each next breath, and panic. Was he getting enough air? He breathed deeply again, and held the breath, then released. This was how he fell asleep, or tried to, these days.

He felt the end coming.

Those stirrings, the slip and slide of the heartbeat, the errant syncopation that was beyond control. He did not want to leave so much undone.

George swallowed hard and fiddled absently with the bedclothes. He stared up at the white ceiling. His heart stalled and stopped and then turned over. Forward march, again. He took another deep breath and felt the end coming toward him, aiming at him with impeccable accuracy.

George wondered what he would do if he had a gun. He had wondered this before, often and idly. Usually, it was in an everyday situation. Someone cut him off on the highway. The cashier at the drugstore was stupid or incompetent or rude or all three. A colleague was ignorant. A gas station attendant seemed to harbor anti-Arab sentiment. Now he wondered: If I had a gun, could I use it—on Ahmed? Would I even dream of such a thing? And wouldn't it be wonderful! He wanted to erase Ahmed's contented, self-satisfied expression. In the other room, Philip was dragging chairs across the rug to the table. George imagined a shiny metal revolver, light like a toy. His eyes shut. He was half asleep.

He's handling the gun, a present from his father, polished and shiny. It's Christmastime in Jerusalem, snow on the palm trees. In the conference room at Orient House, George is walking slowly toward Ahmed. Sandra is standing in a thin, deep blue silk dressing gown in the corner. Ahmed strides across the room to meet George with open arms. George smiles, whips out the gun, and fires. Goodbye, you clever dog. Philip is calling him from the other room.

Doctor?

George half awakens. Ahmed falls to the floor. Why not? Half conscious, now, George adds a pool of blood for effect. Good, looks good. A few coffee cups strewn shattered across the floor. Faces aghast.

Doctor?

Why not? After all, Ahmed deserves it. In his grandiose tent on a bluff overlooking the city; ever the sheikh. And George has nothing to lose. He's sick: anyone can see that. Any act is permitted, because George will feel no consequence for very long. Philip can get me a gun, George thought. Would he?

"Doctor, Doctor," Philip was calling from the other room. "Your food is here."

I want one, George thought as he began to fall asleep again. I want one.

CHAPTER TWENTY-TWO

*P*HILIP HAD GONE OUT TO THE HOTEL LOBBY TO PREPARE THE way. From the top drawer of his dresser, George pulled out the little money bag his father had always carried, a small French leather thing. He opened it and took out the key. No chance the lock it once fitted would still be there, but he put it in his pocket, anyway. His lucky charm. He went out. The courtyard was bright and crowded with warmly dressed guests eating croissants and eggs and drinking coffee in the cold. Ramadan did not seem to be having much effect here.

George looked fixedly down at the path and the shrubbery in order not to have to talk to anyone who might consider accosting him. He gave a small nod hello to his friend the upside-down goldfish. It was another very sunny day: two in a row might mean the rains were ending. He hoped so. The rains had depressed him, they seemed to carry everything away with them, rubble, stones, litter, people, places, history. In the lobby, he found Philip standing with a cup of coffee.

"No necktie?" he said to Philip.

"My concession to Israeli informality," Philip said.

"I wouldn't grant them even that," George said. "Make 'em squirm! You're too well brought up, Philip."

Philip laughed. He put his cup down on an empty brass table.

In the hotel's driveway stood several minivans and Jeeps.

"Taking subjects and dignitaries to Gaza to offer tithes to the Chairman, I suppose?" George said, gesturing at the vehicles.

"Something like that," Philip said. "Amr just left."

George nodded.

Philip looked at him.

"Come on, then," Philip said. "We're over here."

George walked at his side to the Uno. He was feeling virtually spry, keeping pace with Philip footstep for footstep. He felt like sprinting. He wished suddenly that he had a woman here at his side and not his dutiful Philip. A woman in a very tight skirt and fashionable silk blouse, and high heels; or failing that, barefoot, in jeans and a skimpy tee shirt.

A small man buzzing like a mosquito came running up to them, and when he came near enough, George realized the buzzing sound was French. The little fellow identified himself as a reporter for Agence France-Presse. He pulled a notebook out of his pocket, looking at George expectantly.

"*Alors?*" the man said.

"*Alors*, what?" George replied.

"*Alors, Docteur Raad, que dites-vous de la campagne 'trouvez le soldat'?*" he asked. What do you think of the Find the Soldier campaign?

"*Je dis* that I do not give interviews," George said. "So go away. Come on, Philip, please, let's get out of here."

THE GRILLE AT THE TOP of the door was the one his father had put up, an intricate lacework of deer and trees, but it seemed lower and smaller, somehow. There were three shiny newish locks on the door. Even at home, the Israelis were security obsessed. On the other hand, in such a situation, who wouldn't change the lock? He nodded at Philip with his chin, and Philip rang the bell. On the right-hand side of the doorjamb a mezuzah had been affixed. George shook his head at it. The huge cypress cast its remembered shadow across the front of the house. On the second floor, an unshaded window reflected the cold sky. They waited.

Philip rang again, and just as he lifted his finger from the button, the door opened. A young woman in jeans stood in the doorway, looking at them curiously. We must be an odd apparition, George thought to himself: this formal-looking old Arab man, and the younger one, foreign-seeming as well. She had a dishtowel in her hand.

"Can I help you?" she asked in Hebrew, looking at him curiously. "*Efshar la'azor lecha?*"

"I'm George Raad," George said in English.

She certainly recognized the name, George thought, watching her shocked eyes. She wound a stray lock of hair behind her ear.

"Oh," she said, switching to slightly accented English. She paused.

She looked over her shoulder down the long dark hallway into the house, and then back at the unbidden visitors. "Oh, I'm sorry. I don't know what I'm supposed to do in this situation."

"Me neither," George said. He smiled.

"Oh well, why don't you come in?" She moved out of their way.

The first room was the grandest room, with a domed ceiling. George felt the past surround him. The house felt smaller—he was bigger, that was all. He felt dizzy with the past, as if it were suddenly physical, after all the years of dreaming and remembering and invoking. Here was that wall, these old tiles, that door out to the terrace—and through that window, the suddenly and specifically remembered patch of sun and sky and neighbor's arching roof. His throat caught with a terrible sadness and love. Philip and the girl were watching him. He tried to keep his features arranged. Probably he was not entirely successful, he felt.

The girl walked ahead of them, and George saw his father in a three-piece suit marching up the hallway.

"I think my mother's out in the garden," the girl said.

George knew that his father would be coming into the room to welcome his suppliers, who had traveled in from the countryside for their annual gathering in Jerusalem. George watched them all standing politely in a corner of the big front room. Masri from the Nablus area was biting his nails, and Qawasmi from Hebron was shifting from foot to foot. Like them, the others were important landowners and clan leaders and cultivators in their own regions, and yet there they stood, these tall, grown men, on the elaborate tile floor, the same tile floor, now slightly chipped here and there, but probably slightly chipped back then (yes, there was the jug-shaped chip near the door, oh, familiar chip!). There they stood shifting and nervous in their heavy robes, waiting silently for an audience with the worldly city merchant as if they were illiterate nomads. They looked like shepherds from Bible pictures. And here came his father now, crossing the Israeli girl's path and flinging noisily into the room on a flow of formal but effusive greetings, wrapping one arm around Masri, and the other around some other old robed shadow. The sound of their Arabic, the *kif halak*s and *marhaba*s and the *inshallah*s of course, and then the endless outpourings of numbers and figures and sums. And the eating.

George and Philip followed the girl down the hallway. A long red Shirvan runner used to keep this corridor warm, George remembered. Where was it now? Sold by this girl's family or stored in some musty Israeli bomb shelter, probably. Or carted to Amman by his father and left behind. It didn't matter, he told himself. Things do not matter, houses, rugs, chairs, keys: they are all just symbols of times past and people lost. He missed that rug very badly, just now.

The girl slipped through a door to the right and his mother swept out of a bedroom in her fur coat, with lipstick on—the transformation of his mother from everyday lady to beautiful, mysterious, desirable being, all wrought by a silk dress, and fur and lipstick—and leaned down to kiss him goodbye. The memory of her perfume enveloped him. He held on to to Philip's arm. At the end of the hallway, the tall French doors had been covered in insulating plastic.

They entered what used to be the dining room and study. In the corner, dusting the top of a television, was a woman about George's age.

"Mom, we have visitors," the girl said to the woman in Hebrew.

The woman turned.

George saw a face he would never have recognized anywhere else in the world, but here he recognized it. It was the little girl who lived in back, in the cramped renters' apartment on the first floor. She came from a family of very poor Arabic-speaking Jews from Beirut. He recalled that he and she had once run away from home together and hidden behind a bush in the Rose Garden park a block away until George's mother found them. Leila was her name. She stood there looking at him intently over her reading glasses.

"*Kif halak*, George," she said. He saw that there were sudden tears in her eyes.

He looked at her, and smiled politely, and shook his head. He couldn't respond to her quick emotion.

She couldn't take her eyes off him, and he shifted under her intense gaze.

"I am so sorry about your grandson," she said finally, in what sounded like little-used Arabic.

He kept standing there.

"Do you think we could have a glass of water for Dr. Raad?" Philip asked, after a silence.

"Oh, my God, yes," the girl said, running off.

"Sit down, please," Leila said.

The chair she gestured to was the twin of the chair that sat in front of George's television in Cambridge.

He felt his heart squeezing inside his chest. He shook his head.

"I can't," he said. I want to oblige you, he thought, but I can't. I don't want to make any trouble, but I must. After all, he couldn't very well sit in that chair. Someone was in it already. His mother was there, crossing and uncrossing her legs, making her nylons whisper as she talked to him about school and his maths test and the tennis team. He was a little boy in shorts, sitting, almost lost, in the enormous cushions of the other chair.

"Please," Leila said.

He stared at the chair. She looked at it. He could tell that she hadn't thought about it in twenty years or more, if ever. But she remembered. He heard her take a breath.

"Sit here, then," she said, pointing to the couch.

He walked over stiffly, and sat down. Philip hovered over him.

"I wondered if you would come," Leila said. "I saw you on the television."

The girl brought a glass of water.

It was his mother's dining room table, he could see that now, from the couch. He took a sip of the water.

"*Shukran,*" he said to Leila.

"Oh, George," she said.

She was trying to be matter-of-fact, because she was Israeli, and that was a habit with them. But she couldn't quite manage it, he noticed.

He tried, too, because it was his habit to be diffident and removed, but what he could not do a second time in this place was distance himself.

THE BOY AWOKE to a loud burst of masculine laughter. George's bedroom was adjacent to the dining room and he padded out in his pajamas, rubbing his eyes. There they all were, all the men, in their robes, sitting around the table near the wood-burning stove, hunched over, drinking yet another enormous pot of tea. His father lifted him up and sat him on the table where he remained like a treasured centerpiece for what seemed hours, in memory, incorrectly answering questions about the price of oranges and loquats to pleased laughter from the men, and doing sums concerning the weight of boxes and crates with the seriousness of utter ignorance. The men brought him sweets from Habb Rumman, or sometimes creamy Istanbuli cheese from Zapheriades' grocery. He remembered his father kissing him over and over on the top of his head. It seemed a tableau from another century.

• • •

"You LOOK WELL," Leila said in English.

"But changed, eh?" George said. "After all these years . . ."

"Well, we have all changed." She looked down at her mottled hands and looked back up at him.

"Yup," he said. His eyes moved around the room. He didn't want to make Leila and her daughter miserable by being here and seeing all that was here to see, but what choice did he have? He couldn't shift his view without noticing something else Leila would recognize as belonging to him. Every wall, every square of tile, for example. He felt he was hallucinating.

"How is America?" Leila asked. The daughter sat down in the easy chair.

"Big," he said. "American." What should he ask her in return? He was having trouble with the norms of politesse, which did not seem to fit the situation.

"This is your daughter?" he asked, groping for a subject.

"Oh, yes," Leila said, flustered that she had not introduced them. "This is Noga."

"Hello, Noga," George said. Somehow, the girl was easier. She was new, and not so easily associated with history. She had no memory of those days, that chair. It was hers, as far as she knew.

"Hi," she said, shyly. She was younger than Marina by about ten years, he figured.

"Do you have any others?" George asked Leila.

There was a small but noticeable silence.

"I had a son," she said. She looked away toward the terrace. "He was killed last year in Lebanon."

George found himself speechless, when words of condolence should have popped to his lips. You have to pay *some* price for taking away *my* land and living in *my* house for fifty years and for eternity, he heard himself think. He looked at Leila for too long a time, and he knew she could feel him looking. He knew that she knew what he was thinking. She probably had her own bitter, blaming thoughts about *him*, too.

But this is my childhood acquaintance, he told himself, still looking at her and sizing up in her profile all the puffs and hollows, the lines and droops that age had wrought on the little girl's hopeful face. Like my loss, hers is a human loss also, a real true loss to her, and to this girl Noga. Oh, yes, he thought, he had learned a lesson from Ibrahim's death. You had to pick carefully the things in the name of which you were willing to let people die, and then you had to be certain that that was what they were dying for, and not for your own ambition, or someone else's, or for a plan that looked like the good plan but that actually was something else completely.

The Israelis had told her her boy had died for the Jews and that was almost as big a lie as the Palestinians' trying to convince him that *his* had died for the Palestinians. Only a monster would fail to recognize the parallel, or someone who was shielding his eyes from a distasteful truth, and George was bent on resisting everything that generated blindness and monstrousness. He had not become, overnight—over one particular night—some kind of mush-headed humanist, but he was trying hard to keep in mind the value of what was human, the value of each person's own short-lived story. He was refusing, deliberately, to deny human empathy, no matter between whom. Deny human empathy and go down as a villain, he believed.

It was always wrong for the young to die before their elders, he thought: young soldiers were a clever tool invented by the middle-aged and the elderly to ensure their own continuing comfort. Young martyrs, too. If someone had to die for the cause of Palestine—and history had certainly shown that *someone* did—why not George or Ahmed or even Hassan, why not Leila or the Prime Minister? Instead, his grandson was dead, her son was dead. Maybe in some vast eternal balance, her son deserved to be dead more than his grandson did—to pay back for the house, all the houses, the orchards, the vineyards, the refugees, the war dead, the fifty years (so far!) of statelessness—or perhaps (from the skewed Israeli point of view) Ibrahim was a minor, acceptable sacrifice for saving the Jews from another round of slaughter. But judging it from within the smaller, more precious frame of human reference, both boys should be standing here right now making faces at each other, the little one following the big one around and hanging on his legs.

"I am so sorry," George said to Leila, and meant it, as much as he could. She looked at him gratefully.

History was a sad business.

CHAPTER TWENTY-THREE

DORON WOKE AT DAWN IN THE BACKSEAT OF THE JALOPY. He picked his head up and peered out the window. A red bus bounced past. He was parked out in front of the Peugeot dealership, a block from the Talpiot circle. He felt his face; covered in stubble—no wonder he'd looked like a derelict to himself the night before. He squinted into the mirror and saw what looked like the face of a prisoner who had been held for a long time in the dark and now was brought up into the early morning sunshine. He squinted and blinked. It was a cool morning. His mouth tasted sour.

On his way to Kakal Street, a pair of headlights was trailing his car. He thought so, anyway. It was all Yizhar's fault. Doron mistrusted Yizhar, but at the same time, he believed Yizhar, believed in Yizhar, in the force of his personality, his unwavering sincerity, whether for good or for evil. If Yizhar said he had a security detail on Doron, then he did, that was Doron's thinking. What Yizhar said was always true, at least in its essence. The headlights disappeared. Yizhar knew everything, and was running the game from way up in his aerie at The Building.

A small security detail, Yizhar had said. At this hour, the streets were filling up with red public buses overflowing with soldiers going to and from base. Right now, Doron saw only one other passenger car, a bus or two behind him. He didn't like believing so strongly in someone of whom he was suspicious. But weren't those the same headlights behind him again, here on Kakal Street outside his mother's house? Probably not, probably not. Doron parked in his mother's shelter. The car's motor died with a shudder and a clunk. He thought he heard something sweep behind him as he walked up the short path to his mother's side door. Yizhar *had* put a tail on him.

Or maybe it was Hajimi.

Doron let himself in and flicked lights on in the hallway to the kitchen. His mother was asleep but would be up soon. Not for the first time, he thought it would be nice if he had some money and could get himself his own place. He stood in front of the refrigerator and examined its contents. It was spartan fare, a half dozen eggs and a half liter of low-fat milk and two containers of yogurt, some old hard Bulgarian cheese and a couple of rewrapped pita loaves—the refrigerator of an old person, he thought. He sectioned the one remaining lemon and ate it with some yogurt.

The yellowed photograph of his parents on the shores of the Kinneret was in its place next to the coffee machine on the sideboard, surrounded by bowls of fruit. His father was leaning on his crutch, as usual. He was the only man in the world who looked jaunty with a crutch. He was about Doron's age in the photo. Doron's mother had her eyes locked on her husband, and was holding on to his arm as her skirt blew around her. They were a honeymooning couple, about to make a baby. It was hard imagining them before his birth. To him it seemed as if they had met and fallen in love and gotten married and gone to the Kinneret all with the express purpose of creating him. But why? To set him down in this world to meet his fate? If they had only imagined.

He went into the bathroom to shave, and watched his real self reemerge. In his old room, Doron sat down heavily on the bed. This was now his mother's study. It was filled with her archaeology books, the endless *Encyclopedia Judaica*, books on the Philistines and the Persians, and odd collected artifacts from digs around the Middle East. Sitting on a shelf was *A Land Without People*, written by her mentor, the title a reference to the hopeful Zionist description of pre-Israel Palestine. He kicked off his dusty faux-leather loafers. A land without people, for a people without a land.

He unwrapped his long scarf. He laid it on the bed next to him alongside the wool hat he'd been wearing and looked at these, his accessories. They were utterly alien to him. The disguise was finished. From now on, he would go where he had to go in his own uniform. He hunted for it in the closet. Yes, he would greet misfortune as himself. His father's crutch and cane leaned up against the back wall. He noticed the honeymoon suit, his father's only suit, wrapped up in plastic, left hanging alongside his father's other clothes almost ten years after he'd died. This was the family museum. Doron's old stuff was here, too, miscellaneous athletic gear, his old scrapbook from his first days in the army, photos of the revered tanks of the past and pictures of the heroes—Dayan and Motta Gur, and Gertler, of course—stacked up on the closet floor. Doron shook his head at his former self as he riffled through the hangers to find his uniform. He put on each article of clothing carefully, and checked the embroidered insignias on his sleeves to make sure they were straight.

"You're here?" his mother asked. She stood in the kitchen doorway. "I didn't hear you come in."

"You were asleep," he said. He sat at the kitchen table, staring at the back of a cereal box. The sun was just coming up over the terrace wall. His mother walked past him quickly toward the coffee machine. He knew she didn't like to be seen by anyone, even him, this early in the morning. Her hair stuck out like a lion's ratty mane.

"You're in uniform," she said.

He picked his beret up from the table and put it on.

"It looks good." She went to the refrigerator and pulled a bag of coffee out of the freezer. "You look like your father." She opened the coffee and began spooning it into the filter.

He got up and went over to her. "Good morning," he said. He gave her a kiss.

" . . . Three, four, five. There." She was counting out spoons of coffee, but there were tears in her eyes. She looked away from him.

"You look as if you're about to become head of the Southern Command," she said. She pulled the milk out of the refrigerator. "You going somewhere?"

"Oh, just a sort of a formal dress thing at headquarters," he said. He watched the coffee begin to drip. "Some ceremony."

She looked at him and didn't continue her questioning. The coffeepot hissed.

"Got any more lemons?" he asked. He smiled faintly.

"No, I don't," she said, looking inside the refrigerator. "Someone finished them." She cast him an accusing look.

She poured a cup of coffee for each of them and they carried their cups carefully down the long hall to the terrace. He remembered what his father had taught him: When you're carrying a full cup, don't look at it or it will spill. His father had learned that lesson serving breakfast in the officers' mess. It seemed to Doron like a maxim for leading a successful, unexamined life. And better yet, it was *true*. If you never looked down, the coffee never spilled. But it was hard to resist looking.

He and his mother sat down. It had been a long time since he had seen her with her hair unbrushed and with no makeup at all. Her grayness seemed eerier and more vulnerable when a spear of rising sunlight caught her full in the face. She saw him looking.

She patted his hand.

She wasn't dying, so why did he feel so sad.

"The thing's at headquarters in Tel Aviv?" she asked.

"Yes."

She thought about that for a while.

She looked at the floor and picked absently at the skin around her thumbnail. She ran a fuzzy slipper over the curlicues and arabesques in the old Palestinian floor tiles, making new bright patterns in the dust. Beyond the terrace, palm fronds rustled in the wind like shuffled papers. "You have to face things, sweetheart."

"I am facing them, Mother. Everything is fine."

She watched an airplane descending over the desert. Doron watched her watching.

"I'm not getting that feeling."

"Don't worry." He tried to smile.

Her face knotted up.

The old sofa that long ago had been abandoned on the terrace to the Jerusalem weather creaked beneath his shifting weight. The noise was a noise he was used to; if it hadn't creaked, he would have noticed. The lingering night smell of newly blooming jasmine filled him with a sudden nostalgia for this house when they had just moved into it, this sofa when it was new, for his childhood, his mother when she was young. His father.

"Do you know the story of Gertler, mother?"

She looked at him.

"Gertler? A great, great hero. What do you mean, Ari? Everyone knows the story of Gertler."

"I don't mean as prime minister, Mother."

"Ah, you mean the scandal during the war. Not really, no," she said. They both gazed at the floor as her toe slid along a maroon swirl. "I don't know it. I mean, not particularly, really." She was trying to focus, arising from her bed only to deal with a disappearing son and the old story of Gertler. She picked up her coffee cup. "I mean, I don't know more than the average person, I suppose. We all respected him so much. Your father, too." She sipped carefully.

"Yizhar was involved, I remember," he said. "Isn't that right?"

"Yes," she said, nodding as if she had just recalled it. "Yes, something like that I remember, too."

A siren went off in the distance. They both picked up their heads to listen. It faded.

"They said that Gertler was ruined by drink," she said. "And his friends were not as supportive as they might have been, your father told me. Professional jealousy, I think it was. Now that you mention it, I imagine Yizhar was one of them. Yes, he must have been. He and Gertler were great friends. He was Gertler's protégé."

Doron nodded slowly.

"History is history, Ari," she said. "Character is not immutable. Yizhar is a reputable man. Entirely reputable. I know what you are thinking."

"Some people never change, Mother."

"Maybe." She leaned over and tapped his knee with a forefinger. "Yizhar is not a fool. Maybe he failed to stand by an old friend, back then, but he rescued Gertler, in the end. Yizhar was the one who spoke out for him. Trust him."

He looked at her and raised his eyebrows.

"I have to go out," she said. "Promise me you'll come back here after your whatever it is."

"Of course I will," he said.

She looked at him and he could see that she knew something was wrong.

"Don't do anything stupid, Ari. Remember your father."

"I'm fine, Mother, stop worrying."

"Remember what Daddy used to say: 'When in doubt, wait.'" She picked up their empty coffee cups.

"And ended up rushing into a bullet and a land mine, so much for waiting," he said.

She was headed down the long corridor.

"Wait, let me remember," she said, turning back to him from halfway down the hall. "What was it? Who said it? Let me think, let me think . . . Ben-Gurion? Maybe. Golda?" She stood there in the hallway's shadows, her voice coming out of the darkness. "Ah, I remember, it was Golda: 'Heroes can't always afford to wait and see.'"

"So there," Doron said to her. "So the lesson is: 'When in doubt, wait, but heroes can't always afford to wait.'" He laughed. "There is a motto for everything *and* for its opposite, isn't there?"

She smiled at him.

"The gardener brought the pansies yesterday," she said. "They look so bright from here. Do you like them?"

He didn't answer.

"Well, I'm getting dressed," she said. "I'll be back in a minute."

Doron stood and looked over the side of the terrace. Morning traffic had begun, but it was never very heavy in this neighborhood. A water truck drove by. A few cars were parked on the street, but he recognized all of them. They belonged to the neighbors. He saw the low branches moving on the tree across the street tree. A bird, landing? He heard his mother coming back down the hall.

"What are you looking at?" his mother asked from behind him. He turned around.

"Nothing," he said. "There's nothing to see down there that I haven't seen a million times."

She was wearing her pants suit, and carrying an open bag overflowing with a clipboard, pointer, slides for her presentation, and notes.

They walked into the kitchen together.

"I'll call a taxi," she said. She went to the phone. He watched her. The curve of her back, which had thickened with age, seemed vulnerable. He definitely felt regret about what he was about to do, no matter how it turned out. But there was no choice. He was just waiting till the hour was appropriate.

"Promise me you're coming home later," she said. She looked at him fiercely.

"I promise, I promise," he said. He tried to make it sound light, as if he were imitating a young boy annoyed at his mother's attentions.

"Okay. Okay, then." She looked away from him because she couldn't look at him. "I'm going to wait downstairs for the cab."

"Maybe character *is* immutable, Mother," Doron said. "*You've* never changed, for example."

His mother turned back to him and smiled. "Be careful, Ari," she said, squeezing his arm. She kissed him goodbye.

She left, and he went back to the terrace to watch for her taxi. She waited just below where he stood; he could see only her head and the tip of the pointer sticking out of the bag. The pots of pansies were still in their crates. A garbage truck was parked in the middle of the street, picking up everything on the block from there. The grocer's boy passed by with a cardboard box on his shoulder. Across the street, the low branches of the tree moved again.

A cat? Yizhar's "security detail"? Or what?—the wind?

He could see her taxi stuck behind the garbage truck. The cabby started to honk wildly, and Doron's mother, hearing the commotion, began walking down the street. She got into the cab and the garbage truck turned the corner, and he saw her hand waving out the taxi's back window to him.

CHAPTER TWENTY-FOUR

A T THE HOSPITAL ENTRANCE, PHILIP TURNED TO GEORGE.
"Feeling up to it?" he asked.
"You never feel up to it, Philip," George said. "You just do it because you have to." He nodded at a doctor who walked by and seemed to recognize him.

"I think cardiology is up there," George said, pointing at a long stairway at the end of the hall. "Marina told me there is a terrible staircase the Israelis have put there as their own peculiar way of showing compassion for the sick and disabled." Philip started toward it, but George held him back.

"Let me hold your arm, Philip." He grasped Philip's arm with the strength of a vise.

"You know, I'm supposed to consider myself lucky if I'm well enough to climb these stairs and maybe go through another procedure. But it won't make me feel lucky. Remember the last time?" George stopped their progress for a moment. "I don't want to feel that way again."

He breathed deeply. Three Palestinian women were sitting at the base of the stairwell, waiting. A sort of checkpoint, a security check with a metal detector, was set up at the bottom stair, manned by one soldier.

George wanted to run for the exit. The soldier was as good an excuse as any. But he knew he had to face the soldier, face the stairs, face Dr. Simcha Rodef, and submit. George looked at the metal detector.

"Lord," he said to Philip, sighing.

"*This* will be fun," Philip said.

"And just today, I'm feeling pretty well," George went on, as if neither of them had noticed the coming obstacle. The soldier was looking at them, but of course, he would be looking at anyone who was approaching. George didn't even want to think about what the next few weeks would bring, if another procedure didn't simply finish him off right there on the table. Utter exhaustion, susceptibility to infection, disorientation, weakness, panic, and worst of all, the inability to move, and therefore the necessity of remaining in Jerusalem. He walked slowly along, looking down at the speckled stone floor. What if he were to die in Jerusalem?

George thought of Leila's son; and of Ari Doron. He looked at this soldier here before him: as usual, there was nothing to read in the face. They had illegible faces from a distance, and illegible faces from up close. A boyish face beneath a military beret. The soldier inspected him briefly.

"Yes?" the soldier said, in Hebrew.

"Cardiology," Philip replied in English.

The soldier nodded.

"Yesh lecha nesheck?" he asked.

"What is he saying?" George asked Philip.

Philip looked at the soldier and cocked his head.

The soldier patted his own pockets.

"Vepins. Do you have any vepins?" the soldier asked, this time in English.

"Hah!" George burst out. He could not restrain himself. Weapons. If only, he thought.

"No," Philip answered.

"Go up, then," the soldier said, gesturing toward the stairs.

DR. RODEF'S OFFICE was in a side hall on the cardiology floor. All hospitals are the same, George thought as he walked down the soundproofed linoleum and fluorescent corridor. Philip opened Rodef's office door. They walked in and George briefly gauged the quality of the reading material—old magazines from the Hebrew newspapers, scattered over a corner glass table—before lowering himself into a chrome and plastic chair. Philip spoke with a receptionist who sat behind a standard-issue Formica counter, and then he came to stand next to George, like a sentry.

"We're next," he said. Dr. Rodef had tried to cheer things up with Gauguin prints, but the succulent foliage seemed stunningly out of place in the heart of the heart ward in the depths of Hadassah, up here on a forlorn hilltop overlooking the desert.

This was not a place for the lighthearted. George sank into his uncomfortable chair. He felt right at home. He always felt comfortable on any cardiology floor; it was his turf, after all. But now, more so. Ever since his own personal heart attack, he felt an otherworldly calm descend on him when he was in the heart department. His nerves, his fears about his condition, vanished. It was as if he had finally arrived at his destination, finally he was home, and he could re*lax*. Someone, something, had been following him his whole life, he felt, and here on the cardiology floor, he'd met the man face-to-face. There was horror involved in knowing your own fate, of course, horror because the fellow you'd met face-to-face happened to be carrying a loaded—what was that blunt Hebrew word? *Nesheck*, that was it—a loaded weapon and was quite prepared to fire it. But there was also the relief of recognition. Oh, then, *this* is it! Meeting your fate has its advantages, he thought, looking at the Tahitian girl under the palm. She gazed back with flat eyes.

DR. RODEF was taking blood. George watched it flow away. He had the funny little sensors of an electrocardiogram glued to his chest.

"Just a test," the doctor said, smiling at him, pulling one vial off the needle and sticking on another. Behind the doctor's head was a brightly colored poster explaining the components of blood. In this version, plasma looked particularly forbidding. "Just a test," he repeated.

"Yup," George said. He felt as if he were losing something precious. "Looks pretty red," he said in a chipper voice.

"Yes, it does," Rodef said. He smiled. "The EKG looks good."

George watched the needle going up and down.

"So we'll just have to see, as you know," Rodef said.

Why do doctors have to be so bloody honest all the time?

As you know. That's what irritated him. As if somehow he were implicated in the disgusting physical crisis that was destroying him. He looked up at the poster as the doctor attached yet another vial. Ah, the cells: B and T lymphocytes and all the little thrombocytes; the neutrophil and eosinophil; and let us not forget the blasts: the myeloblast, the monoblast, and the wiggly red proerythroblast. Lovely important little beggars. Why couldn't they just flow nicely through the chambers, doing their work like good boys and girls. Why couldn't his heart behave?

He looked at the huge fleshy model of a heart—with its four removable chambers—that stood on the countertop.

Traitor! Defector! Collaborator! George winced as the doctor removed the needle.

"There you are, then," Dr. Rodef said, removing his gloves. "Results as soon as possible." He smiled the disturbingly smug smile of the man whom you suspect knows more about you than you do. George exhaled and closed his eyes.

Zaire you ahr, zen, he thought.

PHILIP LEFT HIM at poolside with a drink. At poolside with a drink. Had a nice ring to it, but unfortunately, it was off-season. The pool was empty, the air was cold, and the drink was a tall glass of water. George stuck his feet out. He was always horizontal at the wrong time of day: at midmorning in Dr. Rodef's office, and now, again, at lunchtime here at the hotel. Was it a function of his illness or just being, as he supposed he could now theoretically consider himself, on vacation? Here in Palestine, he was on vacation from his real life as a doctor and an American, though no sane person could call this place vacationland.

Beyond the wall that separated the hotel and the adjacent mosque from Nablus Road, the cranes of the new Jerusalem were busy. The builders were counting on peace—Ahmed's peace, as George thought of it—to bring some kind of prosperity to the city, and tourists who would thrill to the tragedies of the Holy Land, the crucifixions, the beheadings, the sieges and massacres, all the martyrdoms, the bombings, death all around. George supposed it was amusing—"interesting," as Philip would say—for them to get a feel for it and then go home to a normal place. Blood was clearly a draw here in Holylandia. The fronds of the poolside palm trees snapped in the wind.

All over town, but especially up here near the Old City, where the Jewish side touched the Palestinian side, hotel construction was at a record high. George hated those cranes; they were like mindless birds pecking away at what he considered his property. The contours of Jerusalem were disappearing beneath the new edifices: archway, stone, pilaster and balustrade, cornice and lintel, rampart and pinnacle, all sinking down beneath what was new. It was like an archaeological dig in reverse. George sipped his water and watched the dance of the cranes. So slow, so graceful, the elegant cross of the vertical and the horizontal, turning and turning. A. Aronson was the name of the contractor, his enormous signs were on all the equipment. Oh, A. Aronson, you know not what you do. George shook his head. Then again, possibly A. Aronson is quite aware . . .

Explosions set to carve out foundations for a farther hotel rocked the ground briefly. Dig with quiet little shovels in Jerusalem, A. Aronson, George thought. Do not disturb the public peace of mind with the sound of bombs, fool. The elevator pulley moved slowly across the shaft and he watched as the nearest crane rotated and the elevator with its load of men and brick rose up, up toward the half-done roof of the new Nova Hotel. Kkk, kkk, kkk. Each notch along the crane's tower clicked as the elevator rose. The cranes were dancing over George's head with outstretched arms.

A. Aronson was winning. Farewell, Jerusalem, George thought. The traitors and collaborators are handing history over to the cranes. The spot where the needle had gone in ached, and blood was seeping around it. Damned blood thinner. George grimaced in pain as he raised his glass to the twirling dancers. *L'chaim*, he thought. It was one of his few Hebrew phrases. To life. His heart wriggled inside him like a caught insect as he raised his glass of water. The palpitations generated a feeling of panic without any external cause for fear.

As he lowered his glass once more, George heard the metallic sound that a coin makes, falling on tile. He looked down next to his lounge chair and saw that the skeleton key to the old house had dropped from his pocket. Aha! He reached down for it. You don't get away so easily, mister, he thought. He held the key up to the sunlight. After all these years with no lock to unfasten, it was still remarkably shiny and bright from the touch of his hand and his father's. George put it back deep in his pocket. As a conjuring tool, it was useless now, after all he had seen today at Lovers of Zion Street. But George wasn't ready to part with it just yet. Not just yet. After all, it had only been, oh, forty years or so. . . . Leave it here on the ground, discarded? Unthinkable. He would give it to Marina. He imagined its reception. Thanks, Dad, she would say, with that gently skeptical tone in her voice and that little ironic smile on her face, both inherited from him, just like the key and so many other catastrophes. From the minaret nearby, he heard the crackle of a recording and then, louder than dynamite, the call to prayer. The water was cool as he drank it down. He listened to the anonymous voice chant praise for Allah and his Messenger. Tiny men in blue began unloading boxes of bricks onto the Nova roof. George watched them pile the neat cubes in a corner. Over the new foundations in the distance, puffs of smoke and dust clouded the low air.

CHAPTER TWENTY-FIVE

No leaving before lunchtime. It would be too early. Afternoon would be good. Doron might catch Marina alone. He hoped so, because since Hajimi had been released, Doron had developed a sincere concern about the man. He had no idea what Hajimi might do, but he was sure he would do something.

Doron had one stop to make before Ramallah. He washed the coffee cups, and stood at the sink, letting the water run. He shut his eyes and listened to its clean sound, like rivers and laundry. The soap smelled good. Who was downstairs waiting for him? Maybe he should slip out over the side terrace, whip through the neighbor's backyard, and hide in the Jerusalem forest. He would eat berries and sleep on a bed of pine needles.

He shook himself out of his reverie, and went to sit on the terrace, waiting for the sun to move up in the sky. Every once in a while, he stood and looked at the tree across the street. It seemed that the later it got, the less it moved. He was probably imagining it. He lay on the couch on the terrace and dozed briefly, wakened suddenly by a sonic boom that was distinguishable from a bomb only by the telltale sound of plane engines after the boom cracked. He looked at his watch. Almost time. His uniform felt stiff and proper. He was going to soil it irrevocably in the eyes of Yizhar and perhaps the rest of his countrymen, but there was no turning back. He remembered the friendly tone of Yizhar's voice from last night, when he called that number from the military phone. "Yes? What is it?" Such a nice voice.

"What is it?"

It's me, it's me. It's the end.

Doron went back into his bedroom and opened the closet. He knew what he would find on the shelf in the back, and there it was, in the shoe box he'd put it in after the night at the checkpoint. The way he'd felt after the boy's funeral, he had never wanted to see the gun again, but now he wanted it. He stuck it in his belt. He went back into the kitchen and rummaged around under the sink until he found his mother's stash of plastic grocery bags. He stuffed one into his pocket. There.

He pulled his beret down to shade his eyes as he opened the side door. From the landing, all he could see were the tops of trees and the empty street. He ran down the outside stairs. When he got to the bottom, he opened the shelter gate quickly and looked around: nothing, no one. No cat, even. He felt ridiculous, but he assumed that that was to be his permanent state. He opened the cold car door and closed it fast, locking it immediately, although he wasn't sure the lock locked. He looked over the seat back to make sure no one was there, hiding. He sat panting behind the wheel.

They know who you are. Doron remembered Yizhar's hooded olive eyes as he said it. He looked out the window toward the tree across the street. Nothing. A cold chill tiptoed up his spine. So what if they're watching me? he told himself, not very convincingly. He felt his pockets for the car keys. The next-door neighbors have a cat. It *was* the cat. He was suddenly afraid to start his car. His stomach tightened as he pulled the key away from the ignition. He sat there, just sitting, listening. He heard wind in the trees, and beyond that, nothing. Then he heard ticking. He straightened in fear. Ticking, he thought. Another cliché. But he definitely heard it. Did bombs still tick? He doubted it. He leaned his head back and put his arms behind his neck, trying to relax. The ticking grew louder.

It was his Swatch! Of course. The damned thing! Limor or Noa had bought it for him, but Tamara said it made more noise than Big Ben; she couldn't stand the ticking. Doron never noticed. His ugly Swatch, with its shiny face and metallic band—he loved the thing right now. God, he loved it! He tapped it with a finger and laughed at himself. The ticking was solid and strong. Once you'd heard it, you kept hearing it. That's what Tamara said, and it turned out she was right. He started his car.

THERE HE GOES. Mahmoud watched Lieutenant Ari Doron come down the stairs. They had a good view of the house and the parking shelter from the side street where they had been waiting.

"Look, Uncle, he's in his car." Jibril pointed, just noticing.

"Thanks," Mahmoud said. And it was lucky he had come down now, and not much later, because they were getting bored and sleepy. And hungry. They'd eaten their last food just before sunrise, and had arrived here in time to see the soldier drive up in that thing he called a car. For the past five hours, they had only left the car to piss against a wall behind a tree. As Doron pulled out of the shelter and began heading up the street, Mahmoud put his car in gear, stepped on the gas, and heard a terrible grinding noise. The car trembled and died. He'd forgotten the clutch *again*. The soldier was cruising down Kakal.

"He's already getting *away*," Jibril hissed.

"Stay calm, Jibril," Mahmoud said.

"I think he's looking back at us," Jibril said.

"He's not looking at us," Mahmoud said. "Please."

He tried the fancy footwork again. This time he remembered how to do it. With a lurch, their car agreed to go forward. He turned onto Kakal and followed Doron. Mahmoud had never owned a car, and had rarely driven. The car he had rented for today was a nameless piece of repaired tin that cost ten dollars a day. He'd got it from a friend who'd rented it for seven dollars a day from another friend. Mahmoud had done a visual comparison early that morning, and decided that his car was in even worse condition than the soldier's.

One good thing, though, and the thing that kept the friend's friend in business, was that the car had yellow Israeli plates instead of blue West Bank plates. It meant that you could go anywhere in the car. Yes, yes, you risked a stoning on the West Bank if people didn't look hard before they threw their rocks, if they assumed you were Israeli—but still the plates were invaluable once you were inside Israel. They added one more positive element to the package Mahmoud had put together to get himself and his nephew across the checkpoint this morning.

He had taken every measure available. He and Jibril had both shaved off their moustaches in order to appear less threateningly Palestinian, because it was well known that the Israelis thought any youngish man with a moustache was a probable terrorist. In the backseat, they had stowed Adnan's wife and her sister and their mother, all three of whom had Jerusalem passes. Women, especially sainted grandmas, provided additional authentication of innocence. Men with wives were also considered a less likely threat than single men. A valid Jerusalem pass could come in handy, though it could also be ignored, if the soldiers felt like it. A granny's pass was less likely to be challenged than anyone else's. And, oh, if only you could get some small children on the bandwagon, that was even better, but Mahmoud had looked around, and none was available. They were all in school, for heaven's sake, when they could have been making themselves useful.

"This is easy," Jibril said, as they drove down Kakal. He giggled nervously. He checked under the attaché case at his feet. There were the handcuffs, borrowed from a friend who worked for the section of the Chairman's security force that occasionally employed Jibril. Under the handcuffs, the knife.

"This part is easy," Mahmoud said. The knife made him edgy. He was glad that the women had already been dropped off at Damascus Gate to go shopping.

Where was this nut of a soldier going? That's what Mahmoud wanted to know. He seemed to be headed right into Palestinian territory. Just as well, from Mahmoud's point of view, but pretty weird for an Israeli soldier.

What? Turning right here? The man was heading for East Jerusalem! Mahmoud didn't understand, but then he saw it. The American Colony Hotel. Mahmoud quickly decided to park the car on the little road across from the hotel's driveway, in front of the work sites for the new hotels. He certainly wasn't going to risk anything here in this hornet's nest of security guys and undercover people and UN forces. It was way too public and international. He'd probably end up getting interviewed by CNN with the cuffed soldier standing behind him, or something.

"What are we doing?" Jibril asked.

"We'll just wait," said Mahmoud. "I don't think he's checking in."

Jibril laughed. He jiggled his foot under the attaché case again and drummed his long fingers on the black rubber of the car's window frame.

DORON WALKED INTO the lobby of the American Colony Hotel. He'd heard about the place—den of iniquity was the consensus among his friends, on those rare occasions when the hotel happened to come up in conversation. Filled with Israel bashers, hatching their evil plots. But he didn't buy anyone's propaganda anymore. The butt of his gun was biting into his back. He tried to adjust it, but it kept pinching.

The hotel was conveniently located down the street from Orient House, the unacknowledged Jerusalem headquarters of the Authority. That was the beauty of it for the Palestinians. They could sneak away from what Doron assumed were their ugly warrens of renovated offices inside beautiful old Orient House and go have a long lunch at the hotel, consort with foreign women, be toasted, feel classy and important, maybe even powerful for a few minutes. He understood. Doron had counseled the police on security for one of the Israeli demonstrations against Orient House last year; he had passed by the hotel in his Humvee, but never gone in. Never even thought about going in.

He had felt odd in his Palestinian wardrobe in Ramallah, but here, in full Israeli uniform with a few medals pinned on and his service pistol visibly tucked into his belt, he felt like some kind of towering monster. Why was he taller than everyone in the lobby? He had made himself into an object of scrutiny, derision, and fear. He wanted it, though—he wanted to be as much of an Israeli soldier as was possible, and he had done it. The men and women milling around seemed like figures seen from a great height, pea-sized and alien. They were carrying dolls' accessories, tiny briefcases and little cups of coffee, and they smoked magical cigarettes: how could anything so small actually be lit, and send off smoke? He saw his immense hands hanging at his sides as he gazed down on the women, who wore little Barbie high heels and seemed to teeter. Did he hear these miniature beings talking? They made a continuous squeaking sound in his ears, like mice at a cocktail party.

Doron looked down at them and they all were looking up at him, taking him in. He wanted to hide from their stares, but of course, he was too big to hide: where was he to run for cover—through a door that would turn out to be a mouse hole?

He was here to take responsibility as an Israeli soldier, and then to surrender his Israeli soldierhood. Take my gun.

He wanted to surrender his gun to the enemy because the enemy was no longer his enemy. The enemy was a two-year-old in a Ninja sweatshirt.

Doron tried to stay still and self-contained in that tiny lobby, and not cause any damage. But he had to find Raad, if Raad was here.

He lumbered toward the reception desk. Why did no one at reception seem to notice the huge creature who required their attention?

"Excuse me," he said, in English, so as not to offend with his Hebrew, but of course, he reminded himself, the uniform was enough offense. He got no response.

"*Slicha,*" he amended, switching to Hebrew.

A young man in an impeccable hotel jacket looked over at him with cold eyes, and then looked away again.

"Oh, come on," Doron said, switching back to his stilted English. "I want just to call one of your guests."

The only woman behind the desk approached him—slowly and cautiously, it was true, but at least she was headed his way.

"Yes, who is it, please?" she asked.

"George Raad," he said.

All three receptionists looked at Doron.

"Well?" he said.

The woman looked at one of the men, and he shrugged at her.

"I'll connect you," the woman said.

GEORGE WAS PLAYING solitaire. He was sitting on the bed with his legs crossed and his hair in disarray, his back bent over at an angle that wasn't comfortable. But you had to, for solitaire. This was the time-honored position, the way he'd always sat down to the game. He liked solitaire, loved it, really. Because if he wasn't winning, he could just out-and-out cheat, which you couldn't do in a game where other people might notice and not take so liberal a view of your cheating as you yourself did. He had tried solitaire once on Philip's computer, but when he realized you couldn't rearrange the cards on that program, he gave up in disgust. The *fun* of the game was cheating. Cheating the cards, cheating fate. What a preposterous idea. But if he could not do a switcheroo, it took everything out of it for George.

Things on the bedspread had come to a stalemate. He dealt himself a seven of hearts. No earthly use.

Let's just slip ourselves the jack of spades or clubs here instead of that damn black ten we keep getting, shall we? He lifted his sleeve and looked at the new gauze pad he had put on his arm. Bloody again. Must be the anticoagulant. Was it an emergency? he wondered. Let's ignore it. Jack of spades, it was.

The fun of being alone, too. Playing alone. No one to fuck you up.

Plus of course you had to win or there would be another heart attack.

I am not winning here.

Oh, let's give the cards one more chance, George thought, reserving the jack of spades under a finger, but leaving it in the deck. This was an extremely fraudulent magic trick. Why the pretense, George? he asked himself. But he always did it this way.

He drew a four of diamonds.

"Shit," he muttered.

"Are you winning?" Philip called across the room. Philip knew that George always won in the end.

"Yeh-sss," George growled at him. He slipped the jack of spades out of the deck into the place it rightly should have occupied all along, if only fate were on his side, which it wasn't, was it? Don't let that thought into your head.

In solitaire, the way George played it, you had only yourself to blame. The phone rang.

"Pick it up, will you, Philip?" George said. His concentration was fierce as he played out the round. Now that the jack was in place, everything was working smoothly. Red, black, red, black.

Ta-da, he thought to himself, as he put the final king on each of the four final stacks. He looked down with satisfaction.

"Again," he said to himself. As he began shuffling for a rematch, George watched Philip on the phone.

Philip put his hand over the mouthpiece.

"He won't say who he is, Doctor," he said in a loud whisper.

George began laying out the new game.

"So tell him I'm busy."

"It's an Israeli, I think."

"Tell him I'm *very* busy." George smiled at Philip over his glasses.

"I think it might be an official, or something," Philip said. "Speaks English, and quite secretive."

"You think I should talk to him?" George asked.

"I think."

George turned over a disappointing hand including not only the three of clubs and the three of spades but also the fours of both those suits, and picked up the receiver. He pulled at his sock.

"Yes?" he said.

"Hello, Dr. Raad?"

"Yes," George said. It was something untoward or sinister, he felt it immediately. He stopped adjusting his sock. Philip came over.

"Who is this?" George asked. The accent on the other end was heavily Hebrew, and the voice was very quiet and low.

"Um, I don't know how to say this."

"Well, just go ahead," George said, dealing out his hand. Why was an Israeli calling him, and wasting his time?

"Come on," George said. "Speak."

"I was the commanding officer at the checkpoint the other night."

Three of clubs, three of spades. George kept his eyes down.

"My God," George said into the receiver. "My God. . . ." Then he thought: But was it some crank? Some insane nutter?

"Tell me your name," George said.

"Doron. Ari Doron," Doron said. "I'm downstairs."

"Oh, Christ," George said. "Why?"

"I wanted to see you," Doron said.

"Why?" George said. He shook his head at Philip, who stood near the bed, watching the conversation. George's heart fluttered in a disorganized way. So this was to be the end of the story, he thought.

"Just to, explain, or, I don't know, apologize, or . . ."

"I feel this is very awkward," George said. His spine stiffened, and yet there was the curiosity, he felt that, too. Would George want to kill this man if he saw him? Well, would he? Would he hate him? George hated him now.

"Please." There was a pause. "Would you come down?" The man was pleading. For what?

George hesitated. He unhooked his legs and dropped his feet to the floor. What would it mean to see this man? Did the soldier wish him harm? That was possible, too, he supposed. In *this* world, anything was possible, even likely.

"You wait there," George said. "I can't decide like this. It's too sudden, or something. You wait. And if I come down, then, then I come down. That's how I can do this. If I can do this at all."

"Okay," said the soldier. "All right. I will wait."

Ole rrrrrhite, George repeated to himself. I *weeel* wait.

DORON WAS TRYING to hide near the newspaper rack in a corner of the lobby where sentimental watercolors of Jerusalem were on display on a series of stand-alone easels. But people kept coming up to find or return a paper, and when they saw him there, lurking and cowering, they turned away, or looked at him with loathing.

But I'm here to humiliate myself, he wanted to tell them.

He kept his eye on the stairway that came up into the lobby from the elevator bank near the bar.

It felt like an assignation. Would the beloved show up? He was frightened that Raad would not come. And he was plain frightened of Raad and that superior stare he had seen on the book jacket. The man would not be impressed by Doron's humility. It would be a miracle if he came down, really. But Doron was counting on curiosity. Oh, fuck, what he really wanted desperately was coffee! You couldn't be in this setting and not want coffee. Everyone in the lobby was drinking coffee. But Doron didn't dare try to order it. He couldn't meet another look of disdain without running away.

The watercolor canvases that nearly hid him from view showed a sun-drenched Jerusalem—monuments and temples, all built of pale pink stone and sprayed over with a spatter of blue skies and yellow sun, and gleams and patches of pink and pale blue. Looking at them while he waited, Doron felt disoriented. Who is right? he wondered. The person who painted those, or me? Does Raad think Jerusalem is like that or could be like that or once was *like that?* Was this some kind of *Palestinian* fantasy? Probably this is their image of Jerusalem *without the Jews.*

Jerusalem is a dark place—Doron always felt it. Even when there was sunlight, the city was stony and rubble-strewn. Even here, at midday, at the hotel, dark was descending, he felt that. Well, at this time of year it *was* dark. He liked dark. He liked those dark corners of stone walls in Yemen Moshe near the old windmill, the angles where the walls meet the stone pathways, and black pebbles and old dirt and bits of gray mortar and old piles of pigeon shit seem to grow like lichen, unprepossessing and unstoppable. Doron was sick of the domes and monuments and holy fucking places. The landmarks of Jerusalem are checkpoints, watchtowers, prisons and crowded unpleasant markets, pedestrian malls, and playgrounds dotted with dog shit. I know, I know. I know the dry, sagging willows overhanging the unused railroad tracks: I *know* those old trees. Don't show me rays of sunlight, and warm walks. I drive a piece of shit through long tunnels to get to ring roads, and I park in dark piss-smelling underground lots. Let's be honest. The real holy place of Jerusalem is some square little colorless synagogue in a remote undistinguished neighborhood, or an unwelcoming cement-block mosque across from a kindergarten, or that Russian immigrant church he had noticed once, down a forbidding alley off Bezalel, with a blond prostitute standing outside, one naked leg exposed to the cold through a slit in her skirt. The real holy place is Best Buy.

• • •

THAT'S HIM. George stood at the bottom of the stair. In the corner over there. It wasn't as if there were any question about it. The man was in uniform, for Chrissakes. George had never seen anything so arrogant before. And yet the soldier seemed to be trying to hide.

Maybe someone called him a name, George thought.

Maybe someone stuck out his tongue at him.

The fellow had a kind of courage, to come *here*, and to see *him*.

Doron picked up his head. He looked searchingly at the door that led away to the elevator near the bar.

George watched him from the other side of the room. Doron was looking for *George*, of course, George realized. The soldier was tall, well made, handsome in uniform, like a propaganda poster's soldier for Zion. My fate, George thought. He contemplated the soldier, quietly. A big boy, he thought—could be Leila's dead son.

And there he was. So very imposing. What was this calm that was washing over George like lake water? It was the same as the quiet he felt in Dr. Rodef's waiting room, on Dr. Rodef's table. The peace of recognition, he told himself. Maybe I should just turn around before he sees me, and go back to my room and finish that bad hand. That's what I'll do. And he had just begun to turn when Doron saw the movement out of the corner of his eye, and turned to him, and started to come across the lobby.

George shook his head. No! Jesus, everyone was watching the soldier. Doron understood immediately, and moved back near his corner, sitting at one of the low brass coffee tables there, behind the newspaper rack. George walked over to reception and picked up his messages. He made a reservation in the dining room for the evening. Anything to put off the inevitable moment and to deflect attention. George hated the man for dressing like that. It was bravura. Yet he admired the soldier's courage.

George walked out into the courtyard, past the fishpond, and then around through the other entrance, past the bar and the bathrooms, and finally into the lobby from the hallway Doron had been watching. He sidled past the bad watercolors into a chair at Doron's table.

And then he didn't know what to say.

They looked at each other, then both looked quickly down.

"So?" George said, finally. He shut his eyes tightly for a moment.

"I brought you something," Doron said in English. He pulled the plastic bag out of his pocket and uncrumpled it. A grocery bag? thought George. An odd gift. George watched the soldier's big, strong hands flatten the plastic against the brass table. He seems so competent, George thought. The soldier took the bag and put it behind his back.

What *is* this? George asked himself. In a day filled with bad magic tricks, was this another?

Doron brought the bag back in front of him, and laid it on the table. Now there was something in it.

"There," Doron said, pushing the bag toward George. This is unseemly, George thought. But he took it.

He knew immediately what was inside. The shape was unmistakable. He felt the tip of the muzzle, the stubby barrel, the sweep of the trigger guard, and the hard, smooth butt. He looked up at the soldier.

"What for?" he asked.

"Oh," the soldier said, trying to seem cool and remote. "To do with whatever you like." But he looked wounded.

"Is it loaded?" George asked. Must be practical, after all.

"Yes, it is."

"And what do *you* suggest I do with it?" he asked Doron.

"Whatever." The soldier looked away from the table. "It's yours."

George looked at the soldier. His eyes were downcast, and his long lashes were like a child's. I don't even know how to shoot a gun, George thought. Don't tell Grandfather. Anyway, George supposed, it couldn't be too hard. I mean, look who usually shoots them.

"I don't even know how to shoot a gun," George said aloud. Does he think I'm some kind of a Vengeful Arab? There were plenty of people George would like to see dead. For example, right now, George wanted to kill the soldier in the way people usually say that: I just want to *kill* him! But he didn't actually want to *kill* him. This soldier was not someone whom he had ever imagined in a pool of blood. He wondered why not.

Doron looked up again. Raad was more wasted and handsome in person than on television, Doron thought. Hollows in the cheeks. Yellowed teeth. And those deep black eyes, like sultans' pools, and the incredible haughty demeanor that was not intended or cruel but was somehow superior and condescending. Don't even know how to shoot a gun. The sound of Raad's voice echoed in Doron's ears. As if knowing how were somehow wrong. . . . Maybe he'll shoot me—that's one way to learn how: use it. Doron thought. And is that what I want? he asked himself. Is that what I'm searching for? To put myself up on the block for retribution? Doron wanted to tell everyone that he was sorry, but he knew it wasn't enough. He didn't want to die, didn't want to be someone's target practice—he wanted coffee, and to *live* for a long time, but with an innocent conscience. What he wanted was impossible. He looked at George. What was the Arab thinking?

Oh, Yizhar would be angry, so hopping mad. No contact with the relatives, that was one of the rules. If there was ever another meeting in his office, Yizhar would definitely take out his gun and not hesitate to use it, especially if Doron were to tell him that he knew, he knew who had given him his orders.

"What were you thinking?" George asked.

Doron tried to focus on him again. He had thought their meeting was at an end. He looked up.

"I'm sorry," Doron said. "What do you mean?"

"I mean, what were you thinking on the night my grandson died?" He was the first person George had dared to ask a specific question about the incident. Not Marina, because it would hurt her. Not Sheukhi, because it hurt George. But this fellow, yes, because he was so obviously in some kind of pain, himself, already, and, as he had put it, he was the commanding officer.

Doron looked down at his hands lying flat on the table.

"You don't really want to know."

"No, you're wrong. I do," George said.

"I was thinking that this can't be happening."

"But it was."

"Yes. I was thinking, This can't be my fault."

"But it was." George felt bad saying this, but it did give him some pleasure to see the man wince.

"Yes, it was."

"My daughter will never recover."

"I know. Believe me."

George could see that what had happened weighed heavily on this person who was sitting here in front of him with his big manly hands and solid, upstanding mien. Good. He deserved to suffer. Ayie noh. Beleef me. He couldn't seriously think that George was either going to forgive him or to execute him here in the lobby of the American Colony Hotel, splattering blood all over the watercolors and inconveniencing the reception desk, but still, just being here showed the beginnings of a proper desire for *some* kind of atonement.

Doron sat there, looking down at his hands through long lashes.

George fiddled with the gun through the plastic bag.

"Why don't you go now," George said, finally.

"What?" Doron asked.

"Why don't you just go now? You've done what you came here to do."

Doron looked at the bag in George's hands.

"Yes, you're right." He stood. "I'll be going, then."

George stood also. The correctness was habitual.

Doron stood there on the other side of the table and openly stared into George's eyes.

George looked back, unfazed.

"Yes," he said, in answer to something unasked. "I'm one of the ones you hurt."

Doron kept looking.

"Now, go," George said.

Doron nodded. Without a backward glance, he turned smartly on his polished heel and went.

GEORGE WENT UP to his room, carrying the bag from the Israeli supermarket up the long staircase. Ahmed is on Jabal Il-Aalam, he was remembering, that empty, disputed hill between Jerusalem and Bethlehem. Har Olam, the Israelis called it—the Hill of the World. Ahmed on his high hill. Making another grand gesture. Har Olam was not more than fifteen minutes from the hotel. George let himself into the room.

Philip was standing in front of the French windows. He looked at George.

"It's okay, Philip," George said. "I'm fine. He was far better than Sheukhi, I must say."

"Well, what did he say?"

George shrugged. "Let's talk about it later, okay?" Sometimes Philip's curiosity got the better of his sense of decorum. "Are you going out?" Philip had his jacket on.

"To Jaffa Gate, for souvenirs," Philip said, with a smile of self-depre-cation.

"Blunderbusses and sabers, Philip," George said. "You can buy them there, right next to the menorahs and the tee shirts that say, you know, 'Shalom ya'll,' et cetera."

Philip smiled.

"And what do we have in the bag?" Philip asked.

"Oh, a blunderbuss." George set the bag down next to the bed and plunked himself down heavily in front of his laid-out game. You can never get away with anything with Philip around. The cards shifted slightly, and George began carefully realigning them.

"A blunderbuss?" Philip raised his eyebrows.

"Don't worry, Philip."

"I worry."

"I'm not a little boy."

"I know."

"I'll be careful. I won't do anything foolish."

"Maybe I shouldn't go out." Philip started taking off his jacket.

"Philip."

"You seem on edge."

"That's my own business. You go on out, now, and leave me alone."

"But . . ." Philip hesitated, his arm halfway out of the jacket sleeve.

"Go . . ."

"You . . ."

"I'm just going to sit here and finish my game, okay?"

Philip stood there, vacillating.

"Philip, I'm fine. I'm not going to whack myself, just yet. So get the hell out, now, will you?" George smiled a nonsmile at him, and started turning over cards. "Go do your errands."

"All right," Philip said. He sounded sad. He began buttoning his jacket.

"Don't put that plaintive tone in your voice, for Chrissake, Philip. I'm *fine*. I'll see you in an hour or so. You'll have your arms laden with goodies, and I'll be sitting here winning another round. Okay? Go on, there's a good boy."

"Okay, okay," Philip said, and walked out the door.

"Good," George said out loud, staring blankly at his cards.

He knew just what he was going to do. It might be an impulse, or it might be his last unswerving belief. But the means had just been put into his hands, and he was finding it uncharacteristically difficult to argue with that. He thought he'd take a taxi.

"There he goes," said Jibril.

Mahmoud had already started the car. "Yeah. We're lucky his car is so recognizable, eh?" He wondered what Doron could have possibly been doing in there for so long. It wasn't a place where they welcomed Israeli soldiers.

"Hard to miss," said Jibril. He rubbed the stubble under his nose. It felt itchy and unaccustomed.

"I am *so* glad your grandmother is taking the bus home with the others," Mahmoud said.

"You're a good planner, Uncle."

The boy always knew *just* what to say.

They were traveling up Nablus Road back toward the Hyatt when they heard a huge explosion.

"Sonic boom?" Jibril said to Mahmoud.

"I don't think so." If it was a bomb, that was a problem. Bombs always complicated life on the ground. For Palestinians, anyway. And it didn't take long.

"Sounded pretty huge, no?" Jibril said.

"Who knows?" Mahmoud said. "Depends where it was. If it was really near, that wasn't such a big sound, but if it was far away, it could be very very huge." He hoped it was a sonic boom. Bombs made life difficult for everyone, especially for people who needed to get across the checkpoint. But he knew it was not a sonic boom. He looked over at Jibril.

Jibril was smiling.

Why did young people like destruction so very much? Mahmoud wondered.

The Israelis were right to try to keep the young ones out.

CHAPTER TWENTY-SIX

DORON TURNED OFF NABLUS ROAD AND WENT PAST THE hulk of the Hyatt toward the road to Ramallah. If I don't think about it, I'll get there. Just drive straight, straight, straight. We've done this before, Ari. Watch the road. Don't hit any schoolchildren. Don't get back-ended by any pickups. Watch the lights.

Not far to the checkpoint. Dr. George Raad with *his* gun. Doron was so happy to be rid of it. He felt unburdened. He was happy to ride into enemy territory unarmed, with only his determination protecting him, which was no defense, he knew. Not far to the checkpoint, now, Doron calculated, even though, when he was stationed there, it always seemed he'd never arrive. Then, suddenly to his right, he'd see Jaffar's Supermarket, and be past the store almost before he noticed it, and then around the bend the checkpoint would emerge.

At the light near the Paz station, schoolgirls waited to cross. What would Raad do with the gun? Nothing, probably. He didn't seem the type, to put it mildly. And that was fine with Doron. Off to his left, the tomb of the prophet Samuel rose pink and yellow on its empty hill like those watercolors at the hotel. On the right on another lesser hill stood the skeletal radio towers of the big Israeli listening post where Doron used to hang out with friends.

Oh, fuck, what was *that*? Doron felt the explosion through the tires of his car, it was so big. He rolled his window down to see if he could hear the trail of a jet, but he could only hear the sound of broken mufflers and honking horns and the backfiring of trucks on the Ramallah road. Other people were looking out their windows and up at the sky, and shouting to each other. Doron had the automatic thoughts: Don't let there be bodies strewn all over, don't let there be too much blood, too many maimed—

that was the worst thing, worse than the deaths—and don't let it be any-one I know, please. Phones were ringing all over Jerusalem already, he knew. Are you okay? Yes, I'm fine. Are you okay?

Oopa! He'd passed Jaffar's and hardly noticed. He turned on the radio, but as usual, could receive only static.

I'm fine, Doron thought. Fine. He drove through the checkpoint, saluting the men.

EACH TIME HE went through the checkpoint in this direction, Mahmoud became angry. It was so *easy* in this direction. He felt nervous, humiliated, and guilty in anticipation of any encounter with Israeli authority, but it was true that the Israelis simply didn't give a shit what you were planning to do on the West Bank. The soldier had just driven through, like that!, no ques-tions asked, and for all they knew, he could be a crazed Zionist intent on blowing up a mosque at prayer time or taking a school of little girls hostage. And now, Mahmoud and Jibril. Mahmoud's heart was pounding, but of course, easy also! The soldiers waved them through—just some Pals on their way home, right? Didn't even stop them to ask what they'd been up to, even though they too had probably been able to hear that bomb. Lax se-curity, as if it could possibly matter who went in one direction but not who went in the other. As if you'd passionately want to know why someone was going to the store, and then not even care to take a look at what he brought home. Who could ever understand the Israelis?

He and Jibril continued tailing the soldier. Beeline for the Hajimi house. This soldier was a strange bird. He seemed to know just exactly where the house was, as if he'd been there before. Mahmoud checked his watch. Almost time for mid-afternoon prayers. Would Hajimi himself be at home? It was possible. The soldier parked the car with its Israeli plates right in front of the garden wall and got out. Mahmoud parked a little way past him, past the low, leafy askadinia tree near the gate, around a corner, and he faced the car out, so that they were hidden by a green dumpster but could make a fast getaway, if necessary.

"I should get things ready, right?" Jibril asked.

"Right," Mahmoud said. After all, Doron might not spend much time at this particular stop. He might receive a less than enthusiastic welcome. Who knew how Hajimi might react if he was home? Mahmoud left the keys in the ignition, and sat there thinking while Jibril chattered.

"I'm a little nervous, Uncle," Jibril said as he straightened up from his preparations and looked out the window.

"Of course," Mahmoud said. So am I. The right thing, he kept telling himself. It is the right thing, and the only thing to do.

"He will fight us," Jibril said.

"Yes, maybe," Mahmoud said. "But we are two and he is only one, even though he is big."

"What if he makes noise?"

"Yes? What if? Who will come to his rescue?"

"I suppose . . ." Jibril pulled on the fringe of his scarf.

"If he makes noise, we will have five, ten more men who will come to help us, that's all. Anyway, we have a gag. The gag goes on first."

"Right."

"Ready to go?"

"Yes, I think so." Jibril checked the bag he had put the stuff in. "Yes, I've got everything."

"Okay." Mahmoud turned off the car. "Once he goes in, let's hide under the askadinia tree, there. Outside the wall."

"Got it," Jibril said.

Mahmoud hoped Hajimi was not at home. He wanted to take the guy now, and he didn't want Hajimi stealing his prize.

HERE HE WAS, opening the garden gate. In his mind, Doron had done this so many times, opened her garden gate next to the low, leafy tree. Now he was doing it. The little catch, push down on it. It opens inward. He closes it behind him. Rows of geraniums and impatiens, looking dusty and half dead. He walks between them. One of his dried-out willows, over the house. Maybe he loves willows after all. He hears the call to prayer sound out through the neighborhood.

He reaches for his gun. It's a reflex. Because what if the husband is here. Never thought of that, now, did you? What if he likes to pray in the mosque, and he's going to burst out that door right now and run into me. What if he's here? Be brave, big Israeli soldier. You have seen the husband on the television: little, crushable. You can crush him in your bare hand. Suck the breath out of the child, crush the husband.

The house looks like a bunker to Doron now, as he approaches: low, with little windows, and set down in the hill. A child's plastic pedal-car is parked up against the house near the door, and a stroller.

He rings the bell.

She opens the door. Her hair is covered. She's so different with her hair covered. She looks so Palestinian. She looks up at him, curious and worried.

I'm an Israeli soldier at your door, he thinks. What am I doing here?

SHE WAS ASLEEP, napping, and the bell woke her up and now she can't help it, as she looks at this big man, this giant, at her door, in that uniform, she has the sudden thought, Maybe they are bringing Ibrahim back to me. It's like a dream: there is a tall Israeli soldier at my door. What else could it be about? Like a dream where the impossible thing you want to have happen is actually happening. She's still half asleep. Maybe there was some terrible mistake and they've had him all this time and now they're bringing him back to her. She felt her arms getting ready to go around him, she starts to reach out for him—give him to me!—and she wants to call out to Hassan that they're bringing the baby back. Hassan's just upstairs praying on the roof, but for this he would break off his prayers. For this. They're bringing the baby back.

"I . . ." Doron stopped.

Marina stared at him and heard his voice.

How could this person be here?

"What do you think you're doing?" she said to him in English. There was a catch in her voice.

Doron didn't know what to say. He stood there, looking down at her. He opened his mouth to say something.

"Why did you have to come?" she asked. She stared at him.

He couldn't read her face. What was there? Shock, anger, pain, what? Her face was like a wall against emotion, and then it collapsed. Her mouth turned down and her eyes shut tight and she pushed her fist against the wall. Her shoulders started to tremble and he saw that she was crying.

"You're the only one who knows. . . ." she said. "The only one who saw it happen. I can't . . ."

"Please," he said to her, leaning down. "I came because I didn't know what else I could do. I'm sorry. Oh, God, I'm making it worse."

She wiped her tears away, but new ones came.

She looked at him. Here he came to her in his uniform to apologize in Ramallah among his enemies at the house of the family he had wronged.

"My *husband* is upstairs," she said.

"I am glad he is out of prison."

The man has no idea, Marina thought.

"You're out of your mind," she said. "He'll kill you if he sees you here. Go away."

"Where am I supposed to go?" Doron asked her.

"Back to your country," Marina said.

"Can't."

"I don't care where you go. Just go, he'll kill you if you stay here. Do you want to destroy my life completely?" she asked. "If he hurts you, they'll take him away from me, too, and then I'll have nothing." Now she was trying to pile all her arguments and emotions up on top of each other as fast as possible, to be as cruel as possible, only get him out and away. His presence, that look on his face, made her heart ache. It was as if he were the first person to show her that he really knew what it had meant. Maybe in fact he *was* the only one who understood.

"What should I do now?"

"Oh, Lieutenant, Lieutenant." She shook her head.

The way she said it, Doron thought.

"I'll do whatever you say," he said.

She put out a hand and touched his arm.

"Go away, now," she said. "Before he comes down. Please."

He looked down at her hand on his sleeve. Then he looked back up at her face. She seemed to smile at him, a smile gone so fast he was hardly sure he'd seen it. Maybe he'd imagined it.

"Go on, go, now," she said. "Prayers are ending."

He looked down again. Her hand was pushing him out the door. He thought she'd been touching him, but really she had just been pushing him away. He backed up. The stone of her lintel was the exact pinkish yellow of the watercolors he'd seen at the hotel. He shook his head. The sun was shining across the yard, and it was growing darker, he could feel it. She was dismissing him into the void. Oh, Marina, please, he wanted to say. After this, there was nothing for him but Yizhar.

"He will come *down*, Lieutenant," she said. The soldier looked so bereft, but Hassan would not be capable of a second of pity if he found this figure in his doorway.

"Go," she said. "Go back to you car and get away.

"Save my husband," she said.

"Forgive me," Doron said to her. He leaned on the door frame and looked at her.

"I'm shutting the door now," she said. "I hear him coming."

The door began closing and he heard a man's voice call "Marina!" and then the door shut in his face.

• • •

DORON WAS STANDING there. Marina's face was gone, and Doron was still standing there, looking at the little golden peephole in the middle of the door and at the grain of the wood showing through the paint. He noticed the peeling door frame and the name of the family in Arabic written near the number of the house, the lovely scratches in Arabic for the number 286, and for the name Hajimi—he sounded it out under his breath—running just below the number in ribbony script, the number and the script looking alien to Doron, like something an archeologist would find on a stone buried in a desert somewhere beneath an ancient citadel, a stone etched with an unimportant message forgotten by generations.

Through the door he could hear them talking, a sound that made him feel lonely and in danger at the same time. She was right. Doron did not want Hajimi to find him there. He turned to go. Each stone in the garden path seemed precious to him as he walked away, each leaf. I will never see her garden again. He pulled open the gate, and stood there under the askadinia tree for a moment, looking at his green dumpster across the street. He wondered what he would do now, where to go. Maybe, maybe just turn around, do it, do it, let Hajimi play the story out.

He heard a rushed whisper like the sound of a hiding child, and he turned his head. A child? Someone grabbed him from behind. What? They had him by the arms and there was something over his mouth. A gag, they were tying a gag around his mouth. What? Was it Hajimi? The leaves of the askadinia tree scratched his face as he was pulled backward into its shadows. He spluttered and felt himself held in an inescapable embrace: one arm around his neck, another around his waist, hands coming from nowhere to bind his hands, the unbending blade of a knife against his cheek. Doron struggled, pulling his face back from the knife, pushing out his elbows to try to loosen the grip. Whoever was holding him wouldn't let go, he wouldn't. Was this a joke? The rope around his wrists . . . a kidnapping. Doron couldn't believe it. He twisted his body first one way, then the other in order to get free, but whoever it was stuck to him.

Who the fuck were they? Hajimi was inside. Doron felt betrayed, but by whom? And what creature could have so many arms? It was a team. He thought of Yizhar and his security detail, but the men behind him, working so hard to secure him, were grunting in Arabic. He tried to relax now into their grip. Why fight it? He would just lose his strength. They have me.

"Good boy," one said to him in poor Hebrew. "We go to the car, now." The flat of the blade pushed a little harder against his cheek.

Doron felt hands tapping all over him. They were patting him down. No one had ever searched him before—he usually did the searching. He looked down. Big hands on him, checking waist, legs, ankles, pockets. He had no weapon. They pushed him out from under the tree and across the street to a terrible-looking car. No elite Israeli forces rushed forward to rescue him.

"Get in," one of the men said. "In back." Big Hands jumped in and stationed himself next to Doron, a scarf wrapped around the bottom of his face. Another man got into the driver's seat. He started up the car. It coughed, and died.

The two men started to hiss and sputter in Arabic. The driver tried the ignition again. It died again.

Now *this* was a Palestinian situation, Doron thought.

Doron was waiting for more guys to clamber into the backseat with them, but no one came. Just him and his two handlers.

So there were only two? And no gun? I could have overpowered them. He looked at Big Hands: he was young, he had young, scared eyes. So easily overpowered. Here just beside the paralytic car, Doron's green dumpster—peace be upon it—was keeping witness.

The car shivered and collapsed yet again. Curses muttered by the men.

The driver, an older man, said something angry in Arabic, and the next thing Doron knew, Big Hands took a black-and-white keffiyeh out from under the front seat and tied it around Doron's eyes and untied the gag. More cursing as the car chugged and sputtered. Doron's throat tightened and his heart raced. But the reason they've taken me is that I asked to be taken, Doron thought. I came here of my own free will. They are doing what I wanted them to do. The car pulled away from the curb. Doron lay against the headrest and stared into the black of his blindfold. The roadbed bounced beneath them.

JUST AFTER THE CAR finally kicked itself into motion, the door to Marina's house swept open and Hajimi came running down the path. He burst through the garden gate into the street. Marina was standing in the doorway, frozen in a patch of sunlight. The car peeled away from the curb. Hajimi came to a sudden and complete halt. He stood there in front of the dumpster with his arms folded at his waist, utterly calm, tapping one foot, watching the soldier disappear in a cloud of dust.

She let him go.

CHAPTER TWENTY-SEVEN

HASSAN STOOD THERE IN THE STREET FOR A MINUTE AS the car sped away. The road was empty, now, but he watched the dust settle. His arms were folded. Marina was still at the front door. After a while, Hassan turned and went to look at the other car that was parked in front of the garden path. He looked at the Israeli license plate. He opened the driver's door and bent to peer inside at the ignition lock. No key. He turned and sat sideways on the driver's seat, his legs dangling outside the car. He could get someone to hot-wire it maybe, but it might take too long to arrange, and he didn't know the neighborhood well enough anymore to know which guys were good. Marina watched him. He sat there looking out at the dumpster. Finally he came back in.

"I think I have to go into hiding," Hassan said. "I can't believe it." He looked at her and anger flitted across his face. "It's unavoidable. The guy's been kidnapped and he left his car in front of our house like a signpost."

He went to get his cell phone, and began setting things up—looking for a place to stay, letting a few friends know. He said very little, looking up at Marina from time to time. She stood there watching him. He hung up the phone, and turned away into the bedroom. Marina followed him.

"I did not ask him to come here," she said.

He didn't respond.

"Now," he was talking to himself, as she remembered he did sometimes when he was unhappy. She'd forgotten so many small things. "Now, just throw some stuff together. . . . Only for a short time." He pulled a small black bag out of the armoire. He wouldn't look at her.

"They might not come, Hassan," she said. "We didn't do anything." He looked up at her and smiled a brief smile.

"It doesn't matter what we did, Marina. The car is in front of our house."

Hassan, Hassan, she was thinking, don't leave.

At the same time she was thinking: Go! Go quickly!

He had just come home and now he was going. Was this to be her last moment with her husband? It was not supposed to be like this. Hassan was intent on business, and didn't have time to calibrate *her* delicate emotions, not right now. But she would have to tell him her plans now, instead of waiting for days or weeks, as she had meant to. She had even hoped that with the passing of time, she might change her mind.

She watched him looking at books, bending over drawers, not taking things out, just looking down, with his shoulders hunched, breathing slowly. His hair hung over his eyes, and he drummed on the dresser with his right hand, a habit he had when he was bored or impatient or concentrating hard. She knew that back, so bony and breakable now, but so strong, he was so strong-willed and resolute, my God! He would go into hiding now, right after he'd been released, and for God knew how long.

And she was supposed to remain, and await whatever new tragedy might lie ahead. She would be permanently on a list of names for someone to read off—the way her lieutenant had read off their names that night at the checkpoint. A list of people waiting for bad news. She was finished with it, finished with the drama and the tragedy, finished with his heroism.

A powerful feeling of nothingness swept over her, something she had never felt before until Ibrahim died. Now it was as if nothing and less than nothing were left. She felt as if she were floating in black water. And she wasn't sure if she wanted a passing ship to save her or whether it might not just be better to go under to the place where you could hang suspended in dark water like a cold tentacled creature. There was no passing ship, in any case.

"I didn't ask him," she repeated.

"I know, I know," Hassan said. He went into the bathroom to get his toothbrush.

"Where will you go?" she asked. He came back into the room.

"I don't know," he said, fiddling with the bristles of the brush. He looked up at her. "I have some friends in the Old City; they say they can take me for a while." He looked pitiful, like a little boy, standing there with his toothbrush. "I really don't want to do this, Marina."

"I know you don't," she said.

"I'm not angry at you," he said.

"Yes, you are."

"Maybe a little. Maybe a little," he said. "You should have called me down from the roof. That's all."

She shook her head, but he didn't see.

He sat down on the bed.

"But really, I just feel frustrated by the whole situation," he said. "I want to be with you and it's impossible. Again. I just don't see . . . Oh God." He buried his face in his hands. "Why can't we just be together for a little while like normal people—why am I always in the middle of this stupid bloody battle?"

"Because you want to be, that's why," she said. His small bag sat open next to him on the bed. It was half empty. Even though he had no idea how long he would be away, he didn't pack much. It was the effect of prison, she thought.

"I think I'm going to have a breakdown one day," he said. He looked up at her with the kindest, most desperate eyes. She hadn't forgotten those eyes, at least. She went over to him and stroked his hair. "I'll come and see you, anyway," he said.

"Poor Hassan," she said. She leaned down and kissed him.

"God, I love you so much, what am I going to do?" he said.

Marina stood again, but kept her hand lightly on the top of his head. He held on to her waist with one arm. She had to tell him, but it felt wrong for the moment, when—according to what she had believed since she was a teenager—she should be adoring her brave commando, supporting him in his struggle, vowing to stand by him no matter what.

"I'm going back to America," she said.

"What?" He dropped his arm.

"Yes, I'm going to go back with my father," she said.

"No," he said. "No, you can't."

He looked at her for a long moment.

"He's ill," she said.

It was as if Hassan hadn't heard. He had shut his eyes. She knew he was trying not to listen to anything she might say that he didn't want to hear, trying to block it out.

"There's nothing left for me here, is there?" she said. He opened his eyes, now.

"I'm here," he said finally, quietly.

"No," she said. "No, you're not, not really."

"I am," he said.

"You're going into hiding. If I'm here, they'll just watch me all the time. I'll never see you, anyway." A trace of hardness had come into her voice and she tried to cover it up.

"Come into hiding *with* me, then," he said.

She laughed abruptly. "Hassan, come on." She took his toothbrush from him and wrapped it in tissue. She put it in a side compartment of his bag. She tried to imagine herself in hiding. A dark place, no friends, no family, strangers. Maybe she was already in hiding. She stood away from him slightly, looking down at him sitting there on the bed next to his bag.

Hassan looked at his watch and reached for her two hands.

She put them out and he grabbed them.

"I'm going to go, Marina," he said. "I think I have to go right now, really, before they find out what happened. Otherwise there might not be enough time for me to get away."

"Okay," she said. "Go then, go. I don't want you to go back to prison."

"Tell me you love me," he said.

"I love you," she said.

"You're saying it, but you don't know if you mean it." He still held her by both hands. "Tell me you mean it."

"I do mean it," she said. She pulled her hands away.

"Oh, Marina," he said.

"I do mean it," she said, "but I feel . . . I feel too many things right now. My father is so sick. He looks so thin, have you noticed? And the bombings today. They make me so angry. I just can't seem to get over it, at all, at all . . . and now you have to go, and *I* have to get out of here, that's all, that's really all . . ." She trailed off.

"You'll go to Cambridge?" he asked. "To the house in Cambridge?"

"Yes."

"I don't believe it," he said. He let his head fall back between his shoulders. He breathed deeply. His closed his eyes and opened them again.

"I was trying to see if I was imagining things," he said. He took one of her hands in both of his, and stroked it. He toyed with her wedding ring, and looked up at her.

"You're leaving me, is what you're saying?" His voice sounded angry, and not brave. In spite of the lines around his eyes, she saw his resemblance to Ibrahim.

"I won't let you," he said.

"You can't stop me, angel," she said. She ran her hand over his jaw-line. "You can't stop me. It's like hide-and-seek, Hassan. If you're hiding, you can't seek."

He stood up and turned away from her.

"What else do I need?" he asked, after a few seconds. She moved around to his side, so that she could see his face. He leaned down, avoiding her regard, peering into his bag that stood open on the unmade bed.

He looked at the bed. She looked at it.

They looked at each other.

He shook his head. There was no time.

"I'll find you. I'll call you," he said.

He leaned toward her and kissed her. "I will come to America and get you if you don't come back to me."

She imagined him arriving at Logan Airport with his little black bag.

"I love you more than anything," he said. He kissed her again and she kissed him back. She knew that what he was saying was true. She opened her mouth to say so, but he just kissed her more deeply and clutched at her, his hands up and down her back. She stepped backward and fell onto the bed. He fell with her, and they lay there together. He pressed against her and kissed her again and again. There was no time. She pushed him away. He disentangled himself. She stood.

"Go. Go, Hassan. You've got to." He looked up at her from where he lay across the bed.

"I'm going," he said. He got up. She handed him his little black bag.

And then he went out the back door and over the wall between their house and the Katuls' garden, and he was gone. Unbelievable. Her commando in his white shirt. She blinked and he was gone.

She went into the kitchen and sat down at the table. It was white and empty in here. No one was with her. Ibrahim's picture of the sun was up on the refrigerator. She looked at the tabletop, remembering Hassan's feigned passion for it the night before, and she began to shake. Everything was over, every possible thing. She *would* go back to America: where she belonged. She held back her tears. There was too much emptiness for her here. She would go home with her father and see him through his illness, and then start over. No love, though, and no babies. Just a small apartment in Cambridge. Some college friends. Long hours watching tennis with Dad . . .

Or something. She thought she could take her time.

CHAPTER TWENTY-EIGHT

REALLY THE VIEW WAS SPECTACULAR FROM UP HERE.
Ahmed folded his arms over his chest and gazed down at
the bucolic scene. Rana stood next to him. She was the
distant cousin of a close family friend, so his boys who were at the base of
the hill, controlling access from the Palestinian side, had agreed to allow
her up even though they knew he was alone. Thank you, boys. Of course
the Israelis wanted this hill—they would probably put a big Hilton and a
pool at its summit and then say: Look down on our lands, Ye Mighty, and
tremble! Those relentless Zionists! He put an arm around his pretty little
princess. She ran a quick, small hand over his stubbled cheek. Oh, dear, he
thought. Where *was* her ride back to Bethlehem? The ride was supposed
to get here a full five minutes ago, and though Ahmed was a practiced
master of small talk and small gestures, he was growing bored. Rana was
too young to spend three hours with, love or no love. He wanted the sunset to himself. He looked down toward Jerusalem, controlled by Them.
The city sparkled in the sun. Soon the glorious desert evening would
come and turn everything orange and purple and blue.

And to my right: Bethlehem. Controlled by Us. It rose in steps on its
own lesser hill. Ahmed was staking his claim, that's how he thought of it.
Planting his flag on the patriarchal ground, squatting up here on Jabal Il-
Aalam, the Hill of the World, in order to claim it for Palestine, or at least
for the Authority. Or, at least, to throw a serious Palestinian wrench into
the Israeli imperialist machinery, which wanted to build another of its
enormous, ugly settlements on Jabal Il-Aalam.

Make the Israelis suffer for every one of their encroachments, was
Ahmed's motto. He had actually pitched a tent here at the summit

(Hillary on Everest, his self-mocking thought as he watched his men drive in the stakes). He'd prefer a Hilton for a long stay, too, but you had to use the means at your disposal, right? as he liked to tell George—and in any case, tent life was making him nostalgic, reminding him of his heyday in the prison camp in Lebanon. Rana walked away from him and looked down over Bethlehem. He loved her so much. As long as her ride arrived in the next five minutes, he loved her.

Outside his tent was a circle of about thirty plastic chairs for meetings of friends—Ahmed's supplicants, sycophants, acolytes, protégés, et al., or (skipping the niceties of the classic tongues) ass-kissers and toadies. He loved the sounds of the old Anglo-Saxon syllables. So accurate and physical and impolite and unlike Arabic in every way. Aha! Far in the distance, he heard the putt-putt-putt that was the unmistakable sound of a Palestinian taxicab. Soon Rana would be on her way. His meeting was scheduled for tomorrow—he was planning to discuss the future of Find the Soldier. The campaign had outlived its usefulness. Safeguarding the Hill of the World for Palestine, now that was important. He wondered if his discussion would be affected by the bombs.

Sunset on the Hill of the World, his view obstructed—enhanced, in fact, in his personal depraved Palestinian opinion—only by a fence of concertina wire the Israelis had put up to keep demonstrators and squatters away. He loved his lonely hours up here with the symbolic razor wire and the sunset. The black night was better than anything, with all the stars, and the prayers rising up from the nearby villages. Last night he lay down on the rocky earth and looked out at all the huge blackness for an hour or so. It gave him a whirling sense of time's speed and life's brevity. He saw the faraway lights of planes; were those satellites going so slowly, too high for aircraft, wheeling in their orbits? And shooting stars, lovely. He had nothing here but his mobile phone and the radio—and a lantern and a daily aluminum tin of food and a bag of coffee, and a charcoal grill for grilling the meats his people brought him in the afternoon and for boiling the water for his coffee, and a tin pot and matches and his journal and the newspapers and about a hundred little coffee cups—and a couple of books. And a generator. Oh, and a heater, for cold nights. And of course the army lamp that swung from the top of his tent. Israeli issue, he thought contentedly.

Rana came up to him and rubbed against him.

"Where's my taxi?" she said.

"It's coming, sweetheart. Listen."

She perked up her head, and then nodded happily. The putt-putt-putt was coming up the dirt path the Israelis had carved into the side of Jabal Il-Aalam. It was nice to have Rana visit today, but that would be that. Ahmed wanted to protect whatever solitude he allowed himself, and besides, the rest of his days up here would be filled with business. The Hill of the World. Tomorrow was day three. *This* was a cause he could stick with.

He and Rana had heard the bomb earlier. Bang. Poof. Bang. It sounded like a major big motherfucker. Rana agreed. Lying side by side in his army cot, they had turned on his radio to hear the Israeli news. Mmmmmmh. Big, big, big. Oh my Christ, as George would say. Sixty or so killed on two buses, simultaneously. Hard to argue with that, eh? Damage done. And it had only been a week or so since the last round. Fools. Cowboys. Ahmed and Rana got out of bed and wrapped sheets around themselves and went to look down at Jerusalem. Little puff of black smoke down there at eleven o'clock, no? Rana agreed. Jaffa Road again.

Ahmed hated bombs. (Preferred assassinations, kidnappings, hostage takings: anything where some element of strategy and intelligence was involved.) No matter when a bomb went off, it ruined everything. You planned, you negotiated, you waited, you traded and bartered and connived and conceded, and you felt on the brink of something, you were just about to achieve something—it was touch and go, but possible. And then everything was brought down by some dumb fuck zipped into a vest full of TNT. Like an angry child kicking over a game he hadn't been invited to play. This bombing would ruin the launch of Hill of the World, no doubt. Ahmed had noticed recently that it was always an uncle or a cousin who'd recruited the suicide bombers. He noticed: they never sent their own sons.

The taxi. *Enfin.* Of course, this was the moment Rana would choose to push back her hair in that way. For a heartbeat, as her hair blew in the wind and fell back over her shoulder, Ahmed wished the bloody taxi away, and Rana back on the army cot.

GEORGE PEERED OUT the window as the taxi came to a stop. He had not planned on the girl. He hadn't planned on much at all, in fact. His heart was pounding away like A. Aronson's jackhammers, and a trickle of blood from Dr. Rodef's puncture had stained his white shirt. He noticed a large hematoma forming under the bandage; it was the first time the anticoagulant had shown signs of such overenthusiasm, he thought. His own blood made this doctor panicky. He put his coat back on, stepped out of the taxi onto the windblown hill, and told the driver to go. This was the end of things. Up here on this empty hill with the friend of his childhood. If he did it, he did it. If he didn't, he didn't. He felt dizzy. Light-headed from the thrumming inside him.

He was not in a calculating frame of mind, in fact. Unless one could call those fleeting memories that he was having on the ride up here calculations: After all our shared history, you let your cronies try to letter-bomb me, of all things. You exploited my dead grandson and my daughter. To say nothing of selling out the Palestinian people. You never really cared at all, did you?

Ahmed stood next to the girl. She looked like a child.

"To what do we owe this unexpected pleasure?" Ahmed asked. He had to shout over the wind, because George had not come very close.

"Just a visit," George said. He decided to ignore the girl's presence, and proceed.

"This is George Raad," Ahmed said to the girl. "An old friend of mine." The girl looked at George and smiled. She knew who he was.

"Come see my tent, George," Ahmed shouted. His voice sounded cheerfully welcoming, but he looked concerned, and curious. He was barefoot. Just out of bed, George thought.

"Actually, I wanted to show *you* something," George said. He reached into his coat pocket and was gratified to see Ahmed inch backward in anticipation of something bad. George looked up at him and smiled. "You look scared," he said, moving in closer. "You know, that was a big bomb back there. Did you hear it?"

He took the gun out of his pocket. He held it hanging at his side. It suddenly looked very big to him.

Ahmed was looking at it, too.

"My God," the girl said. George noticed that she separated herself from Ahmed, rather than move toward him for protection. Smart girl.

"What's that for?" Ahmed said.

George gave a short laugh.

"A better question is whose is it," George said. "Don't you want to know how I got it?"

"I guess so," Ahmed said quietly. He crossed his arms over his chest and looked at George.

"It's Ari Doron's," George said.

Ahmed looked at the gun, processing the name. George watched as he tried to remember. The wind rattled the concertina wire. The girl shivered and drew her little leather jacket tightly around her.

"The soldier," Ahmed said, finally.

"Yes," George said. "That's right. The most astonishing thing, really. He came to the hotel and handed me his gun. Loaded—he bothered to inform me."

"Why don't you put it back in your pocket?" Ahmed said.

"What, and keep it . . . like a souvenir?" George asked.

"Sure," Ahmed said, nodding. The girl was over at the edge of the hill now, far enough away but watching the two men. They could hear George's taxi going back down the hill.

"But the soldier said I should *use* it, Ahmed." George looked at the gun hanging from his hand like an unpleasant artificial limb. "You know, I knew his name all along, Ahmed. My little secret, eh?"

Ahmed's face registered no emotion.

"Let's go sit down, George, and stop this nonsense," he said. "We'll be out of the wind in the tent. Rana will make us coffee."

George looked around. Beautiful spot. High and masterful, like Olympus.

"I have a question for you, Ahmed," George said.

"What is your question, George?"

"It might seem impolite, you know. Propriety disregarded, and all that. Hope you won't mind?" George gestured with his palms in a questioning manner, but he had the gun in one hand, and Ahmed took another step backward.

"Get on with it, George."

"Why did you let them try to kill me?" He looked at Ahmed. He raised his eyebrows.

"What?" Ahmed said, pulling his head back and frowning. "Who?"

"Damascus," George said.

Ahmed shrugged.

"I didn't *let* them, George, don't be a fool," he said. "Nothing was going to stop them, except their own stupidity and incompetence. Which did stop them, actually."

Ah, Ahmed, never at a loss.

"A friend of my son-in-law's says you could have stopped them, but that offending them just then would have been inconvenient for you," George said. "Now, what do you say to that? That sounds just like you, doesn't it? Has the ring of truth. . . ."

"I did what I could, George," Ahmed said. "They certainly didn't kill you, did they? I mean, here you are, now, playing *your* little game."

"It's not a game, Ahmed." George brandished the weapon in a swinging way. It waved in the air very unimpressively, he thought.

"Oh, put down that stupid thing, will you, please?" Ahmed said.

George nodded. Ahmed's face, something about his expression, looked peculiarly diabolical to George. George smiled.

"You're *enjoying* this," Ahmed said.

"What do you expect?"

Ahmed turned his back. His loose white shirt was whipped through with wind. At least this was a more fitting assassin than Sheukhi, Ahmed thought. And this one would never shoot a man in the back. Would he?

No, this one would simply never shoot a man at all.

"Don't you turn your back on me, Amr." George lifted the gun and pointed it at the small of Ahmed's back. Was that a good spot to aim for? His doctor's instinct told him yes. Go for the spine.

George heard the girl gasp. He must have looked as if he intended to shoot. There, *that* was something to be proud of. Ahmed turned around. He looked at George and then started slowly toward him.

George moved back a step. He wanted to keep his distance from Ahmed, who could overpower him so easily.

"I'm bleeding, did you see?" George said. He shrugged off his coat, switching the gun from hand to hand, and moving backward. He let the coat fall in a heap to the ground. He stuck out his bandaged arm and looked at the mess. It really was quite bloody, his sleeve.

Ahmed glanced at George's arm.

"That looks bad," he said. He kept approaching, as if to look more closely at the wound.

"Don't come any farther, please," George said. He moved the gun up slightly, aiming at the heart. At least he knew for sure the damage *that* would do.

Ahmed stopped.

Jesus, thought George, shivering. God, it was cold up here.

"What's wrong with you, George?" Ahmed asked.

"I don't know," George said. "My heart is giving out, I think." He blinked back tears from the stinging wind. His heart was doing strange things. He dropped the arm that held the gun, and he felt the gun hanging there against his leg. For a second he thought, I must look ridiculous; but then the thought was gone.

"Did you hurt yourself?" Ahmed asked.

"They took my blood," George said.

"Ah."

"I'm feeling a little queasy."

"You don't look well at all," Ahmed said.

George nodded.

"Who's the girl?" he asked.

"An old friend," Ahmed said.

"Ah," said George. "Another old friend."

"Stop this right now, George," Ahmed said. "You're scaring her, you're scaring me, and you're making a fool of yourself."

"'Stop this right now, George,'" George said.

Ahmed shook his head in disgust.

George raised the gun again. It seemed very heavy now.

"Put it down," Ahmed said.

George did not lower the gun. He coughed. The wind, it was too much. What am I doing here? This is no place for me. He brought the gun back down to his side, and coughed again. Was it going to be one of those coughs? He started to shake. Where was his coat? This was no place for an ill man. I should be in a library somewhere, in my dressing gown, slippers, a little fire glowing in the corner, wooden paneling, dusty shelves, reading glasses, a deep sofa, dog at my feet. Like Ahmed's father in the study in Amman. Marina bringing tea. Not on this desolate hill.

"Do you remember your father's study in Amman?" George asked Ahmed.

"Yes, I remember it," Ahmed said. "George, you're sick."

"Yes, I'm sick," George said. He coughed again. "Of course I'm sick."

"Look at your arm."

He looked down. The sleeve was soaked in blood.

"I'm dying," he said.

"Well, at any rate, you're not well."

"Look at that," George said, staring at his sleeve. "It's like a medical specimen, for Chrissakes." He looked at the gun in his other hand and suddenly felt the absurdity of his position.

"Ahmed, Ahmed," he said. "Take the fucking gun, would you?" He raised the gun and motioned with it to Ahmed. The motion started him coughing again. Ahmed took the gun. The girl came running back to them, now.

George smiled at her, and the cough began again. It was getting dark. He bent over double with the spasms. Ah, there was his coat, on the ground. He leaned down to pick it up and his heart knocked him over and he felt himself topple.

CHAPTER TWENTY-NINE

THE TEAM HAD GONE OUT TO RAMALLAH ALREADY TO question Hajimi and perhaps to rearrest him. What a joke. As if he would say anything. As if he knew anything. Yizhar sat in a corner of the Thai noodle shop, nursing a Diet Coke. He'd thought he would eat, but he'd discovered as he entered the shop that the idea of feeding himself was repugnant. The smells emanating from behind the counter seemed muddy, rotten, and sickly sweet. Normal people would say that this aversion might come from the fact that he had just walked down Jaffa Road through what was left of the debris of the latest bombing—the glass shards, splintered wood, and crumbled concrete, the red metal scraps of bus, and the black blood splashed across the silver pedestrian barricades and staining the roadbed. But Yizhar was used to all that. The Thais remained miraculously intact among the wreckage, like a mirage, like something the hand of God had protected—probably because they were not Jews.

No, the revulsion was caused by something less palpable. He couldn't quite isolate it, but he knew that it had something to do with himself, a deep disgust with himself. Not for being pragmatic and self-serving and aggressive and obsessively secretive—it was very bad to know these things about yourself, but he thought that overall, these were good attributes. No, he was angry because he had been stupid. All his mistakes. Everything he could have done to prevent what had happened. His first mistake, not letting that woman speed right through with her sick baby. He saw himself clearly on that night, a literal-minded, authoritarian bureaucrat, out-of-touch, talking on the secure phone at his old decaying desk, and he hated that man because he had gotten the real Yizhar—brilliant strategist, clever operator, and patriot—into a difficult situation. He remembered feeling this turning of the stomach once before, when he realized that he was the one who had saved Gertler's career, and thereby had guaranteed his own eternal service on a secondary rung.

His stomach was churning up its ugly juices. Question Hajimi! Re-arrest him! Another idiotic ploy. Another sham. As if Hajimi had anything to do with Doron's disappearance. Hajimi was a Hamas nut, and probably a terrorist, but he wasn't a fool. You don't leave your victim's car outside your house. They were going to question Hajimi on two counts: Doron's disappearance, which no one but the chiefs of staff and a few key opera-tives knew about yet, and the bus bombings, both of which Yizhar highly doubted Hajimi had anything to do with. It just seemed convenient to take one guy in for everything at once. The checkpoints would go crazy.

In any case, Hajimi wouldn't exactly be sitting there in his living room waiting for them to come chat. If he realized what had happened—and of course, he would realize it—Hajimi would already be in hiding somewhere in East Jerusalem, and he'd wait until the whole thing blew over. The smart guys always did. There was always a dark little mildewed room in the back of some crumbling medieval heap, and some deviant asshole waiting to take a guy like Hajimi in.

Publicly, Yizhar was busy blaming the bombings—and anything else that might happen—on a "rogue Hamas element." (He was proud of that phrase, "rogue" and "Hamas" in the same sentence as if that were not redundant, implying, too, that the *nonrogue* faction of Hamas, the *not-as-bad* Hamas faction, was somehow a wing of the Authority. . . .) A "rogue" element doing evil deeds on its own recognizance—that concept kept the Authority clean, and meant that the Israelis could leave their eager, bright-eyed little Foreign Ministry youngsters at the table with the Authority, yap-yapping, and get the process over with.

As if that could ever be. Endings did not happen here. Things did not come to a close, even on the rare occasions when they seemed to. In the Holy Land, you could haggle for a century or two over an inch of unus-able land, and really *mean* it. Yizhar stood and looked at the steaming noodle counter again, but he could not rouse his appetite. He walked blindly out into the grim sunlight of shattered Jaffa Road. Let's be honest. Here was another unsavory aspect of his unfolding character: he felt just the tiniest bit of relief that Doron had disappeared. Oh, the tiniest, but definite. As long as the boy did not reappear on a Gaza podium next to the Chairman, and denounce the State of Israel and its duplicitous agent, Daniel Yizhar, Yizhar was not unhappy to see him go.

If the things that had occurred between Yizhar and Doron—the discussions, the arguments, the near scuffles—had happened between men of good faith, no one would ever have been the wiser, because there were secret battles that like-minded friends fought that they never revealed to another soul. It turned out, however, that Doron was another case entirely. Yizhar had made the mistake of believing that he and the soldier were on common ground. He had looked at the open face and the uniform and thought: We are both a part of the same army. But he had been wrong. In fact, although Yizhar hadn't understood it at the time, he and Doron were fighting over that one inch of unusable land. It made Yizhar want to punch things, this mistake of a lifetime, this second serious mistake of an entire career. It made him furious. Even though the soldier had brought his fate on himself at every point, Yizhar felt that his own standing and his reputation for handling things were undermined by the soldier's conduct. The jerk even paid for his own gas and drove his own car straight into a trap in Ramallah.

Yizhar wanted to want to be the kind of person who said, Let the right thing be done. He was capable of understanding that he should want to be good, pure. He wanted to be able to think to himself, Better that I be destroyed than that any harm come to this uncorrupted, upstanding boy. He wished he were capable of actually entertaining such thoughts. But he wasn't. He couldn't do it, not with sincerity. That kind of correctness was beyond him, and thank the Lord for that. That was turn-the-other-cheek crap. He pushed open the glass doors of The Building. Behind the huge plate-glass window of the public conference room near the elevator bank, old men in strange hats were doing jumping jacks—some old labor-union club, Yizhar assumed, supported by government subsidies, of course. He caught the scent of the chicken soup the men would be having for their lunch. It smelled like baby oil and old garlic and turned schnapps. He pressed the up button and waited. What mattered was that it was better for Yizhar—and better for Israel, he reminded himself—if a boy like this just disappeared.

Yizhar had explained the problem in general terms to the Defense Minister, and the Defense Minister had understood. Whatever was said publicly, the security forces wouldn't be pushing too hard too soon for Doron's rescue. No commando forces rushing into Ramallah in hot pursuit. And Yizhar didn't feel particularly bad about it—he didn't feel remorse about the Hajimi baby's death, didn't feel in the least guilty, and he didn't feel bad about Doron's disappearance. He just didn't.

Still, the familiar creeping nausea followed him as he entered the elevator. It was the nausea you felt when fate might be going against you—fear catching you in the stomach. Yizhar got out on his floor. Maybe he was just holding his breath until he heard that the soldier had been killed, and then his cramps would ease. He opened his office door; he must have done it quietly, because there was Irit, with her feet on the desk and a bucket of soup in her lap, slurping away as happily as a puppy and chatting on the telephone.

Other people were happy, Yizhar thought.

She looked up, saw him, promptly removed her feet from the desk, and then proceeded to extricate herself, with as much dignity as possible in the circumstances, first from her telephone call and then from her bucket of soup. Yizhar stood in front of her desk, his arms folded over his stomach, considering her embarrassment. She was showing the tender line of flesh again. Thank you for the entertainment, Irit. The smell of her snack made his stomach turn over. How she would thrill to a televised denunciation of her boss!

He strode into his office and shut the door crisply. He glanced over his newspapers again and looked at his memos and checked his messages. So far, no one had claimed responsibility for Doron's disappearance, and no one had demanded anything yet in exchange for his release. In the language of terror, these were accepted indicators that the soldier was already dead. Still, Yizhar would appreciate a body. In a ditch, by the side of the road, in the wadi, under an overpass, wherever. Just give me that one final proof.

CHAPTER THIRTY

T HEY'D PUT HIM IN THE CAR. BIG HANDS LIKED TO SHOW bravado—he was shoving and pushing, but the older guy was different. Doron knew that the older guy, who seemed oddly familiar, was the real threat. Old Guy thought he was clever, driving around with Doron pushed down on the floor of the car, driving all over Ramallah to try and confuse him about his whereabouts. The boy kept his feet on Doron's back. But when they'd finally came to a stop, Doron knew exactly where he was. Downtown Ramallah, in a cramped parking lot behind one of those dirty office buildings. It was unmistakable from the noises of the traffic and pedestrians, and the smell of diesel and *za'tar*.

His captors had jumped from the car, and hauled him out, talking to each other the whole time in undertones Doron could barely hear, much less understand. He stumbled as they pulled him over a rubble-strewn lot to a back staircase. Going up the crumbling stairs in a blindfold was terrifying until he realized that if he looked straight down he could see the broken edge of each stair as he climbed. The younger one held Doron by his cuffed hands as he pushed the soldier up the stairs from behind, and it felt like the grip of friendship, as Doron went blindly up.

Old Guy was fiddling with a key when Doron and Big Hands reached the landing, and he muttered when it wouldn't turn in the lock. Doron heard the keys clink together. Then the swoop of the door opening. They shouldered him into a room, pushed him down on the floor, and chained his handcuffs to something. Then they removed his blindfold.

Chained to a desk. Doron was surprised it wasn't a bedstead or a radiator, which was the cliché if you knew about hostage takers. An office desk was very difficult to pull through a door frame by yourself, though, so it was a good enough device. But a radiator was even better, because it was fastened to the floor. Doron looked at the radiator from his vantage point at the side of the desk, and thought, Well, these are pretty good conditions, considering.

He tried to decide, from down on the curling linoleum, whether he was glad or scared to be having this last adventure. Scared. Well, he was not going to escape from this place. Escape was an impossibility. He wouldn't even attempt it. This was his trial, right here on the floor in Ramallah. Finally, they had found the soldier, but only when he had stuck himself in front of them and said, Here I am. Sit here chained to this desk for a century, maybe then you'll have done penance, he thought. Being a good person and regretting the harm you have inflicted does not relieve you of your guilt. Zvili, who was not a good person, could walk around saying to himself, Too bad the kid died. So could Yizhar. Doron wondered whether Yizhar cared at all, really, that Ibrahim had died. Yizhar probably said to himself: There were valid security reasons. He wondered if Yizhar knew that these guys—Doron would call Old Guy and Big Hands clowns, except that they had done a brave thing—he wondered if Yizhar knew they had kidnapped his pesky little soldier.

OLD GUY WANTED to execute him, that much was clear. Doron watched Old Guy sitting on a folding chair a couple of feet away from the desk to which Doron was attached. He was holding the blade of his knife against the flat of his palm. He seemed to be using it as a mirror. Just studying his reflection. Couldn't see much of himself with the bandana around the bottom of his face, though. After a while, the two men removed their face coverings.

Old Guy played with his knife. He looked over at Doron, imagining, debating how to do it, Doron thought. Imagining where to stick the blade, between the ribs, but where exactly? If you hadn't done it ever, it was hard to know how to do it efficiently, even if you had a victim who was trussed and couldn't do much to defend himself.

Doron could tell him what to do if he would just ask. He'd learned how to wield a knife in special-forces training. Just stick it right up against the spot between the ribs and then shove up and to your right. That should do it, pretty handily, Doron recalled. That would be the easiest way. Big Hands was pacing the room, occasionally flicking on the television to watch news of the bus bombings in Jerusalem, then flicking it off again with a curse. The kid was nervous and the stress made him impatient and angry.

Doron knew from the minute it began that this was an amateur adventure, not anything big or well planned or controlled by Iran or run by Hamas. Hamas would have killed him immediately, and then let the Israelis stew, wondering whether their soldier were still alive. The guys Iran managed would have taken him on a much longer and more professional ride, and then used him in some hostage-bargaining deal. In both cases, the car would probably have run better. In both cases, no one would be sitting around, looking at a blade.

It bothered Doron that Old Guy was always looking at him as if they knew each other. It was weird. Oh, yes, and they *did*, Doron finally realized. That's who he was: the fellow at the checkpoint, minus the moustache. Troublemaker. What had Yizhar said? A lawyer from Ramallah, the name was too hard to remember. Lawyer kidnaps soldier. Doron tried to make his face as empty as possible; he didn't want the man to know he'd been recognized. The fellow had an itchy trigger finger, Doron felt, but fortunately, no gun.

MAHMOUD WAS THINKING. It was hard to think with the guy on the floor, there. He looked at his own reflection in the wide blade of the knife. He knew those eyes. They were his own, and very like his brother's. Mahmoud wasn't an old man, or a man whose life should be over. But if he did what he meant to do . . .

He pictured it: that was easy. Ahmed Amr, bored of toying with the soldier, tells his Israeli pals that Mahmoud is probably the kidnapper. Or Ruby Horowitz figures things out. She goes to the Israeli authorities. One way or another, hit squads surround Adnan's house. They don't find Mahmoud there, *inshallah*, but they take Adnan in for questioning, which means a brutal interrogation for his brother, who has no idea what Mahmoud and his own firstborn, beloved son Jibril are up to. Mahmoud meanwhile is hiding in the rundown East Jerusalem apartment of some friend of Jibril's. He pictured a very uncomfortable bed, a bad place to spend your last nights. Bad food, day after day. Poor plumbing. Endless boredom, while his luck lasts. And then the team of elite commandos descends. Imagine the wrath of the army after he's murdered one of their own. He imagines it. They won't arrest him and Jibril. They'll kill them and call it a "work accident," that's their phrase for it: they claim you died when the bomb you were making accidentally exploded. And there are no further questions.

Yet Mahmoud felt his whole life was leading up to this. It was right and honorable to kill the soldier. Any Israeli soldier deserved to die, and this wretch most of all, because he had murdered that poor little boy. Mahmoud knew. The guy had stood there chatting on the phone while the boy suffocated to death in front of them all. Mahmoud saw it all, up to a point, and he did not need to know more. More didn't matter. Israeli soldiers humiliated Palestinians every day all day, and they killed you with their rubber bullets, and they kept the whole fucking Palestinian population in prisons and refugee camps, and this soldier deserved to die.

He put the knife flat against Doron's stomach. The pig was sleeping. Sleeping as if he had a clean conscience. I could gut him now, now, while he's asleep. The uniform with its little proud epaulettes incensed Mahmoud. This guy is so pleased to be representing the oppressor, the usurper. He looked at the soldier's face, made innocent and vulnerable by sleep. The lieutenant's mouth was open, and his breath came quietly and regularly, like a child's. But he was not a child. He was a soldier. Mahmoud lay his knife against the sleeping man's throat.

CHAPTER THIRTY-ONE

"C areful of the IV," Ahmed warned from in front of the window.

Marina and Philip were turning George in his hospital bed. George's feet protruded from beneath the sheet as they lifted him. The skin on the top of his feet was delicate and thin, and on the bottom, callused, his toenails yellowish. Sad, cold feet. Marina covered them. Their vulnerable condition after so much use seemed to her to sum up the whole history of her father's life. The idea that he could be so passive, that she was in charge of him. He was heavy. They straightened him; Philip held his head up while Marina fluffed his pillow. Philip laid him back down, and Marina arranged him. He looked like a king, still. She pushed his hair back from his forehead. He sighed.

The doctors had been pitiless. A massive heart attack, and internal bleeding from the anticoagulant George had been taking for so long, they told Marina, Philip, and Ahmed. His brain function was minimal, his heart was a fluttering, stuttering wreck. Dr. Raad was, in their opinion, really too far gone for any kind of treatment. Sometimes it happened like this, suddenly. In a way, it was a blessing. Let him go, they advised. It won't take long. We'll give him drugs in case he is feeling any pain, which we doubt.

Death is like this. Marina remembered her mother's death, that same feeling of paralysis and inability, combined with the need to be very organized, very efficient, and totally responsible. Back then, she had taken charge of her father. Now, there was nothing left to take charge of.

George lifted his left arm and turned his wrist toward his face. This had been his only movement since he arrived at the hospital yesterday evening. The doctors told her it was a primitive motor reflex, that it was meaningless. But she couldn't help thinking he was trying to see what time it was. His eyes were closed. She kept whispering in his ear. She imagined that Philip and Ahmed thought she was saying things like Daddy, I love you, when in fact she was merely informing him that it was five in the evening.

THE WHOLE VALLEY lay below them. Ahmed had never realized what a good view Hadassah Hospital had of the Arab villages that tumbled down the side of Mount Scopus. He recalled that the Palestinians used to ambush Zionist caravans taking doctors and nurses up here, and now he understood why: the hospital site was a prime military redoubt. From this place, you could see everything. He wished he could discuss it with George.

Ahmed looked over at the bed. Friend of my childhood, farewell. He had grabbed George when he fell, and Rana's taxi had arrived just a few frightening minutes later, and they'd sped George into Jerusalem—a trip that had no checkpoints, luckily. Ahmed had held George in his arms like a baby.

He sat down heavily on the windowsill. Marina looked vacantly toward him. She is so like her father, Ahmed thought. He recalled little George blinded by tears as he watched the Amrs packing to leave Jerusalem back during the Catastrophe. The tears, of course, were not because George was going to miss *me*, Ahmed thought, but because he realized that my fate would soon be his. He remembered George in his short pants, watching Ahmed's father and Mohammed, the houseboy, load box after box of books into the back of the open truck that took the Amrs and the Nassars to Amman. Those were precarious days—and so are these, my friend. He looked at George's hands which lay lifeless on the white sheets. A strip of black Hebrew print down the side of the sheet, next to George's right hand, read HADASSAH HOSPITAL, JERUSALEM. Ahmed smiled. George would laugh at the absurd idea of patients' stealing the sheets.

PHILIP TURNED ON the television. Marina looked up. More scenes from the bus bombings. Apparently, the reporters had got hold of a new piece of videotape. Israelis always seemed to have a videocamera and a cell phone on hand whenever something happened. She watched as people on the street scattered and the camera's shocked lens bounced up to film the roofs and then down to film the moving pavement as the camera's owner also fled from the explosion. The hospital room had gone entirely motionless and silent except for the blip of George's monitor and the jumble of noise from the television. They were all transfixed. A doctor came in, looked at George and the television, and went out. The camera's eye righted itself again and people started running toward the burning buses. They were pulling on arms and legs that stuck out of the windows and doors, trying to free those who were stuck inside, before they burned. Marina closed her eyes for a second. She looked again. Limbs and other unidentifiable blown-apart things littered the street. A baby was screaming in a policeman's arms.

"Dah," Ahmed said, quietly.

Philip winced.

Marina forced herself to think: One, the Enemy; two, they are not innocent; three, an occupied people is justified in striking civilians; four, they stole our land and killed our children. She heard Hassan's voice, making all the arguments, the way he used to. The baby was screaming and his face was wounded, she could see now. Passersby were leaning over the victims on the pavement, holding their heads, talking to them. Ambulances had arrived, with stretchers and emergency workers running crazily around in white-and-orange uniforms. It looked like a battleground. This *is* a battleground, Hassan would say. It's been going on for a hundred years. They do it to us, also.

WHATEVER HAPPENED TO her father, she thought now, she was still leaving. Soon after Hassan had disappeared out the back door into the dark, carrying his sad little bag and looking too thin and too young and too bent under the weight of all his worries, Philip appeared at the front door, with the Uno idling, and his bad news, and now here she was. Marina watched the television screen. The policeman handed the screaming child to a nurse who disappeared from view off to the right.

"We'll just turn it off, shall we?" Philip said.

"No, no," she said. "It's okay." Philip had immediately started to sound like her father.

"But it's upsetting you," he said.

"Oh, Philip," she said. "Everything upsets me. Leave it on." She wanted to say: I need to see it. It reminded her of everything, all her reasons for leaving. Before, she would never have watched it, and would have dismissed all of Their suffering as richly deserved. Now, she knew. The men who were involved in history wanted to argue that this was one way to change how the world worked. They just simply did not care about a baby's bleeding face, if it wasn't their own baby. She was leaving.

She smoothed the sheet next to her father's hand and watched as the television reporter in his fresh clothes talked into his shiny microphone while behind him the chaos was continuing to unfold. It was Hassan's politics that had put Ibrahim on a list, and once she had realized that, she knew she would never recover from it. Hassan Hajimi had believed and spoken and acted, and then Marina and Ibrahim Hajimi were on a list, and then her baby was dead. You could go back forever to decide which side's claims were legitimate, back into the darkest history for a millennium, at least. Hassan would always blame the Zionists. Marina lifted George's hand and held it. It was cool and dry.

We all agree, but in the end, so what? What if we win? If you could establish a utopia on earth at the expense of the eternal suffering of one child and its mother—even a Zionist child and its mother—then Marina did not want that utopia. She wanted to be in a place where nothing mattered very much and nothing was worth it, and no one had to make any final sacrifices. She wanted to remove herself from history. She knew she was lucky to have the ability to flee, and only wished, bitterly wished, that she had done it before. She could have escaped—instead, she had returned. Returned to Ramallah. What had she been thinking? Daddy's fault, she thought again, for glorifying The Cause and romanticizing The Homeland when she was a child.

She remembered her fantasies as an adolescent: life on the run with handsome boys, living in desert caves, talking about raids and revolution. What a child she had been. It *was* her father's fault, but she was what he was: a Palestinian. Soon he would be dead, and blame would be useless, as it was already. A Palestinian. That was why she wanted to escape from history; it pressed down too hard on her. Now, she was dreaming again of the Star Market.

Five-fifteen in the afternoon, she whispered.

GEORGE MOVED his head slightly.

There was babble all around him.

That noise, what was that noise? Sounded like gunfire or explosions. Did Ahmed have the gun? Salah al-Din, charge!

Ahmed threw sand in his eyes, but the castle was rich and splendid. Splendid. Someone was holding his hand, how sweet, nice cool long fingers. Was it Nurse? Or Sandra? Sandra, it must be. Hard to say, it was so dark in here. He tried to open his eyes, but it was too much of an effort for a tired old coot like him. He gave in to the fatigue. Just lie down, stay calm, no one will hurt you.

I have a lucky charm from home here in my pocket.

That girl, gee, she was so pretty. Ahmed's friend.

Don't bait me, Philip! Ahmed is my *friend*. They sent me to kill him, they made me do it, gave me their gun, but an Arab does not kill his Arab brother. Not for any reason besides family, and especially not with *the enemy's* gun.

But it *was* family, there was a question of family.

My, it's nice to lie here quietly.

Family. Yes, that's right, it was the little boy. Don't kick my castle down, little boy. Stop all the clocks. Turn off that ranting, babbling noise.

Where *is* that child?

He's lost, down in the orchard, Grandfather.

Send for him, send for him.

What time is it?

MARINA LOOKED OVER at her father. He was checking his wrist again. It was disturbing to her, this constant checking of his wrist, because she knew he had so little time left. She leaned over to him.

"It's five-thirty, now, Daddy," she whispered. Twilight was spreading over the Arab villages below.

DADDY. DADDY. It's five-thirty in the evening. A lovely day for a picnic, they'd had. We took the horses down through the village. Down the hill through the almond trees to Grandfather's, with the turbulent cousins running among the hooves. The blossoms are pink, the pinkest palest pink like children's skin.

Oh, Grandfather, I've found the boy. Look! He was hiding there behind the cypress, silly thing. Kiss me, little Ibrahim, you scoundrel! Gotcha! I have him by the scruff of the neck. Aren't you glad I found him, Grandfather?

I am glad, so glad. And lucky to find him before nightfall, too, young fellow. Put the darling little one up on my lap.

Send Hamad on the donkey for water with the earthenware jug.

There goes Hamad, disappearing under Grandfather's willow toward the well. Grandfather's put his walking stick down and he's sitting on the terrace with his fez and all his medals, and that sweet little big-eyed boy on his lap. Let's go down among the bushes, shall we, Sandra?

I have a patient and another patient, George the Worm. Twist it into the heart. Carefully, my little angel!

Where's my lucky charm, my shiny silver key?

Marina! Save me, kiss me, where are you? Hold my hand tight.

What time is it?

CHAPTER THIRTY-TWO

O ld Guy thought he was sleeping but Doron was not sleeping. He knew what was lying flat against his throat. It was a final judgment. A sharp and shiny final judgment. Doron willed himself to relax beneath the blade, to keep his breathing calm and regular. His heart was pounding. Easier, he thought, to be his father, hit suddenly, full blast, in the middle of a battle, than to lie here passively, waiting. He could smell the other man, his smoky, garlicky breath. It was definitely the lawyer and not the young one. Somehow he held out more hope for the lawyer than for the kid. The lawyer wanted to do it, but there could be mitigating circumstances. The other was young and probably thought he had nothing to lose. He was like Doron.

THEN SOMETHING CHANGED. The blade was removed and Big Hands started to pummel him into consciousness. He pretended to wake suddenly. Maybe they just wanted to finish him off someplace else. He couldn't make out their Arabic.

"We go now," Big Hands said to him in Hebrew; it was always the younger ones who could speak it; they learned it from the television. Big Hands unchained him from the desk and stood him up. They whisked him to the bathroom—a brief respite. He wondered if the bathroom stop meant they would be going a long distance now.

"Are we going far?" Doron asked Big Hands.

Big Hands looked at him.

"Don't ask questions, you," he said.

He took the gag and the keffiyeh from his back pocket and wrapped them again around Doron's head.

They hustled him down the stairs—he wondered why they didn't wait to put on the blindfold until after the stairs were negotiated; not thinking, probably—and out to the car. They pushed him up against it so that his knees were touching the fender. One of them opened the back door, and while Doron was standing next to the car, waiting for the next thing to happen, someone came up behind him with a whoosh of air and the sound of something descending, and Doron fell into the backseat and blackness.

SHE'D FALLEN ASLEEP in the chair next to George's bed, and when the light came up over the villages below his window, it struck her across the face and woke her. His monitor was still beeping. She'd been dreaming of the soldier. She wondered what had happened to him. Spirited away like that, when his only reason for coming was to express his shame. Well, if you didn't like to be ashamed, you shouldn't be an Israeli soldier, she thought. We were all victims of history.

She looked at her father. He seemed asleep, but deep asleep. A painful lump of sadness swelled in her throat. George's breath came in puddles and falls and great gasps and gulps, as if he were drowning. He tapped his hand against his side, over and over, as if he were feeling his pockets. This was new. He had no pockets, anyway. He was wearing a humiliating hospital robe with Hebrew scrawled all over it.

Ahmed was outside in his car in the parking lot, using his cell phone, and Philip was sleeping on a couch in the waiting room. Marina stood and kissed her father and smoothed his cheek. Even dying like this, in an Israeli hospital, too thin and bleeding and unable to breathe, he was still heroic, still the handsomest man she had ever seen, except for Hassan. He would find it so ironic to be dying under Zionist sheets, in a Zionist robe. She kissed him again, and held his hand briefly. When she let go, he patted his side again.

"I'll be back in a minute," she said to him. Pat, pat, pat.

She went to get coffee from the stand downstairs.

NOW HERE HE WAS. Where was he? Doron shook his head. He had received a terrible blow. His head was pounding. His eyes were wide open but everything was black and his face felt constricted. Why? Doron reached up with a hand he could move—ah, they had uncuffed him—and felt his face: the blindfold. Well, *that* was a good explanation, and it cheered him because he was lying here thinking but not letting himself think that for all he knew they might have blinded him while he was unconscious from that blow. Or was it a blow? Possibly he had fallen, fallen from something, what was the last thing he could remember? Doron tried to gather his wits. His head did hurt.

He was lying somewhere, outside. It was cold. There was something rubbing against his back, now, stones or rubble. It was not car upholstery and it was not linoleum.

He wiggled his back. It was like a massage, all those pebbles or whatever against him, he was having his back scratched. He untied his gag, pulled off the blindfold, and saw the sky. Evening or dawn. He had just about lost track of time but he thought it was night coming on, it seemed the beginning of darkness, rather than the end of it. He loved the night, especially the night without Yizhar. His captors seemed nowhere about. In fact, there was no one near. Only sky. He looked up into it. A few cars passed by. Blue night, blue night. The air was a good fresh cold that roused his brain. Thank God for oxygen and the dark, Doron thought. Above him he could see faint stars, but in the foreground, telephone wires and cables running on and on and poles carrying them, and a huge stone wall rising next to him and obstructing his view, and then the dark blue sky beyond.

Can I stand, he wondered? He bent his legs, and that was not nice, not a nice feeling, not good, he was stiff and felt like old iron. But he did it, and then bent at the waist, and that bent too, with a tearing sensation of a rip on his right side, a huge tear of some kind. He sat on the pavement and felt his side. Wet with ooze. He looked down at his hand. It was like a cup of blood, viscous blood, very black, clotted. He felt himself begin to swoon, but then he recovered. He slapped himself on the face hard with his clean hand, which woke him. He balanced his body away from the pavement and stood. It was a reeling, dizzying moment, and then he righted himself. He stuck his hand back over the wound and felt into it, his fingers went in as if into some kind of wet pocket. It felt shockingly deep and wet and red.

Now he remembered. He had come back to consciousness in the car after a terrible blow. He was lying over the back hump, and his body ached terribly. He gasped or sobbed and heard the lawyer say in Arabic, as plain as day: Let's leave him here. *Khallinah nitriko hon.* The car stopped, then, with a small screech, and Doron was tossed forward on the floor. He remembered Big Hands; Big Hands was pushing him out of the car somewhere and he was half conscious at best with the moon spinning up and over and then down and up and over and then down, and then a blade came up into the air in front of the moon out of nowhere sparkling all of a sudden and Big Hands lifted it high over the stars and struck, and Doron had that moment of thinking, He just can't leave me without a mark of hatred. It would be too humiliating.

He looked down at his side, now. He was bleeding away. Too much, Doron thought. I might bleed to death right here. Well, at least my penance is done. It *is* done, isn't it, Marina? He looked around. He was standing below a high garden wall in Ramallah, and he recognized it—the last wall of the residential area, just where the commercial part of town begins. A pink light stirred at the bottom of the sky, and more cars started to roam the streets. He heard the call to prayer. It was morning, not night. A newspaper blew across the street and over up against the window of a hardware store. In the yellowy light of the dawn, men were trailing into a doorway a block away.

He'd go there, Doron thought. It looked busy—not a place where anyone would think of finishing him off. He dragged himself to the curb and held on to a lamppost. He held on passionately, like a drunk. Finally he summoned up his strength and slowly staggered across the street. My God, I might not make it. He fell at the curb on the other side, but hoisted himself up against the rickety tin of a closed pita stand. For a few minutes, he stood there balancing against it, thinking of Marina's open dreaming eyes and Big Hands' hands. And then he stumbled up a little incline past the tea shop that was closed for Ramadan, and leaning now against the sides of the buildings, hauled himself into a tiny cement-block courtyard where he had seen men gathering. Almost at the door, Doron tried to catch his breath. He heard himself inhale—it sounded like bubbling. Was air escaping from his side? He clung to a bookcase that was filled with shoes. It struck him funny, shoes in a bookcase. His side felt wet, but he didn't want to look down. He closed his eyes and leaned against the wall. He was afraid he might faint before he could get help.

Some kind of murmuring was coming from inside. Doron turned into the open doorway. Exposed bulbs hung down from a low ceiling, and all across the floor, men were on their knees, their backs to him. He felt carpet under his boots. Against the back wall, a sheikh in a white turban was saying something. Doron stood there, facing him across the room. He looked frail and ghostly to Doron in the sparse light. Oh, Sheikh, Sheikh, in your turban and robes, horror and fear spreading over your old face. Rescue me, rescue me. Following the sheikh's stare, the praying men began to turn in unison toward the door. And then, to the amazement of the scattering supplicants, the big soldier lurched forward into the mosque, tracking mud from his boots over the prayer rugs. He stumbled blindly in one direction and then another. Men with angry faces rush toward him. *"Duktor, duktor,"* Doron heard someone shout. His legs were bending beneath him like reeds in the wind, and he reached out to steady himself, but there was nothing there. The room with all the men in it was spinning and spinning. He turned, and turned again, and fell face forward onto the floor.

FATEFUL COFFEE, good and strong but American style, what she'd grown up with. Marina stood there in the hallway with her almost empty Styrofoam cup, standing back from the small crowd that had gathered outside his door. She knew it was over. She'd come back with her coffee to find that group huddled there, mostly patients and doctors from the hospital who had gathered to witness the passing of Israel's fabled opponent. For some reason what came into Marina's mind was the dilapidated suitcase her father had packed to leave her house. The suitcase that had gone everywhere her family had gone.

She'd missed the very moment of his death. Perhaps that was just as well but she knew she would regret it always. She made her way through the cluster at the door. Doctors were all over the place, having failed to resuscitate George, and Ahmed was sitting in the big chair in the corner, with his face in his hands. A pearly glow lit the window behind him. Marina was not ready to feel anything except that it was over. Philip came up to her and put a hand on her shoulder but she shook him off gently.

There was George, the center of attention in death as in life. A Palestinian in an Israeli hospital: it was as good an ending as any, and full of meaning for a man who had never been able finally to say that any slice of humanity was wrong or evil or bad, though he had criticized and denounced with the best. She went over to the bed and touched the side of his face. No amount of advance warning prepared her for the emptiness that death created. There was no end of difference between a living body—even comatose or unconscious or asleep—and a dead one. She stroked his hair.

Ahmed came over to her side.

"I did love him, Marina," Ahmed said. He reached for her hand. "In spite of everything."

She nodded. "I know, Uncle," she said.

"I think he might get up and walk out the door," Ahmed said.

She looked up at him and shook her head.

"But I know what you mean," she said. She picked up George's hand. She looked at it, trying to commit it to memory.

"More than an octave," she said.

Ahmed laughed.

"Yes, I remember that," he said.

SHE WOULD BURY him in the family plot in Nazareth.

A nurse came up to her.

"Personal effects," she said, handing Marina a cardboard box.

Marina put the box down on the windowsill.

"I'll arrange everything, Marina," Philip said. His eyes were red. Poor Philip.

"Thank you, Philip," she said.

She started to sort through what was in the box.

Oh, nothing. His trousers. His wallet, with the Authority identification, his Peter Bent card, a picture of Mom. Socks, underwear, so very pathetic. Shoes. His bloody shirt that Ahmed had told her all about. The gun, for heaven's sake. She didn't touch it. Somehow she would send that back to the soldier—Ahmed had told her everything. To the soldier.

Or to his family.

And George's jacket. She looked at it, holding it up and dusting it off in front of the window through which she could see the day beginning. Cars were starting up on faraway sandy hills, children in groups walked to school, two men on donkeys headed out to their field, and down a rocky path, a shepherd and his son made their way to a distant pasture, with their tawny flock trailing alongside the main road in a desultory fashion. She felt in the pockets of the jacket and found George's passport and some change and the old iron key.

Her childhood toy, always snatched back at the end of a few minutes by her anxious father. She hadn't seen it in years, but it was not something that was ever very far from her mind. It was shiny like something new, but it had the weight and feel of keys made a century ago. She held it in her open hand. It was almost as long as her palm. He carried it everywhere.

"This is rightfully yours, Marina," he used to say to her when she was little. "This and the house it belongs to."

Rightfully. Marina remembered not knowing what that word meant.

"He told me he was going to give that to you," Philip said, from behind her.

I don't want it, I don't want it, she thought. And yet she clutched the key as if she were already going down beneath black water and this were her lifeline back up to the surface, and air.

ACKNOWLEDGMENTS

I am deeply indebted to *All That Remains* and *Before Their Diaspora*, by Walid Khalidi.

And many grateful thanks to Kate Manning, Nihaya Qawasmi, Jessica Lazar, and Jim Wilentz for their careful readings of this manuscript.

Thanks, too, to Alice Mayhew for her continued support, her thoughtful changes and emendations, and her helpful prodding on this project; to Anja Schmidt for all her work, and to Deborah Karl.

Martyrs' Crossing

AMY WILENTZ

A Reader's Guide

A Conversation with Amy Wilentz

Kate Manning and Amy Wilentz have known each other since 1980 when Amy was an editor at The Nation *magazine and Kate was a lowly intern, a fact Amy never let Kate forget. However, when Kate was offered the "job" of housesitting an old French farmhouse outside Avignon, Amy suddenly became Kate's best friend, and came along. While in France, Manning and Wilentz wrote many beginnings of novels, countless short stories, and they began the practice of reading and editing each other's work. The two writers still trade chapters, now using their children— who, incredibly, are friends and classmates—as couriers.*

Kate Manning: People familiar with your work before *Martyrs' Crossing* know you as a journalist, a chronicler of Haitian life and politics, an essayist for *The New Yorker* on the Middle East, and writer of trenchant commentary on many subjects. But I happen to know you've always been a closet fiction writer. Why did you choose fiction to tell this particular story?

Amy Wilentz: For practical and probably mundane reasons. My first book about Haiti was about a place that American readers really don't know about. The Mideast was different. I was new there, and relatively unsophisticated. I was not immersed in an academic way. I didn't have the proper credentials to write a good non-fiction book. There are already lots of very bad non-fiction books about the Middle East, and only a few great ones. No one needed another factual tome on the conflict there. And you're right, I've always wanted to write novels.

KM: *Martyrs' Crossing* is your first one, and over the course of the three years it took you to finish, it often seemed to some of your friends and family that it was excruciating and difficult for you to write. Was it?

AW: I really loved writing it. Loved it.

KM: Liar.

AW: I loved it in retrospect of course. During the writing it was often painful. You think: *How in the world do I get Doron out of this mess?* Or you think: *What would a husband possibly plausibly say to his wife in this situation?* And it seems so daunting, day after day, answering these questions and doing it with some verve. The key to writing a novel is to create at least one character whom everyone will love, so that when he is not there, you want him back. Once I had Doron and George and Ahmed and Marina living and breathing, it became easier. Now

I'd like to write the book all over again. I loved my characters so much and I feel lost without them. I don't know where to go now without them.

KM: At the risk of sounding like girls choosing their favorite Beatle, who is your favorite character?

AW: Ahmed. He's self-centered and self-important and smart and so easy to write because of that. I understood him. He didn't have a soft side, so he was flatter and easier to write. He's based loosely—very loosely—on a real person, a former PLO fighter who is now a Bethlehem political figure, and who really *was* camping up on a mountain, in a tent, protecting the area from Israeli occupation. But in vain. Eventually he left, and the place is now an Israeli settlement. John Le Carre used him in *Little Drummer Girl*, too, I'm told.

KM: Who was the hardest character for you to write?

AW: Marina was the hardest. The write-what-you-know theory in fiction is that the closer a character comes to yourself or your situation the easier it is to write. Marina is supposedly me, in that she's a woman with a child, roughly my age. But my tendency is not toward self-disclosure. Marina had been through a terrible trauma and it's difficult to portray a mother going through that without lapsing into melodrama. So, I concentrated on the physical details. You don't write her thinking, *I am so sad*, you concentrate on her folding the laundry and wondering *Why am I so incompetent at doing the very things which only yesterday were automatic?* It's hard to stay away from cliché when writing about mourning or jealousy or anger.

KM: Or love. Or happiness.

AW: Ugh. Love. Happiness. Happiness should be banned. It's too hard to write it well.

KM: How did you make such good fiction out of a political situation that confounds most people?

AW: You have to be very careful not to put too much politics in it. You write around the politics and write instead about people. You put the politics in the characters' situations. The plot of *Martyrs' Crossing* is based on political circumstances. This story could not happen without the conflict and pain of the Middle East being what it is. So in that sense the politics are unavoidable. In fact, the politics gives you a firm structure to hang your plot on. The inherent conflict makes the plot *go*. And I didn't set out to write some apology or some allegory or some heroic fable of good triumphing over evil. For example, people ask me: *Why did Doron want to make restitution to the Palestinian mother?* He wanted to because that was the kind of man he was, that I made him be. His character is tested by the political situation. I made Doron someone who cared because that made him interesting. He should care. Anyone who watches a child suffer would care—should care. People have argued with me about this, saying, *Why should he be so guilty? He was just doing a job. He's acting on orders. He is an instrument of the state.* But of course, soldiers *do* care, and I wanted to show how the soldier—this soldier, anyway—is human.

The problem—anywhere that politics is so violently felt—is that the human is divided from the political. This is the schizophrenia of politics: that the Tutsi is as human as the Hutu, the Palestinian as human as the Israeli. Some readers have come away with the idea that Doron is going crazy, dressing up in Palestinian clothes, searching out Marina in Ramallah; but I think he's normal. To me he's the only sane one. He comes to see the other side as human and that's what leads him to his suicidal situation in the end.

Both sides, Palestinians and Israelis, have told me that there *is* no soldier like Doron in real life. Israelis are so tough they can't admit that one of theirs could have guilty feelings, which they see as a sign of weakness. Palestinians, on the other hand, see Doron as an attempt to humanize an unfeeling occupying force. But really, I think he does exist. And *Martyrs' Crossing* is, after all, a novel, not an attempt to progandize, fix, find a solution, to lay blame. It's just a novel. A story about real people in a real place.

KM: Do you protest too much? Your book is quite political, in its own way. Doesn't fiction have power? What can fiction do that non-fiction cannot?

AW: It can create a soldier like Doron. It can marry the personal and the political.

KM: So he's one of the martyrs of the title—human beings sacrificed—or used—for a political purpose, as George muses so painfully and amusingly, too, at his grandson's funeral: *"The Palestinian People . . . He could always predict when The Palestinian People would enter the speeches of Palestinians."* He's tired of the idea that somehow the death of a child is a noble thing. It's quite funny, the way George thinks, and I like how he uses his sense of humor as armor against pain.

AW: It's fun, figuring out how to have humor in a book that's not about a humorous subject, such as George's cynicism and his sense of the absurd—waving at the upside down goldfish in his hotel fish tank, being somehow pleased at the discomfort of his protege. George's scenes with Marina were fun for me to write since they were based on personal experience. Especially because my own father died some years ago and I miss him terribly, it was a pleasure to put parts of him in a character, teasing him.

KM: **And I notice you conveniently made him a widower, so you didn't have to write a wife/mother character. Do I remember correctly that in the first draft, George had a living breathing wife? Explain some of the wrong turns you took and why you made changes.**

AW: Yes, George had a wife, but I offed her. She got in the way of his interior monologues. She was extraneous. Also, Doron had a girlfriend. She was first called Becky, and then she was called Noa. I liked her. The scenes I wrote between her and Doron gave the novel glimpses of secular Israeli life; non-military and non-religious, the way life is led by most young people in Israel. Doron and Noa were watching TV and having a pizza party and listening to trance dancing music, smoking cigarettes, having sex. But I cut her because she interrupted the plot. She was a pointless female who was only there to be had sex with and it was bad for her! She wasn't enjoying her role, or the sex, and she felt used, so I offed her. Almost all my sex scenes got cut, thankfully. I also had a character, a Palestinian guy from the refugee camps, who was a suicide bomber. But he was way too stereotypical, and he evolved into the grimy lawyer, Sheukhi.

KM: **You left Jerusalem when you were only halfway through the book. Was this liberating, or did it make your task more difficult?**

AW: There is a kind of nostalgia and an elegiac feeling that I had after leaving Jerusalem that contributed to my writing in a way I like. Sitting here in my New York apartment with the construction next door and the sounds of the subway made me long to get away to the world I had left. You're building a world when you're writing, and when you're far away, you're not constrained by reality. There's a tendency among readers who know a place to say *Oh, there's no such thing there! She should know that!* But that irritates me because in fiction, as long as it's credible, there should be license.

For example, I don't think there really *is* an Army headquarters in Jerusalem, and it's certainly not called *The Building*, as it is in my book. But who cares? My fiction needed it. It *could* exist. Still, there are some bad things writers do, such as describing a place as a city of broad avenues when in fact it's a warren of narrow streets. You do need a certain degree of faithfulness to reality, and since I was writing for a large population of people who've been to Jerusalem and who would love to see it on the page and read about it, I put lots of things in the book to amuse them. But some people have hated it, me writing about dirty playgrounds that smell of dog shit and are full of trash. They saw this as an attack on Israel. They're the ones who only go to the Western Wall and stay in their hotels and never get a feel for the rest of Israeli life. My friends, the moms in the smelly playgrounds and the people in offices with rusting desks, loved those parts, because those parts felt real.

KM: What are you going to write next?

AW: I'm waffling between a novel that would be more personal, with a first-person narrator, set here in the US, or something set abroad, more like this book. I feel more comfortable with this kind of book. Can we talk about boy and girl fiction?

KM: It seems to me most of our conversations are about boy and girl fictions of one kind or another. So explain what you mean.

AW: What I mean is: *Martyrs' Crossing* is very much a guy's novel. It's full of history and politics and explosions and what, I'm told, is a rather ripping plot, amazingly enough, since plot is something I hate thinking about. So for me, the idea of writing a so-called girlish memoir/confession about family life is not entirely appealing. A coming-of-age book! How hateful. I say: skip writing entirely when we are coming of age. I am so glad I missed that. There is one side of my personality that is drawn to things I think of as *girl* subjects: love, domesticity, family encounters, growing up—but I think plot lies elsewhere. The novelists I love are capable of finding plot anywhere—Trollope, for example, George Eliot. But they write against a broader background than many novelists today.

KM: There's so much navel-gazing and self-help-group fiction around.

AW: The navel-staring is so alienating to me. *Aesthetically*. Although I love Proust, who wrote one long navel-staring story but made it into a broad social and political portrait. The reason I really dislike most modern self-regarding fiction comes from a moral feeling I have that it often results in a kind of narcissism, a selfishness, and ultimately, who cares???

KM: Right, who cares? Why do readers like it, except to confirm some banal truth about themselves?

AW: Yes, but plenty of Americans will look at a book set in Jerusalem or any other place that's not *here*, and say: *Who cares what happens there?* You remember how I used to describe *Martyrs' Crossing* as a "comic sex romp through the Middle East?" That was a joke about making people care. It's my job to make them care. The way to do that is to write good characters, strong plotting and a lot of steamy, seedy atmosphere. Sex scenes would help, too. I'm saving them all for my next book.

KATE MANNING's *first novel,* Whitegirl, *a story of race, identity, and love, will be published by the Dial Press in March 2002. She is a two-time Emmy-award-winning producer, writer and reporter of television documentaries made for WNET, the public television station in New York. She graduated from Yale University in 1979, and lives in New York City with her husband and three children.*

A Reader's Guide

Reading Group Questions and Topics for Discussion

1. Who are the martyrs of the title? How does the author use the idea of martyrdom—dying for a cause—throughout the interwoven stories of her characters? What is the author's attitude toward such martyrdom?

2. Who are the heroes of *Martyrs' Crossing*? Discuss how Yizhar, Ahmed, Shuekhi, Zvili, Doron, George Raad and Hassan, too, each act according to (or in spite of) personal codes of honor, morality, and patriotism. In a conversation between Yizhar and Doron, Yizhar says, "I despise heroes . . . Heroes act, and other people suffer." Which character comes closest to the author's idea of a hero? What constitutes a hero for our time?

3. As Marina is crossing the checkpoint with masses of Palestinians, she thinks *They were her own people, standing packed around her. Finally, she was sharing their predicament. She had always thought she wanted to.* Is Marina a certain kind of American naif? Or is she politically committed in a way her father is not? Is her marriage to Hassan the result of naiveté? In what ways has her American upbringing left her unprepared to return to her people? Do Americans romanticize the struggles of disenfranchised people? Do Americans romanticize the Israeli-Palestinian conflict? Why do you think the author chose to give Marina an American past?

4. Underlying the stories in *Martyrs' Crossing* are the twin questions of what constitutes *home*, and, what is the meaning of home? George thinks of his friend Ahmed, (Chapter 10 p. 113) "It had been decades since they leaned against each other in this familiar way, not considering politics and the oceans that divided them. Possibly, George thought, this is the meaning of home." Hassan (p. 153) has been teaching Marina about her homeland, saying "You call yourself a Palestinian?" How is the idea of home different for the various characters in this story? What is your idea of home?

5. In this story, people who are ostensibly on the same side do not appear to trust each other. Allies are enemies and foes might be friends. Doron and Marina, for example, seem to understand that in other circumstances they might have more in common than not. George and Ahmed are described as friends in the early part of the book, and by the end, George is described as Ahmed's "greatest enemy," because of differences in what they believe. Doron thinks: *I am the enemy, I am the enemy*, and he asks Yizhar, "So are we enemies now?" (p. 195) Which characters seem to you to be worthy of the term "enemy"? Which characters seem truly at cross purposes? Which are truly dangerous, and to whom? Who is worthy of trust, and for whom?

6. What are the different ways in which the death of Ibrahim becomes fodder for both the Palestinian and Israeli political machines? Discuss the uses of human tragedy for political purpose. Is this inevitable? Justifiable? How does this kind of propagandizing escalate or ease tension?

7. Discuss George's relationship with Ahmed. Throughout the book, George dwells on his childhood friendship with Ahmed. After Ibrahim's death, George thinks, "If Ahmed was insincere under these circumstances, then Palestine was lost to George." (p. 56) How does their friendship evolve over the course of the book? Do the two men have the same goal? The same beliefs?

8. Examine Yizhar's brand of loyalty to Israel. He spins the death of Ibrahim in the press, (p. 72) and Wilentz writes, "Yizhar felt no remorse. His version of the story was not a lie." Is Yizhar lying? Should he feel remorse? In Yizhar's job, where is the line between good and evil? Discuss the differences between Yizhar and Doron.

9. Is there a particular politics or ideology underlying the story in *Martyrs' Crossing*? Is the book more sympathetic to one side or the other?

10. "Our little Ibrahim was not a brave Palestinian freedom fighter," George says at his grandson's funeral. (p. 178) "If you want to place blame for my grandson's death, look in the mirror as well. Look at yourself and the Authority." Because of that speech, the lawyer Sheukhi believes George Raad to be a traitor. Sheukhi has one rule, (on p. 185) "Never criticize a fellow Palestinian in public." Yizhar, too, seems to have a similar rule about his fellow Israelis. What are the uses of loyalty in a political conflict? Is this unwillingness to criticize one's own a good impulse, or a bad one? What other examples—say, in police departments—of this unwillingness to criticize one's own can you think of? Discuss the characters' choices in terms of moral absolutism and moral relativism. Is George a traitor to his people? Is Doron a traitor to his?

11. Sheukhi makes a choice. Doron makes a different kind of choice. Both men feel a need to act. Contrast their choices.

12. James Baldwin wrote, "We are trapped in history, and history is trapped in us." How are the characters in *Martyrs' Crossing* trapped in history? How is it trapped in them? Do you believe human beings can escape the trap of history? If so, how? Who in this story comes closest to escaping? What historical traps have a grip on Americans?